D0417751

# RIVER GOD
## Volume I

Ancient Egypt. Land of the Pharaohs. A kingdom built on gold. A legend shattered by greed ... Now the Valley of the Kings lies ravaged by war, as weak men inherit the cherished crown. Taita, a formidably gifted and wise eunuch slave, has a dream—to restore the majesty of the Pharaoh of Pharaohs on the glittering banks of the Nile. Through the voice ... lendour and ... ion combine ... ves, of loves, ... h weaves his

**Libraries**
& Information Service

24 hour renewals and
information phoneline
**020 8753 2400**

| | | |
|---|---|---|
| - 5 DEC 2006 | | |
| 8 FEB 2007 | | |
| 2 6 MAR 2007 | | |
| - 2 APR 2007 | | |
| - 3 MAY 2007 | | |
| 2 0 OCT 2008 | | |
| | | |
| | | |
| | | |
| | | |

SHELVED IN RESERVE STOCK
PLEASE APPLY TO STAFF

PERMANENTLY WITHDRAWN FROM HAMMERSMITH AND FULHAM PUBLIC LIBRARIES

PRICE

Please return this book to any library
in the borough on or before the last
date stamped.

**Fines are charged on overdue books**.

Hammersmith
& Fulham
Serving our Community

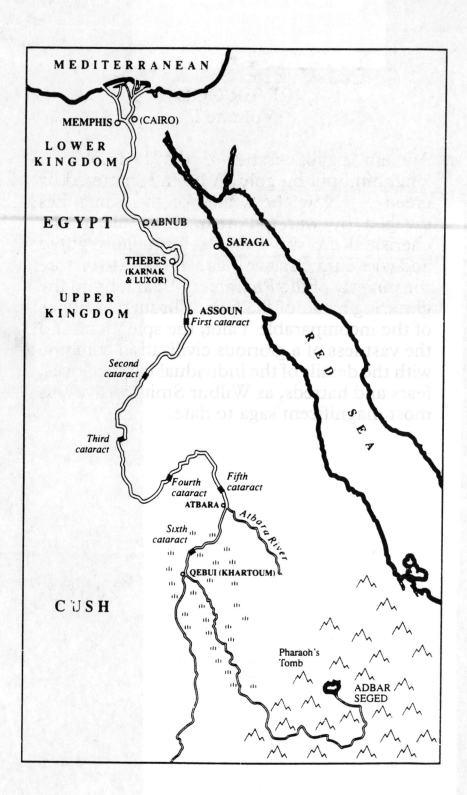

MEDITERRANEAN

MEMPHIS ○ (CAIRO)

LOWER
KINGDOM

EGYPT ○ ABNUB

○ SAFAGA

THEBES ○
(KARNAK
& LUXOR)

UPPER
KINGDOM

○ ASSOUN
■ First cataract

Second
cataract ■

RED SEA

Third
cataract ■

Fourth
cataract ■    Fifth
              cataract ■

ATBARA ○     Athara River

Sixth
cataract ■

○ QEBUI (KHARTOUM)

CUSH

Pharaoh's
Tomb

ADBAR
SEGED

# RIVER GOD

## Volume I

## Wilbur Smith

CHIVERS PRESS

A≤96— 7916 8/96

830 0381

---

**Library of Congress Cataloging-in-Publication Data**

Smith, Wilbur A.
  River god / Wilbur Smith.
    p. cm.
  ISBN 0–7927–2017–2 (hardcover)
  ISBN 0–7927–2016–4 (softcover)
  1. Eunuchs—Egypt—Thebes (Extinct city)—Fiction.
  2. Slaves—Egypt—Thebes (Extinct city)—Fiction.
  3. Thebes (Egypt: Extinct city)—Fiction.
  4. Egypt—History—to 332 B.C.—Fiction.
  5. Large type books.   I. Title.
[PR9405.9.S5R58   1994b]
823—dc20                                          93–49515
                                                      CIP

---

**British Library Cataloguing in Publication Data available**

This Large Print edition is published by Chivers Press, England, and by Chivers North America, 1995.

Published in the U. S. by arrangement with St Martin's Press and in the British Commonwealth with Macmillan London Limited.

U.K. Softcover ISBN 0 7451 3563 3
U.S. Softcover ISBN 0 7927 2016 4

Copyright © Wilbur Smith 1993

All rights reserved. No part of this book may be used or reproduced in any manner without written permission except in the case of brief quotations embodied in critical articles and reviews.

The right of Wilbur Smith to be identified as author of this work has been asserted by him in accordance with the Copyright, Designs and Patents Act 1988.

The hieroglyphs write the name of the god of the Nile inundation, Hapi, from the papyrus of Ani (P BM 10470).

Photoset, printed and bound in Great Britain by
REDWOOD BOOKS, Trowbridge, Wiltshire

This book, like so many others before it, is for my wife, Danielle Antoinette.

The Nile that flows through this story has both of us in her thrall. We have spent days of delight voyaging together upon her waters and idling upon her banks. As we are, so is she a creature of this very Africa of ours.

Yet this great river runs neither so strongly nor so deeply as my love for you, my darling.

# RIVER GOD

The river lay heavily upon the desert, bright as a spill of molten metal from a furnace. The sky smoked with heat-haze and the sun beat down upon it all with the strokes of a coppersmith's hammer. In the mirage the gaunt hills flanking the Nile seemed to tremble to the blows.

Our boat sped close in beside the papyrus beds; near enough for the creaking of the water buckets of the shadoof, on their long, counter-balanced arms, to carry from the fields across the water. The sound harmonized with the singing of the girl in the bows.

Lostris was fourteen years of age. The Nile had begun its latest flood on the very day that her red woman's moon had flowered for the first time, a coincidence that the priests of Hapi had viewed as highly propitious. Lostris, the woman's name that they had then chosen to replace her discarded baby-name, meant 'Daughter of the Waters'.

I remember her so vividly on that day. She would grow more beautiful as the years passed, become more poised and regal, but never again would that glow of virgin womanhood radiate from her so overpoweringly. Every man aboard, even the warriors at the rowing-benches, was aware of it. Neither I nor any one of them could keep our gaze off her. She filled me with a sense of my own inadequacy and a deep and poignant longing; for although I am a eunuch I was gelded only after I had known the joy of a woman's body.

'Taita,' she called to me, 'sing with me!' And when I obeyed she smiled with pleasure. My voice

1

was one of the many reasons that, whenever she was able, she kept me near her; my tenor complemented her lovely soprano to perfection. We sang one of the old peasant love songs that I had taught her, and which was still one of her favourites:

My heart flutters up like a wounded quail
when I see my beloved's face
and my cheeks bloom like the dawn sky
to the sunshine of his smile—

From the stern another voice joined with ours. It was a man's voice, deep and powerful, but it lacked the clarity and purity of my own. If my voice was that of a dawn-greeting thrush, then this was the voice of a young lion.

Lostris turned her head and now her smile shimmered like the sunbeams on the surface of the Nile. Although the man upon whom she played that smile was my friend, perhaps my only true friend, still I felt the bitter gall of envy burn the back of my throat. Yet I forced myself to smile at Tanus, as she did, with love.

Tanus' father, Pianki, Lord Harrab, had been one of the grandees of the Egyptian nobility, but his mother had been the daughter of a freed Tehenu slave. Like so many of her people, she had been fair-headed and blue-eyed. She had died of the swamp fever while Tanus was still a child, so my memory of her was imperfect. However, the old women said that seldom before had such beauty as hers been seen in either of the two kingdoms.

On the other hand, I had known and admired

2

Tanus' father, before he lost all his vast fortune and the great estates that had once almost rivalled those of Pharaoh himself. He had been of dark complexion, with Egyptian eyes the colour of polished obsidian, a man with more physical strength than beauty, but with a generous and noble heart—some might say too generous and too trusting, for he had died destitute, with his heart broken by those he had thought his friends, alone in the darkness, cut off from the sunshine of Pharaoh's favour.

Thus it seemed that Tanus had inherited the best from both his parents, except only worldly wealth. In nature and in power he was as his father; in beauty as his mother. So why should I resent my mistress loving him? I loved him also, and, poor neutered thing that I am, I knew that I could never have her for myself, not even if the gods had raised my status above that of slave. Yet such is the perversity of human nature that I hungered for what I could never have and dreamed of the impossible.

Lostris sat on her cushion on the prow with her slave girls sprawled at her feet, two little black girls from Cush, lithe as panthers, entirely naked except for the golden collars around their necks. Lostris herself wore only a skirt of bleached linen, crisp and white as an egret's wing. The skin of her upper body, caressed by the sun, was the colour of oiled cedar wood from the mountains beyond Byblos. Her breasts were the size and shape of ripe figs just ready for plucking, and tipped with rose garnets.

She had set aside her formal wig, and wore her natural hair in a sidelock that fell in a thick dark rope over one breast. The slant of her eyes was

3

enhanced by the silver-green of powdered malachite cunningly touched to the upper lids. The colour of her eyes was green also, but the darker, clearer green of the Nile when its waters have shrunk and deposited their burden of precious silts. Between her breasts, suspended on a gold chain, she wore a figurine of Hapi, the goddess of the Nile, fashioned in gold and precious lapis lazuli. Of course it was a superb piece, for I had made it with my own hands for her.

Suddenly Tanus lifted his right hand with the fist clenched. As a single man the rowers checked their stroke and held the blades of their paddles aloft, glinting in the sunlight and dripping water. Then Tanus thrust the steering-oar hard over, and the men on the port bank stabbed their backstroke deeply, creating a series of tiny whirlpools in the surface of the green water. The starboard side pulled strongly ahead. The boat spun so sharply that the deck canted over at an alarming angle. Then both banks pulled together and she shot forward. The sharp prow, with the blue eyes of Horus emblazoned upon it, brushed aside the dense stands of papyrus, and she lanced her way out of the flow of the river and into the still waters of the lagoon beyond.

Lostris broke off the song and shaded her eyes to gaze ahead. 'There they are!' she cried, and pointed with a graceful little hand. The other boats of Tanus' squadron were cast like a net across the southern reaches of the lagoon, blocking the main entrance to the great river, cutting off any escape in that direction.

Naturally, Tanus had chosen for himself the northern station, for he knew that this was where the sport would be most furious. I wished it was not so. Not that I am a coward, but I have always the safety of my mistress to consider. She had inveigled herself aboard the *Breath of Horus* only after much intrigue in which, as always, she had deeply involved me. When her father learned, as he surely would, of her presence in the thick of the hunt, it would go badly enough for me, but if he learned also that I was responsible for allowing her to be in the company of Tanus for a full day, not even my privileged position would protect me from his wrath. His instructions to me regarding this young man were unequivocal.

However, I seemed to be the only soul aboard the *Breath of Horus* who was perturbed. The others were simmering with excitement. Tanus checked the rowers with a peremptory hand-signal, and the boat glided to a halt and lay rocking gently upon the green waters that were so still that when I glanced overboard and saw my own reflection look back at me, I was struck, as always, by how well my beauty had carried over the years. To me it seemed that my face was more lovely than the cerulean blue lotus blooms that framed it. I had little time to admire it, however, for the crew were all abustle.

One of Tanus' staff officers ran up his personal standard to the masthead. It was the image of a blue crocodile, with its great coxcombed tail held erect and its jaws open. Only an officer of the rank of Best of Ten Thousand was entitled to his own standard. Tanus had achieved such rank, together with the command of the Blue Crocodile division of Pharaoh's own elite guard, before his twentieth birthday.

5

Now the standard at the masthead was the signal for the hunt to begin. On the horizon of the lagoon the rest of the squadron were tiny with distance, but their paddles began to beat rhythmically, rising and falling like the wings of wild geese in flight, glistening in the sunlight. From their sterns the multiple wavelets of their wakes were drawn out across the placid waters and lay for a long while on the surface, as though moulded from solid clay.

Tanus lowered the gong over the stern. It was a long bronze tube. He allowed the end of it to sink below the surface. When struck with a hammer of the same metal the shrill, reverberating tones would be transmitted through the water, filling our quarry with consternation. Unhappily for my equanimity, I knew that this could readily turn to a murderous rage.

Tanus laughed at me. Even in his own excitation he had sensed my qualms. For a rude soldier he had unusual perception. 'Come up here in the stern-tower, Taita!' he ordered. 'You can beat the gong for us. It will take your mind off the safety of your own beautiful hide for a while.'

I was hurt by his levity, but relieved by the invitation, for the stern-tower is high above the water. I moved to do his bidding without undignified haste, and, as I passed him, I paused to exhort him sternly, 'Have a care for the safety of my mistress. Do you hear me, boy? Do not encourage her to recklessness, for she is every bit as wild as you are.' I could speak thus to an illustrious commander of ten thousand, for he was once my pupil and I had wielded the cane on more than one occasion across those martial buttocks. He grinned at me now as he had in those days, as cocky and impudent as ever.

'Leave that lady in my hands, I implore you, old friend. There is nothing I would relish more, believe me!' I did not admonish him for such a disrespectful tone, for I was in some small haste to take my place in the tower. From there I watched him take up his bow.

Already that bow was famous throughout the army, indeed throughout the length of the great river from the cataracts to the sea. I had designed it for him when he had grown dissatisfied with the puny weapons that, up until that time, were all that were available to him. I had suggested that we should try to fashion a bow with some new material other than those feeble woods that grow in our narrow riverine valley; perhaps with exotic timbers such as the heartwood of the olive from the land of the Hittites or of the ebony from Cush; or with even stranger materials such as the horn of the rhinoceros or the ivory tusk of the elephant.

No sooner had we made the attempt than we came upon a myriad of problems, the first of which was the brittleness of these exotic materials. In their natural state none of them would bend without cracking, and only the largest and therefore the most expensive elephant tusk would allow us to carve a complete bowstock from it. I solved both these problems by splitting the ivory of a smaller tusk into slivers and gluing these together in sufficient girth and bulk to form a full bow. Unfortunately it was too rigid for any man to draw.

However, from there it was an easy and natural step to laminate together all four of our chosen materials—olive wood, ebony, horn and ivory. Of course, there were many months of experimentation with combinations of these materials, and with various types of glue to hold them together. We never did succeed in making a glue strong enough. In the end I solved this last problem by binding the entire bowstock with electrum wire to prevent it from flying apart. I had two big men assist Tanus in twisting the wire on to it with all their combined strength, while the glue was still hot. When it cooled, it set to an almost perfect combination of strength and pliability.

Then I cut strands from the gut of a great black-maned lion that Tanus hunted and killed with his bronze-bladed war spear out in the desert. These I tanned and twisted together to form a bowstring. The result was this gleaming arc of such extraordinary power that only one man out of all the hundreds who had made the attempt could draw it to full stretch.

The regulation style of archery as taught by the army instructors was to face the target and draw the nocked arrow to the sternum of the chest, hold that aim for a deliberate pause, then loose on command. However, not even Tanus had the strength to draw this bow and hold his aim steadily. He was forced to develop a completely new style. Standing sideways to the target, addressing it over his left shoulder, he would throw up the bow with his left arm outstretched and, with a convulsive heave, draw back the arrow until the feathered flights touched his lips and the muscles of his arms and chest stood proud with the effort. In that same instant of full extension, seemingly without aiming, he would loose.

At first, his arrows flew at random as wild bees leave the hive, but he practised day after day and month after month. The fingers of his right hand became raw and bleeding from the chafing of the bowstring, but they healed and toughened. The inside of his left forearm was bruised and excoriated where the bowstring slashed past it on the release of the arrow, but I fashioned a leather guard to protect it. And Tanus stood at the butts and practised and practised.

Even I lost confidence in his ability to master the weapon but Tanus never gave up. Slowly, agonizingly slowly, he gained control of it to the point where, finally, he could launch three arrows with such rapidity that they were all in the air at the same instant. At least two of the three would strike the target, a copper disc the size of a man's head set up at a distance of fifty paces from where Tanus stood. Such was the force of those arrows that they would fly cleanly through the metal which was the thickness of my little finger.

Tanus named this mighty weapon Lanata which was, quite coincidentally, the discarded baby-name of my mistress. Now he stood in the bows with the woman at his side, and her namesake in his left hand. They made a marvellous couple, but too obviously so for my peace of mind.

I called sharply, 'Mistress! Come back here immediately! It is unsafe where you are.' She did not even deign to glance over her shoulder, but made a sign at me behind her back. Every one of the crew of the galley saw it, and the boldest of them guffawed. One of those little black vixens that were her handmaidens must have taught Lostris that gesture, which was more appropriate to the ladies of the riverside taverns than to a highborn daughter of the House of Intef. I

9

considered remonstrating with her, but at once abandoned such an imprudent course, for my mistress is amenable to restraint only in certain of her moods. Instead, I applied myself to beating the bronze gong with sufficient vigour to disguise my chagrin.

The shrill, reverberating tone carried across the glassy waters of the lagoon, and instantly the air was filled with the susurration of wings and a shade was cast over the sun as, from the papyrus beds and the hidden pools and open water, a vast cloud of water-fowl rose into the sky. They were of a hundred varieties: black and white ibis with vulturine heads, sacred to the goddess of the river; flights of honking geese in russet plumage, each with a ruby droplet in the centre of its chest; herons of greenish-blue or midnight black, with bills like swords and ponderous wing-beats; and ducks in such profusion that their numbers challenged the eye and the credibility of the beholder.

Wild-fowling is one of the most ardent pursuits of the Egyptian nobility, but that day we were after different game. At that moment, I saw far ahead a disturbance upon the glassy surface. It was weighty and massive, and my spirits quailed, for I knew what terrible beast had moved there. Tanus also had seen it, but his reaction was altogether different from mine. He gave tongue like a hunting hound, and his men shouted with him and bent to their paddles. The *Breath of Horus* shot forward as though she were one of the birds that darkened the sky above us, and my mistress shrieked with excitement and beat with one small fist upon Tanus' muscled shoulder.

The waters roiled once more and Tanus signalled to his steersman to follow the movement, while I hammered upon the gong to bolster and sustain my courage. We reached the spot where last we had seen movement, and the vessel glided to a standstill while every man upon her decks gazed around eagerly.

I alone glanced directly over the stern. The water beneath our hull was shallow and almost as clear as the air above us. I shrieked as loudly and as shrilly as my mistress had and leapt back from the stern-rail, for the monster was directly under us.

The hippopotamus is the familiar of Hapi, the goddess of the Nile. It was only with her special dispensation that we could hunt it. To that end Tanus had prayed and sacrificed at the goddess's temple that morning, with my mistress close by his side. Of course, Hapi is her patron goddess, but I doubted that alone was the reason for her avid participation in the ceremony.

The beast that I saw beneath us now was an enormous old bull. To my eye, he seemed as large as our galley, a gigantic shape that lumbered along the bottom of the lagoon, his movements slowed down by the drag of the water so that he moved like a creature from a nightmare. He raised puffs of mud from beneath his hooves the same way that a wild oryx stirs the dust as it races across the desert sands.

With the steering-oar Tanus spun the boat about and we sped after the bull. But even at that slow and mannered gallop he rapidly drew away from us. His dark shape faded into the green depths of the lagoon ahead of us.

'Pull! By Seth's foul breath, pull!' Tanus howled

11

at his men, but when one of his officers shook out the knotted lash of the whip, Tanus frowned and shook his head. I have never seen him ply the lash where it was not warranted.

Suddenly the bull broke through the surface ahead of us and blew a great cloud of fetid steam from his lungs. The stink of it washed over us, even though he was well out of bowshot. For a moment his back formed a gleaming granite island in the lagoon, then he drew a whistling breath and with a swirl was gone again.

'After him!' Tanus bellowed.

'There he is,' I cried, as I pointed over the side, 'he's doubling back.'

'Well done, old friend,' Tanus laughed at me, 'we'll make a warrior of you yet.' That notion was ridiculous, for I am a scribe, a sage and an artist. My heroics are of the mind. None the less, I felt a thrill of pleasure, as I always do at Tanus' praise, and my trepidation was, for the moment, lost in the excitement of the chase.

To the south of us the other galleys of the squadron had joined the hunt. The priests of Hapi had kept a strict count of the number of these great beasts in the lagoon, and had given sanction for fifty of them to be slaughtered for the coming festival of Osiris. This would leave almost three hundred of the goddess's flock remaining in the temple lagoon, a number that the priests considered ideal to keep the waterways free of choking weed, to prevent the papyrus beds from encroaching upon the arable lands and to provide a regular supply of meat for the temple. Only the priests themselves were allowed to eat the flesh of the hippopotamus outside the ten days of the festival of Osiris.

So the hunt spun out across the waters like some intricate dance, with the ships of the squadron weaving and pirouetting while the frenzied beasts fled before them, diving and blowing and grunting as they surfaced to dive again. Yet each dive was shorter than the last, and the swirling breaches at the surface became more frequent as their lungs were emptied and could not be fully recharged before the pursuing ships bore down upon them and forced them to dive again. All the while the bronze gongs in the stern-tower of each galley rang out to blend with the excited cries of the rowers and the exhortations of the helmsmen. All was wild uproar and confusion and I found myself shouting and cheering along with the most bloodthirsty of them.

Tanus had concentrated all his attention on the first and largest bull. He ignored the females and younger animals that breached within bowshot, and followed the great beast through all his convolutions, drawing inexorably closer to him each time he surfaced. Even in my excitement I could not but admire the skill with which Tanus handled the *Breath of Horus* and the manner in which his crew responded to his signals. But then, he always had the knack of getting the very best out of those he commanded. How otherwise, with neither fortune nor great patron to sustain him, could he have risen so swiftly to exalted rank? What he had achieved he had done on his own merit, and that despite the malignant influence of hidden enemies who had placed every obstacle in his way.

Suddenly the bull burst through the surface not

13

thirty paces from the bows. He came out gleaming in the sunshine, monstrous black and awful, clouds of steamy vapour spurting from his nostrils like that creature from the underworld that devours the hearts of those who are found wanting by the gods.

Tanus had an arrow nocked and now he threw up the great bow and loosed it in the same fleeting instant. Lanata played her dreadful shimmering music, and the arrow leaped out in a blur that deceived the eye. While it still hissed in flight, another followed it and then another. The bowstring hummed like a lute, and the arrows struck one after the other. The bull bellowed as they buried themselves full-length in his broad back, and he dived again.

These were missiles that I had devised especially for this occasion. The feathered flights had been removed from the arrows and replaced by tiny floats of baobab wood such as the fishermen use to buoy their nets. They slipped over the butt of the shaft in such a way that they were secure in flight but would become dislodged once the beast dived and dragged them through the water. They were attached to the bronze arrow-head by a fine linen thread that was wound around the shaft, but which unravelled once the float was detached. So now, as the bull sped away beneath the water, the three tiny floats popped to the surface and bobbed along behind him. I had painted them bright yellow so that the eye was drawn to them and the bull's position was instantly revealed, even though he was deep in the lagoon.

Thus Tanus was able to anticipate each of the bull's wild rushes and to send the *Breath of Horus* speeding to head him off and to place another set

14

of arrows deep in the glistening black back as it bulged out of the water. By now the bull was towing a garland of pretty yellow corks behind him, and the waters were streaking and swirling red with his blood. Despite the wild emotions of the moment I could not help but feel pity for the stricken creature each time it came bellowing to the surface to be met by another hail of the deadly hissing arrows. My sympathy was not shared by my young mistress, who was in the very thick of the fray and shrieking with the delicious terror and excitement of it all.

Once again the bull came up dead ahead, but this time facing the *Breath of Horus* as she bore down upon him. His jaws gaped so wide that I could see far down his throat. It was a tunnel of bright red flesh that could easily have engulfed a man entirely. The jaws were lined with such an array of fangs that my breath stopped and my flesh chilled. In his bottom jaw they were huge ivory sickles designed to harvest the tough and sinewy stalks of standing papyrus. In his upper jaw they were gleaming white shafts as thick as my wrist that could shear through the hull timbers of the *Breath of Horus* as easily as I would bite through a cake of cornflour. I had recently had the opportunity of examining the corpse of a peasant woman who, while cutting papyrus on the river-bank, had disturbed a cow hippo that had just given birth to a calf. The woman had been severed in half so neatly that it seemed she had been struck with the keenest of bronze blades.

Now this enraged monster with his maw filled with these gleaming teeth was bearing down upon us, and even though I was high in the stern-tower

15

and as far from him as I could possibly be, yet I found myself as incapable of sound or movement as a temple statue, frozen with terror.

Tanus loosed yet another arrow which flew squarely down the gaping throat, yet the creature's agony was already so terrible that he seemed not to notice this further injury, although it must eventually prove fatal. He charged without check or hesitation straight at the bows of the *Breath of Horus*. Such a fearsome roar of fury and of mortal anguish issued from the tortured throat that an artery ruptured deep within it and gouts of blood were sent spraying from his open jaws. The spewing blood turned to clouds of red mist in the sunlight, both beautiful and horrible at the same time. Then the bull crashed headlong into the bows of our galley.

The *Breath of Horus* was cutting through the water at the speed of a running gazelle, but the bull was even swifter in his rage and his bulk was so solid that it seemed as though we had run aground on a rocky shore. The rowers were sent sprawling from their benches, while I was hurled forwards with such force against the rail of the stern-tower that the air was driven from my lungs and replaced by a solid rock of pain in my chest.

Yet even in my own distress my concern was all for my mistress. Through tears of agony I saw her flung forward by the impact. Tanus threw out his arm to try to save her, but he was also off-balance from the shock, and the bow in his left hand hindered him. He was only able to check her impetus for a moment, but then she teetered at the rail with her arms windmilling desperately, and her back arched out over the drop.

'Tanus!' she screamed, and reached out one hand to him. He recovered his balance with the nimbleness of an acrobat and tried to catch her hand. For an instant their fingers touched, then it seemed that she was plucked away and dashed over the side.

From my elevated position in the stern I was able to follow her fall. She flipped over in the air like a cat, and the white skirts streamed upwards to expose the exquisite length of her thighs. To me it seemed that she fell for ever, and my own anguished cry blended with her despairing wail.

'My baby!' I cried. 'My little one!' For I was certain that she was lost. It seemed that all her life, as I had known it, replayed itself before my eyes. I saw her again as a toddling infant and heard the baby endearments that she bestowed on me, her adoring nursemaid. I saw her grow to womanhood, and I remembered every joy and every heartache that she had caused me. I loved her then in the moment of losing her even more than I had done in all those fourteen long years.

She fell upon the vast, blood-splattered back of the infuriated bull, and for an instant lay spread-eagled there like a human sacrifice upon the altar of some obscene religion. The bull whirled about, mounting high out of the water, and he twisted his huge deformed head backwards, trying to reach her. His bloodshot piggy eyes glared with the insanity of his rage, and his great jaws clashed as he snapped at her.

Somehow Lostris managed to gather herself and cling to a pair of the arrow-shafts that protruded from the bull's broad back as though they were handles. She lay with her arms and legs spread

17

wide. She was not screaming now, all her art and strength employed in staying alive. Those curved ivory fangs rang upon each other like the blades of duelling warriors as they gnashed in air. At each bite they seemed to miss her by only a finger's-breadth, and any instant I expected one of her lovely limbs to be pruned away like a delicate shoot from the vine, and to see her sweet young blood mingle with those brutish effusions that streamed from the bull's wounds.

In the prow Tanus recovered swiftly. For an instant I saw his face and it was terrible. He tossed aside the bow, for it was useless to him now, and he seized instead the hilt of his sword and jerked the blade free of its crocodile-skin scabbard. It was a gleaming length of bronze as long as his arm, and the edges were honed until they could shave the hair from the back of his hand.

He leaped up on to the gunwale and balanced there for an instant, watching the wild gyrations of the mortally wounded bull in the water below him. Then he launched himself outwards and dropped like a stooping falcon with the sword held in both hands and pointing downwards.

He dropped across the bull's thick neck, landing astride it as though he were about to ride it into the underworld. The full weight of his body and the impetus of that wild leap were behind the sword as he struck. Half the length of the blade was driven into the hippopotamus's neck at the base of the skull, and, seated upon it like a rider, Tanus worried and worked the keen bronze deeper, using both arms and the strength of those broad shoulders. At the goad of the blade the bull went berserk. His strivings up to that point seemed feeble in comparison to this fresh outburst. The bull reared most of his enormous bulk out of the lagoon, swinging his head from side to side, throwing solid sheets of water so high in the air that they crashed down on the deck of the galley and, like a curtain, almost obscured the scene from my horrified gaze.

Through it all I watched the couple on the monster's back tossed about mercilessly. The shaft of one of the arrows that Lostris was holding snapped, and she was almost thrown clear. If this had happened she would surely have been savaged by the bull and chopped into bloody tatters by those ivory fangs. Tanus reached backwards and with one arm seized and steadied her, while with his right hand he never ceased working the bronze blade deeper into the nape of the bull's neck.

Unable to reach them, the hippopotamus slashed at his own flanks, inflicting terrible gaping wounds in his sides so that for fifty paces around the galley the waters were incarnadined, and both Lostris and Tanus were painted entirely crimson from the tops of their heads to the soles of their feet by the spurting blood. Their faces were turned to grotesque masks from which their eyes whitely glared.

The violent death-throes of the bull had carried them far from the galley's side, and I was the first aboard to recover my wits. I yelled to the rowers, 'Follow them! Don't let them get away,' and they sprang to their stations and sent the *Breath of Horus* in pursuit.

At that instant it seemed that the point of Tanus' blade must have found the joint of the vertebrae in the beast's neck and slipped through.

19

The immense carcass stiffened and froze. The bull rolled on to his back with all four legs extended rigidly, and he plunged below the waters of the lagoon, bearing Lostris and Tanus with him into the depths.

I choked back the wail of despair that rose in my throat, and bellowed an order to the deck below. 'Back-water! Do not overrun them! Swimmers to the bows!' Even I was startled by the power and authority of my own voice.

The galley's forward way was checked, and before I could reflect on the prudence of what I was doing, I found myself heading a rush of hulking warriors across the deck. They would probably have cheered while they watched any other officer drown, but not their Tanus.

As for myself, I had already stripped off my skirt and was naked. Not the threat of a hundred lashes would have made me do this in any other circumstances, for I have let only one other person ever see those injuries that the state executioner inflicted upon me so long ago, and he was the one who had ordered the castrating knife used upon me in the first place. But now, for once, I was totally oblivious of the gross mutilation of my manhood.

I am a strong swimmer, and although in retrospect such foolhardiness makes me shudder, I truly believe that I might have dived over the side and swum down through those blood-dyed waters in an attempt to rescue my mistress. However, as I poised myself at the ship's rail, the waters directly below me opened and two heads bobbed out, both of them streaming water and as close as a pair of mating otters. One was dark and the other fair, but from both of them issued the most unlikely sound I had ever heard. They were laughing. They were howling and shrieking and spluttering with laughter as they floundered towards the ship's side, locked so firmly in each other's arms that I was certain that they were in real danger of drowning one another.

All my concern turned instantly to outrage at this levity, and at the thought of the dreadful folly which I had been on the point of committing. Like a mother whose first instinct on finding her lost child is to thrash it, I heard my own voice lose all its previous deep authority and turn shrill and querulous. I was still berating my mistress with all my famous eloquence as she and Tanus were dragged by a dozen willing hands from the water on to the deck.

'You reckless, unbridled little savage!' I railed at her. 'You thoughtless, selfish, undisciplined little hoyden! You promised me! You swore an oath on the maidenhead of the goddess—'

She ran to me and threw both arms around my neck. 'Oh, Taita!' she cried, still bubbling with laughter. 'Did you see him? Did you see Tanus spring to my rescue? Was it not the noblest deed that ever you heard of? Just like the hero of one of your very best stories.'

The fact that I had been on the point of making a similar heroic gesture was quite ignored, and this only increased my irritation. Added to which I suddenly realized that Lostris had lost her skirt, and that the cold, wet body she pressed to mine was entirely naked. She was displaying to the rude gaze of officers and men the neatest, tightest pair of buttocks in all Egypt.

21

I snatched up the nearest shield and used it to cover both our bodies while I shouted at her slave girls to find another skirt for her. Their giggles only increased my fury, and as soon as both Lostris and I were once again decently covered, I rounded on Tanus.

'As for you, you careless ruffian, I shall report you to my Lord Intef! He will have the skin flogged from your back.'

'You will do no such thing,' Tanus laughed at me, and threw one wet muscled arm around my shoulders to hug me so soundly that I was lifted off my feet, 'for he would have you flogged just as merrily. Nevertheless, thank you for your concern, old friend.'

He looked around quickly, with one arm still encircling my shoulder, and frowned. The *Breath of Horus* was separated from the other ships of the squadron, but by now the hunt was over. Every galley but ours had taken its full share of the bag that the priests had sanctioned us.

Tanus shook his head. 'We did not make the most of our chances, did we?' he grunted, and ordered one of his officers to hoist the recall signal to the squadron.

Then he forced a smile. 'Let us broach a jug of beer together, for now we have a while to wait and this has been thirsty work.' He went to the bows where the slave girls were fussing over Lostris. At first I was still so angry that I would not join their impromptu picnic on the deck. Instead I maintained an aloof dignity in the stern.

'Oh, let him sulk a while,' I heard Lostris' stage-whisper to Tanus as she recharged his cup with foaming beer. 'The old darling gave himself

22

an awful scare, but he will get over it as soon as he is hungry. He does so love his food.'

She is the epitome of injustice, is my mistress. I never sulk, I am no glutton, and at that time I was barely thirty years of age, although to a fourteen-year-old anyone above twenty is an ancient, and I admit that, when it comes to food, I do have the refined tastes of a connoisseur. The roast wild goose with figs that she was ostentatiously displaying was one of my favourite dishes, as she very well knew.

I made them suffer for a while longer, and it was only when Tanus brought me a jug of beer with his own hand and cajoled me with all his charm that I deigned to relent a little and let him lead me to the prow. Still, I was a little stiff with them until Lostris kissed my cheek and said, loud enough for all to hear, 'My girls tell me that you took command of the ship like a veteran, and that you would have dived overboard to rescue me. Oh, Taita, what would I ever do without you?' Only then would I smile at her and accept the slice of goose she pressed upon me. It was delicious, and the beer was of three-palm quality. Even so, I ate sparingly, for I have my figure to consider and her earlier jibe about my appetite still rankled a little.

Tanus' squadron was scattered widely across the lagoon, but now it began to regroup. I saw that some of the other galleys had suffered damage, as we had. Two ships had collided in the heat of the chase, while four others had been attacked by the quarry. However, they reassembled swiftly and took up their battle stations. Then, in line astern and with strings of gay pennants fluttering at the mastheads to proclaim the size of each galley's bag,

23

they dashed past us. The crews raised a cheer as they came level with the *Breath of Horus*. Tanus saluted them with a clenched fist and the Blue Crocodile standard was dipped at the masthead, for all the world as though we had just achieved a famous victory against daunting odds. Boyish display, perhaps, but then I am still enough of a boy to enjoy military ceremonial.

As soon as it was over, the squadron resumed its battle stations and was holding its position against the light breeze that had sprung up, with skilful use of paddles and steering-oars. Of course, there was no sign of the slaughtered hippopotami as yet. Although every galley had killed at least one, while some had killed two and even three, the carcasses had all sunk away into the green depths of the lagoon. I knew that Tanus was secretly lamenting the fact that the *Breath of Horus* had not been the most successful boat, and that our protracted encounter with the bull had limited our score to only that single animal. He was accustomed to excelling. Anyway, he was not his usual ebullient self and he soon left us on the prow and went to supervise the repairs to the hull of the *Breath of Horus*.

The bull's charge had sprung the underwater planking and we were taking enough water to necessitate constant bailing of the bilges with leather buckets. This was a most inefficient procedure which diverted men from their duties as rowers and warriors. Surely it could be improved upon, I thought to myself.

So while we waited for the carcasses of the dead beasts to rise, I sent one of the slave girls to fetch the basket that contained my writing instruments.

24

Then, after a little further thought, I began to sketch out an idea for mechanically removing the water from the bilges of a fighting galley in action, a method which did not demand the efforts of half the crew. It was based on the same principle as the shadoof water buckets. I thought that two men might operate it instead of a dozen at the buckets, as was now the case.

When I had completed the sketch, I pondered on the collision that had caused the original damage. Historically, the tactics used in battles between squadrons of river galleys had always been the same as those of land engagements. The ships would lie alongside each other and exchange volleys of arrows. They would then close and grapple and board, and finish the business with the sword. The galley captains were always careful to avoid collision, as this was considered sloppy seamanship.

'But what if—' I thought suddenly, and I began a sketch of a galley with a reinforced bow. As the idea took firm root I added a horn like that of the rhinoceros at the water line. It could be carved from hardwood and clad with bronze. Angled forwards and slightly downwards, it could be driven through the hull of an opposing vessel to rip out her belly. I was so engrossed that I did not hear Tanus come up behind me. He snatched the papyrus scroll from me and studied it avidly.

Of course, he understood instantly what I was about. When his father had lost his fortune, I had tried everything in my power to find a rich patron to sponsor him to enter one of the temples as a novice scribe, there to continue his studies and his learning. For I truly believed that, with my tutelage, he had every prospect of developing into one of the great minds of Egypt, perhaps in time a name to rank with that of Imhotep who, one thousand years before, had designed those first marvellous pyramids at Saqqarah.

I had been unsuccessful, naturally enough, for the same enemy whose spite and guile had destroyed Tanus' father had set out to bar the way to Tanus himself. No man in the land could prevail against such a baleful influence. So instead I had helped Tanus to enter the army. Despite my disappointment and misgivings, this had been his own choice of career ever since he had first stood upright and wielded a wooden sword on the other infants in the playground.

'By the carbuncles on Seth's buttocks!' he exclaimed now, as he studied my drawings. 'You and that designing-brush of yours are worth ten full squadrons to me!'

Tanus' casual blasphemy on the name of the great god Seth always alarms me. For although both he and I are Horus men, still I do not believe in flagrantly offering offence to any member of the pantheon of Egyptian gods. I personally never pass a shrine without offering a prayer or making a small sacrifice, no matter how humble or unimportant the god it houses. It is, to my mind, simple common sense and good insurance. One has sufficient enemies amongst men without deliberately seeking out others amongst the gods. I am particularly obsequious to Seth, for his formidable reputation terrifies me. I suspect that Tanus knows all this and deliberately does it to tease me. However, my discomfort was soon forgotten in the warm glow of his praise.

'How do you do it?' he demanded. 'I am the soldier, and today I saw everything that you did. Why did not the same ideas occur to me?'

We were instantly immersed in a lively discussion of my designs. Of course, Lostris could not be excluded for long, and she came to join us. Her handmaidens had dried and rebraided her hair and retouched her make-up. Her loveliness was a distraction, especially since she stood beside me and nonchalantly draped one slim arm over my shoulder. She would never have touched a man like that in public, for it would have offended against custom and modesty. But then I am not a man, and though she leaned against me, her eyes never left Tanus' face.

Her preoccupation with him went back to when she had first learned to walk. She had stumbled along adoringly behind the lordly ten-year-old Tanus, faithfully trying to copy his every gesture and word. When he spat, she spat. When he swore, she lisped the same oath, until Tanus had complained bitterly to me, 'Can you not make her leave me alone, Taita? She's just a baby!' He was not doing much complaining now, I noticed.

At last we were interrupted by a hail from the lookout in the bows, and we all hurried forward and peered eagerly across the lagoon. The first hippopotamus carcass was rising to the surface. It came up belly first as the gases in its intestines expanded and the guts distended like a child's balloon made from a goat's bladder. It bobbed on the surface with all its legs extended stiffly. One of the galleys sped across to recover it. A sailor scrambled out on to the carcass and secured a line to one of the legs. As soon as this was done, the

27

galley towed it away towards the distant shore.

By now the huge corpses were surfacing all around us. The galleys gathered them up and dragged them away. Tanus secured two of them to our stern-hawser and the rowers strained at their paddles to move them through the water.

As we approached the shore I shaded my eyes against the slanting sun's rays and peered ahead. It seemed that every man, woman and child in Upper Egypt was waiting upon the bank. They were a vast multitude, dancing and singing and waving palm-fronds to welcome the incoming fleet. The restless movement of their white robes seemed like a storm surf breaking upon the edge of the placid lagoon.

As each galley drew up against the bank, teams of men clad only in the briefest loin-cloths waded out as deep as their armpits to fasten ropes to the bloated carcasses. In their excitement they were oblivious to the ever-present threat of crocodiles lurking in the opaque green waters. Every season these ferocious dragons devour hundreds of our people. Sometimes they are so bold that they rush out on to dry land to seize a child playing near the water's edge or a peasant woman washing clothes or drawing water for her family.

Now, in the vast meat-hunger that gripped them, the people were interested in only one thing. They seized the ropes and hauled the carcasses ashore. As they slithered up the muddy bank, scores of tiny silver fish that had been feasting on the open wounds were slow to relinquish their hold and were drawn out with the carcasses. Stranded upon the mud-banks, they flopped and quivered like stars that had fallen to earth.

Men and women, all wielding knives or axes, swarmed like ants over the bodies. In a delirium of greed they howled and snarled at each other like vultures and hyenas on a lion's kill, disputing each titbit as they hacked at the gigantic carcasses. Blood and bone chips flew in sheets as the blades hacked and hewed. There would be long lines of wounded at the temple that evening, awaiting treatment from the priests for their missing fingers and gashes down to the bone where the careless blades had slipped.

I too would be busy half the night, for in some quarters I have a reputation as a medical doctor that surpasses even that of the priests of Osiris. In all modesty I must admit that this reputation is not entirely unwarranted, and Horus knows my fees are much more reasonable than those of the holy men. My Lord Intef allows me to keep for myself a third part of all that I earn. Thus I am a man of some substance, despite my slave status.

From the stern-tower of the *Breath of Horus* I watched the pantomime of human frailty that was being played out below me. Traditionally the populace is allowed to eat its fill of the meats of the hunt upon the foreshore, just as long as none of the spoils are carried away. Living as we do in a verdant land which is fertilized and watered by the great river, our people are well fed. However, the staple diet of the poorer classes is grain, and months may pass between their last mouthful of meat and the next. Added to which, the festival was a time when all the normal restraints of everyday life were thrust aside. There was licence to excess in all things of the body, in food and drink and carnal passion. There would be sore bellies and aching heads and matrimonial recriminations on the morrow, but this was the first day of the festival and there was no check on any appetite.

I smiled as I watched a mother, naked to the waist and plastered from head to toe with blood and fat, emerge from the belly cavity of a hippopotamus, clutching a running lump of liver which she threw to one of her brood in the jostling, shrieking pack of children that surrounded the carcass. The woman ducked back into the interior of the beast, while, clutching his prize, the child darted away to one of the hundreds of cooking-fires that burned along the shore. There an elder brother snatched the hunk of liver from him and threw it on the coals, while a pack of younger urchins crowded forward impatiently, slavering like puppies.

The eldest child hooked the barely scorched liver off the fire with a green twig, and his brothers and sisters fell upon it and devoured it. Immediately it was consumed they bayed for more, with fat and juice running down their faces and dripping from their chins. Many of the younger ones had probably never tasted the delicious flesh of the river-cow before. It is sweet and tender and fine-grained, but most of all it is fat, fatter than beef or striped wild ass, and the marrow-bones are truly a delicacy fit for the great god Osiris himself. Our people are starved of animal fat and the taste of it drove them wild. They gorged themselves, as was their right on this day.

I was content to keep aloof from this riotous mob, happy in the knowledge that my Lord Intef's bailiffs would secure the finest cuts and marrow-bones for the palace kitchens where the cooks would prepare my personal platter to perfection. My precedence in the vizier's household exceeds all other, even that of his major-domo or the commander of his bodyguard, both of whom are free-born. Of course, it is never openly spoken of, but all tacitly acknowledge my privileged and superior position and few would dare challenge it.

I watched the bailiffs at work now, claiming the share of my lord, the governor and grand vizier of all the twenty-two nomes of Upper Egypt. They swung their long staves with the expertise born of long practice, whacking any bare back or set of naked buttocks that presented themselves as targets, and shouting their demands.

The ivory teeth of the animals belonged to the vizier, and the bailiffs collected every one of them. They were as valuable as the elephant tusks that are brought down in trade from the land of Cush, beyond the cataracts. The last elephant had been killed in our Egypt almost one thousand years ago, in the reign of one of the pharaohs of the Fourth Dynasty, or so the hieroglyphics on the stele in his temple boast. Naturally, from the fruits of the hunt my lord was expected to tithe the priests of Hapi who were the titular shepherds of the goddess's flock of river-cows. However, the amount of the tithe was in my lord's discretion, and I who was in overall charge of the palace accounts knew where the lion's share of the treasure would end up. My Lord Intef does not indulge in unnecessary generosity, even towards a goddess.

As for the hides of the hippopotamus, these belonged to the army and would be turned into

31

war shields for the officers of the guards regiments. The army quartermasters were supervising the skinning-out and the handling of the hides, each of which was almost the size of a Bedouin tent.

The meat that could not be consumed on the bank would be pickled in brine, or smoked or dried. Ostensibly it would be used to feed the army, the members of the law courts, the temples and other civil servants of the state. However, in practice a large part of it would be discreetly sold, and the proceeds would filter down quite naturally into my lord's coffers. As I have said before, my lord was the wealthiest man in the Upper Kingdom after Pharaoh himself, and growing richer every year.

A fresh commotion broke out behind me, and I turned quickly. Tanus' squadron was still in action. The galleys were drawn up in line of battle, stem to stern, parallel to the shore-line, but fifty paces off it on the edge of the deeper water. On each ship harpooneers stood at the rails with their weapons poised and pointed down at the surface of the lagoon.

The taint of blood and offal in the water had attracted the crocodiles. Not only from all over the lagoon, but from as far off as the main course of the Nile, they had come swarming to the feast. The harpooneers were waiting for them. Each long harpoon pole was tipped with a relatively small bronze head, viciously barbed. Spliced to an eye in the metal head was a tough flax rope.

The skill of the harpooneers was truly impressive. As one of these scaly saurians came slipping through the green water, with its great crested tail flailing, moving like a long dark

32

shadow, silent and deadly beneath the surface, they would be waiting for it. They would allow the crocodile to pass beneath the galley, and then, as it emerged on the far side with the harpooneer's movements screened from it by the ship's hull, he would lean out over it and stab downwards.

It was not a violent blow, but an almost delicate dab with the long pole. The bronze head was as sharp as a surgeon's needle, and its full length was buried deep beneath the reptile's thick, scaly hide. The harpooneer aimed for the back of the neck, and so skilful were these thrusts that many of them pierced the spinal cord and killed the creature instantly.

However, when a blow missed its mark, the water exploded as the wounded crocodile burst into wild convulsions. With a twist of the harpoon pole the metal head was detached and remained buried in the reptile's armoured neck. Then four men took the creature on the flax line to control its contortions. If the crocodile was a large one—and some of them were four times the length of a man stretched out on the ground—then the coils of line were whipped away smoking over the gunwale, scorching the palms of the men who were trying to hold it.

When this happened, even the hungry crowds on the beach paused for a while to cheer and shout encouragement, and to watch the struggle as the crocodile was eventually subdued or the rope parted like a whiplash and the sailors were sent tumbling backwards across the deck. More often, the stout flax line held. As soon as the crew were able to turn the reptile's head towards them, it could no longer swim out into the deep water.

They could then drag it in a turmoil of froth and white water to the ship's side where another gang was waiting with clubs to crush the rock-hard skull.

When the carcasses of the crocodiles were dragged to the bank, I went ashore to examine them. The skinners of Tanus' regiment were already at work.

It was the grandfather of our present king who had granted the regiment the honorific 'the Blue Crocodile Guards' and bestowed upon them the standard of the Blue Crocodile. Their battle armour is made from the horny skins of these dragons. Properly treated and cured, it becomes hard enough to stop an arrow or turn the edge of an enemy sword-cut. It is far lighter in weight than metal, and much cooler to wear in the desert sun. Tanus, in his crocodile-skin helmet all decorated with ostrich plumes, and his breastplate of the same hide, polished and starred with bronze rosettes, is a sight to strike terror into the heart of an enemy, or turmoil into the belly of any maiden who looks upon him.

As I measured and noted the length and girth of each carcass, and watched the skinners at work, I felt not even the most fleeting sympathy for these hideous monsters as I had for the slaughtered river-cows. To my mind there is no more loathsome beast in nature than the crocodile, with the possible exception of the venomous asp.

My revulsion was increased a hundredfold when a skinner slit open the belly of one of the largest of these grotesque animals, and out on to the mud slithered the partly digested remains of a young girl. The crocodile had swallowed the entire top half of her body, from the waist upwards. Although the flesh was bleached soft and pasty-white by the digestive juices and was sloughing from the skull, the girl's top-knot was still intact and neatly plaited and coiled above the ghastly, ruined face. As a further macabre touch, there was a necklace around her throat and pretty bracelets of red and blue ceramic beads on the skeletal wrists.

No sooner was this gruesome relic revealed than there came a shriek so high and heart-rending that it cut through the hubbub of the throng, and a woman elbowed aside the soldiers and ran forward to drop on her knees beside the pitiful remains. She tore her clothing and keened the dreadful ululation of mourning.

'My daughter! My little girl!' She was the same woman who had come to the palace the previous day to report her daughter missing. The officials had told her that the child had probably been abducted and sold into slavery by one of the gangs of bandits who were terrorizing the countryside. These gangs had become a force in the land, blatantly conducting their lawless depredations in broad daylight right up to the gates of the cities. The palace officials had warned the woman that there was nothing they could do about recovering her daughter, for the gangs were beyond any control that the state could exert upon them.

For once this dire prediction had proved unfounded. The mother had recognized the ornaments which still decorated the pathetic little corpse. My heart went out to the stricken woman, as I sent a slave to fetch an empty wine jar. Although the woman and her child were both strangers to me, I could not prevent my own tears

35

from welling up as I helped her to gather the remains and place them in the jar for decent burial.

As she staggered away into the uncaring multitude of revellers, carrying the jar clutched to her breast, I reflected that despite all the rites and prayers that the mother would lavish upon her daughter, and even in the unlikely event that she could afford the staggering cost of the most rudimentary mummification, the child's shade could never find immortality in the life beyond the grave. For that to happen, the corpse must be intact and whole before embalming. My feelings were all for the unfortunate mother. It is a weakness of mine that I so often lament, that I take upon myself the cares and sorrows of every unfortunate that crosses my path. It would be easier to have a harder heart, and a more cynical turn of mind.

As always when I am saddened or distressed, I reached for my brush and scroll and began to record all that was taking place around me, everything from the harpooneers, the bereaved mother, the skinning and the butchery of the dead river-cows and crocodiles on the beach, to the unfettered behaviour of the feasting, revelling populace.

Already those who were stuffed with meat and gorged with beer were snoring where they had fallen, oblivious of being kicked and trampled by the others still capable of remaining upright. The younger and more shameless were dancing and embracing and using the gathering darkness and the inadequate cover of the scanty bushes and the trampled papyrus beds to screen their blatant copulations. This wanton behaviour was merely a symptom of the malaise that afflicted the entire land. It would not have been thus if only there had been a strong pharaoh, and a moral and upright administration in the nome of Greater Thebes. The common people take their example from those above them.

Although I disapproved most strongly of it all, still I recorded it faithfully. Thus an hour sped away while I sat cross-legged and totally absorbed upon the poop-deck of the *Breath of Horus*, scribbling and sketching. The sun sank and seemed to quench itself in the great river, leaving a coppery sheen on the water and a smoky glow in the western sky as though it had set fire to the papyrus beds.

The crowds on the beach were becoming ever more raucous and unrestrained. The harlots were doing a brisk trade. I watched a plump and matronly love-priestess, wearing the distinctive blue amulet of her calling upon her forehead, lead a skinny sailor who was half her size from one of the galleys into the shadows beyond the firelight. There she dropped her skirts and fell to her knees in the dust, presenting him with a quivering pair of monumental buttocks. With a happy cry the little fellow was upon her like a dog on a bitch, and within seconds she was yapping as loudly as he was. I began to sketch their antics, but the light faded swiftly, and I was forced to quit for the day.

As I set my scroll aside, I realized with a start that I had not seen my mistress since before the incident with the dead child. I leaped to my feet in a panic. How could I have been so remiss? My mistress had been strictly raised, I had seen to that. She was a good and moral child, fully aware of the duties and obligations which law and custom placed upon her. She was aware also of the honour of the high family to which she belonged, and of her place in society. What was more, she stood in as much awe as I did of her father's authority and temper. Of course I trusted her.

I trusted her as much as I would have trusted any other strong-willed young creature in the first flush of passionate womanhood on a night such as this, alone somewhere in the darkness with the handsome and equally passionate young soldier with whom she was totally infatuated.

My panic was not so much for the fragile maidenhead of my mistress, that ethereal talisman which once lost is seldom mourned, as for the much more substantial risk of damage to my own skin. On the morrow we would return to Karnak and the palace of my Lord Intef, where there would be wagging tongues aplenty to carry the tale of any lapse or indiscretion on any of our parts to him.

My lord's spies permeated every layer of society and every corner of our land, from the docks and the fields to the palace of Pharaoh itself. They were even more numerous than my own, for he had more money to pay his agents, although many of them served both of us impartially and our networks interlocked at many levels. If Lostris had disgraced us all, father, family, and me her tutor and guardian, then my Lord Intef would know of it by morning, and so would I.

I ran from one end of the ship to the other, searching for her. I climbed into the stern-tower and scanned the beach in desperation. I could see nothing of her or of Tanus, and my worst fears were encouraged.

Where to search for them in this mad night I could not begin to think. I caught myself wringing my hands in an agony of frustration, and stopped myself immediately. I am always at pains to avoid any appearance of effeminacy. I do so abhor those obese, mincing, posturing creatures who have suffered the same mutilation as I have. I always try to conduct myself like a man rather than a eunuch.

I controlled myself with an effort and assumed the same coldly determined mien that I had seen on Tanus' features in the heat of battle, whereupon my wits were restored to me and I became rational once again. I considered how my mistress was likely to behave. Of course, I knew her intimately. After all, I had studied her for fourteen years. I realized that she was much too fastidious and conscious of her noble rank brazenly to mingle with the drunken, uncouth throng upon the beach, or to creep away into the bushes to play the beast with two backs, as I had watched the sailor and the fat old harlot do. I knew that I could call upon no one else to assist me in my search, for that would have guaranteed that my Lord Intef would hear all about it. I had to do it all myself.

To what secret place had Lostris allowed herself to be carried away? Like most young girls of her age she was enchanted with the idea of romantic love. I doubted that she had ever seriously considered the more earthy aspects of the physical act, despite the best efforts of those two little black sluts of hers to enlighten her. She had not even displayed any great deal of interest in the mechanics of the business when I had attempted, as was my duty, to warn her, at least sufficiently to

39

protect her from herself.

I realized then that I must look for her in some place that would live up to her sentimental expectations of love. If there had been a cabin on the *Breath of Horus* I would have hurried to it, but our river galleys are small, utilitarian fighting ships, stripped down for speed and manoeuvrability. The crew sleep on the bare deck, while even the captain and his officers have only a reed awning for a night shelter. This was not rigged at the moment, and so there was no place aboard where they could be hiding.

Karnak and the palace were half a day's travel away. The slaves were only now erecting our tents on one of the small inshore islands that had been set aside to give our party privacy from the common herd of humanity. It was remiss of the slaves to be so tardy, but they had been caught up in the festivities. In the torchlight I could see that a few of them were more than a little unsteady on their feet as they struggled with the guy-ropes. They had not yet erected Lostris' personal tent, so the luxurious comforts of carpets and embroidered hangings and down-filled mattresses and linen sheets were not available to the lovers. So where then might they be?

At that moment a soft yellow glow of torchlight farther out on the lagoon caught my attention. Immediately my intuition was aroused. I realized that, given my mistress's connections with the goddess Hapi, her temple on its picturesque little granite island in the middle of the lagoon would be exactly the place that would draw Lostris irresistibly. I searched the beach for some means of reaching the island. Although there were shoals of small craft drawn up on the shore, the ferrymen were mostly falling-down drunk.

Then I spotted Kratas on the beach. The ostrich feathers on his helmet stood high above the heads of the crowd, and his proud bearing marked him out.

'Kratas!' I yelled at him, and he looked across at me and waved. Kratas was Tanus' chief lieutenant and, apart from myself, the firmest of his multitude of friends. I could trust Kratas as I dared trust no other.

'Get me a boat!' I screamed at him. 'Any boat!' I was so distraught and my tone so shrill that it carried clearly to him. It was typical of the man that he wasted not a moment in question or indecision. He strode to the nearest felucca on the shore. The ferryman was lying like a log in his own bilges. Kratas took him by the scruff of the neck and lifted him out bodily. He dropped him on the beach, and the ferryman never moved, but lay in a stupor of cheap wine, twisted in the attitude that Kratas had dumped him in. Kratas launched the craft himself and, with a few thrusts of the punt pole, laid alongside the *Breath of Horus*. In my haste I tumbled from the tower and landed in a heap in the bows of the tiny craft.

'To the temple, Kratas,' I pleaded with him as I scrambled up, 'and may the sweet goddess Hapi grant we are not already too late!'

With the evening breeze in the lateen sail we were whisked across the dark waters to the stone jetty below the temple. Kratas secured the painter to one of the mooring-rings, and made as if to follow me ashore, but I stopped him.

'For Tanus' sake, not mine,' I told him, 'do not

41

follow me, please.'

He hesitated a moment, then nodded. 'I will be listening for your call.' He drew his sword and offered it to me, hilt first. 'Will you need this?'

I shook my head. 'It is not that kind of danger. Besides, I have my dagger. But thank you for your trust.' I left him in the boat and hurried up the granite steps to the entrance of the temple of Hapi.

The rush torches in their brackets on the tall entrance pillars threw a ruddy, wavering light that seemed to bring to life the bas-relief carvings on the walls and make them dance. The goddess Hapi is one of my favourites. Strictly speaking, she is neither god nor goddess, but a strange, bearded, hermaphroditic creature possessed of both a massive penis and an equally cavernous vagina, and bounteous breasts that give milk to all. She is the deification of the Nile, and the goddess of the harvest. The two kingdoms of Egypt and all the peoples in them depend utterly upon her and the periodic flooding of the great river which is her alter ego. She is able to change her gender or, like many of the other gods of this very Egypt, take on the shape of any animal at will. Her favourite guise is that of the hippopotamus. Despite the god's ambiguous sexuality, my mistress Lostris always considered her to be female, and so do I. The priests of Hapi may differ from us on this view.

Her images upon the stone walls were vast and motherly. Painted in hectic primary colours of red and yellow and blue, she beamed down with the head of a kindly river-cow, and seemed to invite all of nature to be fruitful and to multiply. The implied invitation was most inappropriate to my present anxiety. It was my fear that my precious charge might even at this moment be availing herself of the goddess's indulgence.

A priestess was kneeling at the side-altar, and I ran to her, seized her by the hem of her cape and tugged at it urgently. 'Holy sister, tell me, have you seen the Lady Lostris, daughter of the grand vizier?' There were very few citizens of Upper Egypt who did not know my mistress by sight. They all loved her for her beauty, her gay spirit and her sweet disposition, and they clustered around her and cheered her in the streets and marketplaces when she walked abroad.

The priestess grinned at me, all wrinkled and toothless, and she laid one bony finger on the side of her nose with such a sly and knowing expression that all my worst fears were confirmed.

I shook her again, but less gently. 'Where is she, revered old mother? I beseech you, speak!' But instead she wagged her head and rolled her eyes towards the portals of the inner sanctum.

I sped across the granite flags, my heart outrunning my frantic feet, but even in my distress I wondered at the boldness of my mistress. Although as a member of the high nobility she had right of access to the holy of holies, was there another in all of Egypt who would have the nerve to choose such a place for her love tryst?

At the entrance to the sanctum I paused. My instinct had been right. There they were, the two of them, just as I had dreaded. I was so obsessed by my own certainty of what was taking place that I almost yelled aloud to them to stop it. Then I checked myself.

My mistress was fully clad, more so than was usual, for her breasts were covered and she had spread a blue woollen shawl over her head. She was kneeling before the gigantic statue of Hapi. The goddess beamed down upon her, bedecked in wreaths of blue water-lilies.

Tanus knelt beside her. He had laid aside his weapons and his armour. They were piled at the door of the sanctuary. He was dressed only in a linen shift and short tunic, with sandals on his feet. The young couple were holding hands, and their faces were almost touching as they whispered solemnly together.

My base suspicions were refuted, and I was struck with remorse and shame. How could I ever have doubted my mistress? Quietly I began to withdraw, although I would go only as far as the side-altar, where I would give thanks to the goddess for her protection, and from where I could keep a discreet eye on further proceedings.

However, at that moment Lostris rose to her feet and diffidently approached the statue of the goddess. I was so enthralled by her girlish grace that I lingered a moment longer to watch her.

From around her neck she unclasped the lapis lazuli figurine of the goddess which I had made for her. I realized with a pang that she was about to offer it as a sacrifice. That jewel had been crafted with all my love for her, and I hated to see it leave her throat. Lostris stood on tiptoe to hang it on the idol's neck. Then she knelt and kissed the stone foot while Tanus watched, still kneeling where she had left him.

She rose and turned to go back to him, but then she saw me in the doorway. I tried to melt away into the shadows, for I was embarrassed at having spied upon so intimate a moment. However, her face lit with joy and before I could escape, she ran to me and seized my hands.

'Oh, Taita, I am so glad that you are here—you of all people! It is so fitting. It makes it all so perfect.' She led me forward into the sanctum and Tanus rose to his feet and came smiling to take my other hand.

'Thank you for coming. I know we can always count upon you.' I wished that my motives had been as pure as they believed them to be, so I hid my guilty heart from them with a loving smile.

'Kneel here!' Lostris ordered me. 'Here, where you can hear every word we say to each other. You will bear witness for us before Hapi and all the gods of Egypt.' She pressed me to my knees, and then she and Tanus resumed their places in front of the goddess and took each other's hands, looking full into each other's eyes.

Lostris spoke first. 'You are my sun,' she whispered. 'My day is dark without you.'

'You are the Nile of my heart,' Tanus told her quietly, 'The waters of your love feed my soul.'

'You are my man, through this world and all the worlds to come.'

'You are my woman, and I pledge you my love. I swear it to you on the breath and the blood of Horus,' Tanus said clearly and openly, so that his voice echoed through the stone halls.

'I take up your pledge and return it to you one hundredfold,' Lostris cried. 'No one can ever come between us. Nothing can ever part us. We are one, for ever.'

She offered her face to his and he kissed her, deeply and lingeringly. As far as I was aware, it was the first kiss that the couple had ever exchanged. I

45

felt that I was privileged to have witnessed such an intimate moment.

As they embraced, a sudden chill wind off the lagoon swirled through the dimly lit halls of the temple and fluttered the torch flames, so that for an instant the faces of the two lovers blurred before my eyes and the image of the goddess seemed to stir and quiver. The wind passed as swiftly as it had come, but the whisper of it around the great stone pillars was like the distant sardonic laughter of the gods, and I shuddered with superstitious awe.

It is always dangerous to pique the gods with extravagant demands, and Lostris had just asked for the impossible. This was the moment that for years I had known was coming, and which I had dreaded more bitterly than the day of my own death. The pledge that Tanus and Lostris had made to each other could never endure. No matter how deeply they meant it, it could never be. I felt my own heart tearing within me as, at last, they broke the kiss and both turned back to me.

'Why so sad, Taita?' Lostris demanded, her own face flooded with joy. 'Rejoice with me, for this is the happiest day of my life.'

I forced my lips to smile, but I could find no word of comfort or of felicitation for these two, the ones I loved best in all the world. I remained upon my knees, with that fixed, idiotic smile on my lips and desolation in my soul.

Now Tanus lifted me to my feet and embraced me. 'You will speak to Lord Intef on my behalf, won't you?' he demanded as he hugged me.

'Oh yes, Taita,' Lostris joined her plea to his. 'My father will listen to you. You are the only one who can do it for us. You won't fail us, will you, Taita? You have never let me down, never once in all my life. You'll do it for me, won't you?'

What could I say to them? I could not be so cruel as to tell them the blunt truth. I could not find the words to blight this fresh and tender love. They were waiting for me to speak, to express my joy for them, and to promise them my help and support. But I was struck dumb, my mouth was as dry as if I had bitten into an unripe pomegranate.

'Taita, what is it?' I watched the joy wither upon my mistress's beloved countenance. 'Why do you not rejoice for us?'

'You know that I love you both, but—' I could not continue.

'But? But what, Taita?' Lostris demanded. 'Why do you give me "buts" and a long face on this happiest of all possible days?' She was becoming angry, her jaw was setting, but at the same time there were tears gathering deep in her eyes. 'Don't you want to help us? Is this the real value of all the promises you have made to me over the years?' She came to me and thrust her face close to mine in challenge.

'Mistress, please don't talk like that. I do not deserve that treatment. No, listen to me!' I placed my fingers on her lips to forestall another outburst. 'It is not me. It is your father, my Lord Intef—'

'Exactly.' Impatiently Lostris plucked my hand away from her mouth. 'My father! You will go to him and speak to him the way you always do, and it will be all right.'

'Lostris,' I began, and it was a sign of my distress that I used her name in this familiar fashion, 'you are no longer a child. You must not delude yourself with childish fantasies. You know that your father will never agree—'

She would not listen to me, she did not want to hear the truth that I would speak, so she rushed in with words to drown out mine. 'I know that Tanus has no fortune, yes. But he has a marvellous future ahead of him. One day he will command all the armies of Egypt. One day he will fight the battles which will reunite the two kingdoms, and I will be at his side.'

'Mistress, please hear me out. It is not only the lack of Tanus' fortune. It is more, much more.'

'His blood-line and his breeding, then? Is that what troubles you? You know full well that his family is as noble as ours. Pianki, Lord Harrab was my own father's equal and his dearest friend.' She had closed her ears to me. She did not realize the depth of the tragedy on which we were embarking. Neither she nor Tanus did, but then I was probably the only person in the kingdom who understood it fully.

I had protected her from the truth all these years and, of course, I had never been able to tell Tanus either. How could I explain it to her now? How could I reveal to her the depths of the hatred that her father bore towards the young man she loved? It was a hatred born out of guilt and envy, and yet all the more implacable for these reasons.

However, my Lord Intef was a crafty and devious man. He was able to conceal his feelings from those around him. He was able to dissemble his hatred and his spite, and to kiss the one he would destroy and heap rich gifts and lulling flattery upon him. He had the patience of the crocodile buried in the mud at the drinking-place on the river, waiting for the unsuspecting gazelle. He would wait years, even a decade, but when the opportunity arose, he was as swift as that reptile to strike and drag his prey under.

Lostris was blithely unaware of the depths of her father's rancour. She even believed that he had loved Pianki, Lord Harrab, as Tanus' father had loved him. But then how could she know the truth of it, for I had always shielded her from it? In her sweet innocence Lostris believed that the only objections that her father would have to her lover were those of fortune and family.

'You know it is true, Taita. Tanus is my equal in the lists of the nobility. It is written in the temple records for all to see. How can my father deny it? How can you deny it?'

'It is not for me to deny or to accede, mistress—'

'Then you will go to my father for us, won't you, dear Taita? Say you will, please say you will!'

I could only bow my head in acquiescence, and to hide the hopeless expression in my eyes.

The fleet was heavily laden on the return to Karnak. The galleys were low in the water under their cargoes of rawhides and salted meat. Thus our progress against the Nile's current was slower than on our outward journey, but still too swift for my heavy heart and mounting dread.

The lovers were gay and euphoric with their newly declared love and their trust in me to remove the obstacles from their path. I could not bring myself to deny them this day of happiness, for I knew that it would be one of the very last they would share. I think that if I could have found the words or summoned the courage, I would have urged them, there and then, to seek the consummation of their love that I had so opposed the night before. There would never be another chance for them, not after I had alerted my Lord Intef with my foredoomed attempt at matchmaking. Once he knew what they were about, he would come between them and thrust them apart for ever.

So instead I laughed and smiled as gaily as they did, and tried to hide my fears from them. They were so blinded by love that I succeeded, whereas at any other time my mistress would have seen through me immediately. She knows me almost as well as I know her.

We sat together in the prow, the three of us, and we discussed the re-enactment of the passion of Osiris that would be the highlight of the festival. My Lord Intef had made me the impresario of the pageant, and I had cast both Lostris and Tanus in leading roles.

The festival is held every second year, at the rising of the full moon of Osiris. There was a time when it was an annual event. However, the expense and disruption of royal life caused by having to remove the court from Elephantine to Thebes was so great that Pharaoh decreed a greater interval between the festivals. He was always a prudent man with his gold, was our Pharaoh.

The plans for the pageant provided me with a fine distraction from the looming confrontation with my Lord Intef, and so now I rehearsed the two lovers in their lines. Lostris was to play Isis, the wife of Osiris, while Tanus would take on the major role of Horus. They were both vastly amused at the idea of Tanus playing Lostris' son, and I had to explain that the gods were ageless, and it was quite possible that a goddess could appear younger than her offspring.

I had written a new script for the pageant to replace the one that had remained unchanged for almost a thousand years. The language of the ancient one was archaic and unsuitable for a modern audience. Pharaoh would be the guest of honour when the pageant was performed in the temple of Osiris on the final night of the festival, so I was particularly anxious that it should be a success. I had already encountered opposition to my new version of the passion from the more conservative nobles and priests. Only my Lord Intef's intervention had prevailed against their objections.

My lord is not a deeply religious man and would not normally have interested himself in theological arguments. However, I had included a few lines that were designed to amuse and flatter him. I read them to him out of context, and then tactfully pointed out to him that the chief opposition to my version came from the high priest of Osiris, a prissy old man who had once frustrated my Lord Intef's interest in a comely young acolyte. This was a trespass for which my lord had never forgiven the high priest.

Thus it was that my version would be performed for the first time. It was essential that the actors bring out the full glory of my poetry, or it might well be the last time it would be heard.

51

Both Tanus and Lostris possessed marvellous speaking voices, and they were determined to reward me for my promise to help them. They gave me of their best, and thus the rehearsal was so absorbing, their recitations so startling, that for a while I could forget myself.

Then I was brought back from the passion of the gods to my own mundane preoccupations by a cry from the lookout. The fleet was sweeping around the last bend in the river, and there lay the twin cities of Luxor and Karnak, that between them made up Greater Thebes, strung out along the bank before us and sparkling like a necklace of pearls in the stark Egyptian sunlight. Our fantastic interlude had ended, and we must face reality once again. My spirits tumbled as I scrambled to my feet.

'Tanus, you must transfer Lostris and myself to the galley of Kratas before we come any closer to the city. My lord's minions will be watching us from the land. They must not see us in your company.'

'A little late, is it not?' Tanus smiled at me. 'You should have thought of that some days ago.'

'My father will learn about us soon enough,' Lostris endorsed his objection. 'It might make your task easier if we forewarn him of our intentions.'

'If you know better than I, then you must do it your way and I will take no further part in this crazy business of yours.' I put on my most stiff and offended air, and they relented immediately.

Tanus signalled Kratas' galley alongside, and the lovers had only a few moments for their farewells. They dared not embrace before the eyes of half the

52

fleet, but the glances and the loving words they exchanged were almost as fulfilling.

From the stern-tower of Kratas' ship we waved to the *Breath of Horus* as she turned from us, and with her paddles flashing like the wings of a dragonfly, she bore away to her moorings in front of the city of Luxor, while we continued on up-river towards the palace of the grand vizier.

 Immediately we docked at the palace wharf, I made enquiry as to the whereabouts of my master and was relieved to learn that he had crossed the river to undertake a last-minute inspection of Pharaoh's tomb and funerary temple on the west bank. The king's temple and tomb had been under construction for the past twelve years, ever since the first day that he had donned the double white and red crown of the two kingdoms. It was nearing completion at last, and the king would be anxious to visit it as soon as the festival was over and he was free to do so. My Lord Intef was anxious that the king should not be disappointed. One of my lord's many titles and honours was Guardian of the Royal Tombs, and it was a serious responsibility.

His absence afforded me a further day in which to prepare my case and plan my strategy. However, the solemn promise that the two lovers had extracted from me was to speak out for them at the first opportunity, and I knew that would be on the morrow when my lord held his weekly assize.

As soon as I had seen my mistress safely ensconced in the harem, I hurried to my own quarters in that wing of the palace which is reserved for the special companions of the grand vizier.

My Lord Intef's domestic arrangements were as devious as the rest of his existence. He had eight wives, all of whom brought to his marriage-bed either substantial dowry or influential political connections. However, only three of these women had ever borne him children. Apart from my Lady Lostris, there were two sons.

As far as I was aware, and I was aware of everything that happened in the palace and most of what happened outside it, my lord had not visited the harem in the last fifteen years. The getting of Lostris had been the last occasion that he had performed his matrimonial duties. His sexual tastes lay in other directions. The special companions of the grand vizier who lived in our wing of the palace were as pretty a collection of slave boys as you could find in the Upper Kingdom, where over the previous hundred years pederasty had replaced wild-fowling and hunting as the favourite preoccupation of most of the nobility. This was merely another symptom of the ills that beset our lovely land.

I was the eldest of this select company of slave boys. Unlike so many others over the years whom, once their physical beauty had begun to fade or pall, my lord had sent to the auction block in the slave-market, I had endured. He had come to value me for virtues other than my physical beauty alone. Not that this had faded—on the contrary, it had grown more striking as I had matured. You must not think me vain if I mention this, but I have determined to set down nothing but the truth in these accounts. They are remarkable enough without my having to resort to false modesty.

No, my lord seldom pleasured himself with me in those days, a neglect for which I was truly thankful. When he did so, it was usually only to punish me. He knew full well the physical pain and the humiliation his attentions always caused me. Although I had still been a child when I first learned to hide my revulsion, and to simulate pleasure in the perverse acts that he forced upon me, I never succeeded in deceiving him.

Strangely, my feelings of disgust and my loathing for this unnatural congress never detracted from his own enjoyment, rather they seemed to enhance it. He was neither a gentle nor a compassionate man, my Lord Intef. I have counted in the hundreds the slave boys who, over the years, were brought to me weeping and torn after their first night of love with my master. I doctored them and tried my best to comfort them. That is perhaps why they called me *Akh-Ker* in the slave boys' quarters, a name which means Elder Brother.

I might no longer be my master's favourite plaything, but he valued me much more highly than that. I was many other things to him—physician and artist, musician and scribe, architect and bookkeeper, adviser and confidant, engineer and nursemaid to his daughter. I am not so naïve as to believe that he loved me or that he trusted me, but I think that at times he came as close to it as he was capable. That was why Lostris had prevailed upon me to plead on her behalf.

My Lord Intef had no concern for his only daughter, other than to maintain her marriage

55

value at its optimum, and this was another duty that he delegated entirely to me. Sometimes he did not speak a single word to her from one flooding of the Nile to the next. He showed no discernible interest in the regular reports which I made to him of her training and schooling.

Of course, I was always at pains to conceal from him my true feelings for Lostris, knowing that he would certainly use them against me at the first opportunity. I always tried to give him the impression that I found her tuition and her care a tedious duty that I mildly resented having thrust upon me, and that I shared his own disdain and distaste for all of womankind. I don't think he ever realized that, despite my emasculation, I had the feelings and desires of a natural man towards the opposite sex.

My lord's disinterest in his daughter was the reason why I was occasionally tempted, on the urging of my mistress, to run such insane risks as this latest escapade of ours on board the *Breath of Horus*. There was usually at least a chance that we would get away with it.

That evening I retired early to my private quarters, where my first concern was to feed and pamper my darlings. I have a love for birds and animals, and a way with them that amazes even myself. I had an intimate friendship with a dozen cats, for no one can ever claim to own a cat. I owned, on the other hand, a pack of fine dogs. Tanus and I used them to hunt the oryx and the lion out in the desert.

The wild birds flocked to my terrace to enjoy the hospitality I provided for them. They competed raucously amongst themselves for a perch on my shoulder or on my hand. The boldest of them would take food from between my lips. My tame gazelle would brush against my legs like one of the cats, and my two falcons squawk at me from their perches on the terrace. They were the rare desert Sakers, beautiful and fierce. Whenever we were able, Tanus and I would take them out into the desert to fly them against the giant bustards. I took great pleasure from their speed and aerial grace as they stooped down on their prey. Anyone else who attempted to fondle them would feel the cutting edge of those hooked yellow bills, but with me they were as gentle as sparrows.

Only once I had taken care of my menagerie did I call one of the slave boys to bring my evening meal. On the terrace overlooking the wide green expanse of the Nile I savoured the exquisite little dish of wild quail cooked in honey and goat's milk that the head chef had prepared especially to welcome me home. From there I was able to watch for the return of my lord's barge from the far bank. It came with the sunset glowing on the single square sail, and I felt my spirits sink. He might send for me this evening, and I was not ready to face him.

Then with relief I heard Rasfer, the commander of the palace guard, shouting for my lord's favourite of the moment, a sloe-eyed Bedouin lad, barely ten years old. A short while later I heard the child protesting in a terrified treble as Rasfer dragged him past my door towards the curtained entrance of the grand vizier's chambers. Although I had heard it so many times before, I never could harden myself to the sounds of the children, and I felt the familiar pang of pity. Still, I was relieved

57

that it was not I who would be called that evening. I would need a good night's sleep so as to look my best in the morning.

I woke before dawn with the feeling of dread still strong upon me. Even my ritual swim in the cool waters of the Nile did nothing to relieve it. I hurried back to my chamber where two of the slave boys were waiting to oil my body and comb out my hair. I detested the new fashion amongst the nobility of wearing make-up. My own skin and complexion were fine enough not to require it, but my lord liked his boys to use it, and I wanted to please him especially that day.

Even though my image in the bronze mirror reassured me, I could find no appetite for my breakfast. I was the first member of my lord's entourage awaiting his arrival in the water-garden where he held his assize every morning.

While I waited for the rest of the court to assemble I watched the kingfishers at work. I had designed and supervised the building of the water-garden. It was a marvellous complex of channels and ponds which overflowed from one into the other. The flowering plants had been collected from every part of the kingdom and beyond, and they were a dazzle of colour. The ponds were stocked with all the hundreds of varieties of fish that the Nile yields up to the nets of the fishermen, but they had to be replenished daily as a result of the depredations of the kingfishers.

My Lord Intef enjoyed watching the birds hovering in the air like jewels of lapis lazuli, then darting down to hit the water in a flash of spray, and rising again with a silver sliver quivering in their long bills. I think he saw himself as a fellow

58

predator, a fisher of men, and that he looked upon the birds as his kin. He never allowed the gardeners to discourage the birds.

Gradually I was joined by the rest of the court. Many of them were dishevelled and yawning from sleep. My Lord Intef keeps early hours and likes to complete the bulk of the business of state before the main heat of the day. We waited respectfully in the first rays of the sun for my lord's arrival.

'He's in a good mood this morning,' the chamberlain whispered, as he took his place beside me, and I felt a tiny prickle of hope. I might yet be able to escape the serious consequences of my foolhardy promise to Lostris.

There was a stirring and a murmuring amongst us as when the river breeze moves through the papyrus beds, and my Lord Intef came out to us.

His walk was stately and his manner was sumptuous, for he was mighty with the weight of his honours and his power. Around his neck he wore the Gold of Praise, that necklace of red gold from the mines of Lot which Pharaoh had laid upon him with his own hands. His praise-singer preceded him, a stump-legged dwarf chosen for his misshapen body and stentorian tones. It amused my lord to surround himself with curiosities, either beautiful or grotesque. Cavorting and prancing on his bowed legs, the dwarf chanted the lists of my lord's titles and honours.

'Behold the Support of Egypt! Greet the Guardian of the Waters of the Nile! Bow down before Pharaoh's Companion!' These were all titles granted by the king, and many of them imposed specific duties and obligations on him. As Guardian of the Waters, for instance, he was

59

responsible for monitoring the levels and flows of the seasonal floods of the Nile, a duty which was naturally delegated to that faithful, indefatigable slave, Taita.

I had spent half a year with a team of engineers and mathematicians working under me, measuring and carving the rock cliffs at Assoun so that the height of the waters rising up them could be accurately gauged and the volume of the flood calculated. From these figures I was able to estimate the size of the harvest months in advance. This enabled both famine and plenty to be anticipated and planned for by the administration. Pharaoh had been delighted with my work and bestowed further honours and reward upon my Lord Intef.

'Bend the knee for the Nomarch of Karnak and the Governor of all the twenty-two nomes of Upper Egypt! Greet the Lord of the Necropolis and the Keeper of the Royal Tombs!' My lord was by these titles responsible for designing, building and maintaining the monuments to pharaohs long dead and the one still living. Once again, these duties were unloaded upon a long-suffering slave's shoulders. My lord's visit to Pharaoh's tomb the day before had been the first that he had undertaken since the previous festival of Osiris. It was I who was sent out in the dust and the heat to cajole and curse the lying builders and the conniving masons. I often regretted having let my master realize the extent of my talents.

He singled me out now without seeming to have done so. The yellow eyes, as implacable as those of a wild leopard, touched mine, and he inclined his head slightly. I stepped in behind him as he passed,

60

and I was struck as always by his height and the width of his shoulders. He was an outrageously handsome man with long, clean limbs and a flat, hard belly. His head was leonine and his hair dense and lustrous. At this time he was forty years of age, and I had been his slave for almost twenty of those.

My Lord Intef led us to the barrazza in the centre of the garden, a thatched building without enclosing walls, open to the cool breeze off the river. He seated himself cross-legged on the paved floor at the low table on which lay the state scrolls, and I took my usual place behind him. The day's business began.

Twice during the morning my lord leaned back slightly towards me. He did not turn his head nor did he say a word, but he was asking my advice. I barely moved my lips and I kept my voice pitched so low that no one else could hear me and very few were even aware of the exchanges between us.

Once I murmured, 'He is lying,' and a second time, 'Retik is a better man for the post, and he has offered a gift of five gold rings to my lord's private treasury.' And though I did not mention it then, another ring of gold to me if the post were secured.

At noon my lord dismissed the congregation of officials and petitioners and called for his midday meal. For the first time that day we were alone together, except for Rasfer, who was both the commander of the palace guard and the official state executioner. Now he took his post at the gate to the garden, within sight of the barrazza but out of earshot.

With a gesture my lord invited me to move up to his elbow, and to taste the delicious meats and fruits that had been laid out before him. While we

61

waited for the effects of any possible poisoning to manifest themselves upon me, we discussed the morning's business in detail.

Then he questioned me about the expedition to the lagoon of Hapi and the great hippopotamus hunt. I described it all to him and gave him the figures of the profits that he might expect from the meat and hides and teeth of the river-cows. I inflated the estimate of profits a little, and he smiled. His smile is frank and charming. Once you have seen it, it is easier to understand my Lord Intef's ability to manipulate and control men. Even I, who should have known better, was once again lulled by it.

As he bit into a succulent cold cut of river-cow fillet, I drew a breath, screwed up my courage and began my plea. 'My lord should know that I allowed your daughter to accompany me on the expedition.' I could see by his eyes that he already knew this and that he had been waiting for me to attempt to conceal it from him.

'You did not think to obtain my permission beforehand?' he asked mildly, and I avoided his eyes and concentrated on peeling a grape for him as I answered, 'She only asked as we were on the point of departure. As you know, the goddess Hapi is her patron, and she wished to worship and make sacrifice at the lagoon temple.'

'Still you did not ask me?' he repeated, and I offered him the grape. He parted his lips and allowed me to slip it into his mouth. That could only mean that he was well disposed towards me, so obviously he had not yet found out the full truth about Tanus and Lostris.

'My lord was in council with the nomarch of

Assoun at the time. I would not have dared disturb you. Besides, there was no harm in it that I could fathom. It was a simple domestic decision which I thought beneath your concern.'

'You are so glib, aren't you, my darling?' he chuckled. 'And so beautiful today. I like the way you have painted your eyelids, and what is that perfume you are wearing?'

'It is distilled from the petals of the wild violet,' I replied. 'I am happy that you like it, for I have a flask of it as a small gift for you, my lord.' I produced the flask from my purse and went on my knees to offer it to him. He placed his finger under my chin and lifted my face to kiss me on the lips. Dutifully I responded to the kiss until he drew back and patted my cheek.

'Whatever it is you are up to, you are still very attractive, Taita. Even after all these years you can still make me smile. But tell me, you took good care of the Lady Lostris, did you not? You never let her out of your sight or care for a moment, did you?'

'As always, my lord,' I agreed vehemently.

'So there is nothing unusual concerning her that you wish to report to me, is there?'

I was still on my knees in front of him, and my next attempt to speak failed. My voice dried up.

'Do not squeak at me, my old darling,' he laughed, 'speak out like a man, even though you are not.' It was a cruel little jibe, but it steeled me.

'There is indeed something I wish humbly to bring to my lord's attention,' I said. 'And it does indeed concern the Lady Lostris. As I have already reported, your daughter's red moon rose for the first time at the flooding of the great river. Since

63

then the courses of her moon have flowed strongly each month.'

My lord made a small grimace of distaste, the functions of the feminine body repelled him. I found this ironic, considering his own preoccupation with those far less savoury reaches of the masculine anatomy.

I hurried on, 'The Lady Lostris is now of marriageable age. She is a woman of an ardent and loving nature. I believe it would be wise to find a husband for her, as soon as we can.'

'No doubt you have one to suggest?' he asked drily, and I nodded. 'There is indeed a suitor, my lord.'

'Not one, Taita. You mean another one, don't you? I know of at least six, including the nomarch of Assoun and the governor of Lot, who have already made offers.'

'I did mean another one, but this time one that the Lady Lostris approves of. As you recall, she referred to the nomarch as that fat toad, and to the governor as a randy old goat.'

'The child's approval or disapproval is of no interest to me whatsoever.' He shook his head, and smiled and stroked my cheek to encourage me. 'But go on, Taita, tell me the name of this lovelorn swain who will do me the honour of becoming my son-in-law in return for the richest dowry in Egypt.' I steeled myself to reply, but he stopped me. 'No, wait! Let me guess.'

His smile turned into that sly and foxy grin that I knew so well, and I realized that he had been toying with me.

'For Lostris to welcome him, he must be young and handsome.' He pretended to muse on it. 'And

64

for you to speak out for him, he must be a friend or a protégé of yours. There must have been an opportunity for this paragon to declare his suit and to solicit your support. What would be the time and the place for that to have happened, I wonder? Could it have been at midnight in the temple of Hapi, perhaps? Am I on the right trail, Taita?'

I felt myself pale. How did he know so much? He slid his hand around behind my head and caressed the nape of my neck. This was often his prelude to love-making, and he kissed me again.

'I can see by your face that my guesses are close to the target.' He took a handful of my hair and twisted it lightly. 'Now it remains only to divine the name of this bold lover. Could it be Dakka? No, no, Dakka is not so stupid as to incur my wrath.' He twisted my hair just hard enough to bring tears to my eyes. 'Kratas, then? He is handsome and foolhardy enough to take the risk.' He twisted harder and I felt a clump of my hair come away in his hand with a tearing sound. I choked back the whimper in my throat.

'Answer me, my darling, was it Kratas?' He forced my face down into his lap.

'No, my lord,' I whispered painfully. I was not surprised to find that he was fully aroused. He pushed my face down upon himself and held me there.

'Not Kratas, are you sure?' He pretended to be puzzled. 'If it was not Kratas, then I am at a loss to guess who else might be so insolent, so insulting and so mortally stupid as to approach the virgin daughter of the grand vizier of Upper Egypt.'

Abruptly, he raised his voice. 'Rasfer!' he cried. My head was twisted in his lap so that through

65

streaming eyes I could watch Rasfer approach.

In Pharaoh's menagerie on Elephantine Island at Assoun there was a huge black bear brought in many years ago by one of the trade caravans from the East. That vicious, scarred brute always reminded me strongly of the commander of my lord's bodyguard. They both had the same vast, shapeless body and the raw, savage power to crush a man to death. However, in loveliness of face and sweetness of disposition, the bear had been favoured far beyond Rasfer.

I watched Rasfer approach now at a trot that was surprisingly swift and agile for those heavy, tree-like legs and the swell of his hairy gut, and I was transported back over the years to the day that my manhood had been plucked from me.

It all seemed so familiar, as though I was being forced to live once more through that terrible day. Every detail of it was still so clear in my mind that I wanted to shriek aloud. The actors in that long-ago tragedy were the same. My Lord Intef, Rasfer the brute, and me. Only the girl was missing.

Her name had been Alyda. She had been the same age as me, sixteen sweet innocent years. Like me, she had been a slave. I remember her now as having been beautiful, but it is likely that my memory cheats me, for had she been so she would have gone into a harem of one of the great houses and not been relegated to the kitchen. I do know for certain that she had skin the colour and lustre of polished amber that was warm and soft to the touch. I will never forget the feel of Alyda's body, for I will never experience anything like it again. In our misery we had found comfort and deep solace in each other. I never discovered who it was that

66

betrayed us. I am not usually a vengeful man, but I still dream that one day I will find the person who delivered us up.

At that time I had been my Lord Intef's favourite, his special darling. When he discovered that I had been faithless to him, the affront to his self-esteem was such as to drive him to the very frontier of madness.

Rasfer had come to fetch us. He dragged us to my lord's chamber, one of us in each hand, as easily as if we had been a pair of kittens. There he had stripped us naked while my Lord Intef sat cross-legged on the floor, just as he was doing now. Rasfer bound Alyda's wrists and ankles with rawhide thongs. She was pale and shivering but she did not weep. My love for her and my admiration for her courage had never been stronger than at that moment.

My Lord Intef beckoned me to kneel in front of him and he took a lock of my hair and whispered endearments to me. 'Do you love me, Taita?' he asked, and because I was afraid, and because in some dim way I thought that it might spare Alyda's suffering, I answered, 'Yes, my lord, I love you.'

'Do you love anyone else, Taita?' he asked in a voice of silk and, coward and traitor that I was, I answered him, 'No, my lord, I love only you.' It was only then that I heard Alyda begin to weep. It was one of the most harrowing sounds of my life.

He called to Rasfer, 'Bring the slut here. Place her so that they can see each other clearly. Taita must be able to see everything that is done to her.'

As Rasfer pushed the girl into my line of vision I could see that he was grinning. Then my master raised his voice slightly: 'Very well, Rasfer, you may proceed.'

Rasfer slipped a loop of braided rawhide rope over Alyda's forehead. At close intervals the rope was knotted, so that it looked like a headband such as the Bedouin women wear. Standing behind the girl, Rasfer thrust a short, stout baton of olive wood through the rawhide loop and twisted it until it came up tight against her smooth, unblemished skin. The knots of harsh leather bit into her flesh and Alyda grimaced with the pain.

'Slowly, Rasfer,' my lord warned him. 'We still have a long way to go.'

The olive-wood baton seemed like a child's toy in Rasfer's huge, hairy paws. He twisted it with careful deliberation, a quarter of a turn at a time. The knots bit in deeper, and Alyda's mouth dropped open and her lungs emptied in a gasping rush of air. All the colour drained from her skin so that it turned to the colour of dead ashes. She struggled to fill her empty lungs with air and then released it in one long, penetrating scream.

Still grinning, Rasfer twisted the baton and the line of leather knots buried themselves in Alyda's forehead. Her skull changed shape. At first I thought it was a trick of my overwrought mind, then I realized that her head was, in truth, constricting and elongating as the loop tightened. Her scream was now a single unbroken peal that plunged into my heart like a sword-blade. It went on and on for what seemed like for ever.

Then her skull burst. I heard the bone collapse with a sound like a palm-nut crushed in the jaws of a feeding elephant. That terrible, piercing scream was cut off abruptly, as Alyda's corpse sagged in Rasfer's hands, and my soul was filled to

68

overflowing with my sorrow and despair.

After what seemed like an eternity my lord lifted my head and looked into my eyes. His expression was sad and regretful as he told me, 'She has gone, Taita. She was evil and she led you astray. We must make certain that it never happens again. We must protect you from any further temptations.'

Once again he signalled to Rasfer and he took Alyda's naked body by the heels and dragged it out on to the terrace. The back of her crushed head bumped down the steps and her hair streamed out behind her. With a heave of his massive shoulders, Rasfer threw her far out into the river. Her slack limbs flashed and tumbled as she fell and struck the water. She sank swiftly with her hair spreading out around her like trailing fronds of the river-weed.

Rasfer turned away and went to the end of the terrace where two of his men were tending a brazier of burning charcoal. Beside the brazier a full set of surgeon's instruments was laid out on a wooden tray. He glanced over them and then nodded with satisfaction. He returned and bowed before my Lord Intef. 'All is in readiness.'

My master wiped my tear-streaked face with one finger, then lifted the finger to his lips as though he were tasting my sorrow. 'Come, my pretty darling,' he whispered, and lifting me to my feet he led me out on to the terrace. I was so distraught and blinded by my tears that I did not realize my own peril until the soldiers seized me. They threw me down and held me spread-eagled on the terracotta tiles, pinning me at wrists and ankles so that I could move only my head.

My master knelt at my head, while Rasfer knelt

between my spread thighs.

'You will never do this evil thing again, Taita.' Only then did I become aware of the bronze scalpel that Rasfer had concealed in his right hand. My master nodded at him and he reached down with his free hand and seized me and stretched me out, until it felt as though he were plucking my entrails out through my groin.

'What a fine pair of eggs we have here!' Rasfer grinned and showed me the scalpel, holding it up before my eyes. 'But I am going to feed them to the crocodiles, just as I did with your little girl-friend.' He kissed the blade.

'Please, my lord,' I begged, 'have mercy—' but my entreaties ended in a shrill cry as Rasfer slashed down with the blade. It felt as though a red-hot skewer had been thrust up into my belly.

'Say goodbye to them, pretty boy.' Rasfer held up the sac of pale wrinkled skin and its pathetic contents. Then he began to rise, but my lord stopped him. 'You have not finished,' he told Rasfer quietly. 'I want all of it.'

Rasfer stared at him for a moment, not understanding the order. Then he began to chuckle until his belly bounced. 'By the blood of Horus,' he roared, 'from now on pretty boy will have to squat like a girl when he wants to piss!' He struck again, then bellowed with laughter as he held up the finger of flesh that had once been the most intimate part of my body.

'Never mind, boy. You'll walk a lot lighter without that weight to carry around with you.' Staggering with laughter, he started towards the edge of the terrace as if to hurl them into the river, but once again my lord called to him sharply.

70

'Give them to me!' he ordered, and obediently Rasfer placed the bloody fragments of my manhood in his hands. For a few seconds my lord examined them curiously, and then he spoke to me again. 'I am not so cruel as to deprive you for ever of such fine trophies, my darling. I will send these to the embalmers, and when they are ready I will have them placed on a necklace surrounded with pearls and lapis lazuli. They will be my present to you at the next festival of Osiris. Thus at the day of your burial they can be placed in your tomb with you, and if the gods are kind, you may have the use of them in the afterlife.'

Those terrible memories should have ended at the moment when Rasfer staunched the bleeding with a ladle of boiling embalming lacquer from the brazier, and I was plunged into blessed oblivion by the unbearable intensity of the pain, but now I was trapped in the nightmare. It was all happening again. Only this time little Alyda was missing, and instead of the gelding-knife Rasfer held the whip of hippo-hide in his great hairy fist.

The whip was as long as the full stretch of Rasfer's arms and it tapered to the thickness of his little finger at the point. I had watched him whittling it himself, shaving off the coarse outer layer from the long strip of cured hide until the inner skin was exposed, periodically pausing to test the balance and the heft of it, cutting it through the air until it keened and whined like the desert wind through the canyons of the hills of Lot. It was the colour of amber and Rasfer had polished it lovingly until it was smooth and translucent as glass, but so supple that he could bend it into a perfect arc between those bear-like paws. He had allowed the

71

blood of a hundred victims to dry upon it and to dye the thin end of it to a lustrous patina that was aesthetically quite beautiful.

Rasfer was an artist with this awful tool. He could flick out and leave on the tender thigh of a young girl only a crimson weal that never broke the skin, but stung as viciously as a scorpion and left his victim writhing and weeping with the agony of it; or with a dozen hissing strokes he could strip the skin and flesh from a man's back and leave his ribs and the crest of his spine exposed.

He stood over me now and grinned as he flexed the long lash in his hands. Rasfer loved his work, and he hated me with all the force of his envy and the feelings of inferiority that my intelligence and looks and favour engendered in him.

My Lord Intef stroked my naked back and sighed. 'You are so wicked sometimes, my old darling. You try to deceive me to whom you owe the deepest loyalty. Nay, more than simple loyalty—to whom you owe your very existence.' He sighed again. 'Why do you force this unpleasantness upon me? You should know much better than to press the suit of that young jackanapes upon me. It was a ludicrous attempt, but I suppose that I understand why you made it. That childlike sense of compassion is one of your many weaknesses, and one day will probably be the cause of your complete downfall. However, at times I find it rather quaint and endearing and I might readily have forgiven you for it, but I cannot overlook the fact that you have endangered the market value of the goods that I placed in your care.' He twisted my head up so that my mouth was free to answer him. 'For that, you must be punished. Do you understand me?'

'Yes, my lord,' I whispered, but I rolled my eyes to watch the whip in Rasfer's hands. Once again my Lord Intef buried my face in his lap, and then he spoke to Rasfer above my head.

'With all your cunning, Rasfer. Do not break the skin, please. I do not want this delightfully smooth back marred permanently. Ten will do as a start. Count them aloud for us.'

I had watched a hundred or more unfortunates undergo this punishment, some of them warriors and vaunted heroes. Not one of them was able to remain silent under the lash of Rasfer. In any event it was best not to do so, for he took silence as a personal challenge to his skill. I knew this well, having travelled this bitter road before. I was quite prepared to swallow any stupid pride and pay tribute to Rasfer's art in a loud voice. I filled my lungs in readiness.

'One!' grunted Rasfer, and the lash fluted. The way a woman later forgets the full pain of childbirth, I had forgotten the exquisite sting of it, and I screamed even louder than I had intended.

'You are fortunate, my dear Taita,' my Lord Intef murmured in my ear. 'I had the priests of Osiris examine the goods last night. They are still intact.' I squirmed in his lap. Not only from the pain, but also at the thought of those lascivious old goats from the temple probing and prying into my little girl.

Rasfer had his own little ritual to draw out the punishment and to ensure that both he and his victim were able to savour the moment to the full. Between each stroke he jogged in a small circle around the barrazza, grunting exhortations and

73

encouragement to himself, holding the whip at high port like a ceremonial sword. As he completed the circle he was in position for the next stroke, and he raised the lash high.

'Two!' he cried, and I shrieked again.

One of Lostris' slave girls was waiting for me on the broad terrace of my quarters when I limped painfully up the steps from the garden.

'My mistress bids you attend her immediately,' she greeted me.

'Tell her that I am indisposed.' I tried to avoid the summons and, shouting for one of the slave boys to dress my injuries, I hurried through into my chamber in an attempt to rid myself of the girl. I could not face Lostris yet, for I dreaded having to report my failure, and having at last to make her face the reality and the impossibility of her love for Tanus. The black girl followed me, ogling the livid weals across my back with delicious horror.

'Go tell your mistress that I am injured, and that I cannot come to her,' I snapped over my shoulder.

'She told me that you would try to wriggle out of it, but she told me also that I was to stay with you and see to it that you did not.'

'You are insolent for a slave,' I reprimanded her sternly as the boy anointed my back with a healing salve of my own concoction.

'Yes,' agreed the imp with a grin. 'But then so are you.' And she dodged the half-hearted slap I aimed at her with ease. Lostris is much too soft with her handmaidens.

74

'Go tell your mistress that I will come to her,' I capitulated.

'She said I must wait and make sure you did.'

So I had an escort as I passed the guards at the gate of the harem. The guards were eunuchs like myself, but, unlike me, they were portly and androgynous. Despite their corpulence, or perhaps because of it, they were powerful men and fierce. However, I had used my influence to secure both of them this cosy sinecure, so they passed me through into the women's quarters with a respectful salute.

The harem was not nearly as grand nor as comfortable as the quarters of the slave boys, and it was clear where my Lord Intef's real interest lay. It was a compound of mud-brick hutments surrounded by a high mud wall. The only gardens or decorations were those that Lostris and her maids had undertaken, with my assistance. The vizier's wives were too fat and lazy and caught up in the scandals and intrigues of the harem to exert themselves.

Lostris' quarters were those closest to the main gate, surrounded by a pretty garden with a lily pond and song-birds twittering in cages woven of split bamboo. The mud walls were decorated with bright murals of Nile scenes, of fish and birds and goddesses, that I had helped her paint.

Her slave girls were huddled in a subdued group at the doorway, and more than one of them had been weeping. Their faces were streaked with tears. I pushed my way past them into the cool, dark interior, and at once heard my mistress's sobs from the inner chamber. I hurried to her, ashamed that I had been so craven as to try to avoid my duty

75

to her.

She was lying face down on the low bed, her entire body shaking with the force of her grief, but she heard me enter and whirled off the bed and rushed to me.

'Oh, Taita! They are sending Tanus away. Pharaoh arrives in Karnak tomorrow, and my father will prevail upon him to order Tanus to take his squadron up-river to Elephantine and the cataracts. Oh, Taita! It is twenty days' travel to the first cataract. I shall never see him again. I wish I were dead. I shall throw myself into the Nile and let the crocodiles devour me. I don't want to live without Tanus—' All this in one rising wail of despair.

'Softly, my child.' I rocked her in my arms. 'How do you know all these terrible things? They may never happen.'

'Oh, they will. Tanus has sent me a message. Kratas has a brother in my father's personal bodyguard. He heard my father discussing it with Rasfer. Somehow my father has found out about Tanus and me. He knows that we were in the temple of Hapi alone. Oh, Taita, my father sent the priests to examine me. Those filthy old men did horrid things to me. It hurt so, Taita.'

I hugged her gently. It is not too often that I have the opportunity to do so, but now she hugged me back with all her strength. Her thoughts turned from her own injuries to her lover.

'I shall never see Tanus again,' she cried, and I was reminded of how young she truly was, not much more than a child, vulnerable and lost in her grief. 'My father will destroy him.'

'Even your father cannot touch Tanus,' I tried

to reassure her. 'Tanus is a commander of a regiment of Pharaoh's own elite guard. He is the king's man. Tanus takes his orders only from Pharaoh, and he enjoys the full protection of the double crown of Egypt.' I did not add that this was probably the only reason that her father had not already destroyed him, but went on gently, 'While as for never seeing Tanus again, you will be playing opposite him in the pageant. I will make certain that there is a chance for the two of you to speak to each other between the acts.'

'My father will never let the pageant go on now.'

'He has no alternative, unless he is prepared to ruin my production and risk Pharaoh's displeasure, and you can be certain that he will never do that.'

'He will send Tanus away, and have another actor play Horus,' she sobbed.

'There is no time to rehearse another actor. Tanus will play the god Horus. I will make that clear to my Lord Intef. You and Tanus will have a chance to talk. We will find a way out for the two of you.'

She gulped back her tears and looked up at me with complete trust. 'Oh, Taita. I know that you will find a way. You always do—' She broke off suddenly and her expression changed. Her hands moved over my back, exploring the ridged welts that Rasfer's whip had raised across it.

'I am sorry, mistress. I tried to put forward Tanus' suit, as I promised you I would, and all this is the consequence of my stupidity.'

She stepped behind me and lifted the light linen tunic I had donned to hide my injuries, and she gasped. 'This is Rasfer's work. Oh, my poor dear

Taita, why did you not warn me that this would happen, that my father was so violently opposed to Tanus and to me?'

I was hard put not to gasp at this artless piece of effrontery, I who had pleaded and warned them and in return been accused of disloyalty. I managed to hold my peace, however, although my back still throbbed abominably.

At least my mistress's own misery was forgotten for the moment in her concern for my superficial injuries. She ordered me to sit on her bed and remove my tunic while she ministered to me, her genuine love and compassion making up for the lack of her medicinal skills. This distraction lifted her from the utter depths of her despair. Soon she was chattering away in her usual ebullient fashion, making plans to thwart her father's wrath and to reunite herself with Tanus.

Some of these plans demonstrated her good common sense, while others, more far-fetched, merely pointed to her trusting youth and lack of knowledge and experience in the wicked ways of the world. 'I shall play such a fine role of Isis in the pageant,' she declared at one stage, 'and I shall make myself so agreeable to Pharaoh that he will grant me any boon that I ask of him. Then I shall beg him for Tanus as my husband, and he will say—' here she mimicked the king's pompous ceremonial tones so cleverly that I was forced to grin, 'and he will say, "I declare the betrothal of Tanus, Lord Harrab, son of Pianki, and of the Lady Lostris, daughter of Intef, and I raise my good servant Tanus to the rank of Great Lion of Egypt and commander of all my armies. I further order that all the former estates of his father, the

noble Pianki, Lord Harrab be returned to him—"'"
Here she broke off in the middle of her
ministrations to my wounds and flung her arms
around my neck.

'It could happen like that, could it not, dear
Taita? Please say that it could!'

'No natural man could resist you, mistress,' I
smiled at her nonsense. 'Not even great Pharaoh
himself.' If I had known then how close my words
would turn out to being the truth, I think I should
have placed a live coal on my tongue before I
spoke them.

Her face was shining with hope once again. That
was enough reward for me, and I donned my tunic
again to bring to an end her too enthusiastic
ministrations to my back.

'But now, mistress, if you are to make a
beautiful and irresistible Isis, you must get some
rest.' I had brought with me a potion of the
powder of the sleeping-flower which is called the
Red Shepenn. The seeds of this precious flower
had first been brought into this very Egypt by the
trade caravans from a mountainous land
somewhere far to the east. I now cultivated the red
blooms in my garden, and when the petals were
fallen I scratched the seed carapace with a gold
fork of three tines. Thick white milk flowed from
these wounds, which I gathered and dried and
treated in accordance with the formula I had
evolved. The powder could induce sleep, conjure
up strange dreams or smooth out pain.

'Stay with me awhile, Taita,' she murmured as
she settled down on the bed, curled like a sleepy
kitten. 'Cuddle me to sleep like you did when I was
a baby.' She was a baby still, I thought, as I took
79

her in my arms.

'It will all turn out all right, won't it?' she whispered. 'We will live happily ever after, just like they do in your stories, won't we, Taita?'

When she was asleep, I kissed her forehead softly and covered her with a fur rug before I stole from her chamber.

On the fifth day of the festival of Osiris, Pharaoh came down-river to Karnak from his palace on Elephantine Island which was ten days' travel away by swift river galley. He came in full state with all his retinue to officiate at the festival of the god.

Tanus' squadron had left Karnak three days previously, speeding away upstream to meet the great flotilla and escort it on the last stage of the voyage, so neither Lostris nor I had seen him since we had all three returned from the great river-cow hunt. It was a special joy for both of us then to see his galley come flying around the bend in the river, full on the current and with a strong desert wind abeam. The *Breath of Horus* was in the van of the fleet, leading it up from the south.

Lostris was in the grand vizier's train, standing behind her two brothers, Menset and Sobek. The two boys were comely and well-favoured, but there was too much of their father in them for my taste. Menset, the elder of the two, I particularly mistrusted, and the younger followed where his brother led.

I was standing further back in the ruck of courtiers and lesser functionaries from where I

80

could keep an eye both on Lostris and on my Lord Intef. I saw the back of her neck flush with pleasure and excitement at the glimpse she had of Tanus' tall figure on the stern-tower of the *Breath of Horus*. The scales on his crocodile-skin breastplate gleamed in the sunlight, and the spray of ostrich feathers on his helmet floated in the draught of the galley's passage.

Lostris was hopping with excitement and waving both slim arms above her head, but her squeals and her antics were lost in the roar of the vast crowd that lined both banks of the Nile to welcome their pharaoh. Thebes is the most populous city in the world, and I guessed that almost a quarter of a million souls had turned out to welcome the king.

Meanwhile Tanus looked neither left nor right, but stared sternly ahead with his unsheathed sword held before his face in salute. The rest of his squadron followed the *Breath of Horus* in the wide vee of the egret formation, named for the pattern that those birds fly in as they return in the sunset to their roosts. All their standards and battle honours were streaming out in a fluttering blaze of rainbow colours, a noble show that set the crowds cheering and waving their palm-fronds wildly.

It was some time before the first vessel of the main convoy came wallowing round the bend behind them. It was laden with ladies and nobles of the king's entourage. It was followed by another, and then by a great untidy horde of vessels great and small. They came swarming downstream, transports filled with palace servants and slaves and all their accoutrements and paraphernalia, barges laden with oxen and goats and chickens for

81

the kitchens, gilded and gaily painted vessels bearing cargoes of palace furniture and treasure, of nobles and lesser creatures, all uncomfortably jumbled together in a most unseamanlike fashion. In what contrast was the display put up by Tanus' squadron as it rounded-to downstream and held its geometrically spaced formation against the swift Nile current!

At last Pharaoh's state barge lumbered around the bend, and the cheering of the crowd rose to a crescendo. This huge vessel, the largest ever built by man, made its ponderous way towards where we were waiting to welcome it at the stone wharf below the grand vizier's palace.

I had plenty of time in which to study it and to muse how aptly its size and design, and the handling of it, reflected the present state and government of this very Egypt of ours—Egypt as she stood in the twelfth year of the rule of Pharaoh Mamose, the eighth of that name and line, and the weakest yet of a weak and vacillating dynasty. The state barge was as long as five of the fighting galleys laid end to end, but its height and breadth were so ill-proportioned that they gravely offended my artistic instincts. Its massive hull was painted in the riotous colours that were the fashion of the age, and the figurehead of Osiris on the bows was gilded with real gold leaf. However, as she drew closer to the landing where we waited, I could see that the brilliant colours were faded in patches and her sides were zebra-striped in dun where her crew had defecated over the rail.

Amidships stood a tall deck-house, Pharaoh's private quarters, that was so solidly constructed of thick planks of precious cedar, and so stuffed with heavy furniture that the sailing characteristics of the barge were sadly affected. Atop this grotesque edifice, behind an ornate railing that was woven of fresh lilies, beneath a canopy of finely tanned gazelle skins skilfully sewn together and painted with images of all the major gods and goddesses, sat Pharaoh in majestic isolation. On his feet were sandals of gold filigree and his robe was of linen so pure that it shone like the high cumulus clouds of full summer. On his head he wore the tall double crown; the white crown of Upper Egypt with the head of the vulture goddess Nekhbet, combined with the red crown and the cobra head of Buto, the goddess of the Delta.

Despite the crown, the ironic truth was that this beloved sovereign of ours had lost the Delta almost ten years previously. In our turbulent days another pharaoh ruled in Lower Egypt, one who also wore the double crown, or at least his own version of it, a pretender who was our sovereign's deadly adversary, and whose constant wars against us drained both kingdoms of gold and the blood of the young men. Egypt was divided and torn by internal strife. Over the thousand or so years of our history, it had always been thus when weak men took on the mantle of pharaoh. It needed a strong, bold and clever man to hold the two kingdoms in his fists.

In order to turn the unwieldy vessel into the current and bring her to her moorings at the palace wharf, the captain should have steered close in to the far bank. If he had done so, he would have had the full breadth of the Nile in which to complete his turn. However, he had obviously misjudged the strength of wind and current and he began his turn

83

from midstream. At first the barge swung ponderously across the current, listing heavily as the height of the deck-house caught the hot desert wind like a sail. Half a dozen boatswains raged about the lower deck with their whips rising and falling, the snapping of the lash on bare shoulders carrying clearly across the water.

Under the goading of the lash the rowers plied their paddles in a frenzy that churned the waters alongside the hull to foam, one hundred paddles a side pulling against each other and none of them making any effort to synchronize the stroke. Their curses and cries blended with the shouted orders of the four helmsmen who were struggling with the long steering-oar in the stern. Meanwhile, on the poop-deck, Nembet, the geriatric admiral and captain of the barge, alternately combed his fingers through his long scraggy grey beard and flapped his hands in impotent agitation.

High above this pandemonium sat Pharaoh, motionless as a statue and aloof from it all. Oh, verily this was our Egypt.

Then the rate of the barge's turn bled away until she was no longer swinging but heading straight for where we stood on the bank, locked in chains by the pull of the current and the contrary push of the wind. Captain and crew, despite all their wild and erratic exertions, seemed powerless either to complete the manoeuvre and head her into the current, or to heave-to and prevent her from ploughing headlong into the granite blocks of the wharf and staving in her great gilded bows.

As everyone realized what was about to happen, the cheers of the crowd watching from the shore slowly died away and an awful hush fell upon both banks of the Nile into which the shouting and the turmoil on the decks of the huge vessel carried all the more clearly.

Then suddenly all the eyes of the crowd were drawn downstream, as the *Breath of Horus* broke from her station at the head of the squadron and came tearing up-river, driven by the flying paddles. In perfect unison those paddles dipped and pulled and swung and dipped again. She cut in so sharply under the bows of the barge that the crowd gasped with a sound higher than the wind in the papyrus beds. Collision seemed inevitable, but at the last possible moment Tanus signalled with a clenched fist lifted above his head. Simultaneously both banks of rowers backed water and the helmsman put the steering-oar hard over.

The *Breath of Horus* checked and paid away before the ponderous advance of the great barge. The two vessels touched as lightly as a virgin's kiss, and for an instant the stern-tower of the *Breath of Horus* was almost level with the barge's main deck.

In that instant Tanus poised himself on the bulwark of the tower. He had kicked off his sandals, divested himself of his armour, and thrown aside his weapons. Around his waist he had tied the end of a light flax line. With the line trailing behind him he leaped out across the gap between the two vessels.

As though awakening from a stupor, the crowd stirred and shook itself. If there was still one amongst them who did not know who Tanus was, he would know before this day was out. Of course, Tanus' fame had already been won in the river wars against the legions of the usurper in the Lower Kingdom. However, only his own troops

85

had ever seen him in action. The reported deed never carries the same weight as the one that the eye sees for itself.

Now, before the gaze of Pharaoh, the royal flotilla and the entire populace of Karnak, Tanus leaped from one deck to the other and landed as lightly as a leopard.

'Tanus!' I am sure that it was my mistress, Lostris, who first called out his name, but I was next.

'Tanus!' I yelled, and then all those around me took up the cry. 'Tanus! Tanus! Tanus!' They chanted it like an ode to some newly discovered god.

The moment he landed on the deck of the barge, Tanus whirled and raced into the bows, hauling in the thin line hand over hand as he ran. The crew of his galley had spliced a heavy hawser, as thick as a man's arm, to the end of the carrying-line. Now they sent it across as Tanus lay back against the weight of it. With the muscles of his arms and back shining with sweat, he dragged it in.

By this time a handful of the barge's crew had realized what he was about, and rushed forward to help him. Under Tanus' direction they took three turns with the end of the hawser about the barge's bowsprit, and the instant it was secured Tanus signalled his galley away.

The *Breath of Horus* leaped into the current, gathering speed swiftly. Then abruptly she came up short against the hawser, and the weight of the heavy vessel on the other end threw her back on her haunches. For a dreadful moment I thought she might capsize and be dragged under, but Tanus had anticipated the shock and signalled his crew to cushion it by skilfully backing the long paddles.

Although she was dragged down so low that she took in green water over her stern, the galley weathered it, bobbed up and came back taut on the hawser. For a long moment nothing happened. The galley's puny weight made no impression on the great ship's ponderous way. The two vessels were locked together as though a crocodile had an old bull buffalo by the snout but could not drag him from the bank. Then Tanus in the bows of the barge turned to face the disorganized crew. He made one authoritative gesture that caught all their attention, and a remarkable change came over them. They were waiting for his command.

Nembet was the commander of all Pharaoh's fleet with the rank of Great Lion of Egypt. Years ago he had been one of the mighty men, but now he was old and feeble. Tanus took over from him effortlessly, as though it were as natural as the force of the current and the wind, and the crew of the barge responded immediately.

'Pull!' He gestured to the port bank of oarsmen and they bent their backs and pulled with a will.

'Back-water!' He stabbed his clenched fist at the starboard side and they dug in hard with the pointed blades of their paddles. Tanus stepped to the rail and signalled to the helmsman of the *Breath of Horus*, masterfully coordinating the efforts of both crews. Still the barge was bearing down upon the wharf and now only a narrow strip of open water separated the vessel from the granite blocks.

Then at last, slowly, too slowly, she began to respond. The gaudily painted bows began to swing up into the current as the galley dragged them round. Once again the cheering died away and that fateful hush fell upon us all as we waited for the enormous ship to crash into the wharf and tear out her own guts on the rock. When that happened there was no doubt what the consequences must be for Tanus. He had snatched command from the senile admiral and so must bear the full responsibility for all the old man's mistakes. When Pharaoh was dashed from his throne by the collision, when the double crown and all his dignity were sent rolling across the deck, and when the state barge sank beneath him and he was dragged from the river like a drowning puppy before the gaze of all his subjects, then there would be both the insulted Admiral Nembet and my Lord Intef to encourage Pharaoh to bring the full weight of his displeasure to bear upon the presumptuous young upstart.

I stood helplessly and trembled for my dear friend, and then a miracle occurred. The barge was already so close to running aground and Tanus so near to where I stood that his voice carried clearly to me. 'Great Horus, help me now!' he cried.

There is no doubt at all in my mind that the gods often take a hand in the affairs of men. Tanus is a Horus man, and Horus is the god of the wind.

The desert wind had blown for three days and nights out of the western desolation of the Sahara. It had blown at the strength of half a gale without a check for all that time, but now it dropped. It did not taper off, it simply ceased to blow at all. The wavelets that had flecked the surface of the river flattened out, and the palms along the waterfront that had been vigorously shaking their fronds fell still, as though frozen by a sudden frost.

Released from the claws of the wind, the barge rolled back on to an even keel and yielded to the pull of the *Breath of Horus*. Her elephantine bows turned up into the current, and she came parallel with the wharf at the exact moment that her side touched the dressed stone and the rush of the Nile killed her forward-way and stalled her motionless in the water.

One last command from Tanus and, before the ship could gather stern-way, the mooring ropes were cast on to the wharf and swiftly gathered up by eager hands and made fast to the stone bollards. Lightly as a goose-down feather floating on the water, the great barge of state lay safe and serene at her berth, and neither the throne upon which Pharaoh sat, nor the high crown upon his head, had been disturbed by her moorage.

We, the onlookers, burst out in a roar of praise for the feat, and the name of Tanus rather than that of Pharaoh was on all our tongues. Modestly, and very prudently, Tanus made no attempt to acknowledge our applause. To draw any further attention to himself that might detract from the welcome that awaited the king would have been folly indeed, and would certainly have negated any royal favour that his exploit had earned him. Pharaoh was always jealous of his royal dignity. Instead, Tanus surreptitiously signalled the *Breath of Horus* alongside. When she was hidden from our view by the bulk of the barge, he dropped overside on to the galley's deck, quitting the stage on which he had just earned such distinction, and leaving it now to his king.

However, I saw the expression of fury and

chagrin on the face of Nembet, the ancient admiral, the Great Lion of Egypt, as he came ashore behind Pharaoh, and I knew that Tanus had made himself another powerful enemy.

I was able to make good my promise to Lostris that very evening when I put the cast of the pageant through their dress rehearsal. Before the performance began I was able to give the two lovers almost an hour alone together.

In the precincts of the temple of Osiris, which was to be our theatre for the pageant, I had set up tents to act as dressing-rooms for each of the principal players. I had purposely placed Lostris' tent a little apart from the others, screened from them by one of the huge stone columns that support the roof of the temple. While I stood on sentry duty at the entrance to the tent, Tanus lifted the opposite panel and slipped in under it.

I tried not to eavesdrop on their cries of delight as they first embraced, nor to the whispering and cooing, to the muffled laughter and to the small moans and gasps of their decorous love-making which followed. Although at this stage I would not have made any attempt to prevent it, I was convinced that they would not carry this love-making to its ultimate conclusion. Long afterwards both Lostris and Tanus separately confirmed this for me. My mistress had been a virgin on her wedding day. If only any of us had known how close upon us that wedding day was, I wonder how differently we might have acted then.

90

Although I was acutely aware that every minute that they were alone together in the tent increased the danger for all of us, still I could not bring myself to call enough and separate them. Although the welts on my back that Rasfer's whip had raised still burned, and although deep in that morass of my soul where I attempt to hide all my unworthy thoughts and instincts my envy for the lovers burned as painfully, still I let them stay together much longer than I should have done.

I did not hear my Lord Intef coming. He used to have his sandals shod in the softest kid-skin to muffle his footfalls. He moved silently as a ghost, and many a courtier and slave felt either Rasfer's whip or his noose on account of a careless word that my lord overheard on his noiseless peregrinations through the halls and corridors of the palace. However, over the years I developed an instinct that enabled me most times to sense his presence before he materialized out of the shadows. This instinct was not infallible, but that evening it stood me in good stead. When I looked round suddenly he was almost upon me, gliding between the pillars of the hypostyle hall towards me, slim and tall and deadly as an erect cobra.

'My Lord Intef!' I cried loudly enough to startle myself, 'I am honoured that you have come to witness our rehearsals. I would be deeply grateful for any advice or suggestions—' I was gabbling wildly in an attempt to cover my confusion and to alert the lovers in the tent behind me.

In both objects I succeeded better than I had any right to expect. I heard the sudden scuffle of consternation within the dressing-tent behind me as the lovers broke apart, and then the flutter of the

91

rear panel of the tent as Tanus ducked out the way he had entered.

At any other time I would never have succeeded so easily in deceiving my Lord Intef. He would have read the guilt upon my face as clearly as I read the hieroglyphics on the temple walls or my own characters on this scroll; but that evening he was blinded by his own wrath, and intent only on taking me to task for my latest misdemeanour. He did not rage or roar with anger. My Lord is at his most dangerous when his tone is mild and his smile silky.

'Dear Taita.' It was almost a whisper. 'I hear that you have altered some of the arrangements for the opening act of the pageant, despite the fact that I personally ordered them. I could not believe that you have been so presumptuous. I had to come all this way in the heat to find out for myself.'

I knew it was of no avail to feign innocence or ignorance, so I bowed my head and tried to look aggrieved. 'My lord. It was not I who ordered the changes. It was His Holiness, the abbot of the temple of Osiris—'

But my lord broke in impatiently, 'Yes, of course he did, but only after you put him up to it. Do you think I do not know both you and that mumbling old priest? He never had an original thought in his head, while you have nothing but.'

'My lord!' I protested.

'What devious little trick was it this time? Was it one of those convenient dreams sent to you by the gods?' my lord asked, his voice as soft as the rustle of one of the sacred cobras that infested the temple, sliding across the stone flags of the floor.

'My lord!' I did my best to look shocked by the

accusation, although I had indeed given the good abbot a rather fanciful account of how Osiris in the guise of a black crow had visited me in my sleep to complain of the spilling of blood in his temple.

Up until that time the priest had voiced no objection to the realistic piece of theatre that my Lord Intef had planned for the amusement of Pharaoh. I had only resorted to dreams when all my efforts to dissuade my lord had failed. It was deeply abhorrent to me to be party to such an abomination as my lord had ordered to be performed in the first act of the pageant. Of course I am aware that certain savage peoples in the eastern lands make human sacrifice to their gods. I have heard that the Kassites, who live beyond the twin rivers Tigris and Euphrates, cast newborn babes into a fiery furnace. The caravan masters who have travelled in those distant lands speak of other atrocities performed in the name of religion, of young virgins slaughtered to promote the harvest or captives of war beheaded before the statues of a triple-headed god.

However, we Egyptians are a civilized people and we worship wise and just gods, not blood-crazed monsters. I had tried to convince my master of this. I had pointed out to him that only once before had a pharaoh made human sacrifice; when Menotep had slit the throats of the seven rebel princes in the temple of Seth and quartered their corpses and sent the embalmed fragments to the governors of each of the nomes as a warning. History still remembered the deed with distaste. Menotep is known to this day as the Bloody King.

'It is not human sacrifice,' my master had contradicted me. 'Merely a well-merited

93

execution, to be carried out in a rather novel fashion. You will not deny, dear Taita, that the death penalty has always been an important part of our system of justice, will you? Tod is a thief. He has stolen from the royal coffers and he must die, if only as an example to others.'

It sounded reasonable, except that I knew he was not at all interested in justice, but rather in protecting his own treasure and in impressing Pharaoh, who so loved pageant and theatre. This had left me with no alternative but to dream for the benefit of the good abbot. Now my Lord Intef's lip lifted in a smile which exposed his perfect teeth but which chilled my blood and raised the hairs on the nape of my neck.

'Here is a little piece of advice,' he whispered close to my face. 'I suggest that you have another dream tonight, so that whichever god it was that visited you last time has an opportunity to countermand his previous instructions to the abbot and to endorse my arrangements. If this does not happen, I will find some more work for Rasfer—that is my solemn promise to you.' He turned and strode away, leaving me both relieved that he had not discovered the lovers and miserable that I was forced to go ahead with the vile display which he had ordered.

Nevertheless, after my master had left, the rehearsal was a heartening success that revived my spirits. Lostris was in such a glow of happiness after her tryst with Tanus that her beauty was indeed divine, and Tanus in his youth and power was the young Horus incarnate.

Naturally I was perturbed by the entrance of my Osiris to the stage, aware as I now was of the fate that my Lord Intef had ordered for him. My Osiris was played by a handsome, middle-aged man named Tod who had been one of the bailiffs until he had been caught dipping into my Lord Intef's coffers to support a young and expensive courtesan of whom he was enamoured. I was not proud that it was my examination of the accounts that had brought to light the discrepancies.

My lord had released him from custody, where he was awaiting formal trial and sentencing, to play the part of the god of the underworld in the pageant. My lord had promised not to take the matter further if he fulfilled the role of Osiris satisfactorily. The unfortunate Tod was unaware of the hidden menace in this offer and threw himself into the act with pathetic enthusiasm, believing that he was about to earn his pardon. He could not know that, in the meantime, my lord had secretly signed his death warrant and handed the scroll to Rasfer, who was not only the state executioner but my choice to play Seth in our little production. It was my lord's intention that he should combine both roles on the following evening when the pageant was performed before Pharaoh. Although Rasfer was a natural choice for the role of Seth, I regretted having cast him in it as I watched him rehearse the opening scene with Tod, and I shuddered as I imagined how the main performance would differ from the rehearsal.

After the rehearsal it was my most pleasant duty to escort my mistress back to the harem compound. She would not let me leave but kept me late listening to her excited résumé of the day's extraordinary events and the role that Tanus had played in them.

'Did you see how he called upon the great god Horus and how the god came at once to his aid? Surely he has the full favour and protection of Horus, don't you agree? Horus will not let any evil befall us, of that I am now certain.'

There was much more of this happy fantasy, and no more talk of parting and suicide. How swiftly the winds of young love shift!

'After what Tanus did today, the way he saved the state barge from wrecking, surely he must also have earned Pharaoh's high favour, don't you think so, Taita? With favour of both the god and Pharaoh, my father can never succeed in having Tanus sent away now, can he, Taita?'

I was called upon to endorse every happy thought that occurred to her, and I was not allowed to leave the harem until I had memorized at least a dozen messages of undying love which I was sworn to carry to Tanus personally.

When, exhausted, I finally reached my own quarters, there was still no rest for me. Nearly all the slave boys were waiting for me, as excited and as garrulous as my mistress had been. They also wanted to have my opinion of the day's events, and particularly of Tanus' rescue of Pharaoh's ship and the significance of that deed. They crowded around me on the terrace above the river as I fed my pets, and vied with each other for my attention.

'Elder brother, is it true that Tanus called upon the god for his help, and Horus intervened immediately? Did you see it happen? Some even say that the god appeared in his falcon shape and hovered over Tanus' head, spreading protective wings over him. Is it true?'

'Is it true, *Akh*, that Pharaoh has promoted

Tanus to Companion of Pharaoh, and given him an estate of five hundred feddan of fertile land on the riverside as reward?'

'Elder brother, they say that the oracle at the desert shrine of Thoth, the god of wisdom, has cast a horoscope for Tanus. The oracle divines that he will be the greatest warrior in the history of our Egypt and that, one day, Pharaoh will favour him above all others.' It is amusing now to look back on these childish prattles, and to realize the strange truths that were adumbrated in them, but at the time I dismissed them as I did the children, with mock severity.

As I composed myself to sleep, my last thought was that the populace of the twin towns of Luxor and Karnak had taken Tanus to their hearts completely, but that this was an onerous and dubious distinction. Fame and popularity breed envy in high places, and the adulation of the mob is fickle. They often take as much pleasure in tearing down the idols that they have grown tired of, as they did in elevating them in the first place.

It is safer by far to live unseen and unremarked, as I always attempt to do.

On the afternoon of the sixth day of the festival, Pharaoh moved in solemn procession from his villa in the midst of the royal estates in the open country between Karnak and Luxor, down the ceremonial avenue lined with statues of granite lions, to the temple of Osiris on the bank of the Nile.

The great sledge on which he rode was so tall

that the dense crowds lining the avenue were forced to strain their necks backwards to look up at him on his great gilded throne as he trundled by, drawn by twenty pure white bullocks with massive humped shoulders and wreaths of flowers on their horned heads. The skids of the sledge ground harshly over the paving and scarred the stone slabs.

One hundred musicians led the procession, strumming the lyre and the harp, beating the cymbal and the drum, shaking the rattle and the sistrum, and blowing on the long straight horn of the oryx and on the curling horn of the wild ram. A choir of a hundred of the finest voices in Egypt followed them, singing hymns of praise to Pharaoh and that other god Osiris. Naturally I led the choir. Behind us followed an honour guard from the Blue Crocodile regiment led by Tanus himself. The crowds raised a special cheer for him as, all plumed and armoured, he strode past. The unmarried maidens shrieked and more than one of them sank swooning in the dust, overcome by the hysteria that his new-won fame engendered.

Behind the guard of honour came the vizier and his high-office bearers, then the nobles and their wives and children, then a detachment of the Falcon regiment, and finally Pharaoh's great sledge. In all, this was an assembly of several thousand of the most wealthy and influential persons in the Upper Kingdom.

As we approached the temple of Osiris, the abbot and all his priests were drawn up on the staircase between the tall entrance pylons to welcome Pharaoh Mamose. The temple had been freshly painted and the bas-relief on the outer walls was dazzling with colour in the warm yellow glow

98

of the sunset. A gay cloud of banners and flags fluttered from their poles set in the recesses of the outer wall.

At the base of the staircase Pharaoh descended from his carriage and in solemn majesty began the climb up the one hundred steps. The choir lined both sides of the staircase. I was on the fiftieth step and so I was able to study the king minutely during the few seconds that it took for him to pass close to me.

I already knew him well, for he had been a patient of mine, but I had forgotten how small he was—that is, small for a god. He stood not as tall as my shoulder, although the high double crown made him seem much more impressive. His arms were folded across his chest in the ritual posture and he carried the crook and the flail of his royal office and his godhead. I remarked as I had before that his hands were hairless, smooth and almost feminine, and that his feet also were small and neat. He wore rings on all his fingers and on his toes, amulets on his upper arms and bracelets on his wrists. The massive pectoral plate of red gold on his chest was inlaid with many colours of faience depicting the god Thoth bearing the feather of truth. That piece of jewellery was a splendid treasure almost five hundred years old and had been worn by seventy kings before him.

Under the double crown, his face was powdered dead white like that of a corpse. His eyes were dramatically outlined with startling jet black and his lips were rouged crimson. Under the heavy make-up his expression was petulant, and his lips were thin and straight and humourless. His eyes were shifty and nervous, as well they might be, I reflected.

The foundations of this great House of Egypt were cracked, and the kingdom riven and shaken. Even a god has his worries. Once his domain had stretched from the sea, across the seven mouths of the Delta, southwards to Assoun and the first cataract—the greatest empire on earth. He and his ancestors had let it all slip away, and now his enemies swarmed at his shrunken borders, clamouring like hyena and jackal and vulture to feast on the carcass of our Egypt.

In the south were the black hordes of Africa, in the north along the coast of the great sea were the piratical sea-people, and along the lower reaches of the Nile the legions of the false Pharaoh. In the west were the treacherous Bedouin and the sly Libyan, while in the east new hordes seemed to rise up daily, their names striking terror into a nation grown timid and hesitant with defeat. Assyrians and Medes, Kassites and Hurrians and Hittites—there seemed no end to their multitudes.

What advantage remained in our ancient civilization if it were grown feeble and effete with its great age? How were we to resist the barbarian in his savage vigour, his cruel arrogance and his lust for rapine and plunder? I was certain that this pharaoh, like those who had immediately preceded him, was not capable of leading the nation back to its former glories. He was incapable even of breeding a male heir.

This lack of an heir to the empire of Egypt seemed to obsess him even more than the loss of the empire itself. He had taken twenty wives so far. They had given him daughters, a virtual tribe of daughters, but no son. He would not accept that the fault lay with him as sire. He had consulted every doctor of renown in the Upper Kingdom and visited every oracle and every important shrine.

I knew all this because I was one of the learned doctors he had sent for. I admit that at the time I had felt some trepidation in prescribing to a god, and that I had wondered why he should need to consult a mere mortal on such a delicate subject. Nevertheless, I had recommended a diet of bull's testicles fried in honey and counselled him to find the most beautiful virgin in Egypt and take her to his marriage-bed within a year of the first flowering of her woman's moon.

I had no great faith in my own remedy, but bull's testicles, when cooked to my recipe, are a tasty dish, while I reckoned that the search for the most beautiful virgin in the land might distract Pharaoh and prove not only amusing but pleasurable as well. From a practical point of view, if the king bedded a sufficient number of young ladies, then surely one of them must eventually drop a male pup into his harem.

Anyhow, I consoled myself that my treatment was not as drastic as some of the others proposed by my peers, particularly those disgusting remedies dreamed up by the quacks in the temple of Osiris who call themselves doctors. If not actually efficacious, my recommendations would at least do no harm. That was what I believed. How wrong the fates would prove me, and if only I had known the consequences of my folly, I would have taken Tod's place in the pageant rather than have given Pharaoh such frivolous counsel.

I was amused and flattered when I heard that Pharaoh must have taken my advice seriously, and

101

that he had ordered his nomarchs and his governors to scour the length of the land from El Amarna to the cataracts to find bulls with succulent balls and any virgin who might fit my specifications for the mother of his first son. My sources at the king's court informed me that he had already rejected hundreds of aspiring applicants for the title of the most beautiful virgin in the land.

Then the king was swiftly past me and gone into the temple to the keening of the priests and the obsequious bobbing of the abbot. The grand vizier and all his train followed closely, and then there was an undignified rush of lesser citizens to find places from which to watch the passion play. Space in the temple was limited. Only the mighty and the noble and those rich enough to bribe the thieving priests were allowed into the inner courtyard. The others were forced to watch through the gates from the outer court. Many thousands of the citizenry would be disappointed and would have to be content with a secondhand account of the pageant. Even I, the impresario, had great difficulty in fighting my way through the press of humanity, and I only succeeded when Tanus saw my predicament and sent two of his men to rescue me and force a path for me into the precincts reserved for the actors.

Before the pageant could begin, we were obliged to endure a succession of flowery speeches, firstly from the local functionaries and government ministers, and then from the grand vizier in person. This interlude of speechifying gave me the opportunity to make certain that all the arrangements for the pageant were perfect. I went from tent to tent, checking the costumes and the make-up of each of my actors, and soothing last-minute attacks of temperament and stage-fright.

The unfortunate Tod was nervously dreading the possibility that his performance might not please my Lord Intef. I was able to assure him that it most certainly would, and then I administered to him a draught of the Red Shepenn, which would deaden the pain that he was about to have inflicted upon him.

When I came to Rasfer's tent he was drinking wine with two of his cronies from the palace guard and, with a whetstone, laying an edge on his short bronze sword. I had created his make-up to render him even more repulsive, which was not an easy feat given the high plateau of ugliness from which we started. I realized how well I had succeeded as he leered at me with blackened teeth and offered me a cup of the wine.

'How does your back feel now, pretty boy? Have a taste of a man's drink! Perhaps it will give you balls again.' I am accustomed to his taunts and I kept my dignity as I told him that my Lord Intef had countermanded the abbot's orders and that the first act was to be played out in the original form.

'I have spoken to Lord Intef already.' He held up the sword. 'Feel the edge, eunuch. I want to make certain that it meets with your approval.' I left him feeling a little queasy.

Although Tanus would not be on stage until the second act, he was already in costume. Relaxed and smiling, he clasped my shoulder. 'Well, old friend, this is your opportunity. After this evening

103

your fame as a playwright will spread throughout Egypt.'

'As yours has already. Your name is on every lip,' I told him, but he laughed it away with careless modesty as I went on, 'Do you have your closing declamation prepared, Tanus? Would you like to recite it to me now?'

Traditionally, the actor who played Horus would close the pageant with a message to Pharaoh, ostensibly from the gods but in reality from his own subjects. In olden times this had been the one occasion during the year when the populace, through the agency of the actor, could bring to the king's notice matters of concern which they were not able to address to him at any other time. However, during the rule of this last dynasty of kings the tradition had fallen away, and the closing speech had become merely another eulogy to the divine pharaoh.

For days past I had been asking Tanus to rehearse his speech for me, but every time he had put me off with excuses so lame that I was by now thoroughly suspicious of his intentions. 'This is the last opportunity,' I insisted, but he laughed at me.

'I have decided to let my speech be as much a surprise to you as I hope it will be to Pharaoh. That way you should both enjoy it more.' And there was nothing I could do to persuade him. At times he can be far and away the most headstrong and obstinate young ruffian I have ever encountered. I left him in not a little dudgeon, and went to find more convivial company.

As I stooped in through the entrance of Lostris' dressing-tent, I froze with shock. Even though I had designed her costume myself and instructed

104

her handmaidens as to exactly how I wanted her powder and rouge and eye-paint applied, still I was not prepared for the ethereal vision that stood before me now. For a moment I was convinced that another miracle had taken place and that the goddess had indeed risen up from the underworld to take my mistress's place. I gasped aloud and had actually begun to sink to my knees in superstitious awe when my mistress giggled and roused me from my delusion.

'Isn't this fun? I cannot wait to see Tanus in full costume. I am sure he must look like the god himself.' She turned slowly to allow me to appraise her own costume, smiling at me over her shoulder.

'No more godlike than you, my lady,' I whispered.

'When will the play begin?' she demanded impatiently. 'I am so excited that I can wait no longer.'

I cocked my ear to the panel of the tent and listened for a moment to the drone of the speeches in the great hall. I realized that this was the final oration and that at any moment my Lord Intef would call upon my players to perform.

I took Lostris' hand and squeezed it. 'Remember the long pause and the haughty look before you begin your opening speech,' I cautioned her, and she slapped my shoulder playfully.

'Away with you, you old fuss-pot, it will all go perfectly, you'll see.' And at that moment I heard my Lord Intef's voice raised.

'The divine god Pharaoh Mamose, the Great House of Egypt, the Support of the Realm, the Just, the Great, the All-Seeing, the All-Merciful—'

The titles and honorifics continued while I hurried out of Lostris' tent and made my way to my opening position behind the central pillar. I peered around the column and saw that the inner courtyard of the temple was packed and that Pharaoh and his senior wives sat in the front rank on low benches of cedar wood, sipping cool sherbet or nibbling dates and sweetmeats.

My Lord Intef was addressing them from the front of the raised platform below the altar that was our stage. The main body of the stage was still hidden from the audience by the linen curtains. I surveyed it for one last time, although it was too late to do anything further about it now.

Behind the curtains the set was decorated with palms and acacia trees that the palace gardeners had transplanted under my instruction. My masons had been taken from the work on the king's tomb to build a stone cistern at the back of the temple from which a stream could be diverted across the stage to represent the river Nile.

At the rear of the stage, hanging from floor to ceiling, were tightly stretched sheets of linen on which the artists from the necropolis had painted marvellous landscapes. In the half-light of the dusk and the flicker of the torches in their brackets the effect was so realistic as to transport the beholder into a different world in a distant time.

There were other delights that I had prepared for Pharaoh's amusement, from cages of animals, birds and butterflies that would be released to simulate the creation of the world by the great god Ammon-Ra, to flares and torches that I had doctored with chemicals to burn with brilliant flames of crimson and green, and flood the stage with eerie light and smoke-clouds, like those of the underworld where the gods live.

'Mamose, son of Ra, may you be granted eternal life! We your loyal subjects, the citizens of Thebes, beg you to draw nigh and give your divine attention to this poor play that we dedicate to Your Majesty.'

My Lord Intef concluded his address of welcome and resumed his seat. To a fanfare of hidden rams' horns, I stepped out from behind the pillar and faced the audience. They had endured discomfort and boredom on the hard flagstones, and by now were ripe for the entertainment to begin. A raucous cheer greeted my entrance and even Pharaoh smiled in anticipation.

I held up both hands for silence, and only when it was total did I begin to speak my overture.

'While I walked in the sunlight, young and filled with the vigour of youth, I heard the fatal music in the reeds by the bank of the Nile. I did not recognize the sound of this harp, and I had no fear, for I was in the full bloom of my manhood and secure in the affection of my beloved.

'The music was of surpassing beauty. Joyously I went to find the musician, and could not know that he was Death and that he played his harp to summon me alone.' We Egyptians are fascinated by death, and I had at once touched a deep chord within my audience. They sighed and shuddered.

'Death seized me and bore me up in his skeletal arms towards Ammon-Ra, the sun god, and I was become one with the white light of his being. At a great distance I heard my beloved weep, but I could not see her and all the days of my life were as though they had never been.' This was the first public recitation of my prose, and I knew almost at once that I had them, their faces were fascinated and intent. There was not a sound in the temple.

'Then Death set me down in a high place from which I could see the world like a shining round shield in the blue sea of the heavens. I saw all men and all creatures who have ever lived. Like a mighty river, time ran backwards before mine eyes. For a hundred thousand years I watched their strivings and their deaths. I watched all men go from death and old age to infancy and birth. Time became more and more remote, going back until the birth of the first man and the first woman. I watched them at the moment of their birth and then before. At last there were no men upon the earth and only the gods existed.

'Yet still the river of time flowed back beyond the time of the gods into Nun, into the time of darkness and primordial chaos. The river of time could flow no further back and so reversed itself. Time began to run forward in the manner that was familiar to me from my days of life upon the earth, and I watched the passion of the gods played out before me.' My audience were all of them well versed in the theology of our pantheon, but none of them had ever heard the mysteries presented in such a novel fashion. They sat silent and enthralled as I went on.

'Out of the chaos and darkness of Nun rose Ammon-Ra, He-Who-Creates-Himself. I watched Ammon-Ra stroke his generative member, masturbating and spurting out his seminal seed in mighty waves that left the silver smear that we know as the Milky Way across the dark void. From this seed were generated Geb and Nut, the earth and the heaven.'

'*Bak-her*!' a single voice broke the tremulous silence of the temple.

'*Bak-her! Amen!*' The old abbot had not been able to contain himself, and now he endorsed my vision of the creation. I was so astonished by his change of heart that I almost forgot my next line. After all, he had been my sternest critic up to that time. I had won him over completely, and my voice soared in triumph.

'Geb and Nut coupled and copulated, as men and women do, and from their dreadful union were born the gods Osiris and Seth, and the goddesses Isis and Nephthys.'

I made a wide gesture and the linen curtains were drawn slowly aside to reveal the fantasy world that I had created. Nothing like this had ever been seen in Egypt before and the audience gasped with amazement. With measured tread I withdrew, and my place upon the stage was taken by the god Osiris. The audience recognized him instantly by the tall, bottle-shaped head-dress, by his arms crossed over his chest and by the crook and the flail he held before him. Every household kept his statuette in the family shrine.

A droning cry of reverence went up from every throat, and indeed the sedative that I had administered to Tod glittered weirdly in his eyes and gave him a strange, unearthly presence that was convincingly godlike. With the crook and the flail Osiris made mystical gestures and declaimed in sonorous tones, 'Behold Atur, the river!'

Once more the audience rustled and murmured as they recognized the Nile. The Nile was Egypt and the centre of the world.

109

'*Bak-her!*' another voice called out, and, watching from my hidden place amongst the pillars, I was astonished and delighted as I realized who had spoken. It was Pharaoh. My play had both secular and divine endorsement. I was certain that from now on mine would become the authorized version, replacing the thousand-year-old original. I had found my place in immortality. My name would live on down the millennium.

Joyfully I signalled for the cistern to be opened and the waters began to flow across our stage. At first the audience did not comprehend, and then they realized that they were actually witnessing the revelation of the great river, and a shout went up from a thousand throats, '*Bak-her! Bak-her!*'

'Behold the waters rise!' cried Osiris, and obediently the Nile was swollen by the inundation.

'Behold the waters fall!' cried the god, and they shrank at his command. 'Now they will rise again!'

I had arranged for buckets of dye to be added to the water as it poured out of the cistern at the rear of the temple. First a green dye to simulate the low-water period, and then, as it rose again, a darker dye that faithfully emulated the colour of the silt-laden waters of the high inundation.

'Now behold the insects and birds upon the earth!' ordered Osiris, and the cages at the rear of the stage were opened and a shrieking, chattering, swirling cloud of wild birds and gorgeously coloured butterflies filled the temple.

The watchers were like children, enchanted and enthralled, reaching up to snatch the butterflies from the air and then release them again to fly out between the high pillars of the temple. One of the wild birds, a long-billed hoopoe marvellously

110

patterned in colours of white and cinnamon and black, flew down unafraid and settled on Pharaoh's crown.

The crowd was delighted. 'An omen!' they cried. 'A blessing on the king. May he live for ever!' and Pharaoh smiled.

It was naughty of me, but afterwards I hinted to my Lord Intef that I had trained the bird to single out Pharaoh, and although it was of course quite impossible, he believed me. Such is my reputation with animals and birds.

On the stage Osiris wandered through the paradise that he had created, and the mood was set for the dramatic moment when, with a blood-chilling shriek, Seth bounded on to the stage. Although they had been expecting it, still the powerful and hideous presence shocked the audience, and the women screamed and covered their faces, only to peer out again from between trembling fingers.

'What is this you have done, brother?' Seth bellowed in jealous rage. 'Do you set yourself above me? Am I not also a god? Do you hold all creation to yourself alone, that I, your brother, may not share it with you?'

Osiris answered him calmly, his dignity remote and cool as the drug held him in its thrall. 'Our father, Ammon-Ra, has given it to us both. However, he has also given us the right to choose how we dispose of it, for good or for evil—' The words that I had put into the mouth of the god reverberated through the temple. They were the finest that I had written, and the audience hung upon them. However, I alone of all of them knew what was coming, and the beauty and the power of

111

my own composition were soured as I steeled myself for it.

Osiris drew to the close of his speech. 'This is the world as I have revealed it. If you wish to share it in peace and brotherly love, then you are welcome. However, if you come in warlike rage, if evil and hatred fill your heart, then I order you gone.' He lifted his right arm all draped in the gleaming diaphanous linen of his robe and pointed the way for Seth to leave the paradise of Earth.

Seth hunched those huge, hairy shoulders like a buffalo bull, and he bellowed so that the spittle flew from his lips in a cloud that was flavoured by the rotting teeth in his jaws. I could smell it from where I stood. He lifted high the bronze broad-sword and rushed at his brother. This had never been rehearsed, and it took Osiris completely by surprise. He stood with his right arm still outstretched, and the blade hissed with the power of the stroke as it swung down. The hand was lopped off at the wrist as cleanly as I would prune a shoot from the vine that grows over my terrace. It fell at Osiris' feet and lay there with the fingers fluttering feebly.

The surprise was so complete and the sword so sharp that for a long moment Osiris did not move, except to sway slightly on his feet. The audience must have believed that this was another theatrical trick, and that the fallen hand was a dummy. The blood did not come at once, which lulled them further. They were intensely interested but not alarmed, until suddenly Osiris reeled back and with a dreadful cry clutched at the stump of his lower arm. Only then did the blood burst out between his fingers and sprayed down his white

112

robe, staining it like spilt wine. Still clutching his stump, Osiris staggered across the stage and began to scream. That scream, high and clear with mortal agony, broke the mood of the spectators' complacency. They knew then for the first time that what they were witnessing was not make-believe, but they were trapped in horrified silence.

Before Osiris could reach the edge of the stage, Seth came bounding after him on those thick bow-legs. He seized the stump of Osiris' arm and used it as a handle to drag him back into the centre of the stage, where he threw him sprawling full-length on the stone flags. The tinsel crown tumbled from Osiris' head and the plaits of dark hair fell to his shoulders as he lay in a spreading puddle of his own blood.

'Please spare me,' Osiris shrieked, as Seth stood over him, and Seth laughed. It was a full-throated roar of genuine amusement. Rasfer had become Seth, and Seth was hugely enjoying himself.

That savage laughter woke the audience from its trance. However, the illusion was complete. They no longer believed that they were watching a play, and for all of them this terrible spectacle had become reality. Women screamed and men roared with fury as they witnessed the murder of their god.

'Spare him! Spare the great god Osiris!' they howled, but not one of them rose from his seat or rushed on to the stage to attempt to prevent the tragedy from being played out. They knew that the struggles and passions of the gods were beyond the influence of mortal men.

Osiris reached up and pawed at Seth's legs with

113

his one remaining hand. Still laughing, Seth grabbed his wrist and pulled his arm out to its full length, inspecting it as a butcher might inspect the shoulder of a goat before he sections it.

'Cut it off!' screamed a voice in the crowd, thick with the lust for blood. The mood had swung again.

'Kill him!' screamed another. It has always troubled me how the sight of blood and violent death affects even the mildest of men. Even I was stirred by this terrible scene, sickened and horrified, it is true, but beneath it stirred by a revolting excitement.

With a casual sweep of the blade, Seth struck off the arm, and Osiris fell back, leaving the twitching limb in Seth's red fist. He was trying to rise to his feet, but he had no hands to support himself. His legs kicked spasmodically, and his head whipped from side to side, and still he screamed. I tried to force myself to turn away, but though my gorge rose and scalded the back of my throat, still I had to watch.

Seth hacked the arm into three pieces through the joint of the wrist and the elbow. One at a time he hurled the fragments into the packed ranks of the audience. As they spun through the air they sprinkled those below with drops of ruby. They roared like the lions in Pharaoh's zoo at feeding-time, and held up their hands to catch these holy relics of their god.

Seth worked on with dedicated gusto. Osiris' feet he chopped off at the ankles. Then the calves at the knees, and the thighs at the hip joints. As he threw each of these to them, the mob clamoured for more.

'The talisman of Seth!' howled a voice amongst them. 'Give us the talisman of Seth!' and the cry was taken up. According to the myth, the talisman is the most powerful of all the magical charms. The person who has it in his possession controls all the dark forces of the underworld. It is the only one of the fourteen segments of Osiris' body that was never recovered by Isis and her sister Nephthys from the far corners of the earth to which Seth scattered them. The talisman of Seth is that same part of the body that Rasfer deprived me of, and which forms the centrepiece of that beautiful necklace that was the cynical gift of my Lord Intef.

'Give us the talisman of Seth!' the mob howled, and Seth reached down and lifted the red sodden tunic of the limbless trunk at his feet. He was still laughing. I shuddered as I recognized that merciless sound that I had heard so often at my own punishment sessions. In sympathy I experienced once again the sudden fire in my groin as the short sword flashed in Seth's hairy paw, already wet and running with his victim's blood, and he lifted on high the piteous relic.

The crowd pleaded for it. 'Give it to us,' they begged him. 'Give us the power of the talisman.' The spectacle had transformed them into ravening beasts.

Seth ignored their pleas. 'A gift,' he cried. 'A gift from one god to another. I Seth, god of darkness, dedicate this talisman to the god-Pharaoh, Mamose the divine.' And he hopped down the stone stairs on those powerful bow-legs and placed the relic at Pharaoh's feet.

To my amazement the king leaned forward and gathered it up to himself. His expression beneath

115

the powder and paint was spellbound, as though this was the true relic of the god. I am sure that at that moment he truly believed it was. He held it in his right hand through all that ensued.

His gift accepted, Seth rushed back on to the stage to complete his butchery. The thing that haunts me still is that the poor dismembered creature was alive and sensate to the very end. I realized that the drug I had given Tod had done little to dull his senses. I saw the terrible agony in his eyes as he lay in the lake of his own blood and rolled his head from side to side, the only part that remained to him to move.

For me, then, it came as an intense relief when at last Seth struck off the head and held it up by its thick plaited locks for the crowd to admire. Even then, the poor creature's eyes swivelled wildly in their sockets as he looked for the very last time on this world. At last they dulled and glazed over, and Seth tossed the head to them.

Thus the first act of our pageant ended in swelling and rapturous applause that threatened to shake the granite pillars of the temple from their bases.

 During the intermission my slave helpers cleaned away the gruesome evidence of the slaughter from the set. I was particularly concerned that my Lady Lostris should not realize what had truly taken place in the first act. I wished her to believe that all had gone as we had rehearsed it. So I had arranged that she stay in her tent, and that one of Tanus' men

remain at the entrance to keep her there, and also to ensure that none of her Cushite maidens were allowed to peep out at the first act and rush back to Lostris with a report. I knew that if she realized the truth, she would be too distraught to play her part. While my helpers used buckets of water from our stage Nile to wash away the ghastly evidence, I hurried to my mistress's tent to reassure her and to satisfy myself that my precautions to shield her had been effective.

'Oh, Taita, I heard the applause,' she greeted me happily. 'They love your play. I am so happy for you. You so richly deserve this success.' She chuckled in a conspiratorial fashion. 'It sounded as though they believed the murder of Osiris was real, and the buckets of ox-blood with which you drenched Tod were truly the blood of the god.'

'Indeed, my lady, they seemed totally deceived by our little tricks,' I agreed, although I still felt faint and ill from what I had just lived through.

My Lady Lostris suspected nothing, and when I led her out on to the stage, she barely glanced at the grisly stains that remained upon the stones. I posed her in her opening position, and adjusted the torchlight to flatter her. Even though I was accustomed to it, still her beauty choked my throat and made my eyes sting with tears.

I left her concealed by the linen curtains, and stepped out to face my audience. There was no sarcastic applause to greet me this time. Every one of them, from Pharaoh to the meanest vassal, was captive to my voice, as in my lambent prose I described the mourning of Isis and her sister Nephthys at the death of their brother.

When I stepped down and the curtain was

drawn aside to reveal the grieving figure of Isis, the audience gasped aloud at her loveliness. After the horror and blood of the first act, her presence was all the more moving.

Isis began to sing the lament for the dead, and her voice thrilled through the gloomy halls of the temple. As her head moved to the cadence of her voice, the torchlight was reflected in a darting and flickering shaft from the bronze moon that surmounted her horned head-dress.

I watched Pharaoh attentively as she sang. His eyes never left her face, and his lips moved silently in sympathy with the words that swelled from her throat.

My heart is a wounded gazelle,
torn by the lion claws of my grief—

She lamented and the king and all his train grieved with her.

There is no sweetness in the honeycomb,
no perfume remains in the desert blossom.
My soul is an empty temple,
deserted by the god of love.

In the front rank one or two of the king's wives were snuffling and blubbering, but nobody even glanced at them.

I look on death's grim face with a smile.
Gladly would I follow him,
if he could lead me to the arms of my dear lord.

By now not only the royal wives but every one of

the women were weeping, and most of the men also. Her words and her beauty were too much for them to resist. It seemed impossible that a god should show the same emotions as mortal men, but the slow tears were cutting runnels through the white powder on Pharaoh's cheeks, and he blinked his heavy, kohl-darkened eyelids like an owl as he stared at my Lady Lostris.

Nephthys entered and sang a duet with her sister, then hand-in-hand the two women went in search of the scattered fragments of Osiris' corpse.

Of course I had not placed the actual dismembered portions of Tod's corpse for them to find. During the intermission my helpers had retrieved these and carried them away to the embalmers on my instructions. I would pay for Tod's funeral out of my own purse. It seemed the very least that I could do to compensate the unfortunate creature for my own part in his murder. Despite the missing portion of his anatomy that Pharaoh still held in his hand, I hoped the gods might make an exception in his case and allow Tod's shade to pass into the underworld, and that there he might not think too badly of me. It is wise to have friends wherever you can, in this world and the next.

To represent the body of the god I had the funeral artists from the necropolis build for me a magnificent mummy cartonnage, depicting Osiris in his full regalia and in the death pose with his arms folded across his chest. This container I had cut into thirteen sections that fitted together like a child's building-blocks.

As the sisters retrieved each of these sections they sang a hymn of praise to the god's parts, to his

119

hands and feet, to his limbs and trunk, and finally
to his divine head.

> Such eyes, like stars set in the heavens,
> must shine for ever.
> Death should never dim such beauty,
> nor the funeral wrappings contain such majesty.

When at last the two sisters had reassembled the
complete body of Osiris, except for the missing
talisman, they pondered aloud how they could
return it to life once more.

This was my opportunity to add to the pageant
that essential element that makes any theatrical
production appeal to the popular taste. There is a
broad lascivious streak in most of us, and the
playwright and the poet does well to bear this in
mind if he hopes to have his work appreciated by
the main body of his audience.

'There is but one certain way to bring our dear
lord and brother back to life.' I placed the words in
the mouth of the goddess Nephthys. 'One of us
must perform the act of generation with his
shattered body to make it whole again and to fan
the spark of life within it.'

The audience stirred and leaned forward with
anticipation at this suggestion. It had elements to
appeal to even the most prurient of those present,
including incest and necrophilia.

I had agonized over how I would represent upon
the stage this episode in the myth of the
resurrection of Osiris. My mistress had shocked
me when she had declared herself willing to carry
her role through to the end. She had even had the
effrontery to point out, with that impudent grin of

hers, that she might gain some valuable knowledge and experience from doing so. I was not certain if she was jesting or if she would really have gone through with it; however, I would not give her the opportunity to demonstrate her good faith or lack of it. Her reputation and the honour of her family were too valuable to trifle with.

So it was that at my signal, the linen curtains were drawn once more and my Lady Lostris quickly left the stage. Her place was taken by one of the upper-class courtesans who usually plied her trade in a palace of love near the port. I had hired this wench, from amongst several that I had interviewed, because of her fine young body that so much resembled that of my mistress. Of course, in facial beauty she could not come close to my Lady Lostris, but then I know of none who could.

As soon as the substitute goddess was in position, the torches at the rear of the stage were lit so as to cast her shadow upon the curtain. She began to disrobe in the most provocative manner. The males in the audience cheered on her shadowy gyrations, convinced that they were watching my Lady Lostris. The harlot responded to this encouragement with an increasingly lewd display that was almost as well received as the slaughter of Osiris in the first act.

Now came that action of the play that had given me, the author, considerable pause, for how could I contrive fecundity without a stout peg to hang it on? We had just seen Osiris forcefully deprived of his. In the end I was forced to stoop to that tired old theatrical device that I so scorned in the work of other playwrights, namely the intervention of the gods and their supernatural powers.

121

While my Lady Lostris spoke from the wings, her shadowy alter ego on stage stood over the mummiform figure of Osiris and made a series of mystical gestures. 'My dear brother, by the rare and marvellous powers granted to me by our forefather, Ammon-Ra, I restore to you those manly parts that cruel Seth so brutally tore from you,' intoned my mistress.

I had equipped the mummy case with a device that I could raise by hauling on a length of fine linen twine that ran over a pulley in the temple roof directly above where Osiris lay. At Isis' words the wooden phallus, hinged to the god's pudenda, rose in majestic splendour, as long as my arm, into full erection. The audience gasped with admiration.

When Isis caressed it, I jerked the string to make it leap and twitch. The audience loved it, but loved it even better when the goddess mounted the supine mummy of the god. Judging by the convincing acrobatics of her simulated ecstasy, the harlot I had chosen to play the part must have been one of the truly great exponents of her art. The audience gave full recognition to her superior performance, egging her on with whistling and hooting and shouting ribald advice.

At the climax of this exhibition the torches were extinguished and the temple plunged into darkness. In the darkness the substitution was made once more and when the torches were re-lit my Lady Lostris stood in mid-stage with a new-born infant in her arms. One of the kitchen slaves had been considerate enough to give birth a few days previously, and I had borrowed her whelp for the occasion.

122

'I give you the new-born son of Osiris, god of the underworld, and of Isis, goddess of the moon and of the stars.' My Lady Lostris lifted the infant high and he, astonished by the sea of strangers before him, screwed up his tiny face and turned bright red as he howled.

Isis raised her voice above his and cried, 'Greet the young Lord Horus, god of the wind and the sky, falcon of the heavens!' Half the audience were Horus men and their enthusiasm for their patron was unbounded. They came to their feet in a roaring tumult, and the second act ended in another triumph for me and in mortification for the infant god, who on later examination was found to have prodigiously soiled his swaddling-cloth.

 I opened the final act with another of my recitations describing the childhood and the coming to manhood of Horus. I spoke of the sacred charge laid upon him by Isis, and as I did so, the curtains were drawn aside to reveal the goddess in the centre of the stage.

Isis was bathing in the Nile, attended by her handmaidens. Her wet robe clung to her body so that the pale glory of her skin shone through. The indistinct outlines of her breasts were tipped with tiny rose-buds of virgin pink.

Tanus as Horus entered from the wings, and immediately dominated the stage. In his polished armour and his warrior's pride he was a perfect counterpoint for the beauty of the goddess. The long list of his battle honours in the river wars, together with his most recent exploit in saving the royal barge, had focused the attention of the populace full upon him. For this moment Tanus was the darling of the crowd. Before he could speak, they began to cheer him, and the applause continued so long that the actors were forced to freeze in their opening positions.

While the cheering swirled around Tanus, I picked out certain faces in the audience and watched their reactions. Nembet, the Great Lion of Egypt, scowled and muttered fiercely into his beard, making no attempt to hide his animosity. Pharaoh smiled graciously and nodded slightly, so that those seated behind him were made aware of his approbation, and their own enthusiasm was encouraged. My Lord Intef, never one to fly against the prevailing winds, smiled his most silky smile and nodded his head in concert with his king. His eyes, however, when seen from my vantage-point, were deadly.

At last the applause abated and Tanus could speak his lines, not without difficulty, however, for every time he paused to draw breath another outburst of cheering broke out. It was only when Isis began to sing that complete silence fell upon them once more.

The suffering of your father,
the terrible fate that hangs over our house,
all these must be expunged.

In verse Isis warned her noble son, and held out her arms to him in supplication and in command.

The curse of Seth is upon us all,

and only you can break it.
Seek out your monstrous uncle.
By his arrogance and his ferocity,
you will know him.
When you find him,
strike him down.
Chain him,
bind him to your will,
that the gods and all men
will be freed for ever from his ghastly sway.

Still singing, the goddess withdrew and left her son to his quest. Like children following a well-loved nursery rhyme, the audience knew full well what to expect and leaned forward eagerly and hummed with anticipation.

When at last Seth came leaping back on stage for the cataclysmic battle, the age-old struggle between good and evil, beauty and ugliness, duty and dishonour, the audience was ready for him. They greeted Seth with a chorus of hatred that was spontaneous and unfeigned. In defiance Rasfer leered and gibbered at them, strutting about the stage, cupping his genitalia in his hands and thrusting his hips out at them in a mocking and obscene gesture that drove them wild with fury.

'Kill him, Horus!' they howled. 'Smash in his ugly face!' And Seth pranced before them, stoking their fury.

'Kill the murderer of the great god Osiris!' they roared in a paroxysm of loathing.

'Smash in his face!'

'Rip out his guts!'

The congregation's reaction to him was in no way moderated by the fact that it knew, deep down, that this was Rasfer and not Seth.

'Hack off his head!' they screamed.

'Kill him! Kill him!'

At last Seth pretended to see his nephew for the first time, and swaggered up to him, lolling his tongue out between his blackened teeth, drooling like an idiot so that silver strands of saliva slimed down on to his chest. I would never have believed that Rasfer could make himself more repulsive than nature had already accomplished, but now he proved me wrong.

'Who is this child?' he demanded, and belched full in the face of Horus. Tanus was unprepared for this and stepped back involuntarily, his expression of disgust unfeigned as he smelled Rasfer's breath and the contents of his stomach, the sour wine still fermenting in it.

Tanus recovered swiftly and spoke his next line. 'I am Horus, son of Osiris.'

Seth let out a mocking peal of laughter. 'And what is it you seek, boy child of a dead god?'

'I seek vengeance for the murder of my noble father. I seek the assassin of Osiris.'

'Then search no further,' Seth shouted, 'for I am Seth the vanquisher of lesser gods. I am Seth the eater of stars, and the destroyer of worlds.'

The two gods drew their swords and rushed at each other, to meet in mid-stage with a ringing clash of bronze as blade struck blade. In an attempt to reduce the chances of accidental injury, I had attempted to substitute wooden swords for bronze, but neither of my actors would have any of it. My Lord Intef had intervened when Rasfer had appealed to him. He had ordered that they be allowed to wield their real battle weapons, and I

126

had been forced to yield to this higher authority. At least it added to the realism of the scene as they stood now chest to chest, with blades locked, and glared into each other's face.

They made an extraordinary pair, so totally dissimilar, pointing up the moral of the play, the eternal conflict of good against evil. Tanus was tall and fair and comely. Seth was swarthy and thick-set, bow-legged and hideous. The contrast was direct and visceral. The mood of the audience was as fiery and as fiercely partisan as that of the two protagonists.

Simultaneously they pushed each other backwards and then rushed in again, thrusting and cutting, feinting and parrying. They were both highly trained and skilled swordsmen, amongst the finest in all Pharaoh's armies. Their blades whirled and glinted in the torchlight so that they seemed as insubstantial as the sunlight reflected from the wind-ruffled surface of the great river. The sound of their flight was that of the wings of the birds startled from their roosts in the gloomy heights of the temple, but when they clashed together it was with the heavy ring of hammers at the coppersmith's forge.

What seemed to the observer to be the chaos of real battle was in fact a meticulously choreographed ballet which had been carefully rehearsed. Each man knew exactly how each blow must be launched and each parry timed. These were two superb athletes engaged in the activity for which they had trained their entire warrior's lifetime, and they made it seem effortless.

When Seth thrust, Horus left his parry so late that the point actually touched his breastplate and

127

left a tiny bright scratch on the metal. Then when Horus launched himself forward in riposte, his edge flew so close to Seth's head that a coil of his coarse matted hair was shorn from his skull, as if by a barber's razor. Their footwork was as graceful and intricate as that of the temple dancers, and they were swift as falcons and lithe as hunting cheetahs.

The crowd was mesmerized and so was I. Therefore it must have been some deep instinct that warned me, perhaps even a nudge from the gods, who knows? At any rate, something outside myself made me tear my eyes away from the spectacle and glance at my Lord Intef where he sat in the front row.

Again, was it instinct or my own deep knowledge of him, or the intervention of the god who protects Tanus that placed the thought in my mind? A little of all three of these, perhaps, but I knew with instant and utter certainty the reason for that wolfish smile on my Lord Intef's handsome features.

I knew why he had chosen Rasfer to play Seth. I knew why he had made no effort to exclude Tanus from the role of Horus, even after he had found out about the relationship between him and my Lady Lostris. I knew why he had ordered the use of real swords, and I knew why he was smiling now. The massacre was not over for the evening. He was looking forward to more. Before this act was played out, Rasfer would ply his special talents once again.

'Tanus!' I screamed, as I started forward. 'Beware! It's a trap. He intends—' My cries were drowned out by the thunder of the crowd, and I had not taken a second step when I was seized by each arm from behind. I tried to struggle free, but two of Rasfer's ruffians held me fast and started to drag me away. They had been placed there for just such a moment as this, to prevent me from warning my friend.

'Horus, give me strength!' I rendered up a swift and silent entreaty, and instead of resisting them I hurled myself back in the same direction as they were pulling me. For an instant they were thrown off-balance, and I broke half-free of their grasp. I managed to reach the edge of the stage before they could control me again.

'Horus, give me voice!' I prayed, and then screamed with all my breath, 'Tanus, beware! He means to kill you.'

This time my voice carried above that of the mob, and Tanus heard me. I saw his head flick and his eyes narrow slightly. However, Rasfer heard me as well. He responded instantly, breaking the rehearsed routine. Instead of dropping back before the whirlwind of cuts and thrusts that Tanus was aiming close to his brutish head, he stepped in and, with an upward sweep of his own blade, he forced Tanus' sword-arm high.

Without the benefit of surprise he would never have made the opening into which he now launched a thrust behind which was the full weight of those massive shoulders and mighty trunk. The point of his blade was aimed an inch below the rim of Tanus' helmet and directly at his right eye. It should have skewered his eye and cleaved his skull through and through.

However, my shouted warning had given Tanus that fleeting moment of grace in which to react. He

129

recovered his guard just in time. With the pommel of his sword he managed to touch a glancing blow to Rasfer's wrist. It had just sufficient force to deflect the sword-point a finger's width, and at the same moment Tanus tucked in his chin and rolled his head. It was too late to avoid the blow entirely. However, the stroke that might have skewered his eye and split his skull like a rotten melon, merely laid open his eyebrow to the bone, and then flew on over his shoulder.

Instantly a sheet of blood gushed from the shallow wound and flowed over Tanus' face, blinding his right eye. He was forced to fall back before the savage onslaught that Rasfer now launched at him. Desperately he gave ground, blinking at the blood and trying to wipe it away with his free hand. It seemed impossible that he would be able to defend himself, and if only I had not been held so securely by the palace guards, I would have drawn the little jewelled dagger at my belt and rushed to his aid.

Even without my assistance Tanus was able to survive that first murderous attack. Though he was wounded twice more, a gouge across the left thigh and a nick on the biceps of his sword-arm, he kept weaving and parrying and ducking. Rasfer kept coming at him, never letting him recover his balance or his full vision. Within minutes Rasfer was blowing and grunting like a giant forest hog, and running with sweat, his misshapen torso gleaming in the torchlight, but the speed and fury of his assault never faltered.

Though no great swordsman myself, I am a student of the art. So often had I watched Rasfer at practice in the weapons-yard that I knew his style intimately. I knew he was an exponent of the attack *khamsin,* the attack 'like the desert wind'. It was a manoeuvre that perfectly suited his brute strength and physique. I had seen him practise it on a hundred occasions and now I divined by his footwork that he was gathering himself for it, for that one last effort that would end it all.

Struggling in the grip of my captors, I screamed at Tanus again, '*Khamsin!* Be ready!' I thought that my warning had been drowned and washed away by the uproar that filled the temple, for Tanus showed no reaction. Later he told me he had indeed heard me, and that with his impaired vision that second warning of mine had certainly saved him once again.

Rasfer dropped back a half-pace, the classic prelude to the *khamsin,* relaxing the pressure for an instant to position his opponent for the coup. Then his weight shifted and his left foot swung forward into the lead. He used his momentum and all the strength of his right leg to launch his entire body into the attack, like some grotesque carrion-bird taking to flight. As both his feet left the ground, the point of his blade was aimed at Tanus' throat. It was inexorable. Nothing could prevent that deadly blade from flying true to its mark except the one classic defence, the stop-hit.

At the precise instant that Rasfer was fully committed to the stroke, Tanus launched himself with equal power and superior grace. Like an arrow leaving the bowstring, he flew straight at his opponent. As they met in mid-air Tanus gathered up Rasfer's blade with his own and let it run down on to the pommel, where it came up hard and short, stopping it dead. It was the perfectly

131

executed stop-hit.

The mass and speed of the two big men were thrown on to the bronze blade in Rasfer's fist, and it could not withstand the shock. It snapped cleanly, and left him clutching only the sheared-off hilt. Then they were locked chest-to-chest once more. Although Tanus' sword was still undamaged, Rasfer had got in under his guard and he could not wield it. Both Tanus' hands, the sword still held in his right fist, were locked behind Rasfer's back as the two men heaved and strained at each other.

Wrestling is one of the military disciplines in which every warrior in the Egyptian army is trained. Bound to each other by the crushing embrace of arms, they spun about the stage, each attempting to throw the other off-balance, snarling into each other's eyes, hooking a heel to trip, butting at each other with the visors of their helmets, equally matched thus far in strength and determination.

The audience had long since sensed that this was no longer a mock engagement, but a fight to the death. I wondered that their appetites had not been jaded by all they had witnessed that evening, but it was not so. They were insatiable, howling for blood and yet more blood.

At last Rasfer tore his arm free of Tanus' encircling grip. He still clutched the hilt of the broken sword in his fist, and with the jagged edge he struck at Tanus' face, deliberately aiming at his eyes and the wound in his brow, trying to enlarge and aggravate it. Tanus twisted his head to avoid the blows, catching them on the peak of his bronze helmet. Like a python shifting its coils around its prey, he used the moment to adjust his crushing hold around Rasfer's chest. The strain that he was exerting was such that Rasfer's features began to swell and engorge with blood. The air was being forced out of him, and he struggled against suffocation. He began visibly to weaken. Tanus kept up the pressure until a carbuncle on Rasfer's back was stretched to bursting-point and the yellow pus erupted in a stinking stream and trickled down into the waistband of his kilt.

Already suffocating, Rasfer grimaced at the pain of the bursting abscess and checked. Tanus felt him falter, and he summoned some deep reserve of strength. He changed the angle of his next effort, dropping his shoulders slightly and forcing his opponent backwards and upwards on to his heels. Rasfer was off-balance, and Tanus heaved again and forced him back a pace. Once he had him moving backwards, he kept the momentum going. Still locked to his opponent, he ran Rasfer backwards across the stage, steering him towards one of the gigantic stone pillars. For a moment none of us realized Tanus' intention, and then we saw him drop the point of his sword to the horizontal and press the hilt hard against Rasfer's spine.

At a full run the point of Tanus' sword hit the unyielding column. The metal screeched against the granite, and the shock was transmitted up the blade. It stopped those two big men in their tracks, and the force of it drove the hilt into Rasfer's spine. It would have killed a lesser man, and even Rasfer was paralyzed by it. With the last gust of his foul breath he let out a cry of agony, and his arms flew open. The broken haft of his own sword spun from

133

his grip and skidded away across the stone pavement.

Rasfer's knees buckled, and he sagged in Tanus' arms. Tanus thrust his hip into him, and, with a heave of his upper body, hurled Rasfer over backwards. He landed so heavily that I heard more than one of his ribs crackle like dry twigs in the flames of the camp-fire. The back of his skull bounced upon the stone flags with a sound like a desert melon dropped from on high, and the breath from his lungs whistled out of his throat.

He groaned in agony. He had barely the strength to lift his arms to Tanus in capitulation. Tanus was so carried away by battle-rage, and inflamed by the roar of the crowd, that he was a man berserk. He stood over Rasfer and lifted his sword on high, gripping the hilt with both hands. He was a dreadful sight. Blood from the wound in his forehead had painted his visage into a glistening devil mask. Sweat and blood had soaked the hair of his chest and stained his clothing.

'Kill him!' roared the congregation. 'Kill the evil one!'

The point of Tanus' sword was aimed at the centre of Rasfer's chest, and I steeled myself for the down-stroke that would impale that gross body. I willed Tanus to do it, for I hated Rasfer more than any of them. The gods know that I had reason, for here was the monster who had gelded me, and I longed for my revenge.

It was in vain. I should have known my Tanus better than expect him to skewer a surrendered enemy. I saw the fires of madness begin to fade from his eyes. He shook his head slightly, as if to regain control of himself. Then, instead of

134

stabbing down, he lowered his sword-point slowly until it just pricked Rasfer's chest. The keen point raised a drop of blood, bright as a garnet amongst the coarse hair of Rasfer's chest. Then Tanus picked up the lines of his script.

'Thus I bind you to my will, and I expel you from the light. May you wander through all eternity in the dark places. May you never more have power over the noble and the good amongst men. I give you to rule over the thief and the coward, over the bully and the cheat, over the liar and the murderer, over the grave-robber and the violater of virtuous women, over the blasphemer and the breaker of faith. From henceforth you are the god of all evil. Get you gone, and carry away with you the curse of Horus and of his resurrected father, Osiris.'

Tanus lifted the point of his sword from Rasfer's chest and tossed the weapon aside, deliberately disarming himself in the presence of his enemy to demonstrate his disdain and scorn. The blade clattered on the flagstones and Tanus strode to the running waters of our stage Nile and went down on one knee to scoop a handful and dash it into his own face, washing away the blood. Then he tore a strip of linen from the hem of his kilt and swiftly bound up the wound on his forehead to stem the bleeding.

Rasfer's two apes released me and rushed on stage to succour their fallen commander. They lifted him to his feet, and he staggered between them, heaving and blowing like a great obscene bullfrog. I saw that he was grievously injured. They dragged him from the stage, and the crowd howled its derision and hatred at him.

I watched my Lord Intef, and his expression was for the moment unguarded. I saw every one of my suspicions confirmed there. This was how he had planned to wreak his vengeance on Tanus—to have him slain before the eyes of the entire populace—and on his own daughter: to have her lover killed before her eyes—that was to have been Lostris' punishment for flouting her father's will.

My Lord Intef's frustration and disappointment now were enough to make me feel a smug satisfaction as I considered what retribution must be in store for Rasfer. He might have preferred more of the rough treatment that Tanus had dealt out to him, to the punishment that my Lord Intef would inflict upon him. My master was ever harsh with those who failed him.

Tanus was still gasping from the exertions of the duel, but now, as he moved to the front of the stage, he drew a dozen deep breaths to steady himself for the declamation that would bring the pageant to an end. As he faced the congregation it fell silent, for in blood and anger he was an awe-inspiring sight.

Tanus lifted up both his hands to the temple roof and cried out in a loud voice, 'Ammon-Ra, give me voice! Osiris, give me eloquence!' The traditional entreaty of the orator.

'Give him voice! Give him eloquence!' the crowd responded, and their faces were still rapt with all they had witnessed, but hungry for more entertainment.

Tanus was that unusual creature, a man of action who was also a man of words and ideas. I am sure that he would have been generous enough to admit that many of those ideas were planted in his mind by that lowly slave, Taita. However, once planted, they were in fertile ground.

When it came to oratory, Tanus' exhortations to his squadrons on the eve of battle were famous. Of course, I had not been present at all of these, but they had been relayed to me verbatim by Kratas, his faithful friend and lieutenant. I had copied many of these speeches down on a set of papyrus scrolls, for they were worthy of preservation.

Tanus had the common touch, and the ability to appeal directly to the ordinary man. I often thought that much of this special power of his sprang from his transparent honesty and his forthright manner. Men trusted him and followed willingly wherever he led them, even unto death itself.

I was still overwrought by the conflict we had all just witnessed and the closeness of Tanus' escape from the trap that my Lord Intef had laid for him. Nevertheless, I was eager to listen to the declamation that Tanus had prepared without my help or advice. To be truthful, I was still a little resentful that he had declined my assistance, and more than a little nervous as to what he might come out with. Tact and subtlety have never been Tanus' most notable virtues.

Now Pharaoh made a gesture of invitation to him to speak, crossing and uncrossing the ceremonial crook and flail, and inclining his head gracefully. The congregation was silent and intent, leaning forward eagerly so as not to miss a single word.

'It is I, Horus the falcon-headed, that speaks,' Tanus began, and they encouraged him.

'It is verily the falcon-headed! Hear him!'

'Ha-Ka-Ptah!' Tanus used the archaic form from which the present name of Egypt was derived. Very few realized that the original meaning was the temple of Ptah. 'I speak to you of this ancient land given to us ten thousand years since, in the time when all the gods were young. I speak to you of the two kingdoms that in nature are one and indivisible.'

Pharaoh nodded. This was the standard dogma, approved by both temporal and religious authority that neither recognized the impostor in the Lower Kingdom, nor even acknowledged his existence.

'Oh, *Kemit*!' Tanus used another ancient name for Egypt: the Black Land, after the colour of the Nile mud brought down by the annual inundation. 'I speak to you of this land riven and divided, torn by civil war, bleeding and drained of treasure.' My own shock was mirrored on the faces of all those who listened to him. Tanus had just given voice to the unspeakable. I wanted to rush on to the stage and clap my hand over his mouth to prevent him from going on, but I was transfixed.

'Oh, *Ta-Meri*!' Another old name: the Beloved Earth. Tanus had learned well the history I had taught him. 'I speak to you of old and feeble generals, and admirals too weak and indecisive to wrest back the stolen kingdom from the usurper. I speak to you of ancient men in their dotage who waste your treasure and spill the blood of your finest young men as though it were the lees of bitter wine.'

In the second row of the audience I saw Nembet, the Great Lion of Egypt, flush with anger and scratch furiously with chagrin at his beard. The other elderly military men around him frowned and moved restlessly on their benches, rattling their swords in their scabbards as a sign of their disapproval. Amongst them all, only my Lord Intef smiled as he watched Tanus escape from one trap only to blunder into the next.

'Our *Ta-Meri* is beset by a host of enemies, and yet the sons of the nobles prefer to cut off their own thumbs rather than to carry the sword to protect her.' As he said this, Tanus looked keenly at Menset and Sobek, Lostris' older brothers, where they sat beside their father in the second row. The king's decree exempted from military service only those with such physical disability as to render them unfit. The surgeon priests at the temple of Osiris had perfected the art of removing the top joint of the thumb with little pain or danger of infection, thus rendering it impossible for that hand to wield a sword or pluck a bowstring. The young bucks proudly flaunted their mutilations as they sat gambling and carousing in the riverside taverns. They considered the missing digit a mark not of cowardice, but of sophistication and independent spirit.

'War is the game played by old men with the lives of the young,' I had heard Lostris' brothers argue. 'Patriotism is a myth conceived by those old rogues to draw us into the infernal game. Let them fight as they will, but we want no part of it.' In vain I had remonstrated with them that the privilege of Egyptian citizenship carried with it duties and responsibilities. They dismissed me with the arrogance of the young and ignorant.

Now, however, beneath Tanus' level stare they fidgeted and concealed their left hands in the folds of their clothing. They were both of them right-handed, but had convinced the recruiting officer to the contrary, with their eloquence and a dash of gold.

The common people at the rear of the great hall hummed and stamped their feet in agreement with what Tanus had said. It was their sons who filled the rowing-benches of the war galleys, or marched under arms through the desert sands.

However, in the wings of the stage I wrung my hands in despair. With that little speech Tanus had made an enemy of fifty of the young nobles in the audience. They were men who would one day inherit power and influence in the Upper Kingdom. Their enmity outweighed a hundred times the adoration of the common herd and I prayed for Tanus to cease. In a few minutes he had done enough damage to last us all a hundred years, but he went on blithely.

'Oh, *Ta-Nutri*!' This was yet another ancient name: the Land of the Gods. 'I speak to you of the wrong-doer and the robber who waits in ambush on every hilltop and in every thicket. The farmer is forced to plough with his shield at his side, and the traveller must go with his sword bared.'

Again the commoners applauded. The depredations of the robber bands were a terrible scourge upon them all. No man was safe beyond the mud walls of the towns, and the robber chieftains who called themselves the Shrikes were arrogant and fearless. They respected no law but their own, and no man was safe from them.

Tanus had struck exactly the right note with the people, and suddenly I was moved by the notion that this was all much deeper than it seemed. Revolutions have been forged and dynasties of

140

pharaohs overturned by just such appeals to the masses. With Tanus' next words my suspicion was strengthened.

'While the poor cry out under the lash of the tax-collector, the nobles anoint the buttocks of their fancy boys with the most precious oils of the orient—' A roar went up from the rear of the hall, and my fears were replaced by a tremulous excitement. Had this been carefully planned? Was Tanus more subtle and devious than I had ever given him credit for?

'By Horus!' I cried in my heart. 'The land is ripe for revolution, and who better to lead it than Tanus?' I felt only disappointment that he had not taken me into his confidence and made me party to his design. I could have planned a revolution as skilfully and as cunningly as I could design a water-garden or write a play.

I craned to look over the heads of the congregation, expecting at the very next moment to see Kratas and his brother officers burst into the temple at the head of a company of warriors from the squadron. I felt the hair on my forearms and at the nape of my neck lift with excitement as I pictured them snatching the double crown from Pharaoh's head and placing it upon the blood-smeared brow of Tanus. With what joy I would have joined the cry of 'Long live Pharaoh! Long live King Tanus!'

Heady images swirled before my eyes as Tanus went on speaking. I saw the prophecy of the desert oracle fulfilled. I dreamed of Tanus, with my Lady Lostris beside him, seated on the white throne of this very Egypt, with myself standing behind them resplendent in the apparel of the grand vizier of the

Upper Kingdom. But why, oh why, had he not consulted me before embarking on this perilous venture?

With his next breath he made the reason plain. I had misjudged my Tanus, my honest, plain and good Tanus, my noble, straight and trustworthy Tanus, lacking only in guile and stealth and deceit.

This was no plot. This was simply Tanus speaking his mind without fear or favour. The commoners, who only moments before had been clinging enraptured to every word that fell from his tongue, were now quite unexpectedly given the sharp edge of that organ as he rounded upon them.

'Hear me, oh Egypt! What is to become of a land where the mean-spirited try to suppress the mighty amongst them; where the patriot is reviled; where there is no man of yesterday revered for his wisdom; where the petty and the envious seek to tear down the men of worth to their own base level?'

There was no cheering now as those at the back of the hall recognized themselves in this description. Effortlessly my Tanus had succeeded in alienating every man amongst them, great and small, rich and poor. Oh, why had he not consulted me, I mourned, and the answer was plain. He had not consulted me because he knew I would have counselled him against it.

'What order is there in society where the slave is free with his tongue, and counts himself as equal to those of noble birth?' he blazed at them. 'Should the son revile his father and scorn the wisdom paid for in grey hairs and wrinkled brow? Should the waterfront harlot wear rings of lapis lazuli and set herself above the virtuous wife?'

142

By Horus, he would not spare one of them from the lash of his tongue, I thought bitterly. As always, he was completely oblivious to his own safety in the pursuit of what he saw as the right and open way.

Only one person in the temple was enchanted with what he had to tell them. Lostris appeared at my side and gripped my arm.

'Isn't he wonderful, Taita?' she breathed. 'Every word he utters is the truth. Tonight he is truly a young god.'

I could find neither the words nor the heart to agree with her, and I hung my head in sorrow as Tanus went on relentlessly.

'Pharaoh, you are the father of the people. We cry out to you for protection and for succour. Give the affairs of state and war into the hands of honest and clever men. Send the rogues and the fools to rot on their estates. Call off the faithless priests and the usurious servants of the state, those parasites upon the body of this *Ta-Meri* of ours.'

Horus knows that I am as good a priest-hater as the best of them, but only a fool or very brave man would call down the wrath of every god-botherer in Egypt upon his own head, for their power is infinite and their hatred implacable. While as for the civil servants, their lines of influence and corruption have been set up over the centuries and my Lord Intef was the chief of them all. I shuddered in pity for my dear blunt friend as he went on handing out instructions to Pharaoh on how to restructure the whole of Egyptian society.

'Heed the words of the sage! Oh, king, honour the artist and the scribe. Reward the brave warrior and the faithful servant. Root out the bandits and

143

the robbers from their desert fastnesses. Give the people example and direction in their lives, so that this very Egypt may once again flourish and be great.'

Tanus fell to his knees in the centre of the stage and spread his arms wide. 'Oh, Pharaoh, you are our father. We protest our love to you. In return, show us now a father's love. Hear our entreaties, we beg of you.'

Up to that moment I had been stupefied by the depths of my friend's folly, but now, much too late, I regained my wits and signalled frantically for my stage-hands to drop the curtain before Tanus could do any further damage. As the gleaming folds of cloth floated down and hid him from their view, the audience sat in stunned silence, as though they did not believe all that they had heard and seen that night.

It was Pharaoh himself who broke the spell. He rose to his feet, and his face behind the stiff white make-up was inscrutable. As he swept from the temple, the congregation prostrated itself before him. Before he too went down in obeisance, I saw my Lord Intef's expression. It was triumphant.

 I escorted Tanus back from the temple to his own sparsely furnished quarters close to the dock at which his squadron was moored. Although I walked beside him with my hand on the hilt of my dagger, prepared for the consequences of his foolhardy honesty to be visited on us immediately, Tanus was quite unrepentant. Indeed, he seemed

144

oblivious to the depths of his folly and inordinately pleased with himself. I have often remarked how a man freshly released from terrible strain and mortal danger becomes garrulous and elated. Even Tanus, the hardened warrior, was no exception.

'It was time somebody stood up and said what needed to be said, don't you agree, old friend?' His voice rang clear and loud down the darkened alley, as though he were determined to summon any awaiting assassin to us. I kept my agreement muted.

'You did not expect it of me, did you now? Be honest with me, Taita. It took you quite by surprise, did it not?'

'It surprised us all.' This time I could agree with a little more enthusiasm. 'Even Pharaoh was taken aback, as well he might be.'

'He listened, Taita. He took it all in, I could tell. I did good work this evening, don't you think so?'

When I attempted to raise the subject of Rasfer's treacherous attack upon him and broach the possibility that it might have been inspired by my Lord Intef, Tanus would have none of it. 'That is impossible, Taita. You dreamed it. Lord Intef was my father's dearest friend. How could he wish me ill? Besides, I am to be his son-in-law, am I not?' And despite his injuries he let out such a happy shout of laughter that it roused the sleepers in the darkened huts that we were passing and they shouted grumpily back at us to be quiet. Tanus ignored their protests.

'No, no, I am sure that you are wrong,' he cried. 'It was simply Rasfer working out his spite in his own charming way. Well, he'll know better next time.' He threw his arm around my shoulders and hugged me so hard that it hurt. 'You saved me twice tonight. Without your warnings Rasfer would have had me both times. How do you do these things, Taita? I swear you are a secret warlock, and have the gift of the inner eye.' He laughed again.

How could I stifle his joy? He was like a boy, a big rumbustious boy. I could not help but love him all the more. This was not the time to point out the danger in which he had placed himself and all of us who were his friends.

Let him have his hour, and tomorrow I would sound the voice of reason and of caution. So I took him home and stitched the gash in his forehead, and washed his other wounds and anointed them with my special mixture of honey and herbs to prevent mortification. Then I gave him a stiff draught of the Red Shepenn and left the good Kratas to guard his slumbers.

When I reached my own quarters well after midnight, there were two summonses awaiting me: one from my Lady Lostris and the other from the vanquished Rasfer. There was no doubt as to which of them I would have responded to if I had been given the choice, but I was not. Rasfer's two thugs almost dragged me away to where he lay on a sweat-soaked mattress, cursing and moaning by turns, and calling on Seth and all the gods to witness his pain and his fortitude.

'Good Taita!' he greeted me, raising himself painfully on one elbow, 'you will not believe the pain. My chest is afire. I swear every bone in it is crushed, and my head aches as though it is bound by thongs of rawhide.'

With very little effort I was able to force back my

146

tears of pity, but it is a strange thing about those of us who are doctors and healers that we cannot find it in our hearts to deny our skills to even the most abominable creatures that require them. I sighed with resignation, unpacked the leather bag that contained my medical equipment and set out my instruments and unguents.

I was delighted to find that Rasfer's self-diagnosis was perfectly valid, and that apart from numerous contusions and shallow wounds, at least three of his ribs were broken and there was a lump on the back of his head almost the size of my fist. I had, therefore, a perfectly legitimate reason for adding considerably to his discomfort. One of the broken ribs was seriously out of alignment and there was genuine danger that it might pierce the lung. While his two thugs held him down and Rasfer squealed and howled most gratifyingly, I manipulated the rib back into place and strapped up his chest with linen bandages well soaked in vinegar to shrink as they dried.

Then I addressed myself to the lump on the back of his skull where it had struck the stone paving. The gods are often generous. When I held a lamp to Rasfer's eyes the pupils did not dilate. There was not the least doubt in my mind as to what treatment was required. Bloody fluid was gathering inside that unlovely skull. Without my help Rasfer would be dead by the following sunset. I thrust aside the obvious temptation and reminded myself of the surgeon's duty to his patient.

There are probably only three surgeons in all of Egypt who are capable of trepanning a skull with a good chance of success, and personally I would not

147

put much faith in the other two. Once again I ordered Rasfer's two oafs to take hold of him to control his struggles, and to hold him face down on his mattress. By the roughness of their handling and their obvious disregard for their master's injured ribs, I surmised that they were not exactly overflowing with loving feeling towards their master.

Once again a chorus of howls and squeals turned the night hideous and gladdened my labours, as I made a semi-circular incision around the lump on his scalp, and then peeled a large flap of skin away from the bone. Now not even those two strapping ruffians could hold him down. His struggles were splashing blood as high as the ceiling of the room and sprinkling us all, so that we seemed to be inflicted with a red pox. At last, in exasperation, I ordered them to bind his ankles and wrists to the bedposts with leather straps.

'Oh, gentle and sweet Taita, the pain is beyond belief. Give me but a drop of that flower juice, I beg you, dear friend,' he blubbered.

Now that he was safely bound to the bed, I could afford to be frank with him. 'I understand, my good Rasfer, just how you feel. I also would have been grateful for a little of the flower when last you took the knife to me. Alas, old comrade, my store of the drug is finished, and there will not be another eastern caravan for at least a month,' I lied cheerfully, for very few knew that I cultivated the Red Shepenn myself. Knowing that the best was yet to come, I reached for my bone-drill.

The human head is the only part of the body that puzzles me as a doctor. At the orders of my Lord Intef the corpses of all executed criminals are

148

handed over to me. In addition Tanus has been able to bring me many fine specimens from the battlefield, suitably pickled in vats of brine. All these I have dissected and studied so that I know every bone and how it fits into its exact place in the skeleton. I have traced the route by which food enters the mouth and passes through the body. I have found that great and wondrous organ, the heart, nestling between the pale air-bladders of the lungs. I have studied the rivers of the body through which the blood flows, and I have observed the two types of blood which determine the moods and emotions of man.

There is, of course, that bright joyous blood that, when released by the cut of a scalpel or the headsman's axe, spurts out in regular impulses. This is the blood of happy thoughts and fine emotions, it is the blood of love and kindness. Then there is that darker sullen blood that flows without the vigour and the bounding joy of the other. This is the blood of anger and of sorrow, of melancholic thoughts and evil deeds.

All these matters I have studied, and have filled one hundred papyrus rolls with my observations. There is no man in the world that I know of who has gone to such lengths, certainly none of those quacks in the temple with their amulets and their incantations have done so. I doubt any one of them could tell the liver from the sphincter of the anus without an invocation to Osiris, a casting of the divining dice and a fat fee paid in advance.

In all modesty I can say that I have never met a man who understands the human body better than I, and yet the head is still a puzzle to me. Naturally I understand that the eyes see, the nose smells, the mouth tastes and the ears hear—but what is the purpose of that pale porridge that fills the gourd of the skull?

I have never been able to fathom it myself, and no man has ever been able to offer me a satisfactory explanation, except that Tanus came closest to it. After he and I had spent an evening together sampling the latest vintage of red wine, he had woken in the dawn and suggested with a groan, 'Seth has placed this thing in our heads as his revenge on mankind.'

I once met a man who was travelling with a caravan from beyond those legendary twin rivers, the Tigris and the Euphrates, who professed to have studied the same problem. He was a wise man and together we debated many mysteries over the course of half a year. At one point he suggested that all human emotion and thought sprang not from the heart, but from those soft amorphous curds that make up the brain. I mention this naïve assertion only to demonstrate how gravely even an intelligent and learned man can err.

Nobody who has ever considered that mighty organ, the heart, leaping with its own life in the centre of our body, fed by great rivers of blood, protected by the palisades of bone, can doubt that this is the fountain from which all thought and emotion springs. The heart uses the blood to disseminate these emotions throughout the body. Have you ever felt your heart stir within you and quicken to beautiful music, or a lovely face, or the fine words of a moving speech? Have you ever felt anything leaping around inside your head? Even the wise man from the East had to capitulate before my ruthless logic.

150

No rational man can believe that a bloodless puddle of curdled milk lying inert in its bony jar could conjure up the lines of a poem or the design of a pyramid, could cause a man to love or to wage war. Even the embalmers scoop it out and discard it when they prepare a corpse for the long journey.

There is, however, a paradox here in that if this glutinous mass is interfered with, even by the pressure of trapped fluid upon it, the patient is certainly doomed. It requires an intimate knowledge of the structure of the head and a quite marvellous dexterity to be able to drill through the skull without disturbing the sac that contains this porridge. I have both these attributes.

As I ground down slowly through the bone, encouraged by Rasfer's bellows, I paused regularly to wash away the bone chips and filings by splashing vinegar into the wound. The sting of the liquid added little to the patient's well-being, but revived the flagging volume of his voice.

Suddenly the sharp bronze drill bit cleanly through the skull, and a tiny but perfect circle of bone was blown out of the wound by the pressure within. It was followed immediately by a spurt of dark, clotted blood that hit me in the face. Immediately Rasfer relaxed under me. I knew, not without a sneaking pang of regret, that he would survive. As I stitched the flap of scalp back into place, covering the aperture in the depths of which the dura mater pulsed ominously, I wondered if I had truly done mankind a great service by preserving this specimen of it.

When I left Rasfer with his head swathed in bandages, snoring and whimpering in porcine self-pity, I found that I was completely exhausted.

151

The excitements and alarums of the day had expended even my vast store of energy. However, there was to be no rest for me yet, for my Lady Lostris' messenger still hovered on the terrace of my quarters and pounced on me as I set foot on the first step. I was allowed only sufficient grace to wash away Rasfer's blood and change my soiled raiment.

As I tottered into her chamber, barely able to place one foot before the other, my Lady Lostris met me with blazing eyes and ominously tapping foot. 'Just where do you think you have been hiding yourself, Master Taita?' she lashed out at me immediately. 'I sent for you before the second watch, and it's now not much short of dawn. How dare you keep me waiting so? Sometimes you forget your station. You know full well the punishment for impertinent slaves—' She was in full flight, having let her impatience brew for all these hours. In anger her beauty is stunning, and when she stamped her foot in that adorable gesture that was so typically her own, I thought that my heart must burst with my love for her.

'Don't you stand there grinning at me!' she flared at me. 'I am so truly angry that I could order you flogged.' She stamped her foot again, and I felt the tiredness fall from my shoulders like a heavy load. Her mere presence had the power to revitalize me.

'My lady, what a wondrous role you played this night. It seemed to me and all who watched you that it was indeed the divine goddess that walked amongst us—'

'Don't you dare try your tricks with me.' She stamped for the third time, but without conviction.

152

'You'll not wriggle out of this so easily—'

'Truly, my lady, as I walked back from the temple through the crowded streets, your name was on every tongue. They said your singing was the finest they had ever heard, and had quite stolen every heart.'

'I believe not a word,' she declared, but she was clearly having difficulty sustaining her fury. 'In fact I thought my voice was awful this evening. I was flat at least once, and off-key on numerous—'

'I must contradict you, mistress. You were never better. And what beauty! It lit the whole temple.' She is not truly vain, my Lady Lostris, but she is a woman.

'You awful man!' she cried in exasperation. 'I was ready to have you flogged this time, I truly was. But come and sit beside me on the bed and tell me all about it. I am still so excited that I am sure I will not sleep for a week.' She took my hand and led me to the bed, babbling on happily about Tanus, and how he must have won every heart as well as Pharaoh's with his wonderful performance and fearless speech, and how the infant Horus had beshat her dress, and did I truly think that she had sung even passing well, and wasn't I just saying so?

At last I had to stop her. 'My lady, it is almost dawn and we must be ready to leave with all the court to accompany the king when he crosses the river to inspect his funerary temple and his tomb. You must get some sleep if you are to look your best on such an important state occasion.'

'I'm not sleepy, Taita,' she protested, and went chattering on, only to slump against my shoulder a few minutes later, fallen asleep in mid-sentence.

Gently, I slipped her head down on to the

carved wooden headrest and covered her with a rug of colobus monkey furs. I could not bring myself to leave immediately but hovered beside her bed. At last I placed a gentle kiss upon her cheek. She did not open her eyes, but whispered sleepily, 'Do you think there will be an opportunity for me to speak to the king tomorrow? Only he will be able to prevent my father sending Tanus away.'

I could think of no ready answer for her, and while I still dithered, she fell fully asleep.

 I could scarcely drag myself from my couch at dawn, for I seemed barely to have closed my eyes to sleep before it was time to open them again. My reflection in the bronze mirror was haggard and my eyes were underscored in purple. Swiftly I touched on make-up to cover the worst of my sorry condition, enhancing the hollows of my eyes with kohl and my pale features with a brushing of antimony. Two of the slave boys combed out my hair and I was so pleased with the result that I felt almost cheerful as I hurried down to the grand vizier's private dock where the great state barge lay moored.

I was amongst the last to join the throng upon the quay, but no one seemed to notice my late arrival, not even my Lady Lostris who was already on the deck of the barge. I watched her for a while.

She had been invited to join the royal women. These comprised not only the king's wives, but his numerous concubines and all his daughters. Of course these last were the cause of much of Pharaoh's unhappiness, a flock of them ranging in

154

age from crawlers and toddlers to others of marriageable age, and not a son amongst them. How was Pharaoh's immortality to be maintained without a male line to carry it forward?

It was difficult to believe that, like me, Lostris had not slept more than an hour or two, for she seemed as sweet and fresh as one of the desert roses in my garden. Even in that glittering array of feminine beauty that had been hand-picked by Pharaoh's factors or sent to him in tribute by his satraps at the ends of the empire, Lostris stood out like a swallow in a flock of drab little desert larks.

I looked for Tanus, but his squadron was already lying well upstream, ready to escort Pharaoh's crossing, and the reflection of the rising sun turned the surface of the river into a dazzling silver sheet that blinded the eye. I could not look into it.

At that moment there was the steady boom of a drum, and the populace craned to watch Pharaoh's stately progress down from the palace to the royal barge.

This morning he wore the light *nemes* crown of starched and folded linen, secured around his forehead with the gold band of the *uraeus*. The erect golden cobra, with its hood flared and its garnet eyes glittering, rose up from his brow. The cobra was the symbol of the powers of life and death that Pharaoh held over his subjects. The king was not carrying the crook and flail, only the golden sceptre. After the double crown itself, this was the most holy treasure of all the crown jewels and was reputed to be over a thousand years old.

Despite all the regalia and the ceremonial, Pharaoh wore no make-up. Under the direct rays of the early sun, and without make-up to disguise the fact, Mamose himself was unremarkable. Just a soft little godling of late middle age, with a small round paunch bulging over the waistband of his kilt and features intricately carved with lines of worry.

As he passed where I stood, it seemed he recognized me, for he nodded slightly. I immediately prostrated myself on the paving, and he paused and made a sign for me to approach. I crawled forward on hands and knees, and knocked my forehead three times on the ground at his feet.

'Are you not Taita, the poet?' he asked in that thin and petulant voice of his.

'I am Taita the slave, your Majesty,' I replied. There are times when a little humility is called for. 'But I am also a poor scribbler.'

'Well, Taita the slave, you scribbled to good effect last night. I have never been so well entertained by a pageant. I shall issue a royal edict declaring your poor scribblings to be the official version.'

He announced this loud enough for all the court to hear, and even my Lord Intef, who followed him closely, beamed with pleasure. As I was his slave, the honour belonged to him more than to me. However, Pharaoh was not finished with me yet.

'Tell me, Taita the slave, are you not also the same surgeon who recently prescribed to me?'

'Majesty, I am that same humble slave who has the temerity to practise a little medicine.'

'Then when shall your cure take effect?' He dropped his voice so that only I could hear the question.

'Majesty, the event will take place nine months

156

after you have fulfilled all those conditions that I listed for you.' As we were now in a surgeon-and-patient relationship, I felt emboldened to add, 'Have you followed the diet I set you?'

'By Isis' bountiful breasts!' he exclaimed with an unexpected twinkle in his eye. 'I am so full of bull's balls, it is a wonder that I do not bellow when a herd of cows passes the palace.'

He was in such pleasant mood that I tried a little joke of my own. 'Has Pharaoh found the heifer I suggested?'

'Alas, doctor, it is not as simple as it would seem. The prettiest flowers are soonest visited by the bee. You did stipulate that she must be completely untouched, did you not?'

'Virgin and untouched, and within a season of her first red moon,' I added quickly, making it as difficult as possible to put my recipe to the test. 'Have you found one who meets that description, Majesty?'

His expression changed again, and he smiled thoughtfully. The smile looked out of place on those melancholy features. 'We shall see,' he murmured. 'We shall see.' And he turned and mounted the boarding-ladder of the barge. As my Lord Intef drew level with me, he made a small gesture, ordering me to fall in behind him, and so I followed him up on to the deck of the royal barge.

The wind had dropped during the night and the dark waters of the river seemed heavy and quiet as oil in the jar, disturbed only by those streaks and whirlpools upon the surface where the eternal current ran deep and swift. Even Nembet should be able to make the crossing in these conditions,

157

although Tanus' squadron stood by in most unflattering fashion, as if Tanus was preparing to rescue him from error once again.

My Lord Intef drew me aside as soon as we reached the deck. 'You still have the power to surprise me sometimes, my old darling,' he whispered, and squeezed my arm. 'Just when I was seriously beginning to doubt your loyalty.'

I was taken aback by this sudden flush of goodwill, since the welts from Rasfer's lash across my back still ached. However, I bowed my head to shield my expression and waited for him to give me direction before committing myself, which he did immediately.

'I could not have written a more appropriate declamation for Tanus to recite before Pharaoh if I had tried myself. Where that imbecile Rasfer failed so dismally, you retrieved the day for me in your usual style.' It was only then that it all fell into place. He believed that I was the author of Tanus' monumental folly, and that I had composed it for his benefit. In the uproar of the temple he could not have heard my shouted warnings to Tanus, or he would have known better.

'I am pleased that you are pleased,' I whispered back to him. I felt an enormous sense of relief. My position of influence had not been compromised. It was not my own skin I was thinking of at that moment—well, not entirely. I was thinking of Tanus and Lostris. They would need every bit of help and protection that I could give them during the stormy days that lay ahead for both of them. I was grateful that I was still in a position to be of some use to them.

'It was no less than my duty.' Thus I made the

most of this windfall.

'You will find me grateful,' my Lord Intef replied. 'Do you remember the piece of ground on the canal behind the temple of Thoth that we discussed some time ago?'

'Indeed, my lord.' We both knew that I had hankered after that plot for ten years. It would make a perfect writer's retreat and a place to which I could retire in my old age.

'It is yours. At my next assize, bring the deed to me for my signature.' I was stunned and appalled by the vile manner in which it had come into my possession, as payment for an imagined piece of treachery on my part. For a moment I thought of rejecting the gift, but only for a moment. By the time I had recovered from my shock we were across the river and pulling into the mouth of the canal that led across the plain to Pharaoh Mamose's great funerary temple.

I had surveyed this canal with only minimal help from the royal architects, as I had planned virtually single-handed the whole complicated business of the transport of Pharaoh's body from the place of his death to the funerary temple where the mummification process would take place.

I had assumed that he would die at his palace on lovely little Elephantine Island. Therefore his corpse would be brought down-river in the state barge. I had designed the canal to accommodate the huge ship snugly. So now she slipped into it as neatly as the sword into its scabbard.

Straight as the blade of my dagger, the canal cut through the black loam soil of the riparian plain two thousand paces to the foot of the gaunt Saharan foothills. Tens of thousands of slaves had laboured over the years to build it, and to line it with stone blocks. As the barge nosed into the canal, two hundred sturdy slaves seized the tow-ropes from the bows and began to draw her smoothly across the plain. They sang one of the sad melodious work chants as they marched in ranks along the tow-path. The peasants working in the fields beside the canal ran to welcome us. They crowded to the bank, calling blessing on the king and waving palm-fronds, as the great barge moved majestically by.

When at last we slid into the stone dock below the outer walls of the half-finished temple, the slaves made the tow-ropes fast to the mooring-rings. So precise was my design that the entry port in the bulwark of the state barge lined up exactly with the portals of the main gate to the temple.

As the huge vessel came to rest, the trumpeter in the bows blew a fanfare on his gazelle horn, and the portcullis was raised slowly, to reveal the royal hearse waiting in the gateway attended by the company of embalmers in their crimson robes and fifty priests of Osiris in rank behind them.

The priests began to chant as they trundled the hearse forward on its wooden rollers, on to the deck of the barge. Pharaoh clapped his hands with delight and hurried forward to examine this grotesque vehicle.

I had taken no part in the conception of this celebration of bad taste. It was entirely the work of the priests. Suffice it only to say that in the naked sunlight, the superabundant gold-work shone so brightly as to offend the eye almost as painfully as did the actual design. Such weight of gold forced the priests to pant and sweat as they manhandled the clumsy ark on to the deck, and it listed even the great ship alarmingly. That weight of gold could have filled all the grain stores of the Upper Kingdom, or built and fitted out fifty squadrons of fighting ships and paid their crews for ten years. Thus the inept craftsman attempts to hide the paucity of his inspiration behind a dazzle of treasure. If only they had given me such material to work with, they might have seen something different.

This monstrosity was destined to be sealed in the tomb with Pharaoh's dead body. No matter that its construction had contributed largely to the financial ruin of the kingdom, Pharaoh was delighted with it.

At my Lord Intef's suggestion, the king mounted the vehicle and took his seat on the platform designed to carry his sarcophagus. From there he beamed about him, all his dignity and royal reserve forgotten. He was probably enjoying himself as much as he ever had in all his gloomy life, I reflected with a pang of pity. His death was to be the pinnacle to which most of his living energy and anticipation were directed.

On what was clearly an impulse, he beckoned my Lord Intef to join him on the ark and then looked around the crowded deck as if seeking someone else in the throng. He seemed to find who he wanted, for he stooped slightly and said something to the grand vizier.

My Lord Intef smiled and, following his direction, singled out my Lady Lostris. With a gesture he ordered her to come to him on the ark. She was clearly flustered, and blushed under her make-up, a rare phenomenon for one who was so seldom caught out of countenance. However, she recovered swiftly, and mounted the carriage with girlish, long-legged grace that as usual carried every eye with her.

She knelt before the king and touched her forehead three times to the floor of the platform. Then, in front of all the priests and the entire court, Pharaoh did an extraordinary thing. He reached down and took Lostris' hand, and lifted her to her feet, and seated her beside him on the platform. It was beyond all protocol, there was no precedent for it, and I saw his ministers exchange looks of amazement.

Then something else happened of which even they were not aware. When I was very young there had lived in the boys' quarters an old deaf slave who had befriended me. It was he who had taught me to read men's speech not only by the sound of it, but also by the shape of their lips as they formed the words. It was a very useful accomplishment. With it I could follow a conversation at the far end of a crowded hall, with musicians playing and a hundred men around me laughing and shouting at each other.

Now, before my eyes I saw Pharaoh say softly to my Lady Lostris, 'Even in daylight you are as divine as was the goddess Isis in the torchlight of the temple.'

The shock of it was like the blow of a fist in my stomach. Had I been blind, I berated myself desperately, or had I merely been stupid? Surely any imbecile must have anticipated the direction in which my capricious meddling must incline the order in which the dice of destiny might fall.

My facetious advice to the king must inevitably have had the effect of directing his attention towards my Lady Lostris. It was as though some malignant impulse below the surface of my mind had set out to describe her precisely to him as the mother of his first-born son. The most beautiful virgin in the land, to be taken within the first season after her moon had flowered—it was her exactly. And then, of course, by casting her as the leading female in the pageant, I had managed to display her to the king in the kindest possible light.

What I suddenly realized was about to happen was all of it my fault, as much as though I had deliberately engineered it. What is more, there was nothing I could do about it now. I stood in the sunlight so appalled and stricken with remorse that for a while I was deprived of the powers of speech and of reason.

When the sweating priests shoved the hearse off the deck and through the gateway, the crowd around me started after it and I was borne along with them willy-nilly, as though I were a leaf upon a stream without direction of my own. Before I was able to recover my wits I found myself within the forecourt of the funerary temple. I began to push my way forward, jostling those ahead of me to get past them and to reach the side of the hearse before it came to the main entrance of the royal mortuary.

As one team of priests pushed the vehicle forward, a second team picked up the wooden rollers that were left behind it and ran forward to place them ahead of the ponderous golden vehicle. There was a short delay as the carriage reached that area of the courtyard that had not yet been paved. While the priests spread straw ahead of the rollers to smooth the passage over this rough ground, I slipped quickly around the back of the row of huge carved stone lions that lined the carriageway, and hurried down this clear space until I was level with the ark. When one of the priests tried to bar my way and prevent me reaching the side of the vehicle, I gave him such a look as would have made one of the stone lions quail, and spat a single word at him that was seldom heard in the temple confines and caused him to step hurriedly aside and let me pass.

When I reached the near side of the ark I found myself directly below Lostris, close enough to stretch up and touch her arm, and to hear every word she addressed to the king. I could tell at once that she had completely recovered her poise which Pharaoh's unexpected interest in her had disturbed, and was now setting out to be as agreeable as possible to him. Miserably, I recalled how she had planned to do exactly this, and to use his favour to secure his agreement to her marriage to Tanus. As recently as last evening I had dismissed it as girlish prattle, but now it was happening, and it was beyond my power to prevent it or to warn her of the dangerous waters into which she was steering.

If, earlier in this chronicle, I have given the impression that my Lady Lostris was a flighty child with not a thought in her pretty head other than romantic nonsense and her own frivolous enjoyment of life, then I have fallen short in my efforts as historian of these extraordinary events. Although still so young, she was at times mature far beyond her years. Our Egyptian girls bloom

164

early in the Nile sunlight. She was also a diligent scholar, with a bright mind and a thoughtful and enquiring side to her nature, all of which I had done my very best over the years to foster and develop.

Under my tutelage she had reached the stage where she could debate with the priests the most obscure religious dogma, could hold her own with the palace lawyers on such matters as the Land Tenure Acts and the extremely complicated Irrigation Act that regulated the usage of the waters from the Nile. Of course, she had read and absorbed every single one of the scrolls in the palace library. These included several hundred of which I was the author, from my medical treatises to my definitive essays on the tactics of naval warfare, together with my astrological scrolls on the names and natures of all the heavenly bodies, and my manuals on archery and swordsmanship, horticulture and falconry. She could even argue with me my own principles of architecture, and compare them to those of the great Imhotep.

Thus she was perfectly equipped to discuss any subject from astrology to the practice of war, from politics or the building of temples to the measurement and regulation of the Nile waters, all of which were subjects that fascinated Pharaoh. In addition she could rhyme and riddle and coin an amusing pun, and her vocabulary was almost as extensive as my own. In short, she was an accomplished conversationalist, with a ready sense of humour. She was articulate and had an enchanting voice and a merry little laugh. Truly, no man or god could resist her, especially if she could offer to someone without a son the promise of an heir.

I had to warn her, and yet how could a slave intrude upon the congress of persons so infinitely high above his own station? I skipped nervously beside the carriage, listening to my Lady Lostris' voice at its most enthralling as she set herself out to engage the king's fancy.

She was describing to him the manner in which his funerary temple had been laid out to conform to the most propitious astronomical aspects, those of the moon and the zodiac at the time of Pharaoh's birth. Of course she was merely repeating knowledge that she had gleaned from me, for I was the one who had surveyed and orientated the temple to the heavenly bodies. However, she was so convincing that I found myself following her explanations as though I was hearing them for the first time.

The funeral ark passed between the pylons of the inner court of the temple and rolled down the long colonnaded atrium, past the barred and guarded doors to the six treasuries in which were manufactured and stored the funerary offerings which would go with the king to his tomb. At the end of the atrium the acacia-wood doors, on which were carved the images of all the gods of the pantheon, were swung open, and we entered the mortuary where Pharaoh's corpse would one day be embalmed.

Here in this solemn chapel the king dismounted from the carriage, and went forward to inspect the massive table on which he would lie for the ritual of mummification. Unlike the embalming of a commoner, royal embalming took seventy days to accomplish. The table had been sculpted from a single block of diorite, three paces long and two wide. Into the dark, mottled surface of the stone had been chiselled the indentation that fitted the back of the king's head, and the grooves which would drain the blood and other bodily fluids released by the scalpels and the instruments of the embalmers.

The grand master of the guild of embalmers was standing beside the table, ready to explain the entire process to the king, and he had an attentive audience, for Pharaoh seemed fascinated by every gruesome detail. At one stage it seemed that he might so far forget his dignity as to climb up upon the diorite block and try its fit, very much as though it were a new costume of linen presented by his tailor.

However, he restrained himself with an obvious effort, and instead devoted himself to the mortician's description of how the first incision would be made from his gullet to his groin, and how his viscera would be lifted out cleanly and then divided into their separate parts—liver, lungs, stomach and entrails. The heart, as the hearth of the divine spark, would be left in place, as would the kidneys with their associations with water and thus with the Nile, the source of life.

After this edifying instruction, Pharaoh minutely examined the four Canopic jars that would receive his viscera. They stood on another smaller granite table close at hand. The jars were carved from gleaming translucent alabaster the colour of milk. Their stoppers were fashioned in the shapes of the animal-headed gods: Anubis the jackal, Sobeth the crocodile, Thoth the ibis-headed, Sekhmet with the head of a lioness. They would be the guardians of Pharaoh's divine parts until his awakening in the eternal life.

On the same granite table that held the Canopic jars, the embalmers had laid out their instruments and the full array of pots and amphorae that contained the natron salts, lacquers and other chemicals that they would use in the process. Pharaoh was fascinated by the glistening bronze scalpels which would disembowel him, and when the embalmer showed him the long pointed spoon that would be pushed up his nostrils to scoop out the contents of his skull, those cheesy curds over which I had pondered so long and fruitlessly, the king was fascinated and handled the grisly instrument with reverential awe.

Once the king had satisfied his curiosity at the mortuary table, my Lady Lostris directed his attention to the painted bas-relief engravings that covered the walls of the temple from floor to ceiling. The decorations were not yet completed, but were none the less quite striking in their design and execution. I had drawn most of the original cartoons with my own hand, and had closely supervised the others drawn by the palace artists. These had been traced on to the walls with charcoal sticks. Once the tracings were in place, I had corrected and perfected them in freehand. Now a company of master sculptors was engraving them into the sandstone blocks, while behind them a second company of artists was painting in the completed bas-relief.

The dominant colour I had chosen for these designs was blue in all its variation: the blue of the starling's wing, the blues of the sky and the Nile in the sunlight, the blues of the petals of the desert

168

orchid and the shimmering blue of the river perch quivering in the fisherman's net. However, there were other colours as well, all those vibrant reds and yellows that we Egyptians love so well.

Pharaoh, accompanied closely by my Lord Intef, in his capacity of Keeper of the Royal Tombs, made a slow circuit of the high walls, examining every detail, and commenting on most of them. Naturally the theme I had chosen for the mortuary was the *Book of the Dead*, that detailed map and description of the route to the underworld that Pharaoh's shade must follow, and the depictions of all the trials and dangers he would confront along the way.

He paused for a long while before my drawing of the god Thoth, with his bird head and long curved ibis beak, weighing Pharaoh's disembodied heart on the scales against the feather of truth. Should the heart be impure, it would tip the scales against the feather, and the god would immediately toss it to the crocodile-headed monster that waited close at hand to devour it. Softly, the king quoted the protective mantra laid down in the book to shield himself from such a calamity, and then passed on to my next engraving.

It was almost noon before Pharaoh had completed his inspection of the mortuary temple and led the way out into the forecourt where the palace chefs had laid out a sumptuous open-air banquet.

'Come and sit here, where I can speak to you further on the matter of the stars!' Once again the king ignored precedent to place my Lady Lostris close to him at the banquet table, even moving one of his senior wives to make a place for her. During the meal he directed most of his conversation towards my mistress. She was now completely at her ease and kept the king and all those around her enthralled and merry with her wit and charm.

Of course, as a slave I did not have a seat at the table, nor could I even inveigle myself within range of my mistress to warn her to moderate her demeanour in the king's presence. Instead, I found myself a place on the pedestal of one of the granite lions, from where I could look down the length of the banquet table and watch everything that took place there. I was not the only observer, for my Lord Intef sat close to the king and yet withdrawn, watching it all with glittering, implacable eyes, like a handsome but deadly spider at the centre of his web.

At one stage of the meal a yellow-billed kite wheeled high over head, and uttered a screech, a sardonic and mocking cry. Hurriedly I made the sign against the evil eye, for who knows what god it was that had taken the form of the bird to muddle and confuse our petty endeavours?

After the midday meal it was customary for the court to rest for an hour or so, especially at this the hottest season of the year. However, Pharaoh was so wrought up that today he would have none of it.

'Now we will inspect the treasuries,' he announced. The guards at the doors of the first treasury stood aside and presented arms as the royal party approached, and the doors were swung open from within.

I had planned these six treasuries not only as store-rooms to hold the vast funerary treasure that Pharaoh had been collecting for the past twelve years, ever since his accession to the double throne, but also as workshops in which a small army of craftsmen and artisans was permanently employed in adding to that treasure.

The hall that we entered was the armoury that housed the collection of weapons and accoutrements of the battlefield and the wild chase, both practical and ceremonial, which the king would take with him into the afterworld. With my Lord Intef's concurrence, I had arranged for the craftsmen to be at their benches so that the king would have the opportunity of watching them at work.

As Pharaoh passed slowly down the row of benches, his questions were so astute and technical that those nobles and priests to whom he addressed himself could provide no answers, and they looked around frantically for someone who could. I was summoned hastily from the back of the crowd and pushed forward to face the king's interrogation.

'Ah, yes,' Pharaoh grimaced bleakly as he recognized me. 'It is none other than the humble slave who writes pageants and cures the sick. No one here seems to know the composition of this electrum wire that binds the stock of the war-bow that this man is making for me.'

'Gracious Pharaoh, the metal is a mixture of one part of copper to five parts of silver and four of gold. The gold is of the red variety found only in the mines of Lot in the western desert. No other gives the wire the same pliability or elasticity, of course.'

'Of course,' the king agreed wryly. 'And how do you make the strands so thin? These are no thicker than the hairs of my head.'

171

'Majesty, we extrude the hot metal by swinging it in a special pendulum that I designed for the purpose. Later we can watch the process in the gold foundry, if Your Majesty so wishes.'

Thus during the rest of the tour I was able to remain at the king's side and to deflect some of his attention away from Lostris, but I still could not find the opportunity to speak to her alone.

Pharaoh passed down the armoury to inspect the huge array of weapons and armour already in store. Some of these had belonged to his forefathers and had been employed in famous battles; others were newly manufactured and would never be used in war. All of them were magnificent, each a pinnacle of the armourer's art. There were helmets and breastplates of bronze and silver and gold, battle swords with ivory hilts set with precious stones, full-dress ceremonial uniforms of the commander-in-chief of each of the king's elite regiments, shields and bucklers in hippo-hide and crocodile-skin, all starred with rosettes of gold. It made a splendid array.

From the armoury we crossed the atrium to the furniture store, where a hundred cabinet-makers laboured with cedar and acacia and precious ebony wood to build the funeral furnishings for the king's long journey. Very few substantial trees grow in our riparian valley, and wood is a scarce and costly commodity, worth very nearly its weight in silver. Almost every stick of it must be carried hundreds of leagues across the desert, or shipped downstream from those mysterious lands to the south. Here it was piled in extravagant stacks, as though it were commonplace, and the fragrance of fresh sawdust perfumed the hot air.

We watched while craftsmen inlaid the head-board of Pharaoh's bed with patterns of mother-of-pearl and woods of contrasting colour. Others decorated the arm-rests of the chairs with golden falcons and the backrests of the padded sofas with the heads of silver lions. Not even the halls of the royal palace at Elephantine Island contained such delicate workmanship as would grace the rock cell of the king's tomb.

From the furniture treasury we passed on to the hall of the sculptors. In marble and sandstone and granite of a hundred differing hues, the sculptors whittled and chipped away with chisel and file so that a fine, pale dust hung in the air. The masons covered their noses and mouths with strips of linen on which the dust settled and their features were powdered white with the insidious stuff. Some of the men coughed behind their masks as they worked, a persistent, dry cough that was peculiar to their profession. I had dissected the corpses of many old sculptors who had worked thirty years and died at their trade. I found their lungs petrified and turned to stone in their bodies, thus I spent as little time as possible in the masons' shop lest I contract the same malady.

None the less, their products were wondrous to contemplate, statues of the gods and of Pharaoh himself that seemed to vibrate with life. There were life-sized images of Pharaoh seated on his throne or walking abroad, alive and dead, in his god form or in the shape of a mortal man. These statues would line the long causeway that led from the funerary temple on the valley floor up into the wall of black hills from which his final tomb was even at this moment being excavated. At his death

173

the golden hearse, drawn by a train of one hundred white bullocks, was to bear his massive sarcophagus along that causeway to its final resting-place.

This granite sarcophagus, only partially completed, lay in the centre of the masons' hall. Originally it had been a single block of pink granite quarried from the mines at Assoun, and ferried down-river in a barge especially constructed for that purpose. It had taken five hundred slaves to haul it ashore and drag it over wooden rollers to where it now lay, an oblong of solid stone five paces long, three wide and three tall.

The masons had begun by sawing a thick slab from the top of it. Upon this granite lid a master mason was fashioning the likeness of the mummiform Pharaoh, with his arms crossed and the crook and flail gripped in his dead hands. Another team of masons was now engaged in hollowing out the interior of the main granite block to provide a nest into which the cluster of inner coffins would fit perfectly. Including the huge outer sarcophagus, there would be seven coffins in all, fitting one within the other like a child's puzzle-toy. Seven was, of course, one of the magical numbers. The innermost coffin would be of pure gold, and later we watched it being beaten out of the formless mass of metal in the hall of the goldsmiths.

It was this multiple sarcophagus, this mountain of stone and gold housing the king's wrapped corpse, that the great golden hearse would carry along the causeway to the hills, a slow journey that would take seven whole days to complete. The hearse would stop each night in one of the small shrines that were spaced at intervals along the causeway.

A fascinating adjunct to the hall of statues was the *ushabti* shop at the rear where the servants and retainers who would escort the dead king were being carved. These were perfect little manikins of wood representing all the grades and orders of Egyptian society who would work for the king in the hereafter, so as to enable him to maintain his estate and the style of his existence in the underworld.

Each *ushabti* was a delightfully carved wooden doll dressed in the authentic uniform of his calling and bearing the appropriate tools. There were farmers and gardeners, fishermen and bakers, beer-brewers and handmaidens, soldiers and tax-collectors, scribes and barbers, and hundreds upon hundreds of common labourers to perform every menial task and to go forward in the king's place if ever he were called upon by the other gods to work in the underworld.

At the head of this congregation of little figures there was even a grand vizier whose miniature features closely resembled those of my Lord Intef. Pharaoh picked out this manikin and examined him closely, turning him over to read the description on his back.

My name is Lord Intef, grand vizier of the Upper Kingdom, Pharaoh's sole companion, three times the recipient of the Gold of Praise. I am ready to answer for the king.

Pharaoh passed the doll to my Lord Intef. 'Is your physique truly so muscular, my Lord Intef?' he

175

asked with a smile just below the surface of his dour expression, and the grand vizier bowed slightly.

'The sculptor has failed to do me justice, Your Majesty.'

The last treasury that the king visited that day was the hall of the goldsmiths. The infernal glow of the furnaces cast a strange glow on the features of the jewellers as they worked with total concentration at their benches. I had coached them well. At the entrance of the royal entourage, the goldsmiths knelt in unison to make the triple obeisance to Pharaoh, and then rose and resumed their work.

Even in that large hall the heat of the furnace flames was so sulphurous as almost to stop the breath, and we were soon bathed in our own sweat. However, the king was so fascinated by the treasure displayed for him that he seemed not to notice the oppressive atmosphere. He went directly to the raised dais in the centre of the hall where the most experienced and skilful smiths were at work upon the golden inner coffin. They had perfectly captured Pharaoh's living face in the shimmering metal. The mask would fit exactly over his bandaged head. It was a divine image with eyes of obsidian and rock-crystal, and with the cobra-headed *uraeus* encircling the brow. I truly believe that no finer masterpiece of the goldsmith's art has ever been fashioned in all the thousand years of our civilization. This was the peak and the zenith. All the unborn ages might one day marvel at its splendour.

Even after Pharaoh had admired the golden mask from every angle, he seemed unable to tear himself too far from it. He spent the remainder of the day on the dais beside it, seated on a low stool while box after cedar-wood box of exquisite jewels were laid at his feet and the contents catalogued for him.

I cannot believe that such a treasure was ever before accumulated in one place at one time. To make a bald list of the items does not in the least way suggest the richness and the diversity of it all. None the less, let me tell you at the outset that there were six thousand four hundred and fifty-five pieces already in the cedar-wood boxes, and that each day more were added to the collection as the jewellers worked on tirelessly.

There were rings for Pharaoh's toes as well as his fingers; there were amulets and charms, and gold figurines of the gods and goddesses; there were necklaces and bracelets and pectoral medallions and belts on which were inlaid falcons and vultures and all the other creatures of the earth and the sky and the river; there were crowns and diadems studded with lapis lazuli and garnets and agate and carnelians and jasper and every gemstone that civilized man holds dear.

The artistry with which all this had been designed and manufactured eclipsed all that had been created over the preceding one thousand years. It is often in decline that a nation creates its most beautiful works of art. In the formative years of empire the obsession is with conquest and the building-up of wealth. It is only once this has been achieved that there is leisure and a desire to develop the arts, and—more importantly—rich and powerful men to sponsor them.

The weight of gold and silver already used in the

177

manufacture of the hearse and the funeral mask and all the rest of this breathtaking collection of treasure was in excess of five hundred takhs; thus it would have taken five hundred strong men to lift it all. I had calculated that this was almost one-tenth of the total weight of these precious metals that had been mined in the entire one thousand years of our recorded history. All of this the king intended taking with him to the tomb.

Who am I, a humble slave, to question the price that a king was willing to pay for eternal life? Suffice it only to state that in assembling this treasure, while at the same time conducting the war against the Lower Kingdom, Pharaoh had, almost alone and unaided, plunged this very Egypt of ours into beggary.

No wonder, then, that Tanus in his declamation had singled out the depredation of the tax-collectors as one of the most terrible afflictions visited upon the populace. Between them and the robber bands that ravaged unchecked and unhindered through the countryside, we were all ruined and crushed under the financial yoke that was too heavy for any of us to bear. To survive at all, we had to evade the tax-collector's net. So as he set out to beggar us for his own aggrandizement, the king made criminals of us at the same moment. Very few of us, great or small, rich or poor, slept well at night. We lay awake dreading at any moment the heavy knock of the tax-collector upon the door.

Oh, sad and abused land, how it groaned beneath the yoke!

Lavish quarters had been prepared in the necropolis in which the king would spend that night upon the west bank of the Nile, close to his own final resting-place in the gaunt black hills.

The necropolis, the city of the dead, was almost as extensive as Karnak itself. It was home to all those associated with the building and the care of the funerary temple and the royal tomb. There was a full regiment of the elite guard to protect the holy places, for the usurper in the north was as avaricious for treasure as was our own dear king, while the robber barons in the desert became each day bolder and more daring. The treasuries of the funerary temple were a sore temptation to every predator in the two kingdoms, and beyond.

In addition to the guards there were the companies of the craftsmen and the artisans and all their apprentices to house. I was responsible for the records of wages and rations, so I knew exactly how many there were. On the last pay-day their number had been four thousand eight hundred and eleven. Added to this, there were over ten thousand slaves employed upon the work.

I will not weary myself by listing the numbers of oxen and sheep that had to be slaughtered each day to feed them all, nor the cartloads of fish that were brought up from the Nile, nor the thousands of jars of beer that were brewed daily to slake the summer thirst of this multitude as they laboured under the watchful eye and the ready lash of the overseers.

The necropolis was a city, and in that city was a

palace for the king. It was with relief that we moved into it to spend the night, for it had been a wearying day. But once again there was little rest for me.

I tried to reach my Lady Lostris, but it was almost as if there existed a conspiracy to keep me away from her. According to her little black maids, first she was at toilet, and after that she was in her bath, and then she was resting and could not be disturbed. Finally, as I still waited in the ante-chamber of her quarters, a summons reached me from her father, and I could linger no longer, but must hurry to my master.

As soon as I entered my Lord Intef's bedchamber he dismissed all the others in the room. When we were alone, he kissed me. I was once more surprised by his benevolence and disturbed by his excited manner. Seldom had I seen him in such mood, and always before it had adumbrated calamitous events.

'How often the gateway to power and fortune is found in the most unexpected place!' he laughed at me, and caressed my face. 'This time it lies between the thighs of a woman. No, my old darling, don't play the innocent. I know just what a cunning hand you have taken in all of this. Pharaoh has told me how you cajoled him into it by promising him a male heir to his line. By Seth, but you are the cunning one, are you not? Not a word to me of your design, but you schemed it all on your own account.'

He laughed again, and twisted a lock of my hair between his fingers. 'You must have divined my ultimate ambition all along, even though we have never discussed it openly. So you set out to achieve

180

it for me. Of course, I should have you punished for your presumption,' he twisted the lock of hair until tears started into my eyes, 'but how can I be angry with you when you have placed the double crown within my grasp?' He released the tress of my hair and kissed me again. 'I have just come from the king's presence. In two days, at the culmination of the festival, he will announce his betrothal to my daughter, Lostris.' I felt a sudden darkness behind my eyes, and a chilly dew formed on my skin.

'The wedding will take place the same day, immediately after the closing ceremony of the festival, I saw to that. We don't want any delay in which something might happen to prevent it, do we?'

Such a swift royal wedding was unusual but not unheard of. When brides were chosen to seal a political union, or to consolidate the conquest of a new territory, the wedding often took place the very same day it was decided. Pharaoh Mamose the First, forefather of our present pharaoh, had married the daughter of a conquered Hurrian chieftain on the actual battlefield. However, such historical precedents were of little comfort to me now as I faced the bleak maturation of my worst fears.

My Lord Intef seemed not to notice my distress. He was too concerned with his own immediate interests, and he went on speaking. 'Before I gave my formal consent to the union, I prevailed on the king to concede that if she bore him a son then he would elevate my daughter to the rank of principal wife and queen consort.' He clapped his hands in unrestrained triumph.

'Of course, you realize what that means. If Pharaoh should die before my grandson is of age to rule, then I as his grandfather and closest male line would become regent—' He broke off suddenly and stared at me, and I knew him so well that I understood exactly what was running through his mind. He was bitterly regretting that indiscretion, nobody should ever have heard that thought expressed. It was purest treason. If Lostris bore a son to Pharaoh, then the father would not live long thereafter. We both understood that. My Lord Intef had given voice to regicide, and he was considering removing the only one who had heard it spoken, the humble slave, Taita. We both understood that clearly.

'My lord, I am only grateful that it has turned out the way I planned it. I admit now that I have worked deviously to place your daughter in the king's way, and that I described her to him as the mother of his future son. I used the pageant as a show-piece to focus his attention upon her. However, I could not bring myself to speak to you of such momentous affairs until they had been successfully engineered. But there still remains a great deal for us to do, before we can count ourselves secure—' and I began swiftly to extemporize a list of all that might go awry before he could gain control of the crown and the golden sceptre of Egypt. Tactfully I made it clear how much he still needed me if he were to achieve his design. I saw him relax as he followed my arguments, and I knew that at least for the immediate future I was safe.

It was some time before I could reasonably escape from his presence and hurry to warn my

Lady Lostris of the terrible predicament in which I had placed her. However, before I reached her door I realized that my warning to her would serve no purpose other than to distress her to the point of dementia or even suicide. I could waste no further time if I were to prevent events from rushing to their tragic conclusion.

There was only one person to whom I could turn now.

I left the necropolis and set off alone along the tow-path of the canal, back towards the river-bank where I knew that Tanus' squadrons were encamped. The moon was only three days from full and it lit the jagged hills of the western horizon with a cold yellow radiance and threw black shadows on the plain below.

As I hurried along, I recited to myself a full list of all the possible calamities and misfortunes that might befall Tanus, my Lady Lostris and myself in the days ahead. I was goading myself the same way that a black-maned desert lion lashes up his temper with the bony spike in the end of his tail before he charges at the huntsman. Thus I was in fulminating mood long before I reached the bank of the Nile.

I found Tanus' encampment without difficulty, hard by the bank of the Nile and the mouth of the canal. The ships of the squadron were anchored below the camp. The sentries challenged me and then, when they recognized me, led me to Tanus' tent.

Tanus was at late supper with Kratas and four other of his subordinate officers. He rose to greet me with a smile and offered me the beer tankard in his hand. 'This is such an unexpected pleasure, old friend. Sit down beside me and have a pull of my beer while my slave brings you a cup and platter. You look hot and out of sorts—'

I cut short these pleasantries by rounding on him furiously. 'To Seth with you, you great senseless oaf! Do you not understand what jeopardy you have placed us in? You and that flapping jawbone of yours! Do you have no thought for the safety and the well-being of my mistress?' In truth I had not meant to be so harsh on him, but once I had started, it seemed that I was unable to control my emotions, and all my fear and anxiety came tumbling out in a flood of invective. Not all that I accused him of was true or fair, but it made me feel better to have it out.

Tanus' expression changed and he held up one hand as though to shield himself. 'Whoa! You take me unawares. I am unarmed and unable to defend myself from such a murderous assault.' In front of his officers his tone was jocular, but his smile was thin as he seized my arm and steered me out of the tent into the darkness, and half-dragged me beyond the regimental lines into the open moonlit fields beyond. I was like a child in the grip of that right hand that was trained to wield the sword and draw the great bow Lanata.

'Now puke it up!' he ordered me grimly. 'What has happened to put you in such vile humour?'

I was still angry, but more afraid than angry, and my tongue took flight again. 'I have spent half my life trying to protect you from your own stupidity, and I am sick of it. Don't you understand anything of life? Did you truly believe that you would be allowed to escape unscathed from the incredible folly into which you threw all of us last night?'

'Are you talking about my declamation at the pageant?' He looked puzzled, and released the crushing grip on my arm. 'How can you say it was folly? All my officers, and every other person I have spoken to since then, are all delighted with what I had to say—'

'You fool, don't you see that the opinions of all your officers and all your friends count for the price of a rotten fish in the scheme of things? Under any other ruler you would already be dead, and even this weak and vacillating old man of ours cannot afford to let you escape the consequences of your insolence. It is more than his throne is worth. There will be a bill for you to pay, Tanus, Lord Harrab. Horus knows, it will be a heavy bill.'

'You are speaking in riddles,' he snapped at me. 'I did the king a great service. He is surrounded by fawning toadies who feed him the lies they think he wants to hear. It was past time that he learned the truth, and I know in my heart that once he considers it, he will be grateful to me.'

My anger began to evaporate before his simple and steadfast belief in the triumph of good. 'Tanus, my dearest friend, what an innocent you are! No man is ever grateful for having the unpalatable truth rammed down his throat. But apart from that, you have played directly into the hands of my Lord Intef.'

'My Lord Intef?' he stared at me hard. 'What of my Lord Intef? You speak of him as though he were my enemy. The grand vizier was my father's dearest friend. I know that I can trust him to protect me. He swore an oath to my father as he lay on his death-bed—'

I could see that despite his sunny disposition and our friendship, he was becoming truly angry with me, probably for the first time in his life. I knew also that, although it was slow to rouse, Tanus' anger was something to fear.

'Oh, Tanus!' I curbed my own anger at last. 'I have been unfair to you. There is so much that I should have told you, and never did. Nothing was as you thought it. I was a coward, but I could not tell you that Intef was your own father's deadliest enemy.'

'How can this be true?' Tanus shook his head. 'They were friends, the dearest friends. My earliest memories are of them laughing together. My father told me that I could trust my very life to my Lord Intef.'

'The noble Pianki, Lord Harrab believed that, it is true. His faith cost him his entire fortune, and in the end his life which he placed in Intef's hands.'

'No, no, you must be mistaken. My father was the victim of a series of misfortunes—'

'And every one of those misfortunes was engineered by my Lord Intef. He envied your father for his virtues and his popularity, for his wealth and his influence with Pharaoh. He realized that Lord Harrab would be appointed grand vizier before him and he hated him for all these things.'

'I cannot believe you. I cannot bring myself to believe you.' Tanus shook his head in denial, and the last of my anger was snuffed out.

'I will explain it all to you, as I should have done long ago. I will give you all the proof you need. But

186

there is no time for it now. You must trust me. My Lord Intef hates you even as he hated your father. Both you and my Lady Lostris are in danger. In danger of more than simply life itself, in danger of losing each other for ever.'

'But how is that possible, Taita?' He was confused and shaken by my words. 'I thought that my Lord Intef had agreed to our union. Have you not spoken to him, then?'

'Yes, I have spoken to him,' I cried, and I seized Tanus' hand and thrust it up under the back of my tunic. 'That was his reply. Feel the welts left by the lash! He had me flogged for even suggesting the marriage between you and my Lady Lostris. That is how much he hates you and your family.'

Tanus stared at me speechlessly, but I saw that he believed me at last, and so I was able to come to the subject that was dominating my thoughts more even than his intemperate speech, or the vendetta that the grand vizier had conducted so successfully against him over so many years.

'Hear me now, my dear friend, and brace yourself for the very worst tidings yet.' There was no other way to tell him, except as directly as Tanus would have told me. 'Far from agreeing to your marriage, my Lord Intef has this very night pledged his daughter's hand to another. She is to be married immediately to Pharaoh Mamose, and after she bears his first son she will become his principal wife and consort. The king will make the announcement himself at the end of the festival of Osiris. The marriage will take place that very same evening.'

Tanus swayed on his feet and in the moonlight his face turned ghostly pale. Neither of us could

187

speak for a long while and then Tanus turned away from me and walked out alone into the field of standing corn. I trailed behind him, keeping him in sight, until at last he found an outcrop of black rock and seated himself upon it with the weary air of a very old man. I came up softly and seated myself below him. Deliberately I remained silent until he sighed and asked quietly, 'Has Lostris consented to this marriage?'

'Of course not. As yet she probably knows nothing about it. But do you think for one moment that her objections would count against the will of her father and the king? She will have no say in the matter.'

'What are we to do, old friend?'

Even in my distress I was grateful to him that he used the plural, including me, reassuring me of our friendship. 'There is one other probability that we must face,' I warned him. 'And that is that in the same speech that Pharaoh announces his betrothal to Lostris, he will order your imprisonment, or worse still, issue your death warrant. My Lord Intef has the king's ear and he will certainly put him up to it. In truth he would have good reason. You are certainly guilty of sedition.'

'I do not care to live without Lostris as my wife. If the king takes her from me, then he is welcome to my head as a marriage gift.' He said it simply, without histrionics, so that I had difficulty in feigning anger and putting the edge of contempt into my voice.

'You sound like a weak and pitiful old woman, giving herself up to the fates without a struggle. What a fine and undying love is yours, if you will not even fight for her!'

188

'How do you fight a king and a god?' Tanus asked quietly. 'A king to whom you have sworn allegiance, and a god who is as remote and as unassailable as the sun?'

'As a king he does not deserve your allegiance. You set that out clearly in your declamation. He is a weak and dithering old man who has divided the two kingdoms and brought our *Ta-Meri* bleeding to her knees.'

'And as a god?' Tanus again asked quietly, as though he were not really interested in the answer, although I knew him to be a devout and religious man, as so many great warriors are.

'A god?' I made my tone derisive. 'You have more of the godhead in your sword-arm than he has in all his soft little body.'

'Then what do you suggest?' he asked with deceptive mildness. 'What would you have me do?'

I drew a deep breath and then blurted it out. 'Your officers and your men would follow you to the gates of the underworld. The populace loves you for your courage and your honour—' I faltered, for his expression in the moonlight gave me no encouragement to continue.

He was silent for twenty beats of my racing heart and then he ordered me softly, 'Go on! Say what you have to say.'

'Tanus, you would make the noblest pharaoh that this *Ta-Meri*, this mother-land, has known for a thousand years. You with my Lady Lostris on the throne beside you could lead this land and this people back to greatness. Call out your squadrons, and lead your men down the causeway to where that unworthy pharaoh lies unprotected and vulnerable. By dawn tomorrow you could be ruler

189

of the Upper Kingdom. By this time next year you could have defeated the usurper and have reunited the two kingdoms.' I leaped to my feet and faced him. 'Tanus, Lord Harrab, your destiny and that of the woman you love await you. Seize them in both your strong warrior's hands!'

'Warrior's hands, yes.' He held them up before my face. 'Hands that have fought for my mother-land and have protected her rightful king. You do me a disservice, old friend. They are not the hands of a traitor. Nor is this the heart of a blasphemer, that would seek to cast down and destroy a god, and take his place in the pantheon.'

I groaned aloud in my frustration. 'You would be the greatest pharaoh of the last five hundred years, and you need not proclaim your godhead, not if the idea offends you. Do it, I beseech you, for the sake of this very Egypt of ours, and of the woman that we both love!'

'Would Lostris still love a traitor as she loved a soldier and a patriot? I think not.' He shook his head.

'She would love you no matter what—' I began, but he cut me short.

'You cannot convince me. She is a woman of virtue and of honour. As a traitor and a thief, I would forfeit all right to her respect. What is of equal importance, I would never respect myself again, or consider myself worthy of her sweet love, if I did what you urge. Speak of it no more, as you value our friendship. I have no claim to the double crown, nor will I ever make such claim. Horus, hear me, and turn your face away from me if ever I should break this pledge.'

The matter was closed, I knew him so well, that

great infuriating oaf, whom I loved with all my heart. He meant exactly what he said, and would cleave to it at any cost.

'Then what will you do, damn your stubborn heart?' I flared at him. 'Nothing that I say has any weight with you. Do you want to face this on your own? Are you suddenly too wise to heed my counsel?'

'I'm willing to take your counsel, just as long as it has sense to it.' He reached out and drew me down beside him. 'Come, Taita, help us. Lostris and I need you now as never before. Don't desert us. Help us find the honourable way.'

'I fear there is no such thing,' I sighed, my emotions bobbing and spinning like a piece of flotsam caught in the Nile flood. 'But if you will not seize the crown, then you dare not stay here. You must sweep Lostris up in your arms and bear her away.'

He stared at me in the moonlight. 'Leave Egypt? You cannot be serious. This is my world. This is Lostris' world.'

'No!' I reassured him. 'That is not what I had in mind. There is another pharaoh in Egypt. One who has need of warriors and honest men. You have much to offer such a king. Your fame in the Lower Kingdom is as great as it is here at Karnak. Place Lostris on the deck of the *Breath of Horus* and send your galley flying northwards. No other ship can catch you. In ten days, with this wind and current, you can present yourself at the court of the red pharaoh in Memphis, and swear allegiance to—'

'By Horus, you are determined to make a traitor of me yet,' he cut across me. 'Swear allegiance to

191

the usurper, you say? Then what of the allegiance I swore to the true Pharaoh Mamose? Does that count for nothing with you? What kind of man am I, that can make the same oath to every king or renegade that crosses my path? An oath is not something to be bartered or reclaimed, Taita, it is for life. I gave my oath to the true Pharaoh Mamose.'

'That true Pharaoh is the same one who will marry your love, and will order the strangling-rope to be twisted around your neck,' I pointed out grimly, and this time even he wavered.

'You are right, of course. We should not stay in Karnak. But I will not make myself a traitor or break my solemn oath by taking up the sword against my king.'

'Your sense of honour is too complicated for me.' I could not keep the tone of sarcasm from my voice. 'All I know is that it bodes fair to make corpses of us all. You have told me what you will not do. Now tell me what you will do to save yourself, and rescue my Lady Lostris from a hateful fate.'

'Yes, old friend, you have every right to be angry with me. I asked for your help and advice. When you gave it freely, I scorned it. I beg your patience. Bear with me a while longer.' Tanus sprang to his feet and began to prowl about like the leopard in Pharaoh's menagerie, back and forth, muttering to himself, shaking his head and bunching his fists, as if to face an adversary.

At last he stopped in front of me. 'I am not prepared to play the traitor, but with a heavy heart I will force myself to play the coward. If Lostris agrees to accompany me, and only if she agrees, then I am prepared to take flight. I will take her away from this land we both love so well.'

'Where will you go?' I asked.

'I know that Lostris can never leave the river. It is not only her life and mine, but her god also. We must stay with Hapi, the river. That leaves only one direction open to us.' He raised his right arm, gleaming with muscle in the moonlight, and pointed south. 'We will follow the Nile southwards into the depths of Africa, into the land of Cush and beyond. We will go up beyond the cataracts into the unfathomed wilderness where no civilized man has ever gone before. There, perhaps, if the gods are kind, we will carve out another *Ta-Meri* for ourselves.'

'Who will be your companions?'

'Kratas, of course, and those of my officers and men who are game for the adventure. I'll address them tonight and give them the choice. Five ships, perhaps, and the men to work them. We must be ready to leave by dawn. Will you go back to the necropolis and fetch Lostris to me?'

'And me?' I asked quietly. 'You'll take me with you?'

'You?' He laughed at me. Now that the decision was made, his mood took flight, high as the bating falcon launched from the gloved fist. 'Would you truly give up your garden and your books, your pageants and your building of temples? The road will be dangerous, and the life hard. Do you truly want that, Taita?'

'I could not let you go alone, without my restraining hand upon your shoulder. What folly and danger would you lead my mistress into, if I were not there to guide you?'

'Come!' he ordered, and clapped me on the back. 'I never doubted that you would come with us. I know that Lostris would not leave without you, anyway. Enough chatter! We have work to do. First, we will tell Kratas and the others what we intend, and let them make their choice. Then you must go back to the necropolis and fetch Lostris, while I make the preparations for our departure. I'll send a dozen of my best men with you, but we must hurry. It is past midnight, and well into the third watch.'

Silly romantic fool that I am, but I was as excited as he was as we hurried back to the regiment's encampment below the temple and the causeway. I was so elated that my sense of danger was dulled. It was Tanus who picked out the sinister movement in the moonlight ahead of us and seized my arm and drew me beneath the shelter of a stunted carob tree.

'An armed party,' he whispered, and I saw the glint of bronze spearheads. There was a large band of men, thirty or forty, I estimated.

'Bandits, perhaps, or a raiding party from the Lower Kingdom,' Tanus growled, and even I was alarmed by the stealthy behaviour of the armed men ahead of us. They were not using the tow-path of the canal, but creeping through the open fields, spreading out to surround Tanus' encampment on the river-bank.

'This way!' With a soldier's eye for ground he picked out a shallow wadi that ran down to join the river, and he steered me to it. We jumped down and ran doubled over until we reached the perimeter of the camp. Then Tanus sprang out of the wadi and roused the camp with a bellow.

194

'Stand to arms! On me, the Blues! Form on me!' It was the rallying cry of the Blue Crocodile Guards, and it was taken up at once by the sergeants of each company. Instantly the camp boiled to life. The men sleeping round the fires leaped to their feet and snatched up their stacked weapons, while the officers' tents burst open as though the men within had never slept but had been waiting, tensed and ready for Tanus' command. Sword in hand, they raced to their stations, and I saw Kratas in the forefront.

I was amazed by the swiftness of their response, even though I knew that these were all battle-tested veterans. Before I could draw a dozen excited breaths they had formed in their phalanxes, with overlapping shields and long spears thrust outwards facing the darkness. The strange band out there in the night must have been as startled as I was by this militant display, for although I could still make out the vague shapes of many men and the gleam of their weapons in the gloom, the murderous charge we were all expecting from them never materialized.

The instant that Tanus had his formations in line, he ordered the advance. We had often debated the advantages of offensive action over defence, and now the massed squadrons moved forward, poised to break into a full charge at Tanus' command. It must have been a daunting spectacle to the men out there in the darkness, for a voice hailed us with an edge of panic in its tone. 'We are Pharaoh's men on the king's business. Hold your attack!'

'Hold hard, the Blues!' Tanus stopped the menacing advance, and then called back, 'Which pharaoh do you serve, the red usurper or the true pharaoh?'

'We serve the true king, the divine Mamose, ruler of the Upper and the Lower Kingdoms. I am the king's messenger.'

'Come forward, king's messenger, who creeps around in the night like a thief. Come forward and state your business!' Tanus invited him, but under his breath he told Kratas, 'Be ready for treachery. The smell of it is thick in the air. Have the fires built up. Give us light to see.'

Kratas gave the order and bundles of dry rushes were flung on to the watch-fires. The flames leaped up, and the darkness was thrown back. Into this ruddy glow the leader of the strange band stepped forward and shouted, 'My name is Neter, Best of Ten Thousand. I am the commander of Pharaoh's bodyguard. I bear the hawk seal for the arrest and detention of Tanus, Lord Harrab.'

'By Horus, he lies in his teeth,' Kratas growled. 'You are no felon with a warrant on your head. He insults you and the regiment. Let us at them and I'll thrust that hawk seal up between his buttocks.'

'Hold!' Tanus restrained him. 'Let us hear the fellow out.' He raised his voice again; 'Show us the seal, Captain Neter.'

Neter held it aloft. A small statuette in glistening blue faience, in the shape of the royal hawk. The hawk seal was the king's personal empowerment. The bearer acted with all the force and validity of Pharaoh himself. On pain of death, no man could question or hinder him in the course and commission of the royal business. The bearer answered only to the king.

'I am Tanus, Lord Harrab,' Tanus conceded.

'And I acknowledge the hawk seal.'

'My lord, my lord!' Kratas whispered urgently. 'Do not go to the king. It will mean your certain death. I have spoken to the other officers. The regiment is behind you, nay, the entire army is behind you. Give us the word. We'll make you king before the new day breaks.'

'My ear is deaf to those words,' Tanus told him softly, but with a weight of menace in his tone more telling than any growl or bellow. 'But only this once, Kratas, son of Maydum. Next time that you speak treason, I will deliver you to the king's wrath with my own hands.'

He turned from Kratas to me, and drew me a little to one side. 'It is too late, old friend. The gods frown on our enterprise. I must trust myself to the king's good sense. If he is truly a god, then he will be able to look into my heart and see for himself that it contains no evil.' He touched my arm, and that light gesture was to me more significant than the warmest embrace. 'Go to Lostris, tell her what has happened, tell her why it has happened. Tell her I love her and, whatever happens, I will do so through this life and the next. Tell her I will wait for her, to the ends of eternity, if need be.'

Then Tanus ran his sword back into the scabbard at his side and with empty hands stepped forward to meet the bearer of the hawk seal. 'I stand ready to do the king's bidding,' he said simply.

Behind him his own men hissed and growled, and rattled their swords against their bucklers, but Tanus turned and quieted them with a gesture and a frown, then strode out to confront Neter. The

197

king's guard closed in around him, and then at a trot they moved away along the tow-path of the canal, back towards the necropolis.

The camp was filled with angry, bitter young men when I left it and followed Tanus and his escort at a discreet interval. When I reached the necropolis, I went directly to my Lady Lostris' quarters. I was distressed to find them deserted except for three of her little black maids, who in their usual lazy and lackadaisical manner were packing the last of their mistress's clothing into a cedar-wood chest.

'Where is your mistress?' I demanded, and the eldest and most insolent of them picked her nose as she gave me an airy reply, 'Where you can't reach her, eunuch.' The others tittered at her powers of repartee. They are all of them jealous of my favour with my Lady Lostris.

'Answer me straight, or I'll whip your insolent backside, you little baggage.' I had done so before, so she relented and muttered sulkily, 'They have taken her to Pharaoh's own harem. You have no influence there. Despite your missing balls, the guards will never let you pass amongst the royal women.'

She was right, of course, but still I had to make the attempt. My mistress would need me now, as much as she ever had in all her life.

As I feared, the guards at the gate to the king's harem were intractable. They knew who I was, but they had orders that no one, not even the closest members of Lostris' retinue, was to be allowed to go to her.

It cost me a gold ring, but the best I could achieve, even with that extravagance, was the promise that one of the guards would take my message to her. I wrote it out on a scrap of papyrus parchment, a bland little attempt at encouragement. I dared not relate all that had befallen us, nor the peril in which Tanus now stood. I could not even mention him by name, and yet I had to reassure her of his love and protection. As an investment, it was not worth the price I was forced to pay. Hardest of all to bear, I learned later that my gold had been entirely wasted and that she never received the message. Is there no man we can trust in this perfidious world?

I was not to see either Tanus or my Lady Lostris again until the evening of the last day of the festival of Osiris.

 The festival ended in the temple of the god. It seemed once more that all the populace of Greater Thebes was packed into the courtyards. We were jammed so tightly that I could scarcely breathe in the press and the heat.

I was feeling wretched, for I had slept little for two nights in succession on account of the worry and the strain. Apart from the uncertainty of the fate of Tanus, I had been further burdened by my Lord Intef with the onerous duty of arranging the wedding ceremony of the king to his daughter, a duty that ran so contrary to my own desires. Added to which, I was parted from my mistress, and I could scarcely bear it. I do not know how I came through it. Even the slave boys were concerned about me. They declared that they had never seen my beauty so impaired, or my spirits so low.

Twice during Pharaoh's interminable speech from the throne, I found myself swaying on my feet, on the very point of fainting. However, I forced myself to hold on, while the king droned out the platitudes and half-truths with which he sought to disguise the true state of the kingdom and to placate the populace.

As was only to be expected, he never referred directly to the red pharaoh in the north or the civil war in which we were embroiled, except in such broad terms as 'these troubled times' or 'the defection and insurrection'. However, after he had spoken for a while it suddenly became plain to me that he was referring to every one of the issues that Tanus had raised in his declamation, and attempting to find remedies for each of them.

It was true that he was doing so in his usual inept and vacillating fashion, but the simple fact that he had taken notice of what Tanus had said braced me and focused my wandering attention. I edged forward in the press of humanity until I had a better view of the throne, by which time the king was speaking about the impudence of the slaves and the disrespectful behaviour of the lower classes of our society. This was another issue that Tanus had mentioned, and I was amused to hear Pharaoh's solution. 'From henceforth the slave-owner may order fifty lashes to the insolent slave, without recourse to the magistrate to sanction such punishment,' he announced.

I smiled when I remembered how this same king had almost wrecked the state twelve years previously with another proclamation that ran in the exact opposite direction to this latest pronouncement. Still idealistic at his coronation, he had set out actually to abolish the ancient and honourable institution of slavery. He had wanted to turn every slave in Egypt loose and make him a free man.

Even at this remove in time, such folly is still incomprehensible to me. Though I am myself a slave, I believe that slavery and serfdom are the institutions on which the greatness of nations is founded. The rabble cannot govern itself. Government should be entrusted only to those born and trained to it. Freedom is a privilege, not a right. The masses need a strong master, for without control and direction anarchy would reign. The absolute monarch and slavery and serfdom are the pillars of a system that has allowed us to develop into civilized men.

It had been instructive to see how the slaves themselves had rebelled at the prospect of having freedom thrust upon them. I had been very young at the time, but I too had been alarmed at the prospect of being turned out from my warm and secure niche in the boys' quarters to scavenge on the rubbish-heaps for my next crust of bread with a horde of other freed slaves. A bad master is better than no master at all.

Of course, the kingdom had been thrown into chaos by this folly. The army had been upon the brink of revolt. Had the red pharaoh in the north seized the opportunity, then history might have been written differently. In the end our own pharaoh had hastily withdrawn his misguided decree of manumission, and managed to cling to his throne. Now here he was little more than a decade later proclaiming increased punishments for the impudence of a slave. It was so typical of this hesitant and muddling pharaoh that I pretended to mop my brow in order to cover the first smile that had creased my face in the last two days.

'The practice of self-mutilation for the purpose of avoiding military service will in future be strongly discouraged,' the king droned on. 'Any eligible young man claiming exemption under this dispensation is to appear before a tribunal of three army officers, at least one of whom is to be a centurion or officer of superior rank.' This time my smile was one of reluctant approval. For once Pharaoh was on the right tack. I would dearly love to see Menset and Sobek displaying their missing thumbs to some hardened old veteran of the river wars. What tender sympathy they could expect! 'The fine for such an offence will be one thousand rings of gold.' By Seth's bulging belly, that would make those two young dandies pause, and my Lord Intef would have to meet the fine on their behalf.

Despite my other concerns, I was beginning to feel a little more cheerful, as Pharaoh continued, 'From this day forward it will be an offence punishable by a fine of ten gold rings for a harlot to ply for trade in any public place, other than one set aside by the magistrates for that purpose.' This time I could barely prevent myself from laughing aloud. Vicariously Tanus would make puritans and honest men of all of Thebes. I wondered how the sailors and the off-duty soldiers would welcome this interference in their sporting lives. Pharaoh's period of lucidity had been short-lived. Any fool knows the folly of trying to legislate to man's sexual foibles.

Despite my doubts as to the wisdom of the king's remedies, still I found myself overtaken by a tremulous excitement. It was clear that the king had taken serious notice of every issue that Tanus had brought forward in his declamation. Could he now go on to condemn Tanus for sedition, I wondered?

However, Pharaoh had not finished yet. 'It has been brought to my notice that certain officials of the state have abused the trust and faith that I have placed in them. These officials, concerned with the collection of taxes and the handling of public funds, will be called upon to account for the monies placed in their care. Those found guilty of embezzlement and corruption will be summarily sentenced to death by strangulation.' The populace stirred and sighed with disbelief. Would the king truly seek to restrain his tax-collectors?

Then a single voice at the back of the hall cried out, 'Pharaoh is great! Long live Pharaoh!' The cry was taken up until the temple rang with the cheering. It must have been an unusual sound for the king to hear, that spontaneous applause. Even at the distance that I was from the throne I could tell that he enjoyed it. His lugubrious expression lightened and the double crown seemed to weigh less heavily on his head. I was certain that all of this must improve Tanus' chances of escaping the executioner's noose.

When the cheering eventually subsided, the king went on in his particular style to diminish everything that he had just achieved. 'My trusted grand vizier, the noble Lord Intef, will be placed in sole and absolute charge of this investigation of the civil service, with the full powers of search and arrest, of life and of death vested in him.' There was just the softest echo of applause to greet this appointment, and I used it to disguise a sardonic chuckle. Pharaoh was sending a hungry leopard to count the birds in his chicken-coop. What sport my Lord Intef would have amongst the royal treasuries, and what a redistribution of the nation's wealth would now take place with my master doing the counting, and milking the tax-collectors of their secret hoards of savings!

Pharaoh had a rare talent for capsizing or running the noblest sentiments and intentions on to the rocks with his blundering helmsmanship. I wondered what other folly he would manage to perpetrate before he finished speaking that day, and I did not have too long to wait.

'For some time it has been a cause for great concern to me that a state of lawlessness exists in the Upper Kingdom, placing the lives and the estates of honest citizens in the gravest jeopardy. I had made dispositions to deal with this state of affairs at an appropriate time. However, the matter was recently presented to me in such an untimely and ill-advised manner as to reek of sedition. It was done under the dispensation of the festival of Osiris. However, that dispensation does not cover treason or the crime of blasphemy, an attack on the person and divinity of the king.' Pharaoh paused significantly. It was clear that he was speaking of Tanus, and I was once again critical of his judgement. A strong pharaoh would not explain his motives to the people, or seek to win their approval for his actions. He would simply have pronounced sentence and have had done with the matter.

'I speak, of course, of Tanus, Lord Harrab who played the role of the great god Horus at the pageant of Osiris. He has been arrested for the crime of sedition. My councillors are divided on the subject of this person's guilt. There are those amongst them who wish him to pay the supreme penalty—' I saw my Lord Intef, standing below the throne, avert his gaze for a moment, and it confirmed what I already knew, that he was the chief amongst those who wished to see Tanus executed '—and there are those who feel that his declamation at the festival was indeed inspired by divine forces and that it was not the voice of Tanus, Lord Harrab, that spoke out on these matters, but the veritable voice of the god Horus. If this latter be the case, then clearly there can be no culpability to the mortal through whom the god chose to speak.'

The reasoning was fair, but what pharaoh worth the double crown would deign to explain it to this horde of common soldiers and sailors and farmers, of tradesmen and labourers and slaves, most of whom were still suffering from the ill-effects of too much wine and revelry? While I still pondered this, the king gave a command to the captain of his bodyguard who stood below the throne. I recognized him as Neter, the officer who had been sent to arrest Tanus. Neter marched away smartly and returned a moment later, leading Tanus from the sanctuary at the rear of the hall.

My heart leaped at the sight of my friend, and then with joy and hope I realized that he was unbound, there were no chains on his ankles.

Although he carried no weapons and wore no badge of rank, and was dressed in a simple white kilt, he walked with his accustomed elastic step and jaunty grace. Apart from the healing scab on his forehead where Rasfer had struck him, he was unmarked. He had not been beaten or tortured, and I felt my optimism revived. They were not treating him as a condemned man.

A moment later all my hopes were dashed to pieces. Tanus made his obeisance before the throne, but when he rose to his feet again, Pharaoh looked down upon him severely and spoke in a voice without pity. 'Tanus, Lord Harrab, you stand accused of treason and sedition. I find you guilty of both these crimes. I sentence you to death by strangulation, the traditional punishment of the traitor.'

As Neter placed the noose of linen rope around Tanus' neck to mark him as one condemned to die, a groan went up from the people who watched. A woman wailed, and soon the temple was filled with cries of lamentation and the ululation of mourning. Never before had such a display accompanied the passing of the death sentence. Nothing could demonstrate more clearly the love which the populace bore Tanus. I wailed with them and the tears broke from my lids and streamed down my face to pour like a waterfall on to my chest.

The bodyguards fell upon the crowd, using the butts of their long spears in an attempt to beat the mourners into silence. It was in vain, and I screamed out over their heads, 'Mercy, bountiful Pharaoh! Mercy for the noble Tanus!'

One of the guards struck me on the side of the

head, and I fell to the ground half-stunned, but my cry was taken up. 'Mercy, we beseech you, oh divine Mamose!' It took all the efforts of the guards to restore some order, but still a few of the women were sobbing.

Only when Pharaoh raised his voice again were we at last silent, so that every one of us heard his next pronouncement. 'The condemned man has complained of the lawless state of the kingdom. He has called upon the throne to stamp out the bands of robbers who ravage the land. The condemned man has been called a hero, and there are those who say that he is a mighty warrior. If this be true, then he himself would be better suited than any other to carry out those measures he demands.'

Now the people were confused and silent, and I struck the tears from my face with my forearm as I strained to catch the next word. 'Therefore, the sentence of death is deferred for two years. If the condemned man was truly inspired by the god Horus when he made his seditious speech, then the god will assist him in the task I now place upon him.'

The silence was profound. None of us seemed able to understand what we were hearing, although hope and despair filled my soul in equal measure.

At a signal from the king one of the ministers of the crown stepped forward and offered Pharaoh a tray on which lay a tiny blue statuette. Pharaoh held it aloft and announced, 'I issue to Lord Harrab the hawk seal of the pharaohs. Under the auspice of the seal he may recruit all the men and materials of war that he deems necessary to his task. He may employ whatever means he chooses, and no man may prevent him. For two full years he is the king's man, and he answers only to the king. At the end of that time, on the last day of the next festival of Osiris, he will come before the throne once again, wearing the noose of death around his neck. If he has failed in his task, the noose will be tightened and he will be strangled to death on the spot where he now stands. If he has completed his task, then I, Pharaoh Mamose, will lift the noose from around his neck with my own hands and replace it with a chain of gold.'

Still none of us could speak or move, and we stared in fascination as Pharaoh made a gesture with the crook and the flail. 'Tanus, Lord Harrab, I charge you with the task of eradicating from the Upper Kingdom of Egypt the outlaws and robber bands that are terrorizing this land. Within two years you will restore order and peace to the Upper Kingdom. Fail me at your peril.'

A roar went up from the congregation, wild as the sound of storm surf beating on a rocky shore. Though they cheered unthinkingly, I lamented. The task that Pharaoh had set was too great for any mortal man to achieve. The cloud of death had not been lifted from over Tanus. I knew that in two years from today he would die on the very same spot where he now stood so young and proud and tall.

Forlorn as a lost waif, she stood alone in the midst of the multitude, with the river that was her patron god at her back and before her a sea of faces.

The long linen shift that fell to her ankles was dyed with the juice of shellfish to the colour of the finest wine, a colour that proclaimed her as a virgin bride. Her hair was loose. It flowed down on to her shoulders in a soft dark tide that shone in the sunlight as though with an inner fire. On those shining locks she wore the bridal wreath woven from the long stems of the water-lily. The blossoms were an unearthly cerulean blue, with throats of the clearest gold.

Her face was as white as freshly ground cornflour. Her eyes were so large and dark that they reminded me heartbreakingly of the little girl whom, in years gone by, I had so often woken from the grip of nightmare, and lit the lamp and sat beside her cot until she slept again. This time I could not help her, for the nightmare was reality.

I could not go to her, for the priests and Pharaoh's guard surrounded her, as they had all these days past, and they would not let me near unto her. She was lost to me for ever, my little girl, and I could not support the thought of it.

The priests had built the wedding canopy of river rushes on the bank above the Nile, and my Lady Lostris waited beneath it for her bridegroom to come to claim her. At her side stood her father, with the Gold of Praise glittering around his neck and the smile of the cobra on his lips.

The royal bridegroom came at last, to the

solemn beat of the drum and the bleat of gazelle-horn trumpets, and to me this wedding march was the saddest sound in all the earth.

Pharaoh wore the *nemes* crown and carried the sceptre, but behind the pomp and the regalia, he was still a little old man with a pot-belly and a sad face. I could not help but think of the other bridegroom who might have stood under the canopy beside my mistress, if only the gods had been kinder.

Pharaoh's ministers and high officials attended him so closely that my view of my mistress was obscured. Despite the fact that it was I who had been forced to arrange every detail of it, I was excluded from the wedding, and I had only glimpses of my Lady Lostris during the ceremony.

The high priest of Osiris washed the hands and the feet of both the bride and the groom with water freshly drawn from the Nile to symbolize the purity of their union. Then the king broke a morsel from the ritual corn-loaf and offered it to his young bride as a pledge. I glimpsed my mistress's face as he placed the crust between her lips. She could neither chew nor swallow but stood with it in her mouth as though it were a stone.

Once again she was hidden from my view, and it was only when I heard the crunch of the empty jug that had contained the marriage wine as the bridegroom shattered it with a blow of his sword, that I knew that it was done and that Lostris was for ever more beyond the reach of Tanus' arms.

The crowd beneath the canopy opened and Pharaoh led his newest bride forward to the front of the platform to present her to the people. They showed their love for Lostris in a chorus of adulation that went on and on until my ears rang and my head swam.

I wanted to escape from the press and go to find Tanus. Although I knew that he had been released from detention and was once again at liberty, he had not attended the ceremony. He was perhaps the only man in Thebes who had not come to the riverside today. I knew that wherever he might be, he stood in as dire need of me as I was of him. The only small comfort that either of us might find on this tragic day was with each other. However, I could not tear myself away. I had to see it out to the final harrowing moment.

At last my Lord Intef came forward to take his farewell of his daughter. As the crowd subsided into silence he embraced her.

Lostris was like a corpse in his embrace. Her arms hung limply at her side, and her face was pale as death. Her father released her, but kept a grip on her hand as he turned and faced the congregation to offer the ritual gift to his daughter. Traditionally, this gift was made over and above the dowry that went directly to the bridegroom. However, only the nobility observed this custom, which was designed to give the bride an independent income.

'Now that you go from my house and from my protection to the house of your husband, I bestow upon you the gift of parting, that you will remember me always as the father that loved you.' The words were inappropriate to the circumstances, I thought bitterly. My Lord Intef had never loved another living soul. However, he continued the ancient formula, as though the sentiments were his own. 'Ask any boon of me, my beloved child. I will refuse you nothing on this joyous day.'

It was the usual practice for the extent of the gift to be agreed in private between father and daughter before the ceremony. In this case, however, my Lord Intef had told his daughter unequivocally what she was entitled to ask for. He had done me the honour of discussing the matter with me the previous day, before informing Lostris of his decision. 'I don't want to be extravagant, but on the other hand I do not wish to appear parsimonious in Pharaoh's eyes,' he had mused. 'Let us say, five thousand gold rings and fifty feddan of land—not on the riverfront, mind you.'

He had, with my prompting, finally decided on five thousand gold rings and one hundred feddan of prime irrigable land as being a suitable gift for a royal wedding. On his instruction I had already drawn up the deed of grant for the land, and set aside the gold from a secret store that my master kept out of the way of the tax-collectors.

The matter was settled. It remained only for Lostris to give voice to the request before her groom and all the wedding guests. But she stood pale and silent and withdrawn, seeming neither to see nor hear what was going on around her.

'Speak up, my child. What is it that you desire from me?' My Lord Intef's tones of paternal love were becoming strained, and he shook his daughter's hand to rouse her. 'Come, tell your father what he can do to make this happy day complete.'

My Lady Lostris stirred as though coming awake from a dreadful dream. She looked about her and her tears welled up and threatened to break over her quivering eyelids. She opened her mouth to speak, but what came from her throat was the weak little cry of a wounded bird. She closed her lips again and shook her head speechlessly.

'Come, child. Speak out.' My Lord Intef was having difficulty sustaining an expression of paternal affection. 'Name your marriage gift, and I will give it to you, whatever it is that you desire.'

The effort that Lostris had to make was apparent to me, even though I stood so far from her, but this time when she opened her mouth her request rang out over our heads, clear as the music of the lyre. There could not have been a soul in the crowd who did not hear every word of it.

'For my gift give me the slave, Taita!'

My Lord Intef reeled back a pace as though she had thrust a dagger into his belly. He stared at her aghast, his mouth opening and closing without a sound escaping. Only he and I knew the value of the gift that Lostris had demanded. Not even he, with the store of wealth and treasure that he had garnered over a lifetime, could afford such a payment.

He recovered swiftly. His expression was once more calm and benign, though his lips stretched tight. 'You are too restrained, my darling daughter. A single slave is no fitting gift for Pharaoh's bride. Such stinginess is not in my nature. I would rather you accepted a gift of real value, five thousand rings of gold and—'

'Father, you have always been too generous with me, but I want only Taita.'

My Lord Intef smiled a white smile, white teeth, white lips and white rage. While he still stared at Lostris I could see that his mind was racing.

I was the most valuable of all his possessions. It was not simply my wide range of extraordinary talents that made up the full measure of my worth to him. Even more, it was that I knew intimately every convoluted thread of the intricate tapestry of his affairs. I knew every informer and spy in his network, every person whom he had ever bribed and who had bribed him. I knew which favours were outstanding on each account, which favours remained to be settled, and which grudges were still to be paid off.

I knew all his enemies, a long list; and I knew those he counted his friends and allies, a much shorter list. I knew where every nugget of his vast treasure was hidden, who were his bankers and his agents and his nominees, and how he had concealed the ownership of great tracts of land and stores of precious metals and gemstones in the legal labyrinth of deeds and titles and servitudes. All of this was information that would delight the tax-collectors and cause Pharaoh to revise his opinion of his grand vizier.

I doubted that my Lord Intef himself could remember and trace all his wealth without my assistance. He could not properly order and control his sprawling, shadowy empire without me, for he had kept himself aloof and separated from the most unsavoury aspects of it. He had preferred to send me to take care of those details which, if discovered, might incriminate him.

So it was that I knew a thousand dark secrets, and I knew of a thousand fearful deeds, of embezzlement and extortion, of robbery and bloodiest murder, all of which taken together could destroy even a man as powerful as the grand vizier.

I was indispensable. He could not let me go. And yet, before Pharaoh and the entire population of Thebes, he could not deny Lostris her request.

My Lord Intef is a man full of ire and hatred. I have seen such rage in him that must have made Seth, the god of anger, start up and take notice. But I had never seen such fury as now that his own daughter had him cornered.

'Let the slave Taita stand forward,' he called, and I saw that it was a ruse for him to gain a respite. I pushed my way as swiftly as I was able to the foot of the wedding platform, to give him as little time as possible to plan his next mischief.

'I am here, my lord,' I cried, and he stared down at me with those deadly eyes. We have been together so long that he can speak to me with a look almost as clearly as with the spoken word. He stared at me in silence until my heart was racing and my fingers fluttered with fear, then at last he said in soft, almost affectionate tones, 'Taita, you have been with me since you were a child. I have come to regard you as a brother more than as a slave. Still, you have heard my daughter's request. I am by nature a fair and kind man. After all the years it would be inhuman of me to discard you against your wishes. I know that it is unusual for a slave to be given a say in his own disposal, but then your circumstances are indeed unusual. Choose, Taita. If you wish to stay in your home, the only home you have ever known, then I cannot find the heart to send you away. Not even at the request of my own daughter.' He never took his eyes off me, those terrible yellow eyes. I am not a coward but I am careful of my safety. I realized that I was staring into the eyes of death, and I could not find my voice.

I tore my gaze from his, and looked towards my Lady Lostris. There was such appeal there, such loneliness and terror, that my own safety counted for nothing. I could not desert her now, not at any price or under any threat.

'How can a poor slave deny the wish of Pharaoh's wife? I am ready to do the bidding of my new mistress,' I cried out at the top of my lungs, and I hoped that my voice had a manly ring to it and was not as shrill as it sounded in my own ears.

'Come, slave!' my new mistress ordered. 'Take your place behind me.'

As I mounted the platform, I was forced to pass close to my Lord Intef. His white, stiff lips barely moved as he spoke for my ears alone. 'Farewell, my old darling. You are a dead man.'

I shuddered as though a poisonous cobra had slid across my path and I hurried to take my place in the retinue of my mistress, as though I truly believed that I could find safety in her protection.

I stayed close to Lostris during the rest of the ceremony and I waited on her personally at the wedding feast, hovering at her elbow and trying to make her eat a little of the meats and fine fare that was spread before her. She was so wan and sickly that I was certain that she had eaten nothing in the last two days, not since her betrothal and the condemnation of Tanus.

In the end I succeeded in getting her to take a

216

little watered wine, but that was all. Pharaoh saw her drink and thought that she was toasting him. He lifted his own gold chalice, and smiled at her over the rim as he returned the toast, and the wedding guests cheered the couple delightedly.

'Taita,' she whispered to me as soon as the king's attention was diverted by the grand vizier who sat at his other hand, 'I fear that I am going to vomit. I cannot stay here another moment. Please take me back to my chamber.'

It was an impudence and a scandal, and had I not been able to adopt the role of surgeon, I could never have achieved it, but I was able to creep on my knees to the king's side, and to whisper to him without causing an undue comment amongst the wedding guests, most of whom were well along in wine at this stage.

As I grew to know him better, I found that Pharaoh was a kindly man, and this was the first proof he gave me of it. He listened to my explanations and then clapped his hands and addressed the guests. 'My bride will go to her chamber now to prepare for the night ahead,' he told them, and they leered and greeted the announcement with lewd comment and lascivious applause.

I helped my mistress to her feet, but she was able to make her obeisance to the king and leave the banquet hall without my support. In her bedchamber she threw up the wine she had drunk into the bowl that I held for her, and then she collapsed upon the bed. The wine was all her stomach contained and my suspicion that she had been starving herself was confirmed.

'I don't want to live without Tanus.' Her voice

217

was weak, but I knew her well enough to recognize that her will was as strong as ever.

'Tanus is alive,' I tried to console her. 'He is strong and young and will live for another fifty years. He loves you and he promises to wait for you to the end of time. The king is an old man, he cannot live for ever—'

She sat up on the fur bedcover and her voice became stern and determined. 'I am Tanus' woman and no other man shall have me. I would rather die.'

'We all die in the end, mistress.' If only I could distract her for the first few days of this marriage, I knew I could see her through. But she understood me too well.

'I know what you are up to, but all your pretty words will do you no good. I am going to kill myself. I order you to prepare a draught of poison for me to drink.'

'Mistress, I am not versed in the science of poison.' It was a forlorn attempt, and she crushed it effortlessly.

'Many is the time that I have seen you give poison to a suffering animal. Do you not remember your old dog, the one with abscesses in its ears, and your pet gazelle that was mauled by a leopard? You told me that the poison was painless, that it was the same as going to sleep. Well, I want to go to sleep and be embalmed and go on to the other world to wait for Tanus there.'

I had to try other persuasion. 'But what about me, mistress? You have only this day taken possession of me. How can you abandon me? What will become of me without you? Have pity on me.' I saw her waver, and I thought I had her, but she lifted her chin stubbornly.

'You will be all right, Taita. You will always be all right. My father will take you back gladly after I am dead.'

'Please, my little one,' I used the childhood endearment in a last attempt to cajole her, 'let us talk of this in the morning. Everything will be different in the sunlight.'

'It will be the same,' she contradicted me. 'I will be parted from Tanus, and that wrinkled old man will want me in his bed to do horrid things to me.' Her voice was raised so that the other members of the king's harem might hear every word. Fortunately most of them were still at the wedding feast, but I trembled at the thought of her description of him being relayed to Pharaoh.

Her voice became shriller with the edge of hysteria in it. 'Mix me the poison draught now, this instant, while I watch you do it. I order you to do it. You dare not disobey me!' This command was so loud that even the guards at the outer gates must be able to hear her, and I dared not argue longer.

'Very well, my lady. I will do it. I must fetch my chest of medicine from my rooms.'

When I returned with the chest under my arm, she was up from the bed and pacing around her chamber with glittering eyes in that pale, tragic face.

'I am watching you. Don't try any of your tricks on me now,' she warned me, as I prepared the draught from the scarlet glass bottle. She knew that colour warned of the lethal contents.

When I handed the bowl to her, she showed no fear, and paused only to kiss my cheek. 'You have been both father and loving brother to me. I thank you for this last kindness. I love you, Taita, and I shall miss you.'

She lifted the bowl in both hands as though it were a wassail cup rather than a fatal potion.

'Tanus, my darling,' she toasted him with it, 'they shall never take me from you. We shall meet again on the far side!' And she drained the bowl at a swallow, then dropped it to shatter on the floor. At last, with a sigh, she fell back upon the bed.

'Come, sit beside me. I am afraid to be alone when I die.'

Taken on her empty stomach, the effect of the draught was very rapid. She had only time to turn her face to me and whisper, 'Tell Tanus again how much I loved him. Unto the portals of death, and beyond.' Then her eyes closed and she was gone.

She lay so still and pale that for a moment I was truly alarmed, afraid that I had misjudged the strength of the powder of the Red Shepenn which I had substituted for the essence of the deadly Datura Pod. It was only when I held a bronze hand-mirror to her mouth that the clouded surface reassured me she still breathed. I covered her gently, and tried to convince myself that in the morning she would be resigned to the fact that she was still alive, and that she would forgive me.

At that moment there was a peremptory knock upon the door of the outer chamber and I recognized the voice of Aton, the royal chamberlain, demanding entrance. He was another eunuch, one of the special brotherhood of the emasculated, so I could count him as a friend. I hurried through to greet him.

'I have come to fetch your little mistress to the

king's pleasure, Taita,' he told me, in high girlish tones so incongruous with such a large frame. He had been gelded before puberty. 'Is she ready?'

'There has been a small mishap,' I explained, and led him through to see Lostris for himself.

He puffed out his rouged cheeks with consternation when he saw her condition. 'What can I tell Pharaoh?' he cried. 'He will have me beaten. I will not do it. The woman is your responsibility. You must answer to the king, and stand before his wrath.'

It was not a duty that I relished, but Aton's distress was real, and at least I had my medical status to afford me some protection from the king's frustrated expectations. Reluctantly, I agreed to accompany him to the royal bedchamber. However, I made sure that there was one of the older and more reliable slave maids in attendance in my mistress's outer chamber before I left her alone.

Pharaoh had removed his crown and his wig. His head was shaved as bare and white as an ostrich egg. The effect startled even me, and I wondered how my mistress would have responded to the sight. I doubt that it would have raised either her ardour or her opinion of him.

The king seemed as startled to see me as I was to see him. We stared at each other for a moment before I fell to my knees and made my obeisance.

'What is this, Taita the slave? I sent for another—'

'Merciful Pharaoh, on behalf of the Lady Lostris I come to beg your understanding and indulgence.' I launched into a harrowing description of my Lady Lostris' condition, larding it with obscure

221

medical terms and explanations that were intended to divert the royal appetite. Aton stood beside me, nodding in emphatic corroboration of all I had to say.

I am sure that it would not have worked with a younger and more vigorous bridegroom, ready and rearing to get to the business, but Mamose was an old bull. It would have been impossible to tally all the lovely women who over the past thirty years or so had enjoyed his services. In single file they would probably have encircled the city of Thebes of a hundred gates, possibly more than once.

'Your Majesty,' Aton interrupted my explanations at last, 'with your permission, I will fetch you another female companion for the night. Perhaps the little Hurrian with the unusual control of her—'

'No, no,' the king dismissed him. 'There will be plenty of time for it when the child is recovered from her indisposition. Leave us now, chamberlain. There is some other matter that I wish to discuss with the doctor—I mean, with this slave.'

As soon as we were alone the king lifted his shift to display his belly. 'What do you think is the cause of this, doctor?' I examined the rash that adorned his protuberant paunch, and found it to be an infestation of the common ringworm. Some of the royal women washed less frequently than is desirable in our hot climate. I have noted that filth and the contagious itch go together. The king had probably contracted the infection from one of them.

'Is it dangerous? Can you cure it, doctor?' Fear makes commoners of us all. He was deferring to

222

me now as would any other patient.

With his permission, I went to my quarters to fetch my medicine chest, and when I returned, I ordered him to lie on the ornate gold and ivory marquetry bed while I massaged an ointment into the inflamed red circle of skin on his belly. The ointment was of my own concoction and would heal the rash within three days, I assured him.

'In a great measure you are responsible for the fact that I have married this child who is your new mistress,' he told me as I worked. 'Your ointment may cure my rash, but will your other treatment provide me with a son?' he demanded. 'These are troubled times. I must have an heir before I am another year older. The dynasty is in jeopardy.'

We physicians are always reluctant to guarantee our cures, but then so is the lawyer and the astrologer. While I procrastinated he gave me the escape I was searching for.

'I am no longer a young man, Taita. You are a doctor and I can tell you this. My weapon has been in many a fierce battle. Its blade is no longer as keen as once it was. Of late it has failed me when I most had need of it. Do you have something in that box of yours that would stiffen the wilting stem of the lily?'

'Pharaoh, I am pleased that you have discussed this with me. Sometimes the gods work in mysterious ways—' we both made the sign to avert evil before I went on, 'your first congress with my virgin mistress must be perfectly executed. Any faltering, any bending from our purpose, any failure to raise on high the royal sceptre of your manhood, will frustrate our efforts. There will be only one opportunity, the first union must be

223

successful. If we have to try again there will be the danger of your fathering yet another female.' My medical grounds for this prognosis were rather insubstantial. Nevertheless, we both looked grave, he graver than I did.

I held up my forefinger. 'Had we made the attempt tonight, and—' I said no more, but let my forefinger droop suggestively, and shook my head. 'No, we are fortunate to have been given another chance by the gods.'

'What must we do?' he demanded anxiously, and I was silent for a long while, kneeling in deep thought beside his bed.

It was difficult not to let my relief and satisfaction become apparent. Within the first day of my mistress's marriage, I was already working my way into a position of influence with the king, and I had been offered a perfect excuse for keeping her maidenhead intact for at least a little longer, long enough perhaps for me to be able to prepare her for the brutal shock of her first act of procreation with a man whom she did not love and who was, indeed, physically distasteful to her. I told myself that with clever management of the situation, I might be able to draw out this period of grace indefinitely.

'Yes indeed, Your Majesty, I can help you, but it will take some time. It will not be as easy as curing this rash.' My mind was racing. I had to wring every drop out of this sponge. 'We will have to go on to a very strict diet.'

'No more bull's balls, I beseech you, doctor.'

'I think you have had enough of those now. However, we will need to warm your blood and sweeten your generative fluids for the fateful

224

attempt. Goat's milk, warm goat's milk and honey three times a day, and of course the special potions I will prepare for you from the horn of the rhinoceros and the root of the mandrake.'

He looked relieved. 'You are certain this will work?'

'It has never failed before, but there is one other measure that is essential.'

'What is that?' His relief evaporated, and he sat up and peered at me anxiously.

'Complete abstinence. We must allow the royal member to rest and regain its full strength and force once again. You must forsake your harem and all its pleasures for a while.' I said this with the dogmatic air of the physician that cannot be gainsaid, for it was the one sure way to ensure that my Lady Lostris would remain untouched. However, I was worried by what his reaction would be. He could conceivably have flown into a rage at the thought of being denied his conjugal pleasures. He might have rejected me, and I could have lost all the advantage that I had so newly won. But I had to take the risk for the benefit of my mistress. I had to protect her just as long as I was able.

The king's reaction surprised me. He simply lay back on his headrest and smiled complacently to himself. 'For how long?' he asked quite cheerfully, and I was struck by the realization that my strictures had come as a relief to him. For me, to whom the act of love with a beautiful woman would always be an unattainable and elusive dream, it took an immense effort to understand that Pharaoh was content to be relieved of a once pleasurable duty that, by reason of being so often performed, had become onerous.

There must have been at least three hundred wives and concubines in his harem at that time, and some of those Asian women were notorious for their insatiable appetites. I tried to sympathize with the effort that it must require to act like a god night after night, and year after year. The prospect did not daunt me as the actuality seemed to have wearied the king.

'Ninety days,' I said.

'Ninety days?' he repeated thoughtfully. 'Nine Egyptian weeks of ten days each?'

'At least,' I said firmly.

'Very well.' He nodded without rancour and changed the subject easily.

'My chamberlain tells me, doctor, that apart from your medical skills, you are also one of the three most eminent astrologers in this very Egypt of ours?'

I wondered why my friend the chamberlain had qualified his assertion. For the life of me I could not think who the other two might be, but I inclined my head modestly. 'He flatters me, Your Majesty, but perhaps I do have some little knowledge of the heavenly bodies.'

'Cast a horoscope for me!' he ordered, sitting up eagerly.

'Now?' I asked with surprise.

'Now!' he agreed. 'Why not? For on your orders there is nothing that I should rather be doing at this moment.' That unexpected smile of his was really quite endearing, and despite what he meant to Tanus and my mistress, I found myself liking him.

'I shall have to fetch some of my scrolls from the

226

palace library.'

'We have all night,' he pointed out. 'Fetch whatever you need.'

The exact time and date of the king's birth were well documented and I had in the scrolls all the observations of the movements of the heavenly bodies made by fifty generations of astrologers before me. While the king watched avidly, I made the first cast of the royal horoscope, and before I had half finished it I saw the character of the man, as I had observed it, perfectly endorsed by his stars. The great red wandering star, that we know as the eye of Seth, dominated his destiny. It was the star of conflict and uncertainty, of confusion and war, of sadness and misfortune, and in the end of violent death.

But how could I tell him all these things?

I extemporized and put together a scantily veiled résumé of the well-documented facts of his life, and laced these with a few less well-known details that I had gathered from my spies, one of whom was the royal chamberlain. Then I followed with the usual assurances of good health and long life that every client wants to hear.

The king was impressed. 'You have all the skills that your reputation made me expect.'

'Thank you, Your Majesty. I am pleased that I have been able to be of service.' I began to gather up my scrolls and my writing instruments preparatory to taking my leave. It was very late by now. From the darkness beyond the palace walls I had already heard the first cockerel crow.

'Wait, Taita. I have not given you permission to leave. You have not told me what I really want to know. Will I have a son and will my dynasty

227

survive?'

'Alas, Pharaoh, those matters cannot be predicted by the stars. They can give only the general inclination of your fate, and the overall direction that your life will take, without making clear such details—'

'Ah, yes,' he interrupted me, 'but there are other means of seeing into the future, are there not?' I was alarmed by the direction in which his questions were leading, and I attempted to head him off, but he was determined.

'You interest me, Taita, and I have made enquiry about you. You are an adept of the Mazes of Ammon-Ra.' I was distressed. How had he found this out? Very few knew of this esoteric gift of mine, and I wanted it to remain thus. However, I could not blatantly deny it, so I remained silent.

'I saw the Mazes hidden at the bottom of your medicine chest,' he said, and I was relieved that I had not attempted to deny my gift and been caught out in the lie. I shrugged with resignation, for I knew what was coming.

'Work the Mazes for me, and tell me if I am to have an heir and whether or not my dynasty will survive,' he ordered.

A horoscope is one thing; it requires only a knowledge of the configuration of the stars and their properties. Some little patience, and the correct procedure will result in a fairly accurate prediction. A divination by the Mazes of Ammon-Ra is another matter entirely. It requires an expenditure of the life-forces, a burning up of something deep inside the seer that leaves him worn out and exhausted.

These days I will go to lengths to avoid having to

228

exercise this gift. It is true that on rare occasions I can still be persuaded to work the Mazes, but then for days thereafter I am spiritually and physically depleted. My Lady Lostris, who knows of this strange power of mine, also knows of the effect that it has upon me, and she has forbidden me, for my own sake, to practise it, except occasionally on her behalf.

However, a slave cannot deny a king, and with a sigh I reached for the leather bag in the bottom of my chest that contained the Mazes. I set the bag aside and prepared a mixture of the herbs that are necessary to open the eyes of the soul, to enable them to look into the future. I drank the potion, and then waited until the familiar but dreaded sensation of rising out of my own body assailed me. I felt dreamy and far from reality as I brought out the leather bag which contained the Mazes.

The Mazes of Ammon-Ra consist of ten ivory discs. Ten is the mystical number of the greatest potency. Each disc represents a single facet of human existence, from birth to death and the hereafter. With my own hands I had carved the symbols on the face of each of the Mazes. Each one was a tiny masterpiece. By constantly handling and breathing upon them over the years I had endowed them with part of my own life-force.

I poured them from the bag and began to fondle them, concentrating all my powers upon them. Soon they began to feel warm as living flesh to my touch, and I experienced the familiar sensation of depletion as my own strength flowed from me into the ivory discs. I arranged the Mazes face-down in two random stacks and invited Pharaoh to take up each pile in turn, to rub them between his fingers and to concentrate all his attention upon them at the same time as he repeated his questions aloud: 'Will I have a son? Will my dynasty survive?'

I relaxed completely and opened my soul to allow the spirits of prophecy to enter. The sound of his voice began to penetrate into my soul, deeper and deeper with each repetition, like missiles from a slingshot striking upon the same spot.

I began to sway slightly where I sat, the same way that the cobra dances to the flute of the snake-charmer. The drug took its full effect. I felt as though my body had no weight to it and that I was floating in air. I spoke as if from a great distance and my voice echoed strangely in my own head, as though I sat in a cavern below the surface of the earth.

I ordered the king to breathe upon each stack and then to divide it into halves, setting aside one half and retaining the other. Again and again I made him split each pile and then combine the remainder, until he was left with only two of the coin-shaped Mazes.

For the last time he breathed upon them and then at my instruction placed one in each of my hands. I held them tightly and pressed them to my breast. I could feel my heart pounding against my clenched fists as it absorbed the influence of the Mazes.

I closed my eyes and from the darkness saw shapes begin to emerge, and strange sounds filled my ears. There was no form or coherence to them, it was all confusion. I felt dizzy, and my senses blurred. I felt myself grow lighter still, until I seemed to float in space. I allowed myself to be carried upwards as though I were a blade of dry grass caught in a whirlwind, one of those dust devils of the Saharan summer.

The sounds in my head became clearer, and the dark images firmed.

'I hear a new-born infant cry.' My voice was distorted, as though my palate had been riven at birth.

'Is it a boy?' Pharaoh's question throbbed in my head, so that I felt rather than heard it.

Then slowly my vision began to harden, and I looked down a long tunnel through the darkness to a light at the far end. The ivory Mazes in my hands were hot as embers from the hearth and seared the flesh of my palms.

In the nimbus of light at the end of the tunnel I saw a child, lying in the bloody puddle of its own birth-waters, with the fat python of the placenta still coiled upon its belly.

'I see a child,' I croaked.

'Is it a boy?' Pharaoh demanded from out of the surrounding darkness.

The infant wailed and kicked both legs in the air, and I saw rising from between the chubby thighs a pale finger of flesh surmounted by a cap of wrinkled skin.

'A boy,' I confirmed, and I felt an unexpected tenderness towards this phantom of my mind, as though it were truly flesh and blood. I reached out to it with my heart, but the image faded, and the birth cry receded and was lost in the blackness.

'The dynasty? What will become of my line? Will it endure?' The king's voice reached me, and then was lost in a cacophony of other sounds that filled my head—the sound of battle trumpets, the shouts of men in mortal conflict, and the ring of bronze

231

on bronze. I saw the sky above me, and the air was dark with flights of arrows arcing overhead.

'War! I see a mighty battle that will change the shape of the world,' I cried to make myself heard above the sounds of conflict that filled my head.

'Will my line survive?' The king's voice was frantic, but I paid it no heed, for there was a mighty roaring in my ears, like the sound of the *khamsin* wind, or the waters of the Nile boiling through the great cataracts. I saw a strange yellow cloud that obscured the horizon of my vision, and the cloud was shot through with flashes of light, which I knew were the reflection of the sun from weapons of war.

'What of my dynasty?' Pharaoh's voice tugged at my mind, and the vision faded. There was a silence in my head and I saw a tree standing upon the bank of the river. It was a great acacia in full leaf, and its branches were heavy with fruit pods. On the topmost branch was perched a hawk, the royal hawk, but even as I watched, the hawk changed shape and colour. It was transformed into the double crown of Egypt, red and white, the papyrus and the lotus of the two kingdoms entwined. Then, before my eyes, the waters of the Nile rose and fell, and rose and fell again. Five times in all I saw the waters flood.

While still I stared with burning eyes, abruptly the sky above the tree darkened with flying insects, and a dense cloud of locusts descended upon the tree. They covered it completely. When they rose again the tree was devastated and bare of the last trace of green. Not a leaf remained on the dry brown twigs. Then the dead tree toppled and fell ponderously to earth. The fall shattered the trunk

232

and the crown was smashed into pieces. The fragments turned to dust and were blown away on the wind. Nothing remained but the wind and the driven sands of the desert.

'What is it that you see?' Pharaoh demanded, but it all faded and I found myself once more seated on the floor of the king's bedchamber. I was gasping for breath, as though I had run a great distance, and salt sweat scalded my eyes and poured down my body in rivulets to soak the linen of my kilt and to form a pool on the tiles beneath me. I was shaking with a burning fever and there was that familiar sick and heavy feeling in the pit of my stomach that I knew would be with me for days to come.

Pharaoh was staring at me and I realized what a haggard and dreadful sight I presented to him. 'What did you see?' he whispered. 'Will my line survive?'

I could not tell him the truth of my vision, so I invented another to satisfy him. 'I saw a forest of great trees that reached to the horizon of my dream. There was no end to their number and on top of each tree there was a crown, the red and the white crown of the two kingdoms.'

Pharaoh sighed and covered his eyes with his hands for a while. We sat in silence, he in the release that my lie had given him, and I in sympathy for him.

At last I lied softly. 'The forest that I saw was the line of your descendants,' I whispered, to spare him. 'They reach to the boundaries of time, and each of them wears the crown of Egypt.'

He uncovered his eyes, and his gratitude and his joy were pathetic to watch. 'Thank you, Taita. I

233

can see how the divination has taxed your strength. You may go now and rest. Tomorrow the court will sail for my palace on Elephantine Island. I will have a galley set aside for the safe passage of you and your mistress. Guard her with your life, for she is the vessel that contains the seeds of my immortality.'

I was so weak that I had to use the frame of the bed to lift myself to my feet. I tottered to the door and steadied myself against the jamb. However, I was not so weakened that I could not think of my duty to my mistress.

'There is the matter of the marriage sheet. The populace will expect to have it displayed,' I reminded him. 'Both your reputation and that of my mistress is at stake.'

'What do you suggest, Taita?' This soon he was relying on me. I told him what must be done, and he nodded. 'See to it!'

Carefully I folded the sheet that covered the royal bed. It was of the finest linen, white as the high cirrus clouds of summer, embroidered with the rare silk thread that the trade caravans occasionally bring in from the East. I carried the folded sheet with me when I left the king's bedchamber and made my way back through the still dark and silent palace to the harem.

My mistress was sleeping like a dead woman, and I knew that with the amount of the Red Shepenn I had given her, she would sleep the day away and would probably only wake that evening. I sat beside her bed for a while. I felt exhausted and depressed for the Mazes had drained my soul. The images they had evoked still troubled me. I felt certain that the infant I had seen was that of my mistress, but then how could the rest of my vision be explained? There seemed to be no answer to the riddle, and I set the thought aside for I still had work to do.

Squatting beside Lostris' bed, I spread the embroidered sheet upon the floor. The blade of my dagger was sharp enough to shave the hair from my forearm. I picked out one of the blue rivers of blood beneath the smooth skin on the inside of my wrist, and I pricked it with the point of the dagger and let the dark slow blood trickle on to the sheet. When I was satisfied with the extent of the stain, I bound up my wrist with a strip of linen to staunch the bleeding, and bundled the soiled sheet.

The slave girl was still in attendance in the outer chamber. I ordered that Lostris was to be allowed to sleep undisturbed. Knowing that she would be well cared for, I was content to leave her, and climb the ladder to the top of the outer wall of the harem.

The dawn was only just breaking, but already an inquisitive crowd of old women and loiterers had gathered below the walls. They looked up expectantly when I appeared.

I made a show of shaking out the sheet before I draped it over the ramparts of the outer wall. The bloodstain in the centre of the cloud-white ground was the shape of a flower, and the crowd buzzed with gossip at this badge of my mistress's virginity and her bridegroom's virility.

At the rear of the crowd stood a figure taller than those around him. His head was covered by a striped woollen shawl. It was only when he threw this back and exposed his face and his head of red-gold hair that I recognized him.

235

'Tanus!' I shouted. 'I must speak to you.'

He looked up at me upon the wall, and his eyes were filled with such pain as I wished never to see again. That stain upon the sheet had destroyed his life. I also had known the agony of lost love and remembered every detail of it even after all the long years. Tanus' heart wound was fresh and bleeding still, more agonizing than any hurt that he had received on the battlefield.

He needed my help now, if he were to survive it. 'Tanus! Wait for me.'

He threw the shawl over his head, covering his face, and he turned from me. Unsteady as a drunkard, he stumbled away.

'Tanus!' I shouted after him. 'Come back! I must talk to you.' He did not look round, but quickened his pace.

By the time that I had climbed down from the wall and run out of the main gates, he had disappeared into the maze of alleys and mud huts of the inner city.

I searched for Tanus half the morning, but his quarters were deserted and nobody had seen him in any of his customary haunts.

At last I had to abandon the search, and make my way back to my own rooms in the quarters of the slave boys. The royal flotilla was preparing to sail for the south. I had still to assemble and pack my possessions if my mistress and I were to be ready for the departure. I forced aside the sense of gloom that the Mazes and my glimpse of Tanus had left me, and I set about

236

bundling up my possessions and breaking up the only home that I had ever known.

My animals seemed to sense that something untoward was happening. They fretted and chirped and whined, each trying in his own way to attract my attention. The wild birds hopped and fluttered on the paved terrace outside, while in the corner nearest my bed, my beloved Saker falcons stretched their wings and raised the feathers along their backs, and screeched at me from their perches. The dogs and the cats and the tame gazelle crowded around my legs, trying to brush against me, and hindered my efforts to pack my possessions.

In exasperation I noticed the jug of soured goat's milk beside my bed. It is one of my favourite drinks, and the slave boys make certain that the jug is always refilled. My animals also enjoy the thickened milk, so to distract them I carried the jug out on to the terrace and filled their clay drinking-bowls. They crowded around the bowls, pushing and shoving each other, and I left them and went back to my task, closing the awnings of rush matting to keep them out.

It is curious how many possessions even a slave can gather about him over a lifetime. The boxes and bundles were piled high against one wall before I was at last finished. By this time my mood of depression and weariness was almost prostrating, but I was still sufficiently alert to be aware of the silence. I stood for a while in the centre of my room, listening uneasily. The only sound was the jingle of the tiny bronze bells on the jesses of my female falcon where she sat in the far corner and watched me with that intent, implacable gaze of the raptor. The tiercel, smaller but more handsome than she, was asleep on his own perch in the other corner, with the soft leather hood of the rufter covering his eyes. None of my other pets made a sound. Not one of the cats mewed or hissed at the dogs, nor did the wild birds chirrup or sing, none of my puppies growled or tumbled over each other in boisterous play.

I went to the rush awning and drew it aside. The sunlight burst into the room and blinded me for a moment. Then my vision returned and I cried out with horror. They were scattered upon the terrace and down into the garden every bird and animal.

They lay in the abandoned attitudes of death, every one of them where he had fallen. I rushed out to them, calling my favourites by name, kneeling to pick one of them up in my arms and hugging the slack warm body as I searched for signs of life. There was no flicker of it in any of them, though I went to each of them. The birds were small and light in my hand, their marvellous plumage undimmed by death.

I thought that my already heavy heart must now burst with the sheer weight of my grief. I knelt on the terrace with my family scattered around me and I wept.

It was some time before I could bring myself to think about the cause of this tragedy. Then I stood up and went to one of the empty bowls that lay on the tiles. They had licked it clean, but I sniffed at it to try and fathom the nature of the poison that had been intended for me. The odour of soured milk disguised any other smell; all I knew was that it had been swift and deadly.

I wondered who had placed the jug beside my

bed, but it did not matter whose hand had carried the vessel to me. I knew with utter certainty who had given the order for it. 'Farewell, my old darling. You are a dead man,' Lord Intef had told me, and he had not waited long to transform the words into the deed.

The anger that seized me was a form of madness. It was aggravated by my unsteady state and sombre mood. I found that I was shaking with a rage that I had never known before. I drew the little dagger from my belt and before I realized what I was doing, I was rushing down the steps of the terrace with the naked blade in my hand. I knew that at this time of the morning Intef would be in his water-garden. I could no longer bear to think of him as my Lord Intef. The memory of every outrage he had ever visited upon me, every agony and every humiliation, was bright and clear in my mind. I was going to kill him now, stab him a hundred times through that cruel and evil heart.

I was in sight of the gate to the water-garden before I regained my sanity. There were half a dozen guards at the gate, and there would be as many more beyond. I would never get within dagger-thrust of the grand vizier before they cut me down. I forced my flying feet to check and turn back. I slipped the dagger into the jewelled leather sheath, and brought my breathing under control. I walked slowly back to the terrace and gathered up the pathetic bodies of my pets.

I had planned to plant a row of sycamore trees along the border of my garden. The holes to take them had already been dug. The trees would never be planted now that I was leaving Karnak, and the pits would serve as graves for my beloved

239

creatures. It was the middle of the afternoon before I had filled the last grave, but my rage was unabated. If I could not yet have my full vengeance, at least I could give myself a foretaste of it.

There was still a little of the sour milk left in the jug beside my bed. I held the jug in my hands and tried to think of some way in which I could get it to the grand vizier's kitchens. It would be so fitting to pay him his own vile coin, although I knew in my heart that the idea was futile. Lord Intef was far too cunning to be taken so easily. I myself had helped him devise the system he used to keep himself secure from poison and assassination. He could not be reached without much careful planning. What was more, he would be especially on his guard now. I would have to be patient, but that was impossible. Even if I could not kill him yet, I could exact some lesser payment as a deposit against what I was determined must follow.

Still carrying the fatal jug, I slipped out of one of the side-doors of the boys' quarters into the street. I did not have to go far to find a milkman surrounded by his flock of nanny-goats. While I waited he stripped the rich milk from the swollen udders of one of them, topping the jug to the brim. Whoever had prepared the poison had used enough to murder half the citizens of Karnak. I knew that more than sufficient remained in the jug for my purpose.

One of the grand vizier's bodyguards loafed at the door to Rasfer's chamber. The fact that he had him under guard proved to me that Rasfer was still valuable to Lord Intef, and the loss of his personal lieutenant would annoy if not seriously discommode him.

The guard recognized me and waved me into the sick-room that smelled like a sty. Rasfer lay on his filthy bed, basting in his own sweat. However, I could tell at once that my surgery had been successful, for he opened his eyes and cursed me weakly. He must also be so certain of his own eventual recovery that he need no longer toady to me.

'Where have you been, you ball-less freak?' he growled at me, hardening my resolve and ridding me of the last traces of any pity that I might have felt for him. 'I have been in agony ever since you drilled into my skull. What kind of physician are you—'

There was much more in this style, which I pretended to ignore as I unwound the soiled bandage from around his head. My interest was purely academic as I examined the small wound that the trepan had left in his scalp. It was another perfectly executed operation, and I felt a certain professional regret that it would be wasted.

'Give me something for the pain, eunuch!' Rasfer tried to seize the front of my tunic, but I was too quick for him and stepped back out of his reach.

I made a fuss of shaking a few crystals of harmless salt from a glass vial into his drinking-bowl, and then topped it up with milk from my jug.

'If the pain becomes too bad, this will relieve it,' I told him as I set the bowl near to his hand. Even at this stage, I could not bring myself to hand it to him directly.

He heaved himself up on one elbow and reached

241

for the bowl to guzzle it down. Before his fingers touched it, I pushed it out of his reach with my foot. At the moment I thought that this was merely a desire to prolong the anticipation, and I felt satisfaction at his distress as he whined at me, 'Good Taita, give me the potion. Let me drink. This pain in my head will drive me mad.'

'First let's talk a while, good Rasfer. Did you hear that the Lady Lostris asked for me as her parting gift from Lord Intef?'

Even in his pain, he grinned at me. 'You are a fool if you think he will let you go. You are a dead man.'

'The very words Lord Intef used. Will you mourn for me, Rasfer? Will you weep for me when I am gone?' I asked softly, and he began to chuckle, then broke it off and glanced at the bowl.

'In my own way, I have always been rather fond of you,' he grunted. 'Now let me have the bowl.'

'How fond of me were you when you castrated me?' I asked, and he stared up at me.

'Surely you do not still bear a grudge for that? It was long ago, and besides, I could not disobey the orders of Lord Intef. Be reasonable, Taita, let me have the bowl.'

'You laughed as you cut me. Why did you laugh? Did you enjoy it so much?'

He shrugged and then winced at the pain that the movement caused him. 'I am a jovial man. I always laugh. Come now, old friend, say you forgive me and let me have the bowl.'

I nudged it towards him with my foot. He reached out and seized it, his movements still uncoordinated. A few drops slopped over the rim as he raised it greedily to his mouth.

I didn't realize what I was about to do, until I had leapt forward and struck the bowl out of his hands. It hit the floor without shattering and rolled into the corner, splashing milk up on to the wall.

Rasfer and I stared at each other. I was appalled by my own stupidity and my weakness. If ever a man deserved a death by the agony of poison, it was this one. But then I saw again the contorted bodies of my pets strewn across the terrace, and I knew why I had not been able to allow Rasfer to drink. Only a fiend could commit such an act. I have too high a regard for myself ever to descend to the ignominy of the poisoner.

I saw understanding dawn in Rasfer's bloodshot eyes. 'Poison,' he whispered. 'The bowl was poisoned.'

'It was sent to me by Lord Intef.' I don't know why I told him this. Perhaps I was trying to excuse myself for the atrocity that I had almost committed. I don't know why I was behaving so strangely. Maybe it was still the after-effects of working the Mazes. I staggered slightly as I turned for the door.

Behind me Rasfer began to laugh, softly at first and then louder, until great gusty bellows of laughter seemed to shake the walls.

'You are a fool, eunuch,' he roared after me as I ran. 'You should have done it. You should have killed me, for now as surely as I have a hole between my buttocks, I will kill you.'

As I had expected, when at last I returned to her chamber my Lady Lostris was still asleep. I settled at the foot of her bed, intending to wait for her to wake on her own. However, the rigours and the exertions of the past day and night had been too much for me. I slumped down and fell asleep, curled like a puppy on the tiles.

I woke under attack. Something struck the side of my head such a painful blow that I was on my feet before I was properly awake. The next blow took me across the shoulder and stung like the bite of a hornet.

'You cheated me!' my Lady Lostris screamed at me. 'You did not let me die.' She swung the fan again. It was a formidable weapon, the bamboo handle was as long as twice the span of my arms, and the comb at its head that held the fan of ostrich feathers was of solid silver. Fortunately she was still groggy from the drug and from oversleeping, and her aim was erratic. I ducked under the blow, and the momentum of it swung her around so that she collapsed on the bed again.

She dropped the fan and burst into tears. 'I wanted to die. Why did you not let me die?'

It was some time before I could approach her, and put one arm around her to comfort her. 'Did I hurt you, Taita?' she asked. 'I have never beaten you before.'

'Your first attempt was a very good one,' I congratulated her ruefully. 'In fact you are so good at it that I do not think you need practise it further.' Theatrically I rubbed the side of my head, and she smiled through her tears.

'Poor Taita. I do treat you so badly. But you did deserve it. You cheated me. I wanted to die and you disobeyed me.'

I saw it was time to change the subject. 'Mistress, I have the most remarkable news for you. But you must promise to tell no one of it, not even your maids.' Not since she had first learned to talk had she been able to resist a secret, but then what woman can? The promise of one had always been enough to distract her, and it worked yet again.

Even with her heart broken and the threat of suicide hanging over her, she sniffed back the last of her tears and ordered, 'Tell me!'

Recently, I had accumulated a good store of secrets to choose from, and I paused for a moment to make my selection. I would not tell her of the poisoning of my pets, of course, nor of my glimpse of Tanus. I needed something to cheer her rather than to depress her further.

'Last night I went to Pharaoh's bedchamber and I spoke to him for half the night.'

The tears rose to the surface of her eyes once more, 'Oh, Taita, I hate him. He's an ugly old man. I don't want to have to—'

I wanted no more in that vein, in moments she would be weeping again, so I hurried on, 'I worked the Mazes for him.' Instantly I had her complete attention. My Lady Lostris is totally fascinated by my powers of divination. If it were not for the deleterious effect that the Mazes have upon my health, she would make me work them every single day.

'Tell me! What did you see?' She was riveted. No thought of suicide now, all sadness forgotten. She was still so young and artless that I felt ashamed of my trickery, even though it was for her own good.

245

'I had the most extraordinary visions, mistress. I have never had such clear images, such depths of sight—'

'Tell me! I declare I will die of impatience if you don't tell me immediately.'

'First you must swear secrecy. Not another soul must ever know what I saw. These are affairs of state and dire consequence.'

'I swear. I swear.'

'We cannot take these matters lightly—'

'Get on with it, Taita. You are teasing me now. I order you to tell me this very moment or, or,' she groped for a threat to coerce me, 'or I shall beat you again.'

'Very well. Listen to my vision. I saw a great tree upon the bank of the Nile. Upon the summit of the tree was the crown of Egypt.'

'Pharaoh! The tree was the king.' She saw it at once, and I nodded. 'Go on, Taita. Tell me the rest of it.'

'I saw the Nile rise and fall five times.'

'Five years, the passing of five years!' She clapped her hands with excitement. She loves to unravel the riddles of my dreams.

'Then the tree was devoured by locusts, and thrown down and turned to dust.'

She stared at me, unable to utter the words, so I spoke for her. 'In five years Pharaoh will be dead, and you will be a free woman. Free from your father's thrall. Free to go to Tanus, with no man to stop you.'

'If you are lying to me, it will be too cruel to bear. Please say it is true.'

'It is true, my lady, but there is more. In the vision, I saw a new-born babe, a boy child, a son. I

246

felt my love go out to the infant, and I knew that you were the mother of the child.'

'The father, who was the father of my baby? Oh, Taita, tell me please.'

'In the dream I knew with absolute certainty that the father was Tanus.' This was the first deviation from the truth that I had allowed myself, but once again I had the consolation of believing that it was for her benefit.

She was silent for a long time, but her face shone with an inner glow that was all the reward I could ever ask for. Then at last she whispered, 'I can wait for five years. I was prepared to wait all eternity for him. It will be hard, but I can wait five years for Tanus. You were right not to let me die, Taita. It would have been an offence in the face of the gods.'

My relief buoyed me up, and I now felt more confident that I would be able to steer her safely through all that lay ahead.

At dawn the following day the royal flotilla sailed south from Karnak. As the king had promised, my Lady Lostris and all her entourage were on board one of the small, fast galleys of the southern squadron.

I sat with my mistress on the cushions under the awning on the poop that the captain had arranged especially for her. We looked back at the lime-washed buildings of the city shining in the first tangerine tints of the rising sun.

'I cannot think where he has gone.' She was fretting over Tanus as she had a score of times since we had set sail. 'Did you look everywhere for him?'

'Everywhere,' I confirmed. 'I spent half the morning scouring the inner city and the docks. He has disappeared. But I left your message with Kratas. You can be sure Kratas will deliver it to him.'

'Five years without him, will they ever pass?'

 The voyage up-river passed pleasantly enough in long, leisurely days spent sitting on the poop-deck in conversation with my mistress. We discussed every detail of our changed circumstances in great depth, and examined all that we might expect and hope for in the future.

I explained to her all the complexities of life at the court, the precedent and the protocol. I traced for her the hidden lines of power and influence, and I listed all those whom it would be in our interest to cultivate and those whom we could safely ignore. I explained to her the issues of the day, and how Pharaoh stood on each of them. Then I went on to discuss with her the feeling and the mood of the citizenry.

In a large measure I was indebted to my friend Aton, the royal chamberlain, for all this intelligence. It seemed that over the last dozen years every ship that had come down-river from Elephantine Island to Karnak had carried a letter from him to me full of these fascinating details, and on its return to Elephantine Island had carried a golden token of my gratitude back to my friend,

Aton.

I was determined that we would soon be at the centre of the court and in the mainstream of power. I had not trained my mistress all these years to see the weapons that I had placed in her armoury rust with disuse. The sum of her many accomplishments and her talents was already formidable, but I was patiently adding to it each day. She had a keen and restless mind. Once I had helped her to throw off the black mood that had threatened to destroy her, she was, as always, open to my instruction. Every chance I had, I fired up her ambition and her eagerness to take up the role I had planned for her.

I soon found that one of the most effective means of enlisting her attention and cooperation was to suggest that all this would be to the eventual benefit and advantage of Tanus. 'If you have influence at court, you will be better able to protect him,' I pointed out to her. 'The king has set him an almost impossible task to fulfil. Tanus will need us if he is to succeed, and if he fails only you will be able to save him from the sentence that the king has placed upon him.'

'What can we do to help him carry out his task?' At the mention of Tanus I immediately had all her attention. 'Tell me truly, will any man be able to stamp out the Shrikes? Is it not too difficult a mission, even for a man like Tanus?'

The bandits that terrorized the Upper Kingdom called themselves the Shrikes, after those fierce birds. Our Nile shrike is smaller than a dove; a handsome little creature with a white chest and throat and a black back and cap, it plunders the nests of other birds and makes a grisly display of

249

the pathetic carcasses of its victims by hanging them on the thorns of the acacia tree. Its vernacular name is the Butcher Bird.

In the beginning the bandits had used it as a cryptic name to conceal their identity and to hide their existence, but since they had grown so strong and fearless, they had adopted it openly and often used the black and white feather of the Butcher Bird as their emblem.

In the beginning they would leave the feather on the doorway of a home they had robbed or on the corpse of one of their victims. But in those days, so bold and so organized had they become that at times they might send a feather to an intended victim as a warning. In most cases that was all that was necessary to make the victim pay over a half of all he owned in the world. That was preferable to having all of it pillaged, and having his wives and daughters carried off and raped, and he and his sons thrown into the burning ruins of their home to boot.

'Do you think it possible that even with the power of the hawk seal Tanus will be able to carry out the king's mission?' my mistress repeated. 'I have heard that all the bands of the Shrikes in the whole of the Upper Kingdom are controlled by one man, someone that they call the Akh-Seth, the brother of Seth. Is that true, Taita?'

I thought for a moment before I answered. I could not yet tell her all I knew of the Shrikes, for if I did so, then I would be forced to reveal how such knowledge had come into my possession. At this stage that would not be much to her advantage, nor to my credit. There might be a time for these disclosures later.

'I have also heard that rumour,' I agreed cautiously. 'It seems to me that if Tanus were to find and crush this one man, Akh-Seth, then the Shrikes would crumble away. But Tanus will need help that only I can give him.'

She looked at me shrewdly. 'How can you help him?' she demanded. 'And what do you know about this business?'

She is quick, and hard to deceive. She sensed at once that I was hiding something from her. I had to retreat swiftly and to play on her love of Tanus and her trust in me.

'For Tanus' sake, ask me no more now. Only give me your permission to do what I can to help him complete the task that Pharaoh has set him.'

'Yes, of course we must do all in our power. Tell me how I can help.'

'I will stay with you at the court on Elephantine Island for ninety days, but then you must give me leave to go to him—'

'No, no,' she interrupted me, 'if you can be of help to Tanus, you must go immediately.'

'Ninety days,' I repeated stubbornly. That was the period of grace that I had won for her. Although I was torn between these two dear children of mine, my first duty was to my mistress. I knew that I could not leave her alone at the court without a friend or a mentor. I also knew that I had to be with her when the king finally sent for her in the night.

'I cannot leave you yet, but don't worry. I have left a message for Tanus with Kratas. They will be expecting me, and I have explained to Kratas all that has to be done before I arrive back at Karnak.' I would not tell her more, and there can be few as

251

obtuse or as evasive as I can be when I set myself to it.

The flotilla sailed only during the day. Neither the navigational skills of Admiral Nembet nor the comfort of the king and his court would stand up to a night passage, so every evening we moored and a forest of hundreds of tents sprang up on the river-bank. Always the royal stewards chose the most congenial spot to pitch camp, usually in a grove of palm trees or in the lee of a sheltering hillock, with a temple or a village nearby from which we were able to draw supplies.

The entire court was still in festive mood. Every camp was treated as a picnic. There was dancing and feasting in the light of the bonfires, while in the shadows the courtiers intrigued and flirted. Many an alliance both political and carnal was struck during those balmy nights, perfumed with the fruity aromas of the irrigated lands along the river and the spicier desert airs blown in from further afield.

I used every moment to the best advantage of both my mistress and myself. Of course she was now one of the royal ladies, but there were already several hundred of those, and she was still a very junior wife. Lord Intef's foresight might change her future status, but only if she bore Pharaoh a son. In the meantime it was up to me.

Almost every evening after we had gone ashore, Pharaoh sent for me, ostensibly to see to the cure of his ringworm, but in reality to review the preparations for begetting a male heir to the double crown. While he watched with interest, I prepared my tonic for potency and virility from grated rhinoceros horn and mandrake root, which

I mixed with warm goat's milk and honey. When he had taken this, I examined the royal member and was delighted for the sake of my mistress to find that it possessed neither the length nor the girth that one would have expected from a god. I was of the opinion that my mistress, even in her virgin state, would be able to cope with its modest dimensions without too much discomfort. Naturally I would do all in my power to avoid the dread moment, but if I was unable to stave it off, then I was determined to ease the passage to womanhood for her.

Having found the king to be healthy if unremarkable in these regions, I recommended a poultice of cornflour mixed with olive oil and honey to be applied to the royal member at night before retiring, and then I went on to deal with the ringworm. To the king's intense gratification my ointment cured the condition within the three days that I had promised, and my already considerable reputation as a physician was enhanced. The king boasted of my accomplishment to his council of ministers, and within days I was in huge demand throughout the court. Then, when it was known that I was not only a healer but also an astrologer whom even the king consulted, my popularity became boundless.

Every evening there came to our tents a succession of messengers bearing expensive gifts for my mistress from this lady or that lord and begging that she allow me to visit them for a consultation. We acceded to only those with whom we wished to make better acquaintance. Once I was in the tent of a powerful and noble lord, he with his kilt up around his waist while I examined his haemorrhoids, it was a simple matter to extol my mistress and bring her many virtues to the attention of my patient.

The other ladies of the harem soon discovered that my Lady Lostris and I sang a beautiful duet together, and that we could compose the most intriguing riddles and tell even more amusing stories. We were in demand throughout the court, and especially amongst the children of the harem. This gave me special pleasure, for if there is anything I love more than animals, it is small children.

Pharaoh, who was responsible for our popularity in the first place, soon had the increase of it reported to him. This further spurred his interest in my mistress, if it were not already sufficiently intense. At sailing time on many mornings she was summoned on board the royal barge to spend the day in the king's company, while most evenings, at the royal invitation, my mistress dined at the king's board, and regaled him and the assembled company with her natural wit and childlike grace. Of course I was always in discreet attendance. When the king made no move to send for her in the night in order to force her to submit to those horrible but rather hazy terrors she had conjured up, her feelings towards him began to moderate.

Beneath his glum exterior Pharaoh Mamose was a kind and decent man. My Lady Lostris soon realized this, and like me, she began to grow quite fond of him. Before we reached Elephantine Island she was treating him like a favourite uncle, and quite unaffectedly would sit on his knee to tell him a story, or would play throwing-sticks with him on the deck of the royal barge, both of them flushed with the exertion and laughing like children. Aton confided to me that he had never seen the king so gay.

All this was watched and noted by the court, who very soon recognized her as the king's favourite. Soon there were other visitors to our tents in the evening, those who had a petition which they wished my mistress to bring to Pharaoh's notice. The gifts they proffered were even more valuable than those offered for my services.

My mistress had rejected her father's gift in favour of a single slave, so she had begun the journey southwards as a pauper, dependent on my own modest savings. However, before the voyage was done she had accumulated not only a comfortable fortune, but also a long list of favours owed by her new rich and powerful friends. I kept a careful accounting of all these assets.

I am not so conceited that I should pretend that my Lady Lostris would not have achieved this recognition without my help. Her beauty and her cleverness and her sweet, warm nature must have made her a favourite in any circumstances. I only suggest that I was able to make it happen a little sooner and a little more certainly.

Our success brought with it some drawbacks. As always, there was jealousy from those who felt themselves displaced in Pharaoh's favour, and there was also the matter of Pharaoh's mounting carnal interest in my mistress. This was aggravated by the period of abstinence that I had enforced upon him.

One evening in his tent after I had administered his rhinoceros horn, he confided in me, 'Taita, this cure of yours is really most efficacious. I have not felt so virile since I was a young man, way back before my coronation and my divinity. This morning when I awoke I had a stiffening of the member which was so gratifying that I sent for Aton to view it. He was mightily impressed and he wished forthwith to fetch your mistress.'

I was thoroughly alarmed by this news, and I put on my sternest expression and shook my head and sucked air through my teeth and tut-tutted to show my disapproval. 'I am grateful for your good sense in not agreeing to Aton's suggestion, Your Majesty. It could so easily have undone all our efforts. If you want a son, then you must follow my regime meticulously.'

This brought home to me the swift passage of time, and how soon the ninety days of grace would be up. I began to condition my mistress for that night which Pharaoh would soon insist upon.

First I must prepare her mind, and I set about this by pointing out to her that it was inevitable, and that if she wished to outlive the king and eventually to go to Tanus, then she would have to submit to the king's will. She was always a sensible girl.

'Then you will have to explain exactly what it is he expects of me, Taita,' she sighed. I was not the best guide in this area. My personal experience had been ephemeral, but I was able to outline the fundamentals and to make it seem so commonplace as not to alarm her unduly.

'Will it hurt?' she wanted to know, and I hastened to reassure her.

'The king is a kind man. He has much experience of young girls. I am sure he will be

256

gentle with you. I will prepare an ointment for you that will make things much easier. I will apply it every night before you retire. It will open the gateway. Think to yourself that one day Tanus will pass through those same portals, and that you are doing this to welcome him and no other.'

I tried to remain the aloof physician and take no sensual pleasure in what I had to do to help her. The gods forgive me, but I failed in my resolution. She was so perfect in her womanly parts as to overshadow the most lovely blossom that I had ever raised in my garden. No desert rose ever bore petals so exquisite. When I smoothed the ointment upon them they raised their own sweet dew, more oleaginous and silky to the touch than any unguent that I could concoct.

Her cheeks turned rosy and her voice was husky as she murmured, 'Up until now, I thought that part of me was meant for only one purpose. Why is it that when you do that, I long so unbearably for Tanus?'

She trusted me so implicitly, and had so little understanding of these unfamiliar sensations, that it required the exercise of all my ethics as a physician to proceed with the treatment only as long as was necessary. However, I slept only fitfully that night, haunted by dreams of the impossible.

As we sailed deeper into the south, so the belts of green land on each side of the river narrowed. Now the desert began to squeeze in upon us. In places brooding cliffs of black granite trod the verdant fields under foot and pressed so close as to overhang the turgid waters of the Nile.

The most forbidding of these narrows was known as the Gates of Hapi, and the waters were whipped into a wild and wilful temper as they boiled through the gap in the high cliffs.

We made the passage of the Gates of Hapi, and came at last to Elephantine, the largest of a great assembly of islands that were strung through the throat of the Nile, where the harsh hills constricted its flow and forced it through the narrows.

Elephantine was shaped like a monstrous shark pursuing the shoal of lesser islands up the narrows. On either side of the river the encroaching deserts were distinct in colour and character. On the west bank, the Saharan dunes were hot orange and savage as the Bedouin who were the only mortals able to survive amongst them. To the east, the Arabian desert was dun and dirty grey, studded with black hills that danced dreamlike in the heat mirage. These deserts had one thing in common—both of them were killers of men.

What a delightful contrast was Elephantine Island, set like a glistening green jewel in the silver crown of the river. It took its name from the smooth grey granite boulders that clustered along its bank like a herd of the huge pachyderms and also from the fact that the trade in ivory brought

258

down from the savage land of Cush beyond the cataract had for a thousand years centred upon this place.

Pharaoh's palace sprawled over most of the island, and the wags suggested that he had chosen to build it here at the southernmost point in his kingdom to be as far from the red pretender in the north as possible.

The wide stretch of water that surrounded the island secured it from the attack of an enemy, but the remainder of the city had overflowed on to both main banks. After great Thebes, west and east Elephantine together made up the largest and most populous city in the Upper Kingdom, a worthy rival to Memphis, the seat of the red pretender in the Lower Kingdom.

As at no other place in the whole of Egypt, Elephantine Island was clad with trees. Their seeds had been brought down by the river on a thousand annual floods, and they had taken root in the fertile loams that had themselves been transported by the restless waters.

On my last visit to Elephantine, when I had come up-river to do a survey of the river gauges for my Lord Intef in his capacity as Guardian of the Waters, I had spent many months on the island. With the assistance of the head gardener, I had catalogued the names and natural histories of all the plants in the palace gardens, so I was able to point them out to my mistress. There were *ficus* trees the like of which had never been seen elsewhere in Egypt. Their fruits grew not upon the branch but on the main trunk, and their roots twisted and writhed together like mating pythons. There were dragon's blood trees whose bark, when

259

cut, poured out a bright red sap. There were Cushite sycamores and a hundred other varieties that spread a shady green umbrella over the lovely little island.

The royal palace was built upon the solid granite that lay below the fertile soil and formed the skeleton of the island. I have often wondered that our kings, the long line of pharaohs of fifty dynasties that stretches back over a thousand years, have each of them devoted so much of his life and treasure to the building of vast and eternal tombs of granite and marble, while in their lifetimes they have been content to live in palaces with mud walls and thatched roofs. In comparison to the magnificent funerary temple that I was building for Pharaoh Mamose at Karnak, this palace was a very modest affair, and the dearth of straight lines and symmetry offended the instincts of both the mathematician and the architect in me. I suppose the sprawling jumble of red clay walls and roofs canted at odd angles did have a sort of bucolic charm, yet I itched to get out my ruler and plumb-line.

Once we had gone ashore and found the quarters that had been set aside for us, the true appeal of Elephantine was even more apparent. Naturally we were lodged in the walled harem on the northern tip of the island, but the size and the furnishings of our lodgings confirmed our favoured position, not only with the king but with his chamberlain as well. Aton had made the allocation, and he, like most others, had proved completely defenceless against my mistress's natural charm, and was now one of her most shameless admirers.

He placed at our disposal a dozen spacious and airy rooms with our own courtyard and kitchens. A side-gate in the main wall led directly down to the riverside and a stone jetty. That very first day I purchased a flat-bottomed skiff which we could use for fishing and water-fowling. I kept it moored at the jetty.

As to the rest of our new home, however comfortable it might have been, neither my mistress nor I was satisfied, and we immediately set about improving and beautifying it. With the cooperation of my old friend the head gardener, I laid out and planted our own private garden in the courtyard, with a thatched barrazza under which we could sit in the heat of the day, and where I kept my Saker falcons tethered on their perches.

At the jetty I set up a shadoof to lift from the river a constant flow of water that I led through ceramic pipes to our own water-garden with lily-ponds and fish-pools. The overflow from the pools drained away in a narrow gutter. This gutter I directed through the wall of my mistress's chamber, across a screened corner of the room and out the far side, from whence it returned to the main flow of the Nile. I carved a stool of fragrant cedar wood, with a hole through the seat, and placed this over the gutter so that anything dropped through the bottom of the seat would be borne away by the never-ending flow of water. My mistress was delighted with this innovation and spent far more time perched upon the stool than was really necessary to accomplish the business for which it was originally intended.

The walls of our quarters were bare red clay. We designed a set of frescoes for each room. I drew the

261

cartoons and transposed them on to the walls and then my mistress and her maids painted in the designs. The frescoes were scenes from the mythology of the gods, with fanciful landscapes peopled by wonderful animals and birds. Of course, I used my Lady Lostris as my model for the figure of Isis, but was it any wonder that the figure of Horus was central to every painting, or that on the insistence of my mistress, he was depicted as having red-gold hair and that he looked amazingly familiar?

The frescoes caused a stir throughout the harem and every one of the royal wives took turns to visit us, to drink sherbet and to view the paintings. We had set a fashion, and I was prevailed upon to advise on the redecoration of most of the private apartments in the harem, at a suitable fee, of course. In this process we made many new friends amongst the royal ladies and added considerably to our financial estate.

Very soon the king heard about the decorations and came in person to examine them. Lostris gave him the grand tour of her chambers. Pharaoh noticed her new water-stool of which my mistress was so proud that when the king asked her to demonstrate it for him she did so without hesitation, perching upon it and giggling as she sent a tinkling stream into the gutter.

She was still so innocent as not to realize the effect that this display had upon her husband. I could tell by his expression that any attempt that I might make to delay him beyond the promised ninety days was likely to be difficult.

After the tour, Pharaoh sat under the barrazza and drank a cup of wine while he actually laughed aloud at some of my mistress's sallies. At last he turned to me. 'Taita, you must build me a water-garden and a barrazza just like this—only much bigger, and whilst you are about it, you can make a water-stool for me as well.'

When at last he was ready to leave, he commanded me to walk a little way alone with him, ostensibly to discuss the new water-garden, but I knew better. No sooner had we left the harem than he was at me.

'Last night I dreamed of your mistress,' he told me, 'and when I awoke, I found that my seed had spilled out upon the sheets. That has not happened to me since I was a boy. This little vixen of yours has begun to fill my thoughts both sleeping and waking. I have no doubt that I can make a son with her, and that we should delay no longer. What do you think, doctor, am I not yet ready for the attempt?'

'I counsel you most strongly to observe the ninety days, Majesty. To make the attempt before that would be folly.' It was dangerous to label the king's desire as folly, but I was desperate to contain it. 'It would be most unwise to spoil all our chances of success for so short a period of time.' In the end I prevailed, and left him looking glummer than ever.

When I returned to the harem, I warned my mistress of the king's intentions, and so thoroughly had I conditioned her to accept the inevitable that she showed no undue distress. She was by this time completely resigned to her role as the king's favourite, while my promise that there would be a term to her captivity here on Elephantine Island made it easier for her to bear. In all fairness, our

263

sojourn on the island could not truly be described as captivity. We Egyptians are the most civilized men on earth. We treat our women well. I have heard of others, the Hurrians and the Cushites and the Libyans, for example, who are most cruel and unnatural towards their wives and daughters.

The Libyans make of the harem a true prison in which the women live their entire lives without sight of a living male apart from the eunuchs and the children. They say that even male dogs and cats are forbidden to pass through the gates, so great is their possessive frenzy.

The Hurrians are even worse. Not only do they confine their women and make them cover their bodies from ankle to wrist, but they force them to go masked as well, even within the confines of the harem. Thus only a woman's husband ever lays eyes upon her face.

The primitive tribes of Cush are the worst of all of them. When their women reach the age of puberty they circumcise them in the most savage manner. They cut away the clitoris and the inner lips of the vagina to remove the seat of sexual pleasure so that they may never be tempted to stray from their husbands.

This may seem so bizarre as to defy belief, but I have seen the results of this brutal surgery with my own eyes. Three of my mistress's slave girls were captured by the slavers only after they were matured and had been subjected to the knife by their own fathers. When I examined the gaping, scar-puckered pits they had been left with, I was sickened, and my instincts as a healer were deeply offended by this mutilation of that masterpiece of the gods, the human body. It has been my observation that this circumcision does not achieve its object, for it seems to deprive the victim of the most desirable female traits, and leaves her cold and calculating and cruel. She becomes a sexless monster.

On the other hand, we Egyptians honour our women and treat them, if not as equals, at least with consideration. No husband may beat his wife without recourse to the magistrate, and he has a legal duty to dress and feed and maintain her in accordance with his own station in society. A wife of the king, or of one of the nobles, is not confined to the harem, but, if suitably escorted by her entourage, may walk abroad in city street or countryside. She is not forced to hide her charms, but, according to the fashion of the moment and her own whim, she may sit at her husband's dinner-table with her face uncovered and her breasts bared, and entertain his male companions with conversation and song.

She may hold, in her own right, slaves and land and fortune separately from the estate of her husband, although the children she bears belong to him alone. She may fish, and fly hawks, and even practise archery, although such masculine endeavours as wrestling and swordsmanship are forbidden to her. There are, quite rightly, certain activities from which she is barred, such as the practice of law and architecture, but a high-born wife is a person of consequence, possessed of legal rights and dignity. Naturally it is not the same for the concubine or for the wife of a common man. They have the same rights as the bullock or the donkey.

Thus my mistress and I were free to wander

abroad to explore the twin cities on each bank of the Nile and the surrounding countryside. In the streets of Elephantine my Lady Lostris was very soon a favourite, and the common people gathered round her to solicit her blessing and her generosity. They applauded her grace and beauty, just as they had done in her native Thebes. I was instructed by her always to carry a large bag of cakes and sweetmeats from which she stuffed the cheeks of every ragamuffin we encountered who seemed to her to require nourishing. Wherever we went, we seemed always to be surrounded by a shrieking, dancing flock of children.

My mistress always seemed happy to sit in the doorway of a poor shanty with the housewife, or under a tree in the field of a peasant farmer and listen to their woes and grievances. At the first opportunity she would take these up with Pharaoh. Often he would smile indulgently and agree to the redress that she suggested. So her reputation as a champion of the common man was born. When she passed through even the saddest, poorest quarters of the city, she left smiles and laughter behind her.

On other days we fished together from our little skiff in the backwaters of the lagoons that the inundation of the Nile had created, or we laid out decoys for the wild duck. I had made a special bow for my mistress which was suited to her strength. Of course, it was nothing like the great bow, Lanata, that I had designed for Tanus, but it was adequate for the water-fowl we were after. My Lady Lostris was a better marksman than most men I have watched at the archery butts, and when she loosed an arrow it was very seldom that I was not required to plunge overside and swim out to retrieve the carcass of a duck or a goose.

Whenever the king went out hawking, my mistress was invited to attend. I would walk behind her with my Saker falcons on my arm, as we skirted the edge of the papyrus beds. As soon as a heron rose with heavy wing-beats from a hidden pool in the reeds, she would take one of the falcons from me and kiss its hooded head. 'Fly fast and true, my beauty!' she would whisper to it, and slip the rufter to unmask the fierce yellow eyes, and launch the splendid little killer aloft.

We would watch entranced as the falcon towered high above the quarry, and then folded those sickle wings and stooped with a speed that made the wind sing over his dappled plumage. The shock of impact carried clearly to us over a distance of two hundred paces. A puff of pale blue feathers was smeared across the darker blue of the sky, and then was carried away like smoke on the river breeze. The falcon bound to its prey with hooked talons to bring it smashing to earth. My mistress shrieked in triumph and ran as fast as a boy to retrieve the bird, to lavish praise upon it and pamper it, and then to feed it the severed head of the heron.

I love all creatures of the water and the land and the air. My mistress has the same feelings. Why is it then, I often wonder, that both of us are so moved by these sports of the chase? I have puzzled over it without finding an answer. Perhaps it is simply that man, and woman also, are the earth's fiercest predator. We feel a kinship with the falcon, with his beauty and his speed. The heron and the goose were given to the falcon by the gods as his rightful prey. In the same way, man has been given dominance over all other creatures on earth. We cannot deny these instincts with which the gods have endowed us.

From the earliest age, when she had first developed the strength and the stamina to stay with us, I had allowed my Lady Lostris to accompany Tanus and myself on our hunting and fishing forays. For, perhaps to mask his hatred of his rival, Lord Harrab, my Lord Intef consented to my hunting sorties with young Tanus.

Years before, Tanus and I had taken possession of a deserted fisherman's shack which we had discovered on the fringe of the swamp below Karnak. We had made this our secret hunting-lodge. It was only a short distance from the shack to the edge of the true desert. So from this comfortable base we had the options of fishing the lagoon or of wild-fowling or of hawking that noble bird, the giant bustard, in the open desert.

In the beginning Tanus had resented the intrusion of this gawky nine-year-old girl, skinny and flat-chested as a boy, into our private world. Soon, however, he had grown accustomed to her presence and even found it convenient to have someone to run errands for him and perform the irksome little chores around camp.

Thus, little by little, Lostris had picked up the lore and the wisdom of the outdoors, until she knew every fish and bird by its proper name, and could wield a harpoon or a hunting-bow with equal skill. In the end Tanus had become as proud of her as if it had been he who had invited her to join us in the first place.

She had been with us in the black rock hills

above the river valley on the day that Tanus had hunted the cattle-killer. The lion was a scarred old male with a black mane that waved like a field of corn in the wind as he walked, and a voice like the thunder of the heavens. We set my pack of hounds upon him and followed them as they bayed the lion up from the paddock beside the Nile where he had killed his last bullock. The dogs cornered him at the head of a rocky defile. The lion fixed on us as soon as we came up and brushed the dogs aside as he charged through them.

As he came grunting and roaring towards us, my mistress had stood unwavering, only a pace behind Tanus' left shoulder, with her own puny little bow at full draw. Of course, it had been Tanus who had killed the beast, sending an arrow from the great bow Lanata hissing down his gaping throat, but we had both seen Lady Lostris' courage displayed in full measure.

I think it was probably on that day that Tanus first became aware of his true feelings for her, while for my mistress, the hunt and the chase were for ever bound up with the images and memories of her lover. She had remained ever since an avid huntress. She had learned from Tanus and myself to respect and to love the quarry, but not to burden herself with guilt when she exercised her god-given rights over the other creatures of the earth, to use them as beasts of burden, to consume them as food, or to pursue them as game.

We may have dominance over the beasts, but in the same way, all men and women are Pharaoh's cattle, and none may gainsay him. Promptly on the ninetieth night the king sent Aton to fetch my mistress.

Because of our friendship and his own feelings for my mistress, Aton had given me ample warning before he came. I was able to make my final preparations well in advance of his arrival.

For the last time I rehearsed my mistress in exactly what to say to the king and how to behave towards him. Then I applied the ointment that I had reserved for this occasion. It was not only a lubricant, but contained also the essence of a herb that I use on other patients to deaden the pain of tooth-ache and other minor afflictions. It had the property of numbing the sensitive mucous membranes of the body.

She was brave right up to the moment that Aton appeared in the doorway of her chamber, and then her courage deserted her and she turned to me with tears brimming against her lids. 'I cannot go alone. I am afraid. Please come with me, Taita.' She was pale beneath the make-up that I had applied so carefully, and a fit of shivering took hold of her so that her small white teeth chattered together softly.

'Mistress, you know that is not possible. Pharaoh has sent for you. This once I cannot help you.'

It was then that Aton came to her aid. 'Perhaps Taita could wait in the ante-chamber of the king's bedroom, with me. After all, he is the royal physician, and his services may be needed,' he suggested in his reedy voice, and my mistress stood on tiptoe to kiss his fat cheek.

'You are so kind, Aton,' she whispered, and he

blushed.

My Lady Lostris held my hand tightly as we followed Aton through the labyrinth of passages to the king's apartments. In the ante-chamber she squeezed it hard, and then dropped my hand and went to the doorway to the king's chamber. She paused and looked back at me. She had never looked so lovely or so young and vulnerable. My heart was breaking, but I smiled at her to give her courage. She turned from me and stepped through the curtains. I heard the murmur of the king's voice as he greeted her and her soft reply.

Aton seated me on a stool at the low table, then without a word set up the bao board between us. I played without attention, moving the polished round stones in the cups carved into the wooden board, and Aton won three quick games in succession. He had very seldom beaten me before, but I was distracted by the voices from the room beyond, although they were too low for me to catch the actual words.

Then quite clearly I heard my mistress say, exactly as I had coached her, 'Please, Your Majesty, be gentle with me. I beseech you, do not hurt me,' and the appeal was so moving that even Aton coughed softly and blew his nose upon his sleeve, while it was all I could do to restrain myself from leaping to my feet and rushing through the curtain to drag her away.

For a while there was silence and then a single high, sobbing cry that rent my soul, and once again silence.

Aton and I sat hunched over the bao board, no longer making any pretence at playing. I do not know how long we waited, but it must have been in the last watch of the night when I heard at last the sound of an old man's snores from beyond the curtain. Aton looked up at me and nodded, then he rose ponderously to his feet.

Before he reached the curtains, they parted, and my mistress stepped through them and came directly to where I sat. 'Take me home, Taita,' she whispered.

Without thinking about it I picked her up in my arms, and she hugged me around the neck and laid her head on my shoulder, just like she used to as a little girl. Aton took up the oil lamp and lit the way for us back to the harem. He left us at the door to my mistress's bedchamber. I laid her on the bed, and while she drowsed I examined her gently. There was a little blood, just a smear of it on those silken thighs, but it had staunched itself.

'Is there any pain, my little one?' I asked softly, and she opened her eyes and shook her head.

Then quite unexpectedly she smiled at me. 'I don't know what all the fuss was about,' she murmured. 'In the end, it was not much worse than using your water-stool, and it didn't take much longer either.' And she curled herself in a ball and fell asleep without another sound.

I almost wept with relief. All my preparations and the numbing herbs I had employed had seen her through without damage to either her body or her sweet spirit.

In the morning we went out hawking as though nothing untoward had happened, and my mistress mentioned the subject only once during the day. As we picnicked on the bank of the river, she asked thoughtfully, 'Will it be the same with Tanus, do you think, Taita?'

'No, mistress. You and Tanus love each other. It will be different. It will be the most wonderful moment in your entire life,' I assured her.

'Yes, I know deep in my heart that is how it should be,' she whispered, and involuntarily both of us looked northwards along the sweep of the Nile, towards Karnak far below the horizon.

Although I knew well where my duty towards Tanus lay, life on the island was so idyllic, and I so much enjoyed the exclusive company of my mistress, that I delayed my departure with the excuse that she still needed me. In truth, although Pharaoh sent for her night after night, my mistress had a tough and resilient streak in her and was blessed with the instinct of survival in full measure. Very swiftly she learned how to please the king, but at the same time to remain untouched and emotionally unmoved by it. She did not need me as much as Tanus did. Indeed, it was she who began to nag me to leave her at Elephantine and to journey down-river once again.

I procrastinated until one evening, after a full day out in the field with the king, we returned late to the palace. I saw to it that my mistress was bathed and her evening meal was laid out for her before I went to my own rooms.

273

As I entered my chamber the delicious odour of ripe mangoes and pomegranates filled the air. In the centre of the floor stood a large closed basket which I could tell was filled with these two favourite fruits of mine. I was not surprised to find it there, for never a day passed without gifts being sent to my mistress and me by someone seeking our favours.

I wondered who it was this time, and my mouth filled with saliva as another whiff of the fragrance filled my nostrils. I had not eaten since noon. As I lifted the woven lid and reached for the reddest and ripest of the pomegranates, the fruit spilled and rolled across the floor. There was a sharp hissing sound and a great black ball of writhing coils and gleaming scales flopped out of the basket and lashed out at my legs.

I leaped backwards, but not fast enough. The open jaws of the serpent struck the leather heel of my sandal with such force that I very nearly lost my balance. A cloud of venom was released from the curved fangs. The clear but deadly fluid drenched the skin of my ankle, but with another leap, I managed to evade the second strike that followed immediately upon the first. I threw myself back against the wall in the far corner of the room.

The cobra and I confronted each other across the width of the floor. Half its body was coiled upon itself, but the front portion of it was raised as high as my shoulder. Its hood was extended to display the broad black and white bands which patterned it. Like some dreadful black lily of death swaying upon its stem, it watched me with those glittering, beady eyes, and I realized that it stood between me and the only door to the chamber.

It is true that some cobras are kept as pets. They are given the run of the household, and they keep down the numbers of rats and mice that infest the building. They will drink milk from a jug and become as tame as kittens. There are others of these serpents that are trained by methods of torment and provocation to become deadly tools of the assassin. I was in no doubt as to which kind of cobra this was standing before me now.

I sidled along the wall, trying to outflank it and to reach safety. It launched itself at me, and the gape of its jaw was a pale sickly yellow and tendrils of venom drooled from the tips of its fangs. Involuntarily I yelled with terror as I sprang away from it and cowered in my corner again. The serpent recovered swiftly from the strike, and reared upright. It was still between me and the doorway. I knew that its poison sacs were charged with sufficient venom to kill a hundred strong men. As I watched, its lower body uncoiled slowly and it began to glide across the floor towards me, its flaring head held high and those terrible, bright little eyes fastened upon me.

I have seen one of these snakes mesmerize a fowl so that it made no move to escape at this sinuous approach, but lay before it with a patent air of resignation. I was paralyzed in the same way, and found that I could neither move nor cry out again as death glided towards me.

Then suddenly I saw a movement beyond the swaying cobra. My Lady Lostris appeared in the doorway, summoned by my first terrified cry. I found my voice again, and I screamed at her, 'Be careful! Come no closer!'

She paid no heed to my warning as she took in

the scene at a glance. A moment's delay or hesitation on her part, and the serpent would have struck at me for the third and last time. My mistress had been at her dinner when she heard my cry for help. She stood now with a half-eaten melon in one hand and a silver knife in the other, and she reacted with the swift instinct of a true huntress.

Tanus had taught her to forsake the awkward double-jointed manner of throwing that is natural to the female, and she hurled the melon she held with the force and aim of a trained javelineer. It struck the cobra upon the back of its extended hood, and for a fleeting instant the blow knocked it flat upon the tiled floor. Like the release of a war bow, the serpent whipped erect and turned its dreadful head towards my mistress and then sped at her across the room in full attack.

I was released from my trance at last and started forward to help her, but I was too slow. Using its tail as a fulcrum, the cobra swung forward and aimed at her with its jaws so widely distended that venom sprayed from its erect fangs in a fine, pale mist. My mistress leaped back, agile and swift as a gazelle before the rush of the hunting cheetah. The cobra missed its strike, and for an instant the impetus threw it flat at her feet, extended to its full glistening, scaly length.

I do not know what possessed her, but she had never lacked in courage. Before the cobra could recover, she hopped forward again and landed with both those neat little sandalled feet upon the back of its head, pinning it to the tiles with her full weight.

Perhaps she had expected to crush its spine, but

the snake was as thick as her wrist and resilient as the lash of Rasfer's whip. Although its head was pinned, the rest of its long body whipped up and over and coiled around her legs. A woman of lesser sense and nerve might have tried to escape that loathsome embrace. If she had done so my mistress would have died, for the instant the cobra's head was freed the death-strike would have followed.

Instead, she kept both feet planted firmly upon the writhing serpent, spreading her arms to balance herself, and she screamed out, 'Help me, Taita!'

I was already halfway across the room, and now I dived full length and thrust my hands into the coils of the serpent's body that boiled around her legs. I groped along its sinuous length, down to where it narrowed into the neck, and I seized it and locked both my hands around the cobra's throat, with my fingers entwined.

'I have him!' I yelled, almost incoherent with my own horror and loathing for this cold, scaly creature that struggled in my grip. 'I have him! Get away from us! Stand clear!'

My mistress leaped back obediently, and I came to my feet clutching the creature with a frantic strength, trying to keep its gaping jaws away from my face. The tail whipped back and wound around my shoulders and my neck, threatening to strangle me as I clung to the head. With this grip upon me the snake now had purchase, and its strength was terrifying. I found that I could not hold it, even with both my fists locked around its throat. It was gradually forcing its head free, drawing it inexorably back through my fingers. I realized that

277

the instant it broke out of my grip, it would lash out at my unprotected face.

'I can't hold it!' I screamed, more to myself than to Lady Lostris. I was holding it at arm's-length, but it was pulling itself towards my face, drawing closer to my eyes every moment as waves of power pulsed through it, contracting and tightening the coils around my throat, forcing the head back through my fingers.

Although my knuckles were white with the strength of my grip, the cobra was so close to my face that I could see the fangs flicking back and forth in the roof of its wide gaping jaws. The cobra was able to erect or to flatten them at will. They were bony white needles, and pale, smoky jets of venom spurted from their tips. I knew that if even a droplet of that poison entered my eyes, it would blind me, and the burning pain of it might drive me half-mad.

I twisted the snake's head away from my face so that the spray of poison was discharged into the air, and I screamed again in despair, 'Call one of the slaves to help me!'

'On the table!' my mistress spoke close beside me. 'Hold its head on the table!' I was startled. I had thought that she had obeyed my order and run to find help, but she was at my side, and I saw that she still brandished the silver table-knife.

Carrying the cobra with me, I staggered across the floor and fell to my knees beside the low table. With a supreme effort I managed to force the snake's head down across one edge of the table, and to hold it there. It gave my mistress a chopping-block against which to wield the knife. She hacked at the base of the cobra's neck, behind

278

the hideous head.

The snake felt the first cut and redoubled its struggles. Coil after coil of rubbery flesh lashed and contorted around my head. Hissing bursts of air flew from its gape, almost deafening us, the awful din mingling with the spurts of venom from its fangs.

The little blade was sharp, and the scaly flesh parted under it. Slippery, cool, ophidian blood welled up over my fingers, but the blade bit down to the bone of the spine. With all her strength and with her face contorted by the effort, my mistress sawed at the bone, but now my fingers were lubricated by the cobra's blood. I felt the head slither out between them and the serpent was free, but at the same moment the knife found the joint between the vertebrae and slipped through, cleaving the spine.

Dangling by a thread of skin, the head was thrown about loosely by the cobra's death-throes. Although almost severed from the body, the fangs still flickered and oozed poison. The lightest touch would be enough to drive them into my flesh. I tore at the body with frenzied, bloody fingers and at last managed to unwind it from around my throat, and to hurl it to the floor.

As the two of us backed away to the door, the snake continued its grotesque contortions, knotting itself and coiling into a ball, scaly turns sliding over each other.

'Are you harmed, my lady?' I asked, without being able to tear my eyes away from the death-throes of the carcass. 'Is there any of the venom in your eyes or on your skin?'

'I am all right,' she whispered. 'And you, Taita?'

The tone of her voice alarmed me enough to make me forget my own distress, and I looked at her face. The reaction from danger had already seized her, and she was beginning to shake. Her dark green eyes were too large to fit that glassy white face. I had to find some way to release her from the icy grip of shock.

'Well,' I said briskly, 'that takes care of tomorrow evening's dinner. I do so love a nice piece of roast cobra.'

For a moment she stared at me blankly and then she let out a peal of hysterical laughter. My own laughter was no less wild and unrestrained. We clung helplessly to each other and laughed until tears poured down our cheeks.

I would not trust our cook with it, so I prepared the cobra myself. I skinned and gutted it and stuffed it with wild garlic and other herbs, together with a dollop of mutton fat from the tail of a prime ram. Then I coiled it in a ball and wrapped it in banana leaves and covered the whole bundle with a thick coating of wet clay. I built over the lump of clay a hot fire which I kept burning all day.

That evening when I cracked open the hard-baked ball of clay, the aroma released by the succulent white flesh flooded our mouths with saliva. There are those who have dined at my table who say they have never eaten tastier food than that which I prepare, and who am I to contradict my friends?

I served the flaky fillets to my mistress with a

wine of five-palm quality that Aton had chanced upon in Pharaoh's store-rooms. My Lady Lostris insisted that I sit with her under the barrazza in the courtyard and share the meal. We agreed that it was better than the tail of crocodile, or even than the flesh of the finest perch from the Nile.

It was only when we had eaten our fill and sent the rest of it to her slave maidens that we broached the matter of who it was that had sent me the gift of the basket of fruit.

I tried not to alarm my mistress, and made a joke of it: 'It must have been somebody who does not like my singing!' However, she was not to be put off so easily.

'Don't play the clown with me, Taita. It is one direction in which you have little talent. I think you know who it was, and I think I do as well.'

I stared at her, not sure how to deal with what I suspected was coming. I had always protected her, even from the truth. I wondered how far she had seen through me.

'It was my father,' she said with such finality that there was no reply or denial I could give her. 'Tell me about him, Taita. Tell me all the things I should know about him, but which you never dared tell me.'

It came hard at first. A lifetime of reticence cannot be overcome in a moment. It was still difficult to realize that I was no longer completely under the thrall of Lord Intef. Deeply as I had always hated him, he had dominated me body and soul since my childhood, and there persisted a kind of perverse loyalty that made it difficult for me to speak out freely against him. Weakly I attempted to fob her off with only the barest outlines of her

281

father's clandestine activities, but she cut across me impatiently.

'Come now! Don't take me for a fool. I know more about my father than you ever dreamed. It is time for me to learn the rest of it. I charge you straight, tell me everything.'

So I obeyed her, and there was so much to tell that the full moon was halfway up the sky before I was done. We sat in silence for a long time afterwards. I had left out nothing, nor had I tried to deny or to excuse my own part in any of it.

'No wonder he wants you dead,' she whispered at last. 'You know enough to destroy him.' She was silent a little longer, and then she went on, 'My father is a monster. How is it possible that I am any different from him? Why, as his daughter, am I not also possessed by such unnatural instincts?'

'We must thank all the gods that you are not. But mistress, do you not despise me also for what I have done?'

She reached across and touched my hand. 'You forget that I have known you all my life, since the day that my mother died giving birth to me. I know what you really are. Anything you did, you were forced to do, and freely I forgive you for it.'

She sprang to her feet and paced restlessly around the lily pond before she returned to where I sat.

'Tanus is in terrible danger from my father. I never realized just how much until this evening. He must be warned so that he will be able to protect himself. You must go to him now, Taita, without delaying another day.'

'Mistress—' I began, but she cut me off

brusquely.

'No, Taita, I will not listen to any more of your sly excuses. You will leave for Karnak tomorrow.'

So before sunrise the next morning I set out fishing, alone in the skiff. However, I made certain that at least a dozen slaves and sentries saw me leave the island.

In a backwater of the lagoon I opened the leather bag in which I had concealed a tom-cat that had befriended me. He was a sad old animal riddled with mange and with agonizing canker in both ears. For some time I had been steeling myself to give him release from his misery. Now I fed him a lump of raw meat laced with Datura essence. I held him on my lap and stroked him as he ate, and he purred contentedly. As soon as he slipped painlessly into oblivion, I cut his throat.

I sprinkled the blood over the skiff, and dropped the carcass of the cat overboard where I knew that the crocodiles would soon dispose of it. Then, leaving my harpoons and lines and other gear on board, I pushed the skiff out into the slow current and waded through the papyrus beds to hard ground.

We had agreed that my mistress would wait until nightfall before she raised the alarm. It would be noon tomorrow before they found the blood-smeared skiff and concluded that I had been taken by a crocodile or been murdered by a band of the Shrikes.

Once I was ashore, I changed swiftly into the

costume I had brought with me. I had chosen to impersonate one of the priests of Osiris. I would often ape their stilted gait and pompous manners for the amusement of my mistress. It needed only a wig, a touch of make-up and the correct costume to make the transformation. The priests are always on the move, up and down along the river, travelling between one temple and another, begging or rather demanding alms along the way. I would excite little interest, and my disguise might help to discourage an attack by the Shrikes. On superstitious grounds they were often reluctant to interfere with the holy men.

I skirted the lagoon and entered the town of West Elephantine through the poor quarter. At the docks I approached one of the barge captains who was loading a cargo of corn in leather bags and clay jugs of oil. With the right degree of arrogance I demanded free passage to Karnak in the name of the god, and he shrugged and spat on the deck, but allowed me to come aboard. All men are resigned to the extortions of the brotherhood. They may despise the priests, but they also fear their power, both spiritual and secular. Some say that the priesthood wields almost as much power as does Pharaoh himself.

The moon was full and the barge captain a more intrepid mariner than Admiral Nembet. We did not anchor at night. With the breeze and the full flood of the Nile behind us, we made a fair passage and on the fifth day rounded the bend of the river and saw the city of Karnak lying before us.

My stomach was queasy as I went ashore, for this was my town and every beggar and idler knew me well. If I were recognized, Lord Intef would hear about it before I could reach the city gates. However, my disguise held up, and I kept to the back alleys as I hurried in a purposeful and priestly manner to Tanus' house near the squadron base.

His front door was unbarred. I entered as though I had the right, and closed the door securely behind me. The starkly furnished rooms were deserted and when I searched them, I found nothing to give me any indication of his whereabouts. Tanus had obviously been gone for a long time, possibly since my mistress and I had left Karnak. The milk in a jug by the window had thickened and dried like hard cheese, and a crust of sorghum bread on the plate beside it was covered with a blue mould.

As far as I could see, nothing was missing; even the bow Lanata still hung on its rack above his bed. For Tanus to have left that was extraordinary. Usually it was like an extension of his body. I hid it away carefully in a secret compartment below his sleeping-place, which I had built for him when first he had moved into these lodgings. I wished to avoid moving around the city in daylight, so I remained in Tanus' rooms for the rest of that afternoon, occupying myself with cleaning up the dust and filth that had accumulated.

At nightfall I slipped out and went down to the riverside. I saw immediately that the *Breath of Horus* was at her moorings. She had obviously been in action since last I had seen her, and had suffered battle damage. Her bows were shattered and her timbers amidships had been scorched and charred.

I noted with a stir of proprietary pride that Tanus had made the modifications to her hull that

I had designed. The gilded metal horn protruded from her bows, just above the water-line. From its battered condition I surmised that it had done fierce execution amongst the fleets of the red pretender.

However, I could see that neither Tanus nor Kratas was on deck. A junior officer whom I recognized had the watch, but I discarded the idea of hailing him, and instead set out to tour the sailors' haunts around the area of the docks.

It says a great deal for the morals and the sanctity of the priests of Osiris that I was welcomed in the dives and whorehouses like an habitué. In one of the more respectable taverns I recognized the impressive figure of Kratas. He was drinking and playing at dice with a group of his brother officers. I made no move to approach him, but I watched him across the crowded room. Meanwhile I fended off the advances of a succession of pleasure-birds of both sexes who were progressively lowering their tariffs in their efforts to tempt me out into the dark alleyway to sample their well-displayed charms. None of them were in the least deterred by my priestly collar of blue glass beads.

When Kratas at last gave his companions a hearty goodnight and made his way out into the alley, I followed his tall figure with relief.

'What is it you want from me now, beloved of the gods?' he growled at me with scorn when I hurried up beside him. 'Is it my gold or my bum-splitter you crave?' Many of the priests had taken enthusiastically to this modern vogue for pederasty.

'I'll take the gold,' I told him. 'You have more of

that than the other, Kratas.' He stopped dead in his tracks and stared at me suspiciously. His bluff and handsome features were only a little flushed and befuddled by liquor.

'How do you know my name?' He seized me by the shoulder and dragged me into a lighted doorway, and studied my face. At last he snatched the wig from off my head. 'By the piles between Seth's buttocks, it's you, Taita!' he roared.

'I'd be obliged if you would refrain from shouting out my name to all the world,' I told him, and he turned serious at once.

'Come! We'll go to my rooms.'

Once we were alone, he poured two mugs of beer. 'Haven't you had enough of that?' I asked, and he grinned at me.

'We'll only know the answer to that in the morning. How now, Taita! Don't be too strict with me. We have been down-river raiding the red usurper's fleet for the past three weeks. Sweet Hapi, but that bow-horn of yours works wonders. We cut up nearly twenty of his galleys and we chopped the heads off a couple of hundred of his rascals. Although it was thirsty work, not a drop of anything stronger than water has passed my lips in all that time. Don't begrudge me a mouthful of beer now. Drink with me!' He raised his mug, and I was also thirsty. I saluted him in return, but as I put the mug down again, I asked, 'Where is Tanus?'

He sobered instantly. 'Tanus has disappeared,' he said, and I stared at him.

'Disappeared? What do you mean, disappeared? Did he not lead the raid down-river?'

Kratas shook his head. 'No. He's gone.

287

Vanished. I have had my men scour every street and every house in all of Thebes. There is no sign of him. I tell you, Taita, I am worried, really worried.'

'When did you last see him?'

'Two days after the royal wedding, after the Lady Lostris married the king, on the evening of the day that you sailed with the royal flotilla for Elephantine. I tried to talk some sense into his thick head, but he would not listen.'

'What did he say?'

'He handed over the command of the *Breath of Horus* and the entire squadron to me.'

'He could not do that, surely?'

'Yes, he could. He used the authority of Pharaoh's hawk seal.'

I nodded. 'And then? What did he do?'

'I have just told you. He disappeared.'

I sipped at the mug of beer as I tried to think it out. Meanwhile Kratas went to the window and urinated through it. It splashed noisily into the street below and I heard a startled passer-by shout up at him, 'Careful where you spray, you filthy pig!'

Kratas leaned out and quite cheerfully offered to crack his skull for him, and the man's grumblings receded rapidly. Chortling with this small victory, Kratas came back to me and I asked, 'What mood was Tanus in when he left you?'

Kratas turned serious again. 'The blackest and most ugly temper I have ever witnessed. He cursed the gods and Pharaoh. He even cursed the Lady Lostris and called her a royal whore.'

I winced to hear it. Yet I knew that this was not my Tanus speaking. It was the voice of despairing and hopeless love.

'He said that Pharaoh could carry out his threat to have him strangled for sedition and he would welcome the release. No, he was in terrible straits and there was nothing that I could do or say to comfort him.'

'That was all? He gave you no hint as to what he intended?' Kratas shook his head and refilled his beer mug.

'What happened to the hawk seal?' I asked.

'He left it with me. He said he had no further use for it. I have it safe aboard the *Breath of Horus*.'

'What of the other arrangements that I discussed with you? Have you done what I asked?'

He looked into his mug guiltily and muttered, 'I began to make the arrangements, but after Tanus was gone, there seemed no point to it. Besides, I have been busy down-river since then.'

'It is not like you, Kratas, to be so unreliable.' I had found that with Kratas hurt disappointment was more effective than anger. 'My Lady Lostris was relying on you. She told me that she trusted you completely. Kratas is a great rock of strength—those were her exact words.'

I could see that it was working yet again, for Kratas is also one of my mistress's ardent admirers. Even a hint of her displeasure would move him.

'Damn you, Taita, you make me sound like a weak-kneed idiot—' I kept silent, but silence can be more irksome than words. 'What in the name of Horus does the Lady Lostris want me to do?'

'Nothing more than I asked you to do before I left for Elephantine,' I told him, and he slammed down his mug.

'I am a soldier. I cannot leave my duties and take half the squadron to go off on some mad adventure. It was one thing when Tanus had the hawk seal—'

'You have the hawk seal now,' I told him softly.

He stared at me. 'I cannot use it without Tanus—'

'You are his lieutenant. Tanus gave you the hawk seal to use. You know what to do with it. Do it! I will find Tanus and bring him back, but you must be ready by then. There is desperate and bloody work ahead, and Tanus needs you. Don't let him down, not again.'

He flushed with anger at the jibe. 'I'll make you swallow those words,' he promised.

'And that will be the finest meal you could set for me,' I told him. I love brave and honest men, they are so easily manipulated.

I was uncertain as to how I would make good my promise to find Tanus, but I left Kratas to sleep off his debauch, and I went out into the town again to try. Once more I made the rounds of every one of his old haunts and questioned anyone who could possibly have seen him. I had no illusions as to the risk I was taking in pursuing my enquiries about Tanus, or as to just how flimsy was my disguise if I should run into anybody who knew me well, but I had to find him. I kept going through the night, until even the shebeens and whorehouses along the waterfront had thrown out the last drunken customers and doused their lamps.

As the dawn broke over the river, I stood tired and disconsolate on the bank of the Nile, and tried to think if there was some possibility I had overlooked. A wild honking cry made me look up. High above me a straggling skein of Egyptian geese was outlined against the pale gold and coppery tones of the eastern sky. Immediately they brought to my mind those happy days that the three of us, Tanus and the Lady Lostris and myself, had spent wild-fowling in the swamps.

'Fool!' I reviled myself. 'Of course that's it.'

By this time the alleyways of the souk were filled with a noisy, jostling crowd. Thebes is the busiest city in the world, no man is idle here. They blow glass and work gold and silver, they weave flax and throw pots. The merchant deals and haggles, the lawyer cants, the priest chants and the whore swives. It is an exciting, flamboyant city and I love it.

I forced my way through the throng and the hubbub of banter and bargaining as the merchants and the farmers displayed their wares for the housewives and the bailiffs of the rich households. The souk stank fulsomely of spices and fruits, of vegetables and fish and meats, some of which were far from fresh. Cattle bellowed and goats bleated and added their dung to the human contribution of excrement that trickled down the open gutters towards old Mother Nile.

I thought of buying an ass, for it would be a long walk in this hottest season of the year, and there were some sturdy beasts on offer. In the end I decided against such extravagance, not only on the grounds of economy, for I knew that once I was out in the open countryside, an expensive animal would certainly attract the attention of the Shrikes. For such a prize they might overcome their religious scruples. Instead, I purchased only a few handfuls of dates and a loaf of bread, a leather bag to carry these provisions and a gourd water-bottle. Then I set out through the narrow streets for the main gate of the city.

I had not reached the gates when there was a commotion in the street ahead of me and a detachment of the palace guards came towards me, using their staves to force a passage through the market crowds. Close behind them a half-dozen slaves carried an ornate and curtained litter at a jog-trot. I was trapped against the clay-daub walls of one of the buildings and though I recognized both the litter and the commander of the bodyguards, I could not avoid a confrontation.

Panic seized me. I might survive a casual scrutiny from Rasfer, but I was certain that even under my disguise, my Lord Intef would know me instantly. Standing beside me was an old slave woman with breasts like two great amphorae of olive oil and a backside like a hippopotamus's. I wriggled sideways until her bulk hid me. Then I settled my wig over my eyes and peeped out from behind her.

Despite my fears I felt a tingle of professional pride that Rasfer was on his feet again so soon after my surgery. He led his troop of bodyguards towards where I hid, but it was only when he drew almost level that I noticed that one side of his face had collapsed. It was as though his unlovely features had been modelled in wax and then held close to a naked flame. This condition is often the consequence of even the most skilful trepanning.

The other half of his face was set in its customary scowl. If Rasfer had been hideous before, now he should cause the children to cry and their elders to make the sign against the evil eye when they looked upon him.

He passed close by where I stood, and the litter followed him. Through a chink in the embroidered curtains I caught a glimpse of Lord Intef as he sprawled elegantly on pillows of pure silk imported from the East that must have cost at least five gold rings each.

His cheeks were freshly shaved and his hair was dressed in formal ringlets. On top of his coiffure was set a cone of perfumed beeswax that would melt in the heat and trickle over his scalp and down his neck to cool and soothe his skin. One hand, the fingers stiff with jewelled rings, lay languidly on the smooth brown thigh of a pretty little slave boy who must have been a recent addition to his collection, for I did not recognize him.

I was taken off-guard by the strength of my own hatred as I looked at my old master. All the countless injuries and humiliations that I had suffered at his hands rushed back to torment me, and these were aggravated by his most recent outrage. By sending the cobra to me he had endangered the life of my mistress. If I had been able to forgive all else, I would never be able to forgive him that.

He began to turn his head in my direction, but before our eyes could meet, I sank down behind the mountainous woman in front of me. The litter was borne away down the narrow alley, and as I stared after it, I found that I was trembling just as I had after my struggle with the cobra.

'Divine Horus, hear this plea. Grant me no rest until he is dead and gone to his master, Seth,' I whispered, and I pushed my way on towards the city gate.

The inundation was at its height, and the lands along the river were in the fecund embrace of the Nile. As she had done every season from the beginning of time, she was laying down on our fields another rich layer of black silt. When she receded again, those glistening expanses would once more bloom with that shade of green that is peculiar to this very Egypt. The rich silt and the sunshine would raise three crops to harvest before the Nile poured over its banks once more to deliver its bounty.

The borders of the flooded fields were hemmed with the raised dykes that controlled the flood and also served as roadways. I followed one of these footpaths eastward until I reached the rocky ground along the foothills, then I turned southward. As I went, I paused occasionally to turn over a rock beside the path, until I found what I was looking for. Then I struck out with more determination.

I kept a wary eye on the rough and broken ground on my right-hand side, for that was just the type of terrain that would afford a fine ambush for a band of Shrikes. I was crossing one of the rocky ravines that lay across the pathway when I was hailed from close at hand.

'Pray for me, beloved of the gods!' My nerves

were so tightly strung that I had let out a startled cry and leapt in the air before I could prevent it.

A shepherd boy sat on the edge of the ravine just above me. He was not more than ten years old, but he seemed as old as man's first sin. I knew that the Shrikes often used these children as their scouts and their sentinels. This grubby little imp looked perfect for that role. His hair was matted with filth, and he wore a badly tanned goat's skin that I could smell from where I stood. His eyes were as bright and as avaricious as those of a crow as he ran them over me, assessing my costume and my baggage.

'Where are you headed, and what is your business, good father?' he asked, and blew a long warbling note on his reed flute that could have been a signal to somebody hidden further up the hillside.

It took another few moments for my heart to steady its wild pace, and my voice was a little breathless as I told him, 'You are impertinent, child. What business is it of yours who I am or where I go?'

Immediately he changed his demeanour towards me. 'I am starved, gentle priest, an orphan forced to fend for myself. Don't you have a crust for me in that big bag of yours?'

'You look well-nourished to me.' I turned away, but he scrambled down the bank and danced beside me.

'Let me see in your bag, kind father,' he insisted. 'Alms, I beg of you, gentle sir.'

'Very well, you little ruffian.' Out of the bag I brought a ripe date. He reached out for it, but before his fingers touched it, I closed my hand and when I opened it again the date had been transformed into a purple scorpion. The poisonous insect lifted its tail menacingly over its head, and the boy screamed and fled back up the bank.

At the top he paused only long enough to howl at me, 'You are not a priest. You are one of the desert djinn. You are a devil, not a man.' Frantically he made the sign against the evil eye and spat three times on the ground, and then he raced away up the hill.

I had captured the scorpion from under a flat rock farther back along the path. Naturally, I had nipped the sting from the end of its tail before slipping it into my bag in readiness for just such an eventuality. The old slave who had taught me to read lips, had showed me a few other tricks while he was about it. One of them was sleight-of-hand.

At the shoulder of the next hill I paused to look back. The shepherd boy was on the crest far above me, but he was not alone. There were two men with him. They stood in a group looking down at me, and the child was gesticulating vehemently. As soon as they saw I had spotted them, all three of them disappeared over the skyline. I doubted they would want further truck with a demon priest.

I had not gone much farther when I saw movement on the track ahead of me, and I stopped short and shaded my eyes against the dazzle of the noonday sun. I was relieved to make out a small and innocent-seeming party coming in my direction. I moved forward cautiously to meet it, and as we drew together, my heart leaped as I thought I recognized Tanus. He was leading a donkey. The doughty little animal was heavily burdened. Atop the large bundle on its back sat a woman and a child, but it trotted on gamely. I saw that the woman was herself heavily burdened, her belly swelling out with her pregnancy. The child balanced behind her was a girl on the verge of puberty.

I was about to hail Tanus and hurry forward to meet him, when I realized that I was mistaken and the man was a stranger. It was his tall, broad-shouldered figure, the limber way he moved and the shining shock of gold-blond hair that had deceived me. He was watching me suspiciously and had drawn his sword. Now he pulled the donkey off the path and interposed himself between me and the precious burden it carried.

'The blessings of the gods upon you, good fellow.' I played out my role as priest, and he grunted and kept the point of the sword aimed at my belly. No man trusted a stranger in this very Egypt of ours.

'You risk the life of your family on this road, my friend. You should have sought out the protection of a caravan. There are brigands in the hills.' I was truly worried for them. The woman seemed gentle and decent, while the child was on the verge of tears at my warning.

'Pass on, priest!' the man ordered. 'Keep your advice for those who value it.'

'You are kind, gentle sir,' the woman whispered. 'We waited a week at Qena for the caravan, and could not wait longer. My mother lives at Luxor, and she will help with the birth of my baby.'

'Silence, woman!' her husband growled at her. 'We want no truck with strangers, even though they wear the robes of the priesthood.'

I hesitated, trying to fathom if there was anything that I could do for them. The girl was a pretty little thing with dark obsidian eyes, and she had quite touched my heart. However, at that moment the husband urged the donkey past where I stood, and with a helpless shrug, I watched them go.

'You cannot bleed for all of mankind,' I told myself. 'Nor can you force your advice on those who reject it.' Without looking back again, I went on northwards.

It was late afternoon before I looked down on the spur of rock that thrust out into the green swampland. Even from this vantage-point it was impossible to pick out the shanty. It was hidden deep in the papyrus beds, and the roof was of papyrus stems, so the concealment was perfect. I ran down the path, leaping from rock to rock, until I reached the edge of the water. This far from the main course of the Nile, the flood was not so significant.

I found our old dilapidated boat tied up at the landing. It was half-flooded and I had to bale it out before committing it to the water. I poled out cautiously along the tunnel through the papyrus. At low ebb of the Nile the shanty stood on dry land, but now there was sufficient water under the stilts that supported it to drown a standing man.

There was an empty boat in better shape than mine tied to one of the hut stilts. I moored mine beside it, climbed the rickety ladder and peered into our old hunting-lodge. It consisted of a single room, and the sunshine streamed in through the holes in the thatched roof, but no matter, for it never rains in Upper Egypt.

The hut had not been in such disorder since the day Tanus and I had first discovered it. Clothing and weapons and cooking-pots were scattered around like the debris of a battlefield. The stink of liquor was even more powerful than that of old food and unwashed bodies.

Those unwashed bodies were lying on an equally unwashed mattress in the far corner. I crossed the littered floor gingerly to inspect them for signs of life, and at that moment the woman grunted and rolled over. She was young and her naked body was full and enticing, with big round breasts and a thatch of crisp curls at the base of her belly. However, even in repose, her face was hard and common. I had no doubt that Tanus had found her on the waterfront.

I had always known him to be fastidious, and he was never a drinking man. This creature and the empty wine jars that were stacked against every wall were merely an indication of how far he had been brought down. I looked at him now as he slept, and hardly recognized him. His face was mottled and bloated with drink and covered with untrimmed beard. It was clear that he had not shaved since last I had seen him outside the harem walls.

At that moment the woman woke. Her eyes focused on me and in a single catlike movement she was off the mattress and reaching for the sheathed dagger hanging on the wall beside me. I snatched the weapon away before she could reach it and offered her the naked point.

'Go!' I ordered softly. 'Before I give you something in your belly that even you have never felt before.'

She gathered up her clothes and pulled them on hurriedly, all the while staring at me venomously.

'He has not paid me,' she said, once she was dressed.

'I am sure you have already helped yourself generously.' I gestured towards the door with the dagger.

'He promised me five rings of gold.' She changed her tone and began to whine. 'I have worked hard for him these last twenty days or more. I have done everything for him, cooked and kept his house, serviced him and cleaned up his puke when he was drunk. I must be paid. I will not leave until you pay me—'

I seized her by a lock of her long black hair and ushered her to the doorway. I helped her, still by means of her hair, into the more dilapidated of the two boats. Once she had poled out of my reach, she turned upon me such a stream of abuse that the egrets and other water-fowl were frightened from the reed-beds around us.

When I returned to where Tanus lay, he had not moved. I checked the wine jars. Most of them were empty, but there were still two or three that were full. I wondered how he had accumulated such a store of liquor, and guessed that he had probably sent the woman back to Karnak to find a ferryman to ship it out to him. There had been enough to keep the entire corps of the Blue Crocodile Guards drunk for a season. Little wonder that he was in such a condition.

I sat beside his mattress for a while, letting my sympathy for him run its full course. He had tried to destroy himself. I understood that, and did not despise him for it. His love for my mistress was such that without it he did not wish to continue living.

Of course I was also angry with him for abusing himself in such a fashion, and for succumbing to such self-indulgent folly. However, even in this pitiful drink-sodden state, I could still find much that was noble and admirable about him. After all, he was not alone in guilt. My mistress had tried to take poison for the very same reason as he had tried to destroy himself. I had understood and forgiven her. Could I do less for Tanus? I sighed for these two young people who were all that I had in life of any real value. Then I stood up and got to work.

Firstly, I stood over Tanus for a while, bolstering my anger to the extent that I could be really harsh with him. Then I took him by the heels and dragged him across the floor of the hut. He came half out of his stupor and cursed weakly, but I took no notice of his protests and tumbled him through the doorway. He plunged into the swamp headfirst and raised a mighty splash as he went under. I waited for him to come up and flounder about groggily on the surface, still only half-conscious.

I dropped in beside him, grabbed a double handful of his hair and thrust his head back under-water. For a moment he struggled only weakly and I was able to hold him under with ease. Then his natural instincts of survival took over and he heaved up with all his old strength. I was lifted clear of the surface and thrown aside like a twig in a storm.

Tanus came out bellowing in the effort to draw breath, and striking out blindly at his unseen adversary. One of those blows would have stunned a hippopotamus, and I backed away hurriedly and watched him from a distance.

Coughing and choking, he floundered to the ladder and hung upon it with his hair streaming into his eyes. He had obviously swallowed so much water and sucked so much of it into his lungs that I felt a tingle of alarm. My cure might have been a little too vigorous. I was just about to go to his aid, when he opened his mouth wide and a foul mixture of swamp water and rotten wine erupted out of him. I was astonished by the quantity of it.

He hung on to the ladder, gasping and gurgling for breath. I swam to one of the stilts of the hut and waited until he had vomited again before I told him, putting all the contempt I could muster into my voice, 'My Lady Lostris would be so proud to see you now.'

He peered about with streaming eyes and focused on me at last. 'Taita, damn you! Was it you that tried to drown me? You idiot, I could have killed you.'

'In your present condition the only damage you could do would be to a jar of wine. What a sorry, disgusting sight you are!' I climbed the ladder into the hut and left him in the water, shaking his head and mumbling to himself. I set about tidying up the mess and the filth.

It was some time before Tanus followed me up the ladder and sat shamefacedly in the doorway. I ignored him and went on with my work, until at last he was forced to break the silence.

'How are you, old friend? I have missed you.'

'Others have missed you also. Kratas, for one. The squadron has been fighting down-river. They could have found use for another sword. My Lady Lostris, for another. She speaks of you every day, and holds her love pure and true. I wonder what she would think of that trollop I chased out of your bed?'

He groaned and held his head. 'Oh, Taita, don't speak your mistress's name. To be reminded of her is unbearable—'

'So broach another jug of wine and wallow in your own filth and your self-pity,' I suggested angrily.

'I have lost her for ever. What would you have me do then?'

'I would want you to have faith and fortitude, as she has.'

He looked up at me pitifully. 'Tell me about her, Taita. How is she? Does she still think of me?'

'More is the pity,' I grunted disgustedly. 'She thinks of little else. She holds herself ready for the day that you two are brought together again.'

'That will never be. I have lost her for ever and I don't want to go on living.'

'Good!' I agreed briskly. 'Then I'll not waste further time here. I'll tell my mistress that you did not want to hear her message.' I pushed past him, swarmed down the ladder and dropped into the skiff.

'Wait, Taita!' he called after me. 'Come back!'

'To what purpose? You want to die. Then get on with it. I'll send the embalmers out to pick up the corpse later.'

He grinned with embarrassment. 'All right, I am being a fool. The drink has fuddled my mind. Come back, I beg of you. Give me the message from Lostris.'

With a show of reluctance I climbed back up the ladder, and he followed me into the hut, staggering only a little.

'My mistress bids me tell you that her love for you is untouched by any of the things that have been thrust upon her. She is still and will always be your woman.'

'By Horus, she puts me to shame,' he muttered.

'No,' I disagreed. 'Your shame is of your own making.'

He snatched his sword from the scabbard that hung above the filthy bed and slashed out at the row of wine amphorae that stood against the far wall. As each one burst, the wine poured out and trickled through the slats of the floor.

He was panting as he came back to me, and I scoffed at him. 'Look at you! You have let yourself go until you are as soft and as short of wind as an old priest—'

'Enough of that, Taita! You have had your say. Mock me no more, or you will regret it.'

I could see he was becoming as angry as I had intended. My insults were stiffening him up nicely. 'My mistress would have you take up the challenge thrown to you by Pharaoh so that you will still be alive and a man of honour and worth in five years' time, when she is free to come to you.'

I had his full attention now. 'Five years? What is this about, Taita? Will there truly be a term to our suffering?'

'I worked the Mazes for Pharaoh. He will be dead in five years from now,' I told him simply. He stared at me in awe and I saw a hundred different emotions pursue each other across his features. He is as easy to read as this scroll on which I write.

'The Mazes!' he whispered at last. Once long ago he had been a doubter, and had disparaged my way with the Mazes. That had changed and he was now an even firmer believer in my powers than my mistress. He had seen my visions become reality too often to be otherwise.

'Can you wait that long for your love?' I asked. 'My mistress swears that she can wait for you through all eternity. Can you wait a few short years for her?'

'She has promised to wait for me?' he demanded.

'Through all eternity,' I repeated, and I thought he might begin to weep. I could not have faced that, not watched a man like Tanus in tears, so I went on hastily, 'Don't you want to hear the vision that the Mazes gave me?'

He thrust back the tears. 'Yes! Yes!' he agreed eagerly, and so we began to talk. We talked until the night fell, and then we sat in the darkness and talked some more.

I told him the things that I had told my Lady Lostris, all the details that I had kept from them both over the years. When I came to the details of how his father, Pianki, Lord Harrab, had been ruined and destroyed by his secret enemy, Tanus' anger was so fierce that it burned away the last effects of the debauchery from his mind, and by the time the dawn broke over the swamps, his resolve was once more clear and strong.

'Let us get on with this enterprise of yours, for it seems the right and proper way.' He sprang to his feet and girded on his sword scabbard. Although I thought it wise to rest a while and let him recover fully from the effects of the wine, he would have no part of it.

'Back to Karnak at once!' he insisted. 'Kratas is

waiting, and the lust to avenge my father's memory and to lay eyes on my own sweet love again burns like a fire in my blood.'

Once we had left the swamp, Tanus took the lead along the rocky path, and I followed him at a run. As soon as the sun came up above the horizon, the sweat burst out across his back and streamed down to soak the waistband of his kilt. It was as though the rancid old wine was being purged from his body. Although I could hear him panting wildly, he never paused to rest or even moderated his pace, but ran on into the rising heat from the desert without a check.

It was I who pulled him up with a shout, and we stood shoulder to shoulder and stared ahead. The birds had caught my attention. I had picked out the commotion of their wings from afar.

'Vultures,' Tanus grunted with ragged breath. 'They have something dead amongst the rocks.' He drew his sword and we went forward cautiously.

We found the man first, and chased the vultures off him in a flurrying storm of wings. I recognized him by the shock of blond hair as the husband I had met on the road the previous day. There was nothing left of his face, for he had lain upon his back and the birds had eaten the flesh away to the bones of the skull. They had picked out his eyes, and the empty sockets stared at the cloudless sky. His lips were gone and he grinned with bloody teeth, as though at the futile joke of our brief existence upon this earth. Tanus rolled him on to his stomach, and we saw at once the stab-wounds in his back that had killed him. There were a dozen of these thrust through his ribs.

'Whoever did this was making sure of the job,' Tanus remarked, hardened to death as only a seasoned soldier can be.

I walked on into the rocks and a buzzing black cloud of flies rose from the dead body of the wife. I have never understood where the flies come from, how they materialize so swiftly out of the searing dry heat of the desert. I guessed that the wife had aborted while they were busy with her. They must have left her alive after they had taken their pleasure with her. With the last of her strength she had taken the infant protectively in her arms. She had died like that, huddled against a boulder, shielding her still-born infant from the vultures.

I went on deeper into the broken ground, and once again the flies led me to where the bandits had dragged the little girl. At least one of them had summoned up the compassion to cut her throat after they had finished with her, rather than let her bleed slowly to death.

One of the flies settled on my lips. I brushed it away and began to weep. Tanus found me still weeping.

'Did you know them?' he asked, and I nodded and cleared my throat to answer.

'I met them on the road yesterday. I tried to warn—' I broke off, for it was not easy to continue. I took a deep breath. 'They had a donkey. The Shrikes will have taken it.'

Tanus nodded. His expression was bleak as he turned away and made a rapid cast amongst the rocks.

'This way!' he called, and broke into a run, heading out into the rocky desert.

'Tanus!' I yelled after him. 'Kratas is waiting—' But he took not the least notice and I was left with no option but to follow him. I caught up with him again when he lost the tracks of the donkey on a bad piece of ground and was forced to cast ahead.

'I feel for that family even more than you do,' I insisted. 'But this is folly. Kratas waits for us. We do not have time to waste—'

He cut me off without even glancing in my direction, 'How old was that child? Not more than nine years? I always have time to see justice done.' His face was cold and vengeful. It was clear to see that he had recovered all his former mettle. I knew better than to argue further.

The image of the little girl was still strong and clear in my mind. I joined him and we picked up the trail again. Now, with the two of us cooperating, we went forward even more swiftly.

Tanus and I had tracked gazelle and oryx, and even lion, in this fashion and we had both become adept at this esoteric art. We worked as a team, running on each side of the spurs that our quarry had left, and signalling every twist or change in it to each other. Very soon our quarry reached a rough track that led eastward from the river and still deeper into the desert. They had joined it, and made our task of catching up with them that much simpler.

It was almost noon, and our water-bottles were empty when at last we spotted them far ahead. There were five of them, and the donkey. It was clear that they had not expected to be followed deep into the desert which was their fastness, and they were moving carelessly. They had not even taken the trouble to cover their back-trail.

Tanus pulled me down behind the shelter of a rock while we caught our breath, and he growled at me, 'We'll circle out ahead of them. I want to see their faces.'

He jumped up and led me in a wide detour out to one side of the track. We overtook the band of Shrikes, but well beyond their line of sight. Then we cut in again to meet the track ahead of them. Tanus had a soldier's eye for ground, and set up the ambuscade unerringly.

We heard them coming from afar, the clatter of the donkey's hooves and the sing-song of their voices. While we waited for them, I had the first opportunity to contemplate the prudence of my decision to follow along so unquestioningly. When the party of Shrikes at last came into view I was convinced that I had been over-hasty. They were as murderous-looking a bunch of ruffians as I had ever laid eyes upon, and I was armed only with my little jewelled dagger.

Just short of where we lay, the tall, bearded Bedouin who was obviously their leader stopped suddenly, and ordered one of the men who followed him to unload the water-skin from the donkey. He drank first and then passed it on to the others. My throat closed in sympathy as I watched them swallow down the precious stuff.

'By Horus, look at the stains of the women's blood on their robes. I wish I had Lanata with me now,' Tanus whispered, as we crouched amongst the rocks. 'I could put an arrow through that one's belly and drain the water from him like beer from the vat.' Then he laid a hand on my arm. 'Don't move until I do, do you hear me? I want no heroics from you now, mind.' I nodded vigorously, and felt not the slightest inclination to protest against these very reasonable instructions.

The Shrikes came on again directly to where we waited. They were all heavily armed. The Bedouin walked ahead. His sword was strapped between his shoulder-blades, but with the handle protruding up over his left shoulder, ready to hand. He had the cowl of his woollen cloak drawn over his head to protect him from the fierce sunlight. It impaired his side-vision and he did not notice us as he passed close in front of us.

Two others followed him closely, one of them leading the donkey. The last two sauntered along behind the animal, engrossed in a listless squabble over a piece of gold jewellery that they had taken from the murdered woman. All their weapons were sheathed, except for the short, bronze-headed stabbing spears carried by the last pair.

Tanus let them all pass, and then he stood up quietly and moved in behind the last two men in the column. He appeared to move casually, as the leopard does, but it was in reality only a breath before he swung his sword at the neck of the man on the right.

Although I had intended backing Tanus up to the full, somehow my good intentions had not been translated into action, and I still crouched behind my comforting rock. I justified myself with the thought that I would probably only have hindered him if I had followed him too closely.

I had never watched Tanus kill a man before. Although I knew that it was his vocation and that he had, over the years, had every opportunity to hone these gruesome skills, still I was astonished by his virtuosity. As he struck, his victim's head leapt from its shoulders like a desert spring-hare from its burrow, and the decapitated trunk actually took another step before the legs buckled under it. As the blow reached the limit of its arc, Tanus smoothly reversed the stroke. With the same movement he struck back-handed at the next brigand. The second neck severed just as cleanly. The head toppled off and fell free, while the carcass slumped forward with the blood fountaining high in the air.

The splash of blood and the weighty thump-thump of the two disembodied heads striking the rocky earth alerted the other three Shrikes. They spun about in alarm, and for a moment stared in bewildered disbelief at the sudden carnage in their ranks. Then with a wild shout they drew their swords and rushed at Tanus in a body. Rather than retreating before them, Tanus charged them ferociously, splitting them apart. He swung to face the man he had isolated from his mates, and his thrust ripped a bloody flesh-wound down the side of his chest. The man squealed and reeled backwards. But before Tanus was able to finish him off, the other two fell upon him from behind. Tanus was forced to spin round to face them, and bronze clashed on bronze as he stopped their charge. He held them off at sword's-length, engaging first one and then the other, until the lightly wounded man recovered and came at him from his rear.

'Behind you!' I yelled at him, and he whipped round only just in time to catch the thrust on his

311

own blade. Instantly the other two were upon him again, and he was forced to give ground in order to defend himself from all sides. His swordsmanship was breathtaking to watch. So swift was his blade that it seemed that he had erected a glittering wall of bronze around himself against which the blows of his enemies clattered ineffectually.

Then I realized that Tanus was tiring. The sweat streamed from his body in the heat, and his features were contorted with the effort. The long weeks of wine and debauchery had taken their toll of what had once been his limitless strength and stamina.

He fell back before the next rush with which the bearded Bedouin drove at him, until he pressed his back to one of the boulders on the opposite side of the track from where I still crouched helplessly. With the rock to cover his back, all three of his attackers were forced to come at him from the front. But this was no real respite. Their attack was relentless. Led by the Bedouin, they howled like a pack of wild dogs as they bayed him, and Tanus' right arm tired and moved slower.

The spear carried by the first man whom Tanus had beheaded had fallen in the middle of the track. I realized that I must do something immediately if I were not to watch Tanus hacked down before my eyes. With a huge effort I gathered up my slippery courage, and crept from my hiding-place. The Shrikes had forgotten all about me in their eagerness for the kill. I reached the spot where the spear lay without any one of them noticing me, and I snatched it up. With the solid weight of the weapon in my hands, all my lost courage came flooding back.

The Bedouin was the most dangerous of the three of Tanus' adversaries, and he was also the closest to me. His back was towards me, and his whole attention was on the unequal duel. I levelled the spear and rushed at him.

The kidneys are the most vulnerable target in the human back. With my knowledge of anatomy, I could aim my thrust exactly. The spearpoint went in a finger's-width to one side of the spinal column, all the way in. The broad spear-head opened a gaping wound, and skewered his right kidney with a surgeon's precision. The Bedouin stiffened and froze like a temple statue, instantly paralysed by my thrust. Then, as I viciously twisted the blade in his flesh the way Tanus had taught me, mincing his kidney to pulp, the sword fell from his fist and he collapsed with such a dreadful cry that his comrades were distracted enough to give Tanus his chance.

Tanus' next thrust took one of them in the centre of his chest, and despite his exhaustion it still had sufficient power in it to fly cleanly through the man's torso and for the blood-smeared point to protrude a hand-span from between his shoulder-blades. Before Tanus was able to clear his blade from the clinging embrace of live flesh and to kill the last Shrike, the survivor spun round and ran.

Tanus took a few paces after him, then gasped, 'I'm all done in. After him, Taita, don't let that murderous jackal get away.'

There are very few men that can outrun me. Tanus is the only one I know of, but he has to be on top form to do it. I put my foot in the centre of the Bedouin's back and held him down as I jerked the spearhead out of his flesh, and then I went after the last Shrike.

I caught him before he had gone two hundred paces, and I was running so lightly that he did not hear me coming up behind him. With the edge of the spear-head I slashed the tendon in the back of his heel, and he went down sprawling. The sword flew out of his hand. As he lay on his back kicking and screaming at me, I danced around him, pricking him with the point of the spear, goading him into position for a good clean killing thrust.

'Which of the women did you enjoy the best?' I asked him, as I stabbed him in the thigh. 'Was it the mother, with her big belly, or was it the little girl? Was she tight enough for you?'

'Please spare me!' he screamed. 'I did nothing. It was the others. Don't kill me!'

'There is dried blood on the front of your kilt,' I said, and I stabbed him in the stomach, but not too deeply. 'Did the child scream as loudly as you do now?' I asked.

As he rolled over into a ball to protect his stomach, I stabbed him in the spine, by a lucky chance finding the gap between the vertebrae. Instantly he was paralysed from the waist down, and I stepped back from him.

'Very well,' I said. 'You ask me not to kill you, and I won't. It would be too good for you.'

I turned away and walked back to join Tanus. The maimed Shrike dragged himself a little way after me, his paralysed legs slithering after him like a fisherman dragging a pair of dead carp. Then the effort was too much and he collapsed in a whimpering heap. Although it was past noon, the sun still had enough heat in it to kill him before it set.

Tanus looked at me curiously as I came back to join him. 'There is a savage streak in you that I never suspected before.' He shook his head in wonder. 'You never fail to amaze me.'

He pulled the water-skin from the back of the donkey and offered it to me, but I shook my head. 'You first. You need it more than I do.'

He drank, his eyes tightly closed with the pleasure of it, and then gasped, 'By the sweet breath of Isis, you are right. I am soft as an old woman. Even that little piece of sword-play nearly finished me.' Then he looked around at the scattered corpses, and grinned with satisfaction. 'But all in all, not a bad start on Pharaoh's business.'

'It was the poorest of beginnings,' I contradicted him, and when he crooked an eyebrow at me I went on, 'We should have kept at least one of them alive to lead us to the Shrikes' nest. Even that one', I gestured towards the dying man lying out there amongst the rocks, 'is too far-gone to be of any use to us. It was my fault. I allowed my anger to get the better of me. We won't make the same mistake again.'

We were halfway back to where we had left the bodies of the murdered family before my true nature reasserted itself, and I began bitterly to regret my callous and brutal treatment of the maimed brigand.

'After all, he was a human being, as we are,' I told Tanus, and he snorted.

'He was an animal, a rabid jackal, and you did a fine job. You have mourned him far too long. Forget him. Tell me, instead, why we must make this detour back to look at dead men, instead of heading straight for Kratas' camp.'

'I need the husband's body.' I would say no more until we stood over the mutilated corpse. The pathetic relic was already stinking in the heat. The vultures had left very little flesh on the bones.

'Look at that hair,' I told Tanus. 'Who else do you know with a bush like that?' For a moment he looked puzzled, and then he grinned and ran his fingers through his own dense ringlets.

'Help me load him on the donkey,' I ordered. 'Kratas can take him into Karnak to the morticians for embalming. We'll buy him a good funeral and a fine tomb with your name on the walls. Then, by sunset tomorrow, all of Thebes will know that Tanus, Lord Harrab perished in the desert, and was half-eaten by the birds.'

'If Lostris hears of it—' Tanus looked worried.

'I'll send a warning letter to her. The advantage we will win by letting the world believe you dead will far outweigh any risk of alarming my mistress.'

Kratas was camped at the first oasis on the caravan road to the Red Sea, less than a day's march from Karnak. He had with him a hundred men of the Blue Crocodile Guards, all of them carefully selected, as I had commanded. Tanus and I reached the encampment in the middle of the night. We had travelled hard and were close to exhaustion. We fell on our sleeping-mats beside the camp-fire and slept until dawn.

At first light, Tanus was up and mingling with

his men. Their delight at having him back was transparent. The officers embraced him and the men cheered him, and grinned with pride as he greeted each of them by name.

At breakfast Tanus gave Kratas instructions to take the putrefying corpse back to Karnak for burial and to make certain that the news of his death was the gossip of all Thebes. I gave Kratas a letter for my Lady Lostris. He would find a trustworthy messenger to carry it up-river to Elephantine.

Kratas selected an escort of ten men, and they prepared to set off with the donkey and its odorous burden, back towards the Nile and Thebes.

'Try to catch up with us on the road to the sea. If you cannot, then you'll find us camped at the oasis of Gebel Nagara. We will wait for you there,' Tanus shouted after him, as the detachment trotted out of the encampment. 'And remember to bring Lanata, my bow, when you return!'

No sooner was Kratas out of sight beyond the first rise on the westerly road than Tanus formed up the rest of the regiment and led us away in the opposite direction along the caravan road towards the sea.

The caravan road from the banks of the river Nile to the shores of the Red Sea was long and hard. A large, unwieldy caravan usually took twenty days to make the journey. We covered the distance in four days, for Tanus pushed us in a series of forced marches. At the outset, he and I were probably the only ones of all the company who were not in superb physical condition. However, by the time we reached Gebel Nagara, Tanus had burned the excess fat off his frame and sweated out the last poisons from the wine jar. He was once again lean and hard.

As for myself, it was the first time that I had ever made a forced march with a company of the guards. For the first few days I suffered all the torments of thirst and aching muscles, of blistered feet and exhaustion that the *Ka* of a dead man must be forced to endure on the road to the underworld. However, my pride would not allow me to fall behind, apart from the fact that to do so in this wild and savage landscape would have meant certain death. To my surprise and pleasure, I found that after the first few days, it became easier and easier to keep my place in the ranks of trotting warriors.

Along the way, we passed two large caravans moving towards the Nile, with the donkeys bow-legged under their heavy loads of trade goods, and escorts of heavily armed men far surpassing in number the merchants and their retainers who made up the rest of the company. No caravan was safe from the depredations of the Shrikes unless it was protected by a force of mercenaries such as these, or unless the merchants were prepared to pay the crippling toll money that the Shrikes demanded to allow them free passage.

When we met these strangers, Tanus pulled his shawl over his head to mask his face and hide that golden bush of hair. He was too distinctive a figure to risk being recognized and his continued existence being reported in Karnak. We did not respond to the greetings and questions that were flung at us by these other travellers, but ran past them in aloof silence without even glancing in their direction.

When we were still a day's march from the coast, we left the main caravan route and swung away southwards, following an ancient disused track that had been shown to me some years previously by one of the wild Bedouin whom I had befriended. The wells at Gebel Nagara lay on this old route to the sea, and were seldom visited by humans these days, only by the Bedouin and the desert bandits, if you can call these human.

By the time we reached the wells, I was as slim and physically fit as I had ever been in my life, but I lamented the lack of a mirror, for I was convinced that this new energy and force that I felt within myself must be reflected in my features, and that my beauty must be enhanced by it. I would have welcomed the opportunity to admire it myself. However, there seemed to be no dearth of others to admire it in my place. At the camp-fire in the evenings, many a prurient glance was flashed in my direction, and I received more than a few sly offers from my companions, for even such an elite fighting corps as the guards was contaminated by the new sexual licence that permeated our society.

I kept my dagger beside me in the night and when I pricked the first uninvited visitor to my sleeping-mat with the needle-point, his yells caused much hilarity amongst the others. After that, I was spared any further unwelcome attentions.

Even once we had reached the wells, Tanus would allow us little rest. While we waited for Kratas to catch up, he kept his men exercising at arms, and at competitions of archery and wrestling and running. I was pleased to see that Kratas had chosen these men strictly in accordance with my instructions to him. There was not a single hulking brute amongst them. Apart from Tanus himself, they were all small, agile men aptly suited to the role that I planned for them.

Kratas arrived only two days behind us. Taking into account his return to Karnak and the time taken up by the tasks that Tanus had set for him there, this meant that he must have travelled even more swiftly than we had done.

'What held you up?' Tanus greeted him. 'Did you find a willing maid on the way?'

'I had two heavy burdens to carry,' Kratas replied, as they embraced. 'Your bow, and the hawk seal. I am glad to be rid of both of them.' He handed over both the weapon and the statuette with a grin, delighted as ever to be back with Tanus.

Tanus immediately took Lanata out into the desert. I went with him and helped him stalk close to a herd of gazelle. With these fleet little creatures racing and leaping across the plain, it was an extraordinary sight to watch Tanus bowl over a dozen of them at full run with as many arrows. That night, as we feasted on grilled livers and fillets of gazelle, we discussed the next stage of my plan.

In the morning we left Kratas in command of the guards, and Tanus and I set out alone for the coast. It was only half a day's travel to the small fishing village which was our goal, and at noon we topped the last rise and looked down from the hills on to the glittering expanse of the sea spread below us. From this height we could see clearly the dark outline of the coral reefs beneath the turquoise waters.

As soon as we entered the village, Tanus called for the headman, and so apparent from his bearing was Tanus' importance and authority, that the old man came at a run. When Tanus showed him the hawk seal, he fell to the earth in obeisance, as though it were Pharaoh himself who stood before him, and beat his head upon the ground with such force that I feared he might do himself serious injury. When I lifted him to his feet once more, he led us to the finest lodgings in the village, his own filthy hovel, and turned his numerous family out to make room for us.

Once we had eaten a bowl of the fish stew that our host provided and drunk a cup of the delicious palm wine, Tanus and I went down to the beach of dazzling white sand and bathed away the sweat and the dust of the desert in the warm waters of the lagoon that was enclosed by the jagged barricade of coral that lay parallel to the shore. Behind us the harsh mountains, devoid of the faintest green tinge of growing things, thrust up into the aching blue desert sky.

Sea, mountains and sky combined in a symphony of grandeur that stunned the senses. However, I had little time to appreciate it all, for the fishing fleet was returning. Five small dilapidated vessels with sails of woven palm-fronds were coming in through the pass in the reef. So great was the load of fish that each of them carried, that they seemed in danger of foundering before they could reach the beach.

I am fascinated by all the natural bounty that the gods provide for us, and I examined the catch avidly as it was thrown out upon the beach, and questioned the fishermen as to each of the hundred different species. The pile of fish formed a glittering treasure of rainbow colours, and I wished that I had my scrolls and paint-pots to record it all.

This interlude was too brief. As soon as the catch was unloaded, I embarked on one of the tiny vessels that stank so abundantly of its vocation, and waved back at Tanus on the beach as we put out through the pass in the reef. He was to remain here until I returned with the equipment that we needed for the next part of my plan. Once again, I did not want him to be recognized where I was going. His job now was to prevent any of the fishermen or their families from sneaking away into the desert to a secret meeting with the Shrikes, to report the presence in their village of a golden-headed lord who bore the hawk seal.

The tiny vessel threw up her bows at the first strong scend of the sea, and the helmsman tacked across the wind and headed her up into the north, running parallel to that dun and awful coast. We had but a short way to go, and before nightfall the helmsman pointed over the bows at the clustered stone buildings of the port of Safaga on the distant shoreline.

 For a thousand years Safaga had been the entrepôt for all trade coming into the Upper Kingdom from the East. Even as I stood in the bows of our tiny craft, I could make out the shapes of other much larger vessels on the northern horizon as they

came and went between Safaga and the Arabian ports on the eastern shore of the narrow sea.

It was dark by the time that I stepped ashore on the beach at Safaga, and nobody seemed to remark my arrival. I knew exactly where I was going, for I had visited the port regularly on Lord Intef's nefarious business. At this hour the streets were almost deserted, but the taverns were packed. I made my way swiftly to the home of Tiamat the merchant. Tiamat was a rich man and his home the largest in the old town. An armed slave barred the door to me.

'Tell your master that the surgeon from Karnak who saved his leg for him is here,' I ordered, and Tiamat himself limped out to greet me. He was taken aback when he saw my clerical disguise, but had the good sense not to remark on it, nor to mention my name in front of the slave. He drew me into his walled garden, and as soon as we were alone he exclaimed, 'Is it really you, Taita? I heard that you had been murdered by the Shrikes at Elephantine.'

He was a portly, middle-aged man, with an open, intelligent face and a shrewd mind. Some years previously he had been carried in to me on a litter. A party of travellers had found him beside the road, where he had been left for dead after his caravan had been pillaged by the Shrikes. I had stitched him together, and even managed to save the leg that had already mortified by the time I first saw it. However, he would always walk with a limp.

'I am delighted to see that the reports of your death are premature,' he chuckled, and clapped his hands to have his slaves bring me a cup of cool

323

sherbet and a plate of figs and honeyed dates.

After a decent interval of polite conversation, he asked quietly, 'Is there anything I can do for you? I owe you my life. You have only to ask. My home is your home. All I have is yours.'

'I am on the king's business,' I told him, and drew out the hawk seal from under my tunic.

His expression became grave. 'I acknowledge the seal of Pharaoh. But it was not necessary to show it to me. Ask what you will of me. I cannot refuse you.'

He listened to all I had to say without another word, and when I had finished, he sent for his bailiff and gave him his orders in front of me. Before he sent the man away, he turned to me and said, 'Is there anything that I have forgotten? Anything else you need at all?'

'Your generosity is without limits,' I told him. 'However, there is one other thing. I long for my writing materials.'

He turned back to the bailiff. 'See to it that there are scrolls and brushes and ink-pot in one of the packs.'

After the bailiff had left, we sat on talking for half the night. Tiamat stood at the centre of the busiest trading route in the Upper Kingdom, and heard every rumour and whisper from the farthest reaches of the empire, and from beyond the sea. I learned as much in those few hours in his garden as I would in a month in the palace at Elephantine.

'Do you still pay your ransom to the Shrikes to allow your caravans through?' I asked, and he shrugged with resignation.

'After what they did to my leg, what option do I have? Each season their demands become more exorbitant. I must pay over one-quarter of the value of my goods to them as soon as the caravan leaves Safaga, and half my profits once the goods are sold in Thebes. Soon they will beggar us all, and grass will grow on the caravan roads, and the trade of the kingdom will wither and die.'

'How do you make these payments?' I asked. 'Who determines the amount, and who collects them?'

'They have their spies here in the port. They watch every cargo that is unloaded, and they know what each caravan carries when it leaves Safaga. Before it even reaches the mountain pass, it will be met by one of the robber chieftains who will demand the ransom they have set.'

It was long past midnight before Tiamat called a slave to light me to the chamber he had set aside for me.

'You will be gone before I rise tomorrow.' Tiamat embraced me. 'Farewell, my good friend. My debt to you is not yet paid in full. Call upon me again, whenever you have need.'

The same slave woke me before dawn, and led me down to the seafront in the darkness. A fine trading vessel of Tiamat's fleet was moored inside the reef. The captain weighed anchor as soon as I came aboard.

In the middle of the morning we crept in through the pass in the coral and dropped anchor in front of the little fishing village where Tanus stood on the beach to welcome me.

During my absence Tanus had managed to gather together six decrepit donkeys, and the sailors from Tiamat's ship waded ashore carrying the bales that we had brought with us from Safaga, and loaded them on to these miserable creatures. Tanus and I left the captain of the trading vessel with strict orders to await our return, then, leading the string of donkeys, we headed back inland towards the wells at Gebel Nagara.

Kratas' men had obviously suffered the heat and the sand-flies and the boredom with poor grace, for they accorded us a welcome that was out of keeping with the period that we had been absent. Tanus ordered Kratas to parade them. The ranks of warriors watched as I unpacked the first bale that we had brought in on the donkey train. Almost immediately their interest gave way to mild amusement as I laid out the costume of a slave girl. In its turn, this was replaced by a buzz of speculation and argument as the bales yielded up a further seventy-nine complete female costumes.

Kratas and two of his officers helped me place one of these on the sand in front of each guardsman, and then Tanus gave the order: 'Disrobe! Put on the dress in front of you!' There was a roar of protest and incredulous hilarity, and it was only when Kratas and his officers passed down the ranks with assumed expressions of sternness to reinforce the order, that they began to obey it.

Unlike our women who dress but lightly and often leave their bosom bared and their legs free and naked, the women of Assyria wear skirts that sweep the ground and sleeves that cover their arms to the wrist. For reasons of misplaced modesty they even veil their faces when they walk abroad, although perhaps these restrictions are placed upon them by the possessive jealousy of their menfolk. Then again there is a wide difference between the sunny land of Egypt and those more sombre climes where water falls from the sky and turns solid white upon the mountaintops, and the winds chill the flesh and the bones of men like death.

Once they had weathered the first shock of seeing each other in this outlandish apparel, the men entered into the spirit of the moment. Soon there were eighty veiled slave girls prancing and mincing about in the long skirts that reached to their ankles, tweaking each other's buttocks and casting exaggerated sheep's eyes at Tanus and his officers.

The officers could no longer maintain their gravity. Perhaps it is because of my peculiar circumstances that I have always found the spectacle of men dressed as women to be vaguely repulsive, but it is strange how few other men share my feelings of distaste, and it needs only some hairy ruffian to don a skirt to reduce his audience to a state of incontinence.

In the midst of this uproar, I congratulated myself that I had insisted that Kratas choose only the smallest and slimmest men from the squadron. Looking them over now, I was certain that they would be able to carry through the deception. They would need only a little schooling in feminine deportment.

327

 The following morning our strange caravan passed through the little fishing village and wound its way down on to the beach, where the trading vessel waited. Kratas and eight of his officers made up the escort. Complete lack of any armed escort for such a valuable consignment would surely have aroused suspicion. Nine armed men dressed in the motley garb of mercenaries would be sufficient to allay this, but would not deter a large raiding party of Shrikes.

At the head of the caravan marched Tanus, dressed in the rich robes and beaded head-dress of a wealthy merchant from beyond the Euphrates river. His beard had grown out densely, and I had curled it for him into those tight ringlets that the Assyrians favoured. Many of these Asians, particularly those from the high mountainous regions further north, have the same complexion and skin coloration as Tanus, so he looked the part I had chosen for him.

I followed close behind him. I had overcome my aversion to wearing female garb, and donned the long skirts and veil, together with the gaudy jewellery of an Assyrian wife. I was determined not to be recognized when I returned to Safaga.

The voyage was enlivened by the sea-sickness of most of the slave girls and not a few of the officers, for they were accustomed to sail on the placid waters of the great river. At one stage so many of them were lining the rail to make their offerings to the gods of the sea, that the ship took on a distinct list.

We were all relieved to step on to the beach at Safaga, where we caused much excitement. The Assyrian girls were famous for their skills on the love couch. It was said that some of them were capable of tricks that could bring a thousand-year-old mummy back to life. It was obvious to those who watched us come ashore that behind the veils our slave girls must be images of feminine loveliness. A shrewd Asian merchant would not transport his wares so far and at such expense, unless he was certain of a good price in the slave-markets on the Nile.

One of the Safaga merchants approached Tanus immediately and offered to buy the entire bevy of girls on the spot, and spare him the onerous journey across the desert with them. Tanus waved him away with a scornful chuckle.

'Have you been warned of the perils of the journey that you intend making?' the merchant insisted. 'Before you reach the Nile, you will be forced to pay a ransom for your safe passage that will eat up most of your profits.'

'Who will force me to pay?' Tanus demanded. 'I pay only what I owe.'

'There are those who guard the road,' the merchant warned him. 'And even though you pay what they demand, there is no certainty that they will let you pass unharmed, especially with such tempting goods as you have with you. The vultures on the road to the Nile are so fat from feeding on the carcasses of stubborn merchants that they can hardly fly. Sell to me now at a good profit—'

'I have armed guards', Tanus indicated Kratas and his small squad, 'who will be a match for any robbers we may meet.' And the onlookers who had

329

listened to the exchange tittered and nudged each other at the boast.

The merchant shrugged. 'Very well, my brave friend. On my next journey through the desert, I will look for your skeleton beside the road. I will recognize you by that blustering red beard of yours.'

As he had promised me he would, Tiamat had forty donkeys waiting for us. Twenty of them were laden with filled water-skins, and the remainder with pack-saddles to carry the bales and bundles that we brought ashore from the trading ship.

I was anxious that we should spend as little time as possible in the port, under all those prying eyes. It would take only a single lapse by one of the slave girls to reveal his true gender, and we would be undone. Kratas and his escort hurried them through the narrow streets, keeping the bystanders at a distance, and making certain that the slave girls kept their veils in place and their eyes downcast, and that none of them responded in gruff masculine tones to the ribald comment that followed us, until we were out into the open country beyond the town.

We camped that first night still within sight of Safaga. Although I did not anticipate an attack until we were beyond the first mountain pass, I was certain that we were already being watched by the spies of the Shrikes.

While it was still light, I made sure that our slave girls conducted themselves as women, that they kept their faces and bodies covered, and that when they went into the nearby wadi to attend to nature's demands, they squatted in decorous fashion and did not uncouthly spray their water while standing.

It was only after darkness fell that Tanus ordered the bundles carried by the donkeys to be opened and the weapons they contained to be issued to the slave girls. Each of them slept with his bow and his sword concealed under his sleeping-mat.

Tanus posted double sentries around the camp. After we had inspected them and made sure that they were all well placed and fully alert, Tanus and I slipped away, and in the darkness returned to the port of Safaga. I led him through the dark streets to the house of Tiamat. The merchant was expecting our arrival, and had a meal laid ready to welcome us. I could see that he was excited to meet Tanus.

'Your fame precedes you, Lord Harrab. I knew your father. He was a man indeed,' he greeted Tanus. 'Although I have heard persistent rumours that you died in the desert not a week since, and that even at this moment your body lies with the morticians on the west bank of the Nile, undergoing the ritual forty days of the embalming process, you are welcome in my humble house.'

While we enjoyed the feast he provided, Tanus questioned him at length on all he knew of the Shrikes, and Tiamat answered him freely and openly.

At last Tanus glanced at me and I nodded. Tanus turned back to Tiamat and said, 'You have been a generous friend to us, and yet we have been less than honest with you. This was from necessity, for it was of vital importance that no one should guess at our real purpose in this endeavour. Now I will tell you that it is my purpose to smash the

Shrikes and deliver their leaders up to Pharaoh's justice and wrath.'

Tiamat smiled and stroked his beard. 'This comes as no great surprise to me,' he said, 'for I have heard of the charge that Pharaoh placed upon you at the festival of Osiris. That and your patent interest in those murderous bandits left little doubt in my mind. I can say only that I will sacrifice to the gods for your success.'

'To succeed, I will need your help again,' Tanus told him.

'You have only to ask.'

'Do you think that the Shrikes are as yet aware of our caravan?'

'All of Safaga is talking about you,' Tiamat replied. 'Yours is the richest cargo that has arrived this season. Eighty beautiful slave girls will be worth at least a thousand gold rings each in Karnak.' He chuckled and shook his head at the joke. 'You can be certain that the Shrikes already know all about you. I saw at least three of their spies in the crowd at the waterfront watching you. You can expect them to meet you and make their demands even before you reach the first pass.'

When we rose to take our leave, he walked with us as far as his own door. 'May all the gods attend your endeavours. Not only Pharaoh, but every living soul in the entire kingdom will be in your debt if you can stamp out this terrible scourge that threatens to destroy our very civilization, and drive us all back into the age of barbarism.'

It was still cool and dark the following morning when the column started out. Tanus, with Lanata slung over his shoulder, was at the head of the caravan, with myself, in all my womanly grace and beauty, following him closely.

Behind us the donkeys were harnessed in single file, moving nose to tail down the middle of the well-beaten track. The slave girls were in double columns on the outer flanks of the file of donkeys. Their weapons were concealed in the packs upon the backs of the animals. Any of the men needed only to reach out to lay a hand upon the hilt of his sword.

Kratas had split his escort into three squads of six men each, commanded by Astes, Remrem and himself. Astes and Remrem were warriors of renown and more than deserving of their own commands. However, both of them had, on numerous occasions, refused promotion in order to remain with Tanus. That was the quality of loyalty that Tanus inspired in all who served under him. I could not help thinking yet again what a pharaoh he would have made.

The escorts now slouched along beside the column, making every attempt to forsake their military bearing. It would seem to the spies who were certainly watching us from the hills that they were there solely to prevent any of the slaves from escaping. In truth they were fully occupied with preventing their charges from breaking into marching step and sounding off a chorus of one of the rowdy regimental songs.

'You there, Kemit!' I heard Remrem challenge one of them. 'Don't take such long steps, man, and swing that fat arse of yours a little! Try to make yourself alluring.'

'Give me a kiss, captain,' Kemit called back, 'and I'll do anything you say.'

The heat was rising, and the mirage was beginning to make the rocks dance. Tanus turned back to me. 'Soon I will call our first rest-stop. One cup of water for each—'

'Good husband,' I interrupted him, 'your friends have arrived. Look ahead!'

Tanus turned back, and instinctively gripped the stock of the great bow that hung at his side. 'And what fine fellows they are, too!'

At that moment our column was winding through the first foothills below the desert plateau. On either hand we were walled in by the steep sides of the rocky hills. Now three men stood in the track ahead of us. The one who led them was a tall, menacing figure swathed in the woollen robe of the desert traveller, but his head was bared. His skin was very dark, and deeply pitted with the scars of the smallpox. He had a nose that was hooked like the beak of a vulture, and his right eye was an opaque jelly from the blind-worm that burrows deep into the eyeball of its victims.

'I know the one-eyed villain,' I said softly, so that Tanus alone could hear. 'His name is Shufti. He is the most notorious of the barons of the Shrikes. Be wary of him. The lion is a gentle beast compared to this one.' Tanus gave no sign of having heard me, but lifted his right hand to show that it held no weapon, and called out cheerfully, 'May all your days be scented with jasmine, gentle traveller, and may a loving wife welcome you at your own front door when at last your journey is done.'

'May your water-skins stay filled and cool breezes fan your brow when you cross the Thirsty Sands,' Shufti called back, and he smiled. That smile was fiercer than a leopard's snarl, and his single eye glared horribly.

'You are kind, my noble lord,' Tanus thanked him. 'I would like to offer you a meal and the hospitality of my camp, but I pray your indulgence. We have a long road before us, and we must pass on.'

'Just a little more of your time, my fine Assyrian.' Shufti moved forward to block the path. 'I have something which you need, if you and your caravan are ever to reach the Nile in safety.' He held up a small object.

'Ah, a charm!' Tanus exclaimed. 'You are a magician, perhaps? What manner of charm is this you are offering me?'

'A feather.' Shufti was still smiling. 'The feather of a shrike.'

Tanus smiled, as though to humour a child. 'Very well then, give me this feather and I'll delay you no longer.'

'A gift for a gift. You must give me something in return,' Shufti told him. 'Give me twenty of your slaves. Then, when you return from Egypt, I will meet you on the road again and you will give me half the profits from the sale of the other sixty.'

'For a single feather?' Tanus scoffed. 'That sounds like a sorry bargain to me.'

'This is no ordinary feather. It is a shrike's feather,' Shufti pointed out. 'Are you so

335

ill-informed that you have never heard of that bird?'

'Let me see this magical feather.' Tanus walked towards him with his right hand outstretched, and Shufti came forward to meet him. At the same time Kratas, Remrem and Astes wandered up inquisitively, as though to examine the feather.

Instead of taking the gift from his hand, suddenly Tanus seized Shufti's wrist and twisted it up between his shoulder-blades. With a startled cry, Shufti fell to his knees and Tanus held him easily. At the same time Kratas and his men darted forward, taking the other two bandits by as much surprise as their chief. They knocked the weapons out of their hands, and dragged them to where Tanus stood.

'So, you little birds think to frighten Kaarik, the Assyrian, with your threats, do you? Yes, my fine vendor of feathers, I have heard of the Shrikes. I have heard that they are a flock of chattering, cowardly little fledglings, that make more noise than a flock of sparrows.' He twisted Shufti's arm more viciously, until the bandit yelled with pain and fell flat on his face. 'Yes, I have heard of the Shrikes, but have you heard of Kaarik, the terrible?' He nodded at Kratas, and quickly and efficiently they stripped the three Shrikes stark naked and pinned them spread-eagled upon the rocky earth.

'I want you to remember my name, and fly away like a good little shrike when next you hear it,' Tanus told him, and nodded to Kratas again. Kratas flexed the lash of his slave-whip between his fingers. It was of the same type as Rasfer's famous tool, whittled from the cured hide of a bull hippopotamus. Tanus held out his hand for it, and reluctantly Kratas handed it over to him.

'Don't look so sad, slave-master,' Tanus told him. 'I'll let you have your turn later. But Kaarik, the Assyrian, always takes the first spoonful from the pot.'

Tanus slashed the whip back and forth through the air, and it whistled like the wing of a goose in flight. Shufti squirmed where he lay, and twisted his head around to hiss at Tanus, 'You are mad, you Assyrian ox! Do you not realize that I am a baron of the Shrike clan? You dare not do this to me—' His naked back and buttocks were stippled with pox scars.

Tanus lifted the whip on high, and then brought it down in a full-armed stroke with all his weight behind it. He laid a purple welt as fat as my forefinger across Shufti's back. So intense was the pain of it that the bandit's entire body convulsed and the air hissed out of his lungs, so that he could not scream. Tanus lifted the lash and then meticulously laid another ridged welt exactly parallel to the first, almost, but not quite, touching it. This time Shufti filled his lungs and let out a hoarse bellow, like a buffalo bull caught in a pitfall. Tanus ignored his struggles and his outraged roars, and worked on assiduously, laying on the strokes as though he were weaving a carpet.

When at last he was done, his victim's legs, buttocks and back were latticed with the fiery weals. Not one of the blows had overlaid another. The skin was intact and not a drop of blood had spilled out, but Shufti was no longer wriggling or screaming. He lay with his face in the dirt, his breath snoring in his throat, so that each

337

exhalation raised a puff of dust. When Remrem and Kratas released him, he made no effort to sit up. He did not even stir.

Tanus tossed the whip to Kratas. 'The next one is yours, slave-master. Let us see what a pretty pattern you can tattoo on his back.'

Kratas' strokes hummed with power, but lacked the finesse that Tanus had demonstrated. Soon the bandit's back was leaking like a flawed jar of red wine. The droplets of blood fell into the dust and rolled into tiny balls of mud.

Sweating lightly, Kratas was satisfied at last, and he passed the whip to Astes as he indicated the last victim. 'Give that one something to remind him of his manners, as well.'

Astes had an even more rustic touch than Kratas. By the time he had finished, the last bandit's back looked like a side of fresh beef that had been cut up by a demented butcher.

Tanus signalled the caravan to move forward, towards the pass through the red rock mountains. We lingered a while beside the three naked men.

At last Shufti stirred and lifted his head, and Tanus addressed him civilly. 'And so, my friend, I beg leave of you. Remember my face, and step warily when you see it again.' Tanus picked up the fallen shrike's feather and tucked it into his headband. 'I thank you for your gift. May all your nights be cradled in the arms of lovely ladies.' He touched his heart and lips in the Assyrian gesture of farewell, and I followed him up the road after the departing caravan.

I looked back before we dropped over the next rise. All three Shrikes were on their feet, supporting each other to remain upright. Even at this distance I could make out the expression on Shufti's face. It was hatred distilled to its essence.

'Well, you have made certain that we will have every Shrike this side of the Nile upon us, the moment we take our first step beyond the pass,' I told Kratas and his ruffians, and I could not have pleased them more, had I promised them a shipload of beer and pretty girls.

 From the crest of the pass we looked back at the cool blue of the sea for the last time and then dropped down into that sweltering wilderness of rock and sand that stood between us and the Nile.

As we moved forward, the heat came at us like a mortal enemy. It seemed to enter through our mouths and nostrils as we gasped for breath. It sucked the moisture from our bodies like a thief. It dried out our skin and cracked it until our lips burst open like over-ripe figs. The rocks beneath our feet were hot, as though fresh from the pot-maker's kiln, and they scalded and blistered our feet, even through the leather soles of our sandals. It was impossible to continue the march during the hottest hours of the day. We lay in the flimsy shade of the linen tents that Tiamat had provided, and panted like hunting dogs after the chase.

When the sun sank towards the jagged rock horizon, we went on. The desert around us was charged with such a brooding nameless menace that even the high spirits of the Blue Crocodile Guards were subdued. The long slow column wound like a maimed adder through the black rock outcrops and tawny lion-coloured dunes, following the ancient road along which countless other travellers had passed before us.

When night fell at last, the sky came alive with such a dazzle of stars and the desert was lit so brightly that, from my place at the head of the caravan, I could recognize the shape of Kratas at the tail, although two hundred paces separated us. We marched on for half the night before Tanus gave the order to fall out. Then he had us up before dawn and we marched on until the heat-mirage dissolved the rocky outcrops around us and made the horizon swim so that it seemed to be moulded from melting pitch.

We saw no other sign of life, except that once a troop of dog-headed baboons barked at us from the cliffs of a stark rock tableland as we passed below them, and the vultures soared so high in the hot blue sky that they appeared to be but dust motes swirling in slow and deliberate circles high above us.

When we rested in the middle of the day the whirlwinds pirouetted and swayed with the peculiar grace of dancing houris across the plains, and the cupful of water that was our ration seemed to turn to steam in my mouth.

'Where are they?' Kratas growled angrily. 'By Seth's sweaty scrotum, I hope these little birds will soon puff up their courage and come in to roost.'

Although they were all tough veterans and inured to hardship and discomfort, nerves and tempers were wearing thin. Good comrades and old friends began to snarl at each other for no reason, and bicker over the water ration.

'Shufti is a cunning old dog,' I told Tanus. 'He will gather his forces and wait for us to come to him, rather than hurry to meet us. He will let us tire ourselves with the journey, and grow careless with our fatigue, before he strikes.'

On the fifth day I knew that we were approaching the oasis of Gallala when I saw that the dark cliffs ahead of us were riddled with the caves of ancient tombs. Centuries ago, the oasis had supported a thriving city, but then an earthquake had shaken the hills and damaged the wells. The water had dwindled to a few seeping drops. Even though the wells had been dug deeper to reach the receding water, and the earthen steps reached down to where the surface of the water was always in shade, the city had died. The roofless walls stood forlorn in the silence, and lizards sunned themselves in the courtyards where rich merchants had once dallied with their harems.

Our very first concern was to refill the water-skins. The voices of the men drawing water at the bottom of the well were distorted by the echoes in the deep shaft. While they were busy, Tanus and I made a swift tour of the ruined city. It was a lonely and melancholy place. In its centre was the dilapidated temple to the patron god of Gallala. The roof had fallen in and the walls were collapsing in places. It had but a single entrance through the crumbling gateway at the western end.

'This will do admirably,' Tanus muttered as he strode across it, measuring it with his soldier's eye for fortification and ambuscade. When I questioned him on his intentions, he smiled and shook his head. 'Leave that part of it to me, old friend. The fighting is my business.'

As we stood at the centre of the temple I noticed the tracks of a troop of baboons in the dust at our feet, and I pointed them out to Tanus, 'They must come to drink at the wells,' I told him.

That evening when we sat around the small, smoky fires of dried donkey dung in the ancient temple, we heard the baboons again, the old bull apes barking a challenge in the hills that surrounded the ruined city. Their voices boomed back and forth along the cliffs, and I nodded at Tanus across the fire. 'Your friend, Shufti, has arrived at last. His scouts are in the hills up there watching us now. It is they who have alarmed the baboons.'

'I hope you are right. My blackguards are close to mutiny. They know this is all your idea, and if you are wrong, I might have to give them your head or your backside to appease them,' Tanus growled, and went to speak to Astes at the neighbouring cooking-fire.

Swiftly a new mood infected the camp as they realized that the enemy was near. The scowls evaporated and the men grinned at each other in the firelight, as they surreptitiously tested the edges of the swords concealed beneath the sleeping-mats on which they sat. However, they were canny veterans and they went through the motions of normal caravan life, so as not to alert the watchers in the dark hills above us. At last we were all bundled on our mats, and the fires died down, but none of us slept. I could hear them coughing and fidgeting restlessly all around me in the dark. The long hours drew out, and through the open roof I watched the great constellations of the stars wheel in stately splendour overhead, but still the attack

342

never came.

Just before dawn, Tanus made his round of the sentries for the last time, and then, on his way back to his place beside the cooling ashes of last night's fire, he stopped by my mat for a moment and whispered, 'You and your friends the baboons, you deserve each other. All of you bark at shadows.'

'The Shrikes are here. I can smell them. The hills are full of them,' I protested.

'All you can smell is the promise of breakfast,' he grunted. He knows how I detest the suggestion that I am a glutton. Rather than reply to such callow humour, I went out into the darkness to relieve myself behind the nearest pile of ruins.

As I squatted there, a baboon barked again, the wild, booming cry shattering the preternatural silences of that last and darkest of the nightwatches. I turned my head in that direction and heard, faint and faraway, the sound of metal strike rock, as though a nervous hand had dropped a dagger up there on the ridge, or a careless shield had brushed against a granite outcrop as an armed man hurried to take up his station before the dawn found him out.

I smiled complacently to myself; there are few pleasures in my life compared to that of making Tanus eat his words. As I returned to my mat, I whispered to the men that I passed, 'Be ready. They are here,' and I heard my warning passed on from mouth to sleepless mouth.

Above me the stars began to fade away, and the dawn crept up on us as stealthily as a lioness stalking a herd of oryx. Then abruptly I heard a sentry on the west wall of the temple whistle, a liquid warble that might have been the cry of a nightjar except that we all knew better, and instantly a stir ran through the camp. It was checked by the low but urgent whispers of Kratas and his officers, 'Steady, the Blues! Remember your orders. Hold your positions!' and not a man stirred from his sleeping-mat.

Without rising, and with my shawl masking my face, I turned my head slowly and looked up at the crests of the cliffs that stood higher than the temple walls. The shark's-tooth silhouette of the granite hills began to alter most subtly. I had to blink my eyes to be certain of what I was seeing. Then slowly I turned my head in a full circle, and it was the same in whichever direction I looked. The skyline all about us was picketed with the dark and menacing shapes of armed men. They formed an unbroken palisade around us through which no fugitive could hope to escape.

I knew then why Shufti had delayed his retaliation so long. It would have taken him all this time to gather together such an army of thieves. There must be a thousand or more of them, although in the poor light it was not possible to count their multitudes. We were outnumbered at least ten to one, and I felt my spirits quail. It was poor odds, even for a company of the Blues.

The Shrikes stood as still as the rocks around them, and I was alarmed at this evidence of their discipline. I had expected them to come streaming down upon us in an untidy rabble, but they were behaving like trained warriors. Their stillness was more menacing and intimidating than any wild shouting and brandishing of weapons would have been.

As the light strengthened swiftly, we could make

them out more clearly. The first rays of the sun glanced off the bronze of their shields and their bared sword-blades, and struck darts of light into our eyes. Every one of them was muffled up, a scarf of black wool wound around each head so that only their eyes showed in the slits, eyes as malevolent as those of the ferocious blue sharks that terrorize the waters of the sea we had left behind us.

The silence drew out until I thought that my nerves might tear and my heart burst with the pressure of blood within it. Then suddenly a voice rang out, shattering the dawn silence and echoing along the cliffs. 'Kaarik! Are you awake?'

I recognized Shufti then, despite the scarf that masked him. He stood in the centre of the west wall of the cliff, where the road cut through it. 'Kaarik!' he called again. 'It is time for you to pay what you owe me, but the price has risen. I want everything now. Everything!' he repeated, and flung aside the scarf so that his pock-marked features were revealed. 'I want everything you have, including your stupid and arrogant head.'

Tanus rose from his mat and threw aside his sheepskin rug. 'Then you will have to come down and take it from me,' he shouted back, and drew his sword.

Shufti raised his right arm, and his blind eye caught the light and gleamed like a silver coin. Then he brought his arm down abruptly.

At his signal, a shout went up from the ranks of men that lined the high ground, and they lifted their weapons and shook them to the pale yellow dawn sky. Shufti waved them forward and they streamed down the cliffs in a torrent into the

345

narrow valley of Gallala.

Tanus raced to the centre of the temple court where the ancient inhabitants had raised a tall stone altar to their patron Bes, the dwarf god of music and drunkenness. Kratas and his officers ran to join him, while the slave girls and I crouched on our mats and covered our heads, wailing with terror.

Tanus leaped up on to the altar, and went down on one knee as he flexed the great bow Lanata. It took all of his strength to string it, but when he stood erect again it shimmered in its coils of silver electrum wire, as though it were a living thing. He reached over his shoulder and drew an arrow from the quiver on his back and faced the main gateway through which the horde of Shrikes must enter.

Below the altar, Kratas had drawn up his men into a single rank, and they also had strung their bows and faced the entrance to the square. They made a pitifully small cluster around the altar, and I felt a lump rise in my throat as I watched them. They were so heroic and undaunted. I would compose a sonnet in their honour, I decided on a sudden impulse, but before I could find the first line, the head of the mob of bandits burst howling through the ruined gateway.

Only five men abreast could climb the steep stairway into the opening, and the distance to where Tanus stood on the altar was less than forty paces. Tanus drew and let his first arrow fly. That single arrow killed three men. The first of them was a tall rogue dressed in a short kilt, with long greasy tresses of hair streaming down his back. The arrow took him in the centre of his naked chest and passed through his torso as cleanly as

346

though he were merely a target cut from a sheet of papyrus.

Slick with the blood of the first man, the arrow struck the man behind him in the throat. Although the force of it was dissipating now, it still went through his neck and came out behind him, but it could not drive completely through. The fletchings at the back of the shaft snagged in his flesh, while the barbed bronze arrow-head buried itself in the eye of the third man who had crowded up close behind him. The two Shrikes were pinned together by the arrow, and they staggered and thrashed about in the middle of the gateway, blocking the opening to those who were trying to push their way past them into the courtyard. At last the arrow-head tore out of the third man's skull, with the eye impaled upon the point. The two stricken men fell apart, and a throng of screaming bandits poured over them into the square. The small band around the altar met them with volley after volley of arrows, shooting them down so that their corpses almost blocked the opening, and those coming in from behind were forced to scramble over the mounds of dead and wounded.

It could not last much longer, the pressure of warriors from behind was too great and their numbers too overwhelming. Like the bursting of an earthen dyke unable to stem the rising flood of the Nile, they forced the opening, and a solid mass of fighting men poured into the square and surrounded the tiny band around the altar of the god Bes.

It was too close quarters for the bows now, and Tanus and his men cast them aside and drew their swords. 'Horus, arm me!' Tanus shouted his battle-cry, and the men around him took it up, as they went to work. Bronze rang on bronze as the Shrikes tried to come at them, but they had formed a ring around the altar, facing outwards. No matter from which side they came, the Shrikes were met by the point and the deadly swordplay of the guards. The Shrikes were not short of courage, and they pressed in serried ranks around the altar. As one of them was cut down, another leaped into his place.

I saw Shufti in the gateway. He was holding back from the fray, but cursing his men and ordering them into the thick of it with horrid howls of rage. His blind eye rolled in its socket as he exhorted them, 'Get me the Assyrian alive. I want to kill him slowly and hear him squeal.'

The bandits completely ignored the women who still cowered on their sleeping-mats, their heads covered, wailing and screeching with terror. I wailed with the best of them, but the struggle in the centre of the yard was too uncomfortable for my liking. By this time, there were over a thousand men crowded into the confined space. Choking in the dust, I was kicked and pummelled by the sandalled feet of the battling horde, until I managed to crawl away into a corner of the wall.

One of the bandits turned aside from the fighting and stooped over me. He tore the shawl away from my face and for a moment stared into my eyes. 'Mother of Isis,' he breathed, 'you are beautiful!'

He was an ugly devil with gaps in his teeth and a scar down one cheek. His breath stank like a sewerage gutter as he lusted into my face. 'Wait until this business is over. Then I'll give you something to make you squeal with joy,' he promised, and twisted my face up to his. He kissed me.

My natural instinct was to pull away from him, but I resisted it and returned his kiss. I am an artist of the love arts, for I learned my skills in the boys' quarters of Lord Intef. My kisses can turn a man to water.

I kissed him with all my skill, and he was transfixed by it. While he was still paralysed, I slipped my dagger from its sheath beneath my blouse and slid the point through the gap between his fifth and sixth ribs. When he screamed, I muffled the sound with my own lips and clasped him lovingly to my breast, twisting the blade in his heart until, with a shudder, he relaxed completely against me, and I let him roll over on his side.

I looked around me quickly. In the few moments that it had taken me to dispose of my admirer, the plight of the small group of guards around the altar had worsened. There were gaps in their single rank. Two men were down and Amseth was wounded. He had switched his sword into his left hand, while the other arm hung bleeding at his side.

With a rush of relief I saw that Tanus was still untouched, still laughing with the savage joy of it all as he plied the sword. But he had left it too late to spring the trap, I thought. The entire band of Shrikes were crowded into the square and baying around him like hounds around a treed leopard. Within moments he and his gallant little band must be cut down.

Even as I watched, Tanus killed another of them with a straight thrust through the throat, and then he jerked his blade free of the clinging flesh and stepped back. He threw back his head and let loose a bellow that rang from the crumbling walls around us. 'On me, the Blues!'

On the instant every one of the cringing slave girls leapt up and flung aside their trailing robes. Their swords were already bared and they fell upon the rear of the robber horde. The surprise was complete and overwhelming. I saw them kill a hundred or more before their victims even realized what they were about, and could rally to meet them. But when they did turn to face this fresh attack, they exposed their backs to Tanus and his little band.

They fought well, I'll give them that, though I am sure it was terror, rather than courage, that drove them on. However, their ranks were too close-packed to allow them free play with the sword, and the men they faced were some of the finest troops in Egypt, which is to say the entire world.

For a while yet they held on. Then Tanus bellowed again from the midst of the turmoil. For a moment I thought it was another command, then I realized that it was the opening bar of the battle hymn of the guards. Though I had often heard it spoken in awe that the Blues always sang when the battle was at its height, I had never truly believed it possible. Now all around me the song was taken up by a hundred straining voices:

We are the breath of Horus,
hot as the desert wind,
we are the reapers of men—

Their swords beat an accompaniment to the words, like the clangour of hammers on the anvils of the underworld. In the face of such arrogant ferocity the remaining Shrikes wavered, and then suddenly it was no longer a battle, but a massacre.

I have seen a pack of wild dogs surround and tear into a flock of sheep. This was worse. Some of the Shrikes threw down their swords and fell to their knees begging quarter. There was no mercy shown them. Others tried to reach the gateway, but guardsmen waited for them there, sword in hand.

I danced on the fringes of the fighting, screaming across at Tanus, trying to make myself heard in the uproar, 'Stop them. We need prisoners.'

Tanus could not hear me, or more likely he simply ignored my entreaties. Singing and laughing, with Kratas at his left hand and Remrem on the other, he tore into them. His beard was soaked with the spurted blood of those he had killed, and his eyes glittered in the running red mask of his face with a madness I had never seen in them before. Joyous Hapi, how he thrived on the heady draught of battle!

'Stop it, Tanus! Don't kill them all!' This time he heard me. I saw the madness fade, and he was once more in control of himself.

'Give quarter to those who plead for it!' he roared, and the guards obeyed him. But in the end, out of the original thousand, fewer than two hundred Shrikes grovelled unarmed on the bloody stone flags and pleaded for their lives.

For a while I stood dazed and uncertain on the fringe of this carnage, and then from the corner of my eye I caught a furtive movement.

Shufti had realized that he could not escape through the gateway. He threw down his sword and darted to the east wall of the court, close to where I stood. This was the most ruined section, where the wall was reduced to half its original height. The tumbled mud-bricks formed a steep ramp, and Shufti scrambled up it, slipping and falling, but rapidly nearing the top of the wall. It seemed that I was the only one who had noticed his flight. The guards were busy with their other prisoners, and Tanus had his back turned to me as he directed the mopping-up of the shattered enemy.

Almost without thinking, I stooped and picked up half a mud-brick. As Shufti topped the wall, I hurled the brick up at him with all my strength. It thumped against the back of his skull with such force that he dropped to his knees, and then the treacherous pile of loose rubble gave way beneath him and he came sliding back down in a cloud of dust to land at my feet, only half-conscious.

I pounced upon him where he lay, straddling his chest, and I pressed the point of my dagger to his throat. He stared up at me, his single eye still glazed with the crack I had dealt him.

'Lie still,' I cautioned him, 'or I will gut you like a fish.'

I had lost my shawl and head-dress, and my hair had come down on to my shoulders. He recognized me then, which was no surprise. We had met often, but in different circumstances.

'Taita, the eunuch!' he mumbled. 'Does Lord Intef know what you are about?'

'He will find out soon enough,' I assured him,

and pricked him until he grunted, 'but you will not be the one to enlighten him.'

Without removing the point from his throat, I shouted to two of the nearest guards to take him. They flipped him on to his face and bound his wrists together with linen twine before they dragged him away.

Tanus had seen me capture Shufti, and he strode across to me now, stepping over the dead and wounded. 'Good throw, Taita! You have forgotten nothing that I taught you.' He clapped me on the back so hard that I staggered. 'There is plenty of work for you still. We've lost four men killed, and there are at least a dozen wounded.'

'What about their camp?' I asked, and he stared at me.

'What camp?'

'A thousand Shrikes did not spring up from the sands like desert flowers. They must have pack-animals and slaves with them. Not far from here, either. You must not let them escape. Nobody must escape to tell the tale of today's battle. None of them must be allowed to carry the news to Karnak that you are still alive.'

'Sweet Isis, you are right! But how will we find them?' It was obvious that Tanus was still bemused with battle lust. Sometimes I wondered what he would do without me.

'Back-track them,' I told him impatiently. 'A thousand pairs of feet will have trodden a road for us to follow back to where they came from.' His expression cleared, and he hailed Kratas across the length of the temple. 'Take fifty men. Go with Taita. He will lead you to their base-camp.'

'The wounded—' I began to protest. I had

enjoyed enough fighting for one day, but he brushed my objections aside. 'You are the best tracker I have. The wounded can wait for your care, my ruffians are all as tough as fresh buffalo steaks, very few of them will die before you return.'

 Finding their camp was as simple as I had made it sound.

With Kratas and fifty men following me closely, I made a wide cast around the city, and behind the first line of hills I picked up the broad track that they had made as they came in and deployed to surround us. We followed it back at a trot, and had covered less than a mile before we topped a rise and found the camp of the Shrikes in the shallow valley below us.

Their surprise was complete. They had left fewer than twenty men to guard the donkeys and women. Kratas' men overran them at the first rush, and this time I was too late to save any prisoners. They spared only the women, and once the camp was secure, Kratas let his men have them as part of the traditional reward of the victors.

The women seemed to me to be a more comely selection than I would have expected in such company. I saw quite a few pretty faces amongst them. They submitted to the rituals of conquest with a remarkably good grace. I even heard some of them laughing and joking as the guardsmen threw dice for them. The vocation of camp-follower to a band of Shrikes could not be considered the most delicate calling, and I doubted that any of these ladies were blushing virgins. One

354

by one, they were led by their new owners behind the cover of the nearest clump of rocks, where their skirts were lifted without further ceremony.

New moon follows the death of the old, spring follows winter, none of the ladies showed any signs of mourning for their erstwhile spouses. Indeed, it seemed probable that new and perhaps lasting relationships were being struck up here on the desert sand.

For myself, I was more interested in the pack-donkeys and what they carried. There were over a hundred and fifty of these, and most of them were sturdy animals in prime condition which would fetch good prices in the market at Karnak or Safaga. I reckoned that I should be entitled to at least a centurion's share when the prize money was divided up. After all, I had already dispensed large amounts of my own savings in the furtherance of this enterprise, and should be entitled to some compensation. I would speak seriously to Tanus about it, and could expect his sympathy. His is a generous spirit.

By the time we returned to the city of Gallala, leading the captured pack-animals laden with booty and followed by a straggle of women who had attached themselves quite naturally to their new menfolk, the sun had set.

One of the smaller ruined buildings near the wells had been turned into a field hospital. There I worked through the night, by the light of torch and oil lamp, sewing together the wounded guardsmen. As always, I was impressed by their stoicism, for many of their wounds were grave and painful. None the less, I lost only one of my patients before dawn broke. Amseth succumbed to loss of blood from the severed arteries in his arm. If I had attended to him immediately after the battle, instead of going off into the desert, I might have been able to save him. Even though the responsibility rested with Tanus, I felt the familiar guilt and sorrow in the face of a death that I might have prevented. However, I was confident that my other patients would heal swiftly and cleanly. They were all strong young men in superb condition.

There were no wounded Shrikes to attend. Their heads had been lopped off where they lay on the battlefield. As a physician, I was perturbed by this age-old custom of dealing with the wounded enemy, yet I suppose there was logic in it. Why should the victors waste their resources on the maimed vanquished, when it was unlikely they would have any value as slaves, and, if left alive, might recover to fight against them another day?

I worked all night with only a swallow of wine and a few mouthfuls of food taken with bloody hands to sustain me, and I was almost exhausted, but there was to be no rest for me yet. Tanus sent for me as soon as it was light.

 The unwounded prisoners were being held in the temple of Bes. Their wrists were bound behind their backs, and they were squatting in long lines along the north wall, with the guards standing over them.

As soon as I entered the temple, Tanus called me to where he stood with a group of his officers. I was still in the dress of an Assyrian wife, so I lifted my blood-splattered skirts and picked my way across the floor littered with the debris of the battle.

'There are thirteen clans of Shrikes—isn't that what you told me, Taita?' Tanus asked, and I nodded. 'Each clan with its own baron. We have Shufti. Let's see if you recognize any of the other barons amongst this gathering of the fair and gentle people.' He indicated the prisoners with a chuckle, and took my arm to lead me down the ranks of squatting men.

I kept my face veiled so that none of the prisoners could recognize me. I glanced at each face as I passed, and recognized two of them. Akheku was head of the southern clan that preyed on the lands around Assoun, Elephantine and the first cataract, while Setek was from further north, the baron of Kom-Ombo.

It was clear that Shufti had gathered together whatever men he could find at such short notice. There were members of all the clans amongst those that we had captured. As I identified their leaders with a tap on the shoulder, they were dragged away.

When we reached the end of the line Tanus asked, 'Are you sure that you missed none of them?'

'How can I be sure? I told you that I never met all of the barons.'

Tanus shrugged. 'We could not hope to catch every little bird with one throw of the net. We must count ourselves fortunate that we have taken as many as three so soon. But let us look at the heads. We might be lucky enough to find a few more amongst them.'

This was a gruesome business that might have

affected a more delicate stomach than mine, but human flesh, both dead and living, is my stock-in-trade. While we sat at our ease on the steps of the temple enjoying our breakfast, the severed heads were displayed to us, held up one at a time by the blood-caked hair, tongues lolling from between slack lips, and dull eyes powdered with dust staring into the other world whither they were bound.

My appetite was as healthy as ever, for I had eaten very little during the last two days. I devoured the delicious cakes and fruits that Tiamat had provided, while I pointed out those heads I recognized. There was a score or so of common thieves that I had encountered during the course of my work for Lord Intef, but only one more of the barons. He was Nefer-Temu of Qena, a lesser member of the ghastly brotherhood.

'That makes four of them,' Tanus grunted with satisfaction, and ordered Nefer-Temu's head to be placed on the pinnacle of the pyramid of skulls that he was erecting in front of the well of Gallala.

'So now we have accounted for four of them. We must find the other nine barons. Let us begin by putting the question to our prisoners.' He stood up briskly, and I hastily gulped down the remains of my breakfast and followed him reluctantly back into the temple of Bes.

Although I was the one who had made clear to Tanus the necessity of having informers from within the clans, and indeed it was I who had suggested how we should recruit them, still now that the time to act upon my suggestion had arrived, I was stricken with remorse and guilt. It was one thing to suggest ruthless action, but

358

another thing entirely to stand by and watch it practised.

I made a feeble excuse that the wounded men in the makeshift hospital might need me, but Tanus brushed it away cheerfully. 'None of your fine scruples now, Taita. You will stay with me during the questioning to make certain that you overlooked none of your old friends on your first inspection.'

The questioning was swift and merciless, which I suppose was only appropriate to the character of the men we were dealing with.

To begin with, Tanus sprang up on to the stone altar of Bes, and, with the hawk seal in one hand, he looked down on the ranks of squatting prisoners with a smile that must have chilled them, even though they sat in the full rays of the desert sun.

'I am the bearer of the hawk seal of Pharaoh Mamose, and I speak with his voice,' he told them grimly, as he held the statuette high. 'I am your judge and your executioner.' He paused and let his gaze pass slowly over their upturned faces. As each of them met his eyes, they dropped their own. Not one of them could hold firm before his penetrating scrutiny.

'You have been taken in the act of pillage and murder. If there is one of you who would deny it, let him stand before me and declare his innocence.'

He waited while the impatient shadows of the vultures, circling in the sky above us, criss-crossed the dusty courtyard. 'Come now! Speak up, you innocents.' He glanced upwards at the circling birds with their grotesque pink bald heads. 'Your brethren grow impatient for the feast. Let us not

359

keep them waiting.'

Still none of them spoke or moved, and Tanus lowered the hawk seal. 'Your actions, which all here have witnessed, condemn you. Your silence confirms the verdict. You are guilty. In the name of the divine Pharaoh, I pass sentence upon you. I sentence you to death by beheading. Your severed heads will be displayed along the caravan routes. All law-abiding men who pass this way will see your skulls grinning at them from the roadside, and they will know that the Shrike has met the eagle. They will know that the age of lawlessness has passed from the land, and that peace has returned to this very Egypt of ours. I have spoken. Pharaoh Mamose has spoken.'

Tanus nodded, and the first prisoner was dragged forward and forced to his knees before the altar.

'If you answer three questions truthfully, your life will be spared. You will be enlisted as a trooper in my regiment of the guards, with all the pay and privileges. If you refuse to answer the questions, your sentence will be carried out immediately,' Tanus told him.

He looked down on the kneeling prisoner sternly. 'This is the first question. What clan do you belong to?'

The condemned man made no reply. The blood oath of the Shrikes was too strong for him to break.

'This is the second question. Who is the baron that commands you?' Tanus asked, and still the man was silent.

'This is the third and the last question. Will you lead me to the secret places where your clan hides?' Tanus asked, and the man looked up at

360

him, hawked in his throat and spat. His phlegm spattered yellow upon the stones. Tanus nodded to the guardsman who stood over him with the sword.

The stroke was clean and the head toppled on to the steps at the foot of the altar. 'One more head for the pyramid,' Tanus said quietly, and nodded for the next prisoner to be brought forward.

He asked the same three questions, and when the Shrike answered him with a defiant obscenity, Tanus nodded. This time the headsman mistimed the blow and the corpse flopped about with the neck only half-severed. It took three more strokes before the head bounced down the steps.

Tanus lopped twenty-three heads, I was counting them to distract myself from the waves of debilitating compassion that assailed me, until the first of the condemned men broke down. He was young, not much more than a boy. In a shrill voice he gabbled out the replies before Tanus could actually pose the three questions to him.

'My name is Hui. I am a blood-brother of the clan of Basti the Cruel. I know his secret places, and I will lead you to them.' Tanus smiled with grim satisfaction and gestured for the lad to be led away. 'Care for him well,' he warned his gaolers. 'He is now a trooper of the Blues, and your companion-in-arms.'

After the defection of one of them, it went more readily, although there were still many who defied Tanus. Some of them cursed him, while others laughed their defiance at him until the blade swept down, and their bravado ended with their very last breath that burst from the severed windpipe in a crimson gust.

I was filled with admiration for those who, after a base and despicable life, at the end chose to die with some semblance of honour. They laughed at death. I knew that I was not capable of that quality of courage. Offered that choice, I am certain that I would have responded as some of the weaker prisoners did.

'I am a member of the clan of Ur,' one confessed.

'I am of the clan of Maa-En-Tef, who is baron of the west bank as far as El Kharga,' said another, until we had informers to lead us to the strongholds of every one of the remaining robber barons, and a shoulder-high pile of recalcitrant heads to add to the pyramid beside the well.

One of the matters to which Tanus and I had given much thought was the disposal of the three robber barons we had already captured, and the score of informers we had gleaned from the ranks of the condemned Shrikes.

We knew that the influence of the Shrikes was so pervasive that we dared not keep our captives in Egypt. There was not a prison secure enough to prevent Akh-Seth and his barons from reaching them, either to set them free by bribery or force, or to have them silenced by poison or some other unpleasant means. We knew that Akh-Seth was like an octopus whose head was hidden, but whose tentacles reached into every facet of our government and into the very fabric of our existence.

362

This was where my friend Tiamat, the merchant of Safaga, came into my reckoning.

Marching now as a unit of the Blue Crocodile Guards, and not as a slave caravan, we returned to the port on the Red Sea in half the time that it had taken us to reach Gallala. Our captives were hustled aboard one of Tiamat's trading vessels that was waiting for us in the harbour, and the captain set sail immediately for the Arabian coast, where Tiamat maintained a secure slave-compound on the small off-shore island of Jez Baquan, run by his own warders. The waters around the island were patrolled by packs of ferocious blue sharks. Tiamat assured us that no one who had attempted escape from the island had ever avoided both the vigilance of the warders and the appetites of the sharks.

Only one of our captives was not sent to the island. He was Hui from the clan of Basti the Cruel, the same youngster who had been the first to capitulate to the threat of execution. During the march to the sea, Tanus had kept the lad close to him and had turned all the irresistible force of his personality upon him. By this time Hui was his willing slave. This special gift of Tanus' to win loyalty and devotion from the most unlikely quarters never failed to amaze me. I was sure that Hui, who had buckled so swiftly under the threat of execution, would now willingly lay down his worthless life for Tanus.

Under Tanus' spell, Hui poured out every detail that he could remember of the clan to which he had once sworn a blood-oath. I listened quietly, with my writing-brush poised, as Tanus questioned him and I recorded all he had to tell us.

We learned that the stronghold of Basti the

Cruel was in the fastness of that awful desert of Gebel-Umm-Bahari, on the summit of one of the flat-topped mountains that was protected by sheer cliffs on every side. Hidden and impregnable, but less than two days' march from the east bank of the Nile and the busy caravan routes that ran along its banks, it was the perfect nest for the raptor.

'There is one path to the top, cut like a stairway from the rock. It is wide enough for only one man to climb at a time,' Hui told us.

'There is no other way to the summit?' Tanus asked, and Hui grinned and laid his finger along his nose in a conspiratory gesture.

'There is another route. I have used it often, to return to the mountain after I had deserted my post to visit a lady friend. Basti would have had me killed if he had known I was missing. It is a dangerous climb, but a dozen good men could make it and hold the top of the cliff while the main force came up the pathway to them. I will lead you up it, Akh-Horus.'

It was the first time that I heard the name. Akh-Horus, the brother of the great god Horus. It was a good name for Tanus. Naturally, Hui and our other captives could not know Tanus' real identity. They knew only in their simple way that Tanus must be some kind of god. He looked like a god and he fought like a god, and he invoked the name of Horus in the midst of battle. So, they had reasoned, he must be the brother of Horus.

Akh-Horus! It was a name that all Egypt would come to know well in the months ahead. It would be shouted from hilltop to hilltop. It would be carried along the caravan routes. It would travel the length of the river on the lips of the boatmen,

364

from city to city, and from kingdom to kingdom. The legend would grow up around the name, as the accounts of his deeds were repeated and exaggerated at each telling.

Akh-Horus was the mighty warrior who appeared from nowhere, sent by his brother Horus to continue the eternal struggle against evil, against Akh-Seth, the lord of the Shrikes.

Akh-Horus! Each time the people of Egypt repeated the name, it would fill their hearts with fresh hope.

All that was in the future as we sat in the garden of Tiamat the merchant. Only I knew how hot Tanus was for Basti, and how eager to lead his men into the Gebel-Umm-Bahari to hunt him down. It was not only that Basti was the most rapacious and pitiless of all the barons. There was much more to it than that. Tanus had a very personal score to settle with that bandit.

From me, Tanus had learned that Basti had been the particular instrument that Akh-Seth had used to destroy the fortune of Pianki, Lord Harrab, Tanus' father.

'I can lead you up the cliffs of Gebel-Umm-Bahari,' Hui promised. 'I can deliver Basti into your hands.'

Tanus was silent awhile in the darkness as he savoured that promise. We sat and listened to the nightingale singing at the bottom of Tiamat's garden. It was a sound totally alien from the evil and desperate affairs that we were discussing. After a while Tanus sighed and dismissed Hui.

'You have done well, lad,' he told him. 'Fulfil your promise, and you will find me grateful.'

Hui prostrated himself, as though before a god,

and Tanus nudged him irritably with his foot. 'Enough of that nonsense. Away with you now.'

This recent, unlooked-for elevation to the godhead embarrassed Tanus. No one could ever accuse him of being either modest or humble, but he was at least a pragmatist, with no false illusions of his own station; he never aspired to become either a pharaoh or a divine, and he was always short with any servility or obsequious behaviour from those around him.

As soon as the lad was gone, Tanus turned back to me. 'So often I lie awake in the night and consider all that you have told me about my father. I ache in every fibre of my body and soul for revenge against the one who drove him into penury and disgrace and hounded him to his death. I can barely restrain myself. I am filled by the desire to abandon this devious way that you have devised of trapping Akh-Seth. Instead, I long to seek him out directly, and tear out his foul heart with my bare hands.'

'If you do that, you will lose everything,' I said. 'You know that well. Do it my way and you will restore not only your own reputation, but that of your noble father into the bargain. My way, you will retrieve the estate and the fortune that was stolen from you. My way will not only give you your full measure of revenge, but will also lead you back to Lostris and the fulfilment of the vision that I divined for the pair of you in the Mazes of Ammon-Ra. Trust me, Tanus. For your sake and the sake of my mistress, trust me.'

'If I don't trust you, then who can I trust?' he asked, and touched my arm. 'I know you are right, but I have always lacked patience. For me the swift and direct road has always been easiest.'

'For the time being, put Akh-Seth out of your mind. Think only of the next step along the devious way that we must travel together. Think of Basti the Cruel. It was Basti who destroyed your father's trade caravans as they returned from the East. For five seasons, not one of the caravans of Lord Harrab ever returned to Karnak. They were all attacked and looted along the road. It was Basti who destroyed your father's copper-mines at Sestra and murdered the engineers, and their slave workers. Since then those rich veins of ore have lain untapped. It was Basti who systematically pillaged your father's estates along the Nile, who slaughtered his slaves in the fields and burned the crops, until in the end, only weeds grew in Lord Harrab's fields, and he was forced to sell them at a fraction of their real worth.'

'All that may be true, but it was Akh-Seth who gave Basti his orders.'

'No one will believe that. Pharaoh will not believe that, unless he hears Basti confess it,' I told him impatiently. 'Why are you always so stubborn? We have gone over this a hundred times. The barons first, and then at last the head of the snake, Akh-Seth.'

'Yours is the voice of wisdom, I know it. But it is hard to bear the waiting. I long for my revenge. I long to cleanse the stain of sedition and treason from my honour, and I long—oh, how I long—for Lostris!'

He leaned across and clasped my shoulder with a grip that made me wince. 'You have done enough here, old friend. I could never have accomplished so much without you. If you had not come to find me, I might still be sodden with drink and lying in the embrace of some stinking whore. I owe you more than I can ever repay, but I must send you away now. You are needed elsewhere. Basti is my meat, and I don't need you to share the feast with me. You will not be coming with me to Gebel-Umm-Bahari. I am sending you back where you belong—where I also belong, but where I cannot be—at the side of the Lady Lostris. I envy you, old friend, I would give up my hope of immortality to be going to her in your place.'

I protested most prettily, of course. I swore that all I wanted was another chance at those villains, and that I was his companion and that I would be seriously aggrieved if he would not give me a place at his side in the next campaign. All the time I was secure in the knowledge that when Tanus set his mind on a course of action he was adamant and could not easily be dissuaded, except very occasionally by his friend and adviser, Taita the slave.

The truth was that I had enjoyed my fill of wild heroics and people trying to kill me. I was not by nature a soldier, not some insensitive clod of a trooper. I hated the rigours of campaigning in the desert. I could not bear another week of heat and sweat and flies without even a glimpse of the sweet green waters of Mother Nile. I longed for the feel of clean linen against my freshly bathed and anointed skin. I missed my mistress more than I could express in mere words. Our quiet, civilized life in the painted rooms on the Island of Elephantine, our music and long, leisurely conversations together, my pets and my scrolls, all these exerted an irresistible draw upon me.

Tanus was right, he no longer needed me, and my place was with my mistress. However, to acquiesce too readily to his orders might lower his opinion of me, and I did not want that either.

At last I allowed him to convince me, and, concealing my eagerness, I began my preparations for my return to Elephantine.

Tanus had ordered Kratas back to Karnak, to assemble and bring up reinforcements for the expedition into the desert of Gebel-Umm-Bahari. I was to travel under his protection as far as Karnak, but taking leave of Tanus was not a simple matter. Twice when I had already left the house of Tiamat to join Kratas where he waited for me on the outskirts of the town, Tanus called me back to give me another message to take to my mistress.

'Tell her that I think of her every hour of every day!'

'You have already given me that message,' I protested. 'Tell her that my dreams are filled with images of her lovely face.'

'And that one also. I can recite them by heart. Give me something new,' I pleaded.

'Tell her that I believe the vision of the Mazes, that in a few short years we will be together—'

'Kratas is waiting for me. If you keep me here, how can I deliver your message?'

'Tell her that everything I do is for her. Every breath I draw is for her—' he broke off, and embraced me. 'The truth is, Taita, I doubt I can live another day without her.'

369

'Five years will pass like that single day. When next you meet her, your honour will be restored and you will once more stand high in the land. She can only love you the more for that.'

He released me. 'Take good care of her until I am able to assume that joyous duty from you. Now, away with you. Speed to her side.'

'That has been my intention this hour past,' I told him wryly, and made good my escape.

With Kratas at the head of our small detachment, we made the journey to Karnak in under a week. Fearful of discovery by Rasfer or Lord Intef, I spent as little time in my beloved city as it took me to find passage on one of the barges heading southwards. I left Kratas busily recruiting from amongst the elite regiments of Pharaoh's guards the thousand good men that Tanus had demanded, and I went aboard the barge.

We had the north wind in our sails all the way, and we tied up at the wharf of East Elephantine twelve days after leaving Thebes. I was still dressed in the wig and garb of the priesthood, and nobody recognized me as I came ashore.

For the price of a small copper ring I hired a felucca to take me across the river to the royal island, and it put me down at the steps that led up to the water-gate to our garden in the harem. My heart pounded against my ribs as I bounded up the stairs. I had been away from my mistress far too long. It was at times such as these that I realized the full strength of my feelings for her. I was certain that Tanus' love was but a light river breeze in comparison to the *khamsin* of my own emotions.

One of Lostris' Cushite maidens met me at the gate, and tried to prevent me from entering. 'My mistress is unwell, priest. There is another doctor with her at this moment. She will not see you.'

'She will see me,' I told her, and stripped off my wig.

'Taita!' she squealed, and fell to her knees, frantically making the sign to ward off evil. 'You are dead. This is not you, but some evil apparition from beyond the grave.'

I brushed her aside and hurried to my mistress's private quarters, to be met at the doors by one of those priests of Osiris who consider themselves physicians.

'What are you doing here?' I demanded of him, appalled that one of these quacks had been anywhere near my mistress. Before he could answer, I bellowed at him, 'Out! Get out of here! Take your spells and charms and filthy potions, and don't come back.'

He looked as though he were prepared to argue, but I placed my hand between his shoulder-blades and gave him a running start towards the gate. Then I rushed to my mistress's bedside.

The odour of sickness filled the chamber, sour and strong, and a wild grief seized me as I looked down at the Lady Lostris. She seemed to have shrunk in size, and her skin was pale as the ashes of an old camp-fire. She was asleep or in a coma, I could not be certain which, but there were dark, bruised shadows beneath her closed eyelids. Her lips had that dry and crusty look that filled me with dread.

I drew back the linen sheet that covered her and beneath it she was naked. I stared in horror at her body. The flesh had melted off her. Her limbs were thin as sticks and her ribs and the bones of her pelvis stuck out through the unhealthy skin, like those of drought-stricken kine. Tenderly, I placed my hand in her armpit to feel for the heat of fever, but her skin was cool. What kind of disease was this, I fretted. I had not encountered any like it before.

Without leaving her side, I yelled for her slave girls, but none of them had the courage to face the ghost of Taita. In the end I had to storm into their quarters and drag one of them whimpering from under her bed.

'What have you done to your mistress to bring her to this pass?' I kicked her fat backside to focus her attention on my question, and she whined and covered her face, so as not to have to look upon me.

'She will not eat. Barely a mouthful in all these weeks. Not since the mummy of Tanus, Lord Harrab was laid in his tomb in the Valley of the Nobles. She has even lost the child of Pharaoh that she was carrying in her womb. Spare me, kind ghost, I have done you no harm.'

I stared down at her in bewilderment for a moment, until I realized what had happened. My message of comfort to the Lady Lostris had never been delivered. Intuitively I guessed that the messenger whom Kratas had dispatched from Luxor to carry my letter to my mistress, had never reached Elephantine. He had probably become one more victim of the Shrikes, just another corpse floating down the river with an empty purse and a gaping wound in his throat. I hoped that my letter had fallen into the hands of some illiterate thief, and not been taken to Akh-Seth. There was no time to worry about that now.

I rushed back to my mistress's side and fell on my knees beside her bed. 'My darling,' I whispered, and stroked her haggard brow. 'It is me, Taita, your slave.'

She stirred slightly and mumbled something I could not catch. I realized that there was little time to spare; she was far-gone. It was over a month since Tanus' purported death. If the slave girl had spoken the truth, and she had indeed taken no food in all that time, then it was a wonder that she was still alive.

I leaped up again and ran to my own rooms. Despite my 'demise' nothing had been changed, and my medicine chest was in the alcove where I had left it. With it in my arms, I hurried back to my mistress. My hands were shaking as I lit a twig of the scorpion bush from the flame of the oil lamp beside her bed, and held the glowing end under her nose. Almost immediately she gasped and sneezed and struggled to avoid the pungent smoke.

'Mistress, it is I, Taita. Speak to me.'

She opened her eyes and I saw the dawn of pleasure in them swiftly extinguished by the fresh realization of her bereavement. She held out her thin, pale arms to me, and I took her to my breast.

'Taita,' she sobbed softly. 'He is dead. Tanus is dead. I cannot live without him.'

'No! No! He is alive. I come directly from him with messages of love and devotion from him to you.'

'You are cruel to mock me so. I know he is dead. His tomb is sealed—'

'It was a subterfuge to mislead his enemies,' I cried. 'Tanus lives. I swear it to you. He loves you. He waits for you.'

'Oh, that I could believe you! But I know you so well. You will lie to protect me. How can you torment me with false promises? I hate you so—' She tried to break from my arms.

'I swear it. Tanus is alive.'

'Swear on the honour of the mother you never knew. Swear on the wrath of all the gods.' She hardly had the strength to challenge me.

'On all these I swear, and on my love and duty to you, my mistress.'

'Can it be?' I saw the strength of hope flow back into her, and a faint flush of colour bloom in her cheeks. 'Oh, Taita, can it truly be?'

'Would I look so joyful, if it were not? You know I love him almost as much as you do. Could I smile thus, if Tanus were truly dead?'

While she stared into my eyes, I launched into a recitation of all that had occurred since I had left her side so many weeks ago. I excluded only the details of the condition in which I had discovered Tanus in the old shack in the swamps, and the female company I had found him keeping.

She said not a word, but her eyes never left my face as she devoured my words. Her pale face, almost translucent with starvation, glowed like a pearl as she listened to my account of our adventures at Gallala, of how Tanus led the fighting like a god, and of how he sang with the wild joy of battle.

'And so you see, it is true. Tanus is alive,' I ended, and she spoke for the first time since I had begun.

'If he is alive, then bring him to me. I will not eat a mouthful until I set my eyes upon his face once more.'

374

'I will bring him to your side as swiftly as I can send a messenger to him, if that is what you wish,' I promised, and reached for the polished bronze mirror from my chest.

I held the mirror before her eyes, and asked softly, 'Do you want him to see you as you are now?'

She stared at her own gaunt, hollow-eyed image.

'I will send for him today, if you order it. He could be here within a week, if you really want that.'

I watched her struggle with her emotions. 'I am ugly,' she whispered. 'I look like an old woman.'

'Your beauty is still there, just below the surface.'

'I cannot let Tanus see me like this.' Feminine vanity had triumphed over all her other emotions.

'Then you must eat.'

'You promise,' she wavered, 'you promise that he is still alive, and that you will bring him to me as soon as I am well again? Place your hand on my heart and swear it to me.'

I could feel her every rib and her heart fluttering like a trapped bird beneath my fingers. 'I promise,' I said.

'I will trust you this time, but if you are lying I will never trust you again. Bring me food!'

As I hurried to the kitchen, I could not help but feel smug. Taita, the crafty, had got his own way yet again.

I mixed a bowl of warm milk and honey. We would have to begin slowly, for she had driven herself to the very edge of starvation. She vomited up the contents of the first bowl, but was able to keep down the second. If I had delayed my return by another day, it might have been too late.

 Spread by the chattering slave girls, the news of my miraculous return from the grave swept through the island like the smallpox.

Before nightfall Pharaoh sent Aton to fetch me to an audience. Even my old friend Aton was strained and reserved in my presence. He leaped away nimbly when I tried to touch him, as though my hand might pass through his flesh like a puff of smoke. As he led me through the palace, slaves and nobles alike scurried out of my path, and inquisitive faces watched me from every window and dark corner as we passed.

Pharaoh greeted me with a curious mixture of respect and nervousness, most alien to a king and a god.

'Where have you been, Taita?' he asked, as though he did not really want to hear the answer.

I prostrated myself at his feet. 'Divine Pharaoh, as you yourself are part of the godhead, I understand that you ask that question to test me. You know that my lips are sealed. It would be sacrilege for me to speak of these mysteries, even to you. Please convey to the other deities who are your peers, and particularly to Anubis, the god of the cemeteries, that I have been true to the charge laid upon me. That I have kept the oath of silence imposed upon me. Tell them that I have passed the test that you set me.'

His expression glazed as he considered this, and he fidgeted nervously. I could see him forming

376

question after question, and then discarding each of them in turn. I had left him no opening to exploit.

In the end he blurted out lamely, 'Indeed, Taita, you have passed the test I set you. Welcome back. You have been missed.' But I could see that all his suspicions were confirmed, and he treated me with that respect due to one who had solved the ultimate mystery.

I crawled closer to him and dropped my voice to a whisper. 'Great Egypt, you know the reason I have been sent back?'

He looked mystified, but nodded uncertainly. I came to my feet and glanced around suspiciously, as though I expected to be overlooked by supernatural forces. I made the sign against evil before I went on, 'The Lady Lostris. Her illness was caused by the direct influence of—' I could not say the name, but made the horn sign with two fingers, the sign of the dark god, Seth.

His expression changed from confusion to dread, and he shivered involuntarily and drew closer to me, as if for protection, as I went on, 'Before I was taken away, my mistress was already carrying in her womb the treasure of the House of Mamose when the Dark One intervened. Due to her illness, the son she was bearing you has been aborted from her womb.'

Pharaoh looked distraught. 'So that is the reason that she miscarried,' he began, and then broke off.

I picked up my cue smoothly. 'Never fear, Great Egypt, I have been sent back by forces greater than those of the Dark One to save her, so that the destiny that I foresaw in the Mazes of Ammon-Ra may run its allotted course. There will be another

377

son to replace the one that was lost. Your dynasty will still be secured.'

'You must not leave the side of the Lady Lostris until she is well again.' His voice shook with emotion. 'If you save her and she bears me another son, you may ask from me whatever you wish, but if she dies—' he stopped as he considered what threat might impress one who had already returned from beyond, and in the end let it trail away.

'With your permission, Your Majesty, I shall go to her this instant.'

'This instant!' he agreed. 'Go! Go!'

 My mistress's recovery was so swift that I began to suspect that I had unwittingly invoked some force beyond my own comprehension, and I felt a superstitious awe at my own powers.

Her flesh filled out and firmed almost as I watched. Those pitiful empty sacs of skin swelled into plump, round breasts once again, sweet enough to make the stone image of the god Hapi which stood at the doorway to her chamber burn with envy. Fresh young blood suffused the chalk of her skin until it glowed once more, and her laughter tinkled like the fountains of our water-garden.

Very soon it was impossible to keep her to her bed. Within three weeks of my return to Elephantine, she was playing games of toss with her handmaidens, dancing about the garden and leaping high to reach the inflated bladder above the heads of the others, until, fearful that she might overtax her returning strength, I confiscated the ball and ordered her back to her chamber. She would obey me only after we had struck another bargain, and I had agreed to sing with her, or teach her the most arcane formulas of the bao board which would allow her to enjoy her first victory over Aton, who was an addict of the game.

Aton came almost every evening to enquire about my mistress's health on behalf of the king, and afterwards to play the board-game with us. Aton seemed to have decided at last that I was not a dangerous ghost, and although he treated me with a new respect, our old friendship survived my demise.

Each morning my Lady Lostris made me repeat my promise to her. Then she would reach for her mirror and study her reflection without the faintest trace of vanity, assessing every facet of her beauty to determine if it was ready yet to be looked upon by Lord Tanus.

'My hair looks like straw, and there is another pimple coming up on my chin,' she lamented. 'Make me beautiful again, Taita. For Tanus' sake make me beautiful.'

'You have done the damage to yourself, and then you call for Taita to make it better,' I grumbled, and she laughed and threw her arms around my neck.

'That's what you are here for, you old scallywag. To look after me.' Each evening when I mixed a tonic for her and brought the steaming bowl to her as she prepared for sleep, she would make me repeat my promise to her. 'Swear you will bring Tanus to me, just as soon as I am ready to receive him.'

I tried to ignore the difficulties and the dangers that this promise would bring upon us all. 'I swear it to you,' I repeated dutifully, and she lay back against the ivory headrest and went to sleep with a smile upon her face. I would worry about fulfilling my promise when the time came.

From Aton, Pharaoh had a full report of Lostris' recovery and came in person to visit her. He brought her a new necklace of gold and lapis lazuli in the form of an eagle and sat until evening, playing word-games and setting riddles with her. When he was ready to leave, he called me to walk with him as far as his chambers.

'The change in her is extraordinary. It is a miracle, Taita. When can I take her to bed again? Already she seems well enough to bear my son and heir.'

'Not yet, Great Egypt,' I assured him vehemently. 'The slightest exertion on the part of my mistress might trigger a relapse.'

He no longer questioned my word, for now I spoke with all the authority of the once dead, although his previous awe of me had worn a little thin with familiarity.

The slave girls also were becoming accustomed to my resurrection, and were able to look at my face without having to make the sign. Indeed, my return from the underworld was no longer the most popular fare of the palace gossips. They had something else to keep them busy. This was the advent of Akh-Horus into the lives and consciousness of every person living in the land along the great river.

The first time I heard the name Akh-Horus whispered in the palace corridors, I did not immediately place it. The garden of Tiamat beside the Red Sea seemed so remote from the little world of Elephantine, and I had forgotten the name that Hui had bestowed on Tanus. When, however, I heard the accounts of the extraordinary deeds ascribed to this demi-god, I realized who they were speaking about.

In a fever of excitement, I ran all the way back to the harem and found my mistress in the garden, besieged by a dozen visitors, noble ladies and royal wives, for she had so far recovered from her illness as to resume once more her role as court favourite.

I was so wrought up that I forgot my place as a mere slave, and to be rid of them I was quite rude to the royal ladies. They flounced out of the garden squawking like a gaggle of offended geese, and my mistress rounded on me. 'That was unlike you. What on earth has come over you, Taita?'

'Tanus!' I said the name like an incantation, and she forgot all her indignation and seized both my hands.

'You have news of Tanus! Tell me! Quickly, before I die of impatience.'

'News? Yes, I have news of him. What news! What extraordinary news. What unbelievable news!'

She dropped my hands and picked up her formidable silver fan. 'Stop your nonsense this instant,' she threatened me with it. 'I'll not put up with your teasing. Tell me, or I swear you'll have more lumps on your head than a Nubian has fleas.'

'Come! Let's go where nobody can hear us.' I led her down to the jetty and handed her into our little skiff. Out in the middle of the river we were safe from the flapping ears that lurked behind each corner of the palace walls.

'There is a fresh, clean wind blowing through the land,' I told her. 'They call this wind Akh-Horus.'

'The brother of Horus,' she breathed it with reverence. 'Is this what they call Tanus now?'

'None of them know it is Tanus. They think he is a god.'

'He is a god,' she insisted. 'To me, he is a god.'

'That is how they see it also. If he were not a god, how then would he know where the Shrikes are skulking, how else would he march unerringly to their strongholds, how would he know instinctively where they are waiting to waylay the incoming caravans, and to surprise them in their own ambuscades?'

'Has he accomplished all these things?' she demanded in wonder.

'These deeds and a hundred others, if you can believe the wild rumours that are flying about the palace. They say that every thief and bandit in the land runs in terror of his life, that the clans of the Shrikes are being shattered one by one. They say that Akh-Horus sprouted wings, like those of an eagle, and flew up the inaccessible cliffs of Gebel-Umm-Bahari to appear miraculously in the midst of the clan of Basti the Cruel. With his own hands, he hurled five hundred of the bandits from the top of the cliffs—'

'Tell me more!' She clapped her hands, almost capsizing the skiff in her enthusiasm.

382

'They say that at every crossroads and beside every caravan route he has built tall monuments to his passing.'

'Monuments? What monuments are these?'

'Piles of human skulls, high pyramids of skulls. The heads of the bandits he has slain, as a warning to others.'

My mistress shuddered with delicious horror, but her face still shone.

'Has he killed so many?' she demanded.

'Some say he has slain five thousand, and some say fifty thousand. There are even some who say one hundred thousand, but I think those must be exaggerating a little.'

'Tell me more! More!'

'They say he has already captured at least six of the robber barons—'

'And chopped off their heads!' she anticipated me with ghoulish relish.

'No, they say that he has not killed them, but transformed them into baboons. They say he keeps them in a cage for his amusement.'

'Is all of this possible?' she giggled.

'For a god, anything is possible.'

'He is my god. Oh, Taita, when will you let me see him?'

'Soon,' I promised. 'Your beauty burns up brighter every day. Soon it will be fully restored.'

'In the meantime you must gather every story and every rumour of Akh-Horus and bring them to me.'

She sent me to the shipping wharf every day to question the crews of the barges coming down from the north for news of Akh-Horus.

'They are saying now that nobody has ever seen

the face of Akh-Horus, for he wears a helmet with a visor that covers all but his eyes. They say also that in the heat of battle the head of Akh-Horus bursts into flame, a flame that blinds his enemies,' I reported to her after one such visit.

'In the sunlight I have seen Tanus' hair seem to burn with a heavenly light,' my mistress confirmed.

On another morning I could tell her, 'They say that he can multiply his earthly body like the images in a mirror, that he can be in many different places at one time, for on the same day he can be seen in Qena and Kom-Ombo, a hundred miles apart.'

'Is that possible?' she asked, with awe.

'Some say this is not true. They say that he can cover these great distances only because he never sleeps. They say that in the night hours he gallops through the darkness on the back of a lion, and in the day he soars through the sky on the back of an enormous white eagle to fall upon his enemies when they least expect it.'

'That could be true.' She nodded seriously. 'I do not believe about the mirror images, but the lion and the eagle might be true. Tanus could do something like that. I believe it.'

'I think it more likely that everybody in Egypt is eager to set eyes upon Akh-Horus, and that the desire is father to the act. They see him behind every bush. As to the speed of his travels, well, I have marched with the guards and I can vouch for—' She would not allow me to finish, but interrupted primly.

'There is no romance in your soul, Taita. You would doubt that the clouds are the fleece of

Osiris' flocks, and that the sun is the face of Ra, simply because you cannot reach up and touch them. I, for my part, believe Tanus is capable of all these things.' Which assertion put an end to the argument, and I hung my head in submission.

In the afternoons the two of us resumed our old practice of strolling through the streets and the market-places. As before her illness, my mistress was welcomed by an adoring populace, and she stopped to speak with all of them, no matter what their station or their calling. From priests to prostitutes, none was immune to her loveliness and her unfeigned charm.

Always she was able to turn the conversation to Akh-Horus, and the people were as eager as she was to discuss the new god. By this time he had been promoted in the popular imagination from demi-god to a full member of the pantheon. The citizens of Elephantine had already begun a subscription for the building of a temple to Akh-Horus, to which my mistress had made a most generous donation.

A site for the temple had been chosen on the bank of the river opposite the temple of Horus, his brother, and Pharaoh had made the formal declaration of his intention to dedicate the building in person. Pharaoh had every reason to be grateful. There was a new spirit of confidence abroad. As the caravan routes were made secure, so the volume of trade between the Upper Kingdom and the rest of the world blossomed.

Where before one caravan had arrived from the East, now four made a safe crossing of the desert, and as many set out on the return journey. To supply the caravan masters, pack-donkeys were needed in their thousands, and the farmers and breeders drove them into the cities, grinning at the expectation of the high prices they would receive.

Because it was now safe to work the fields furthest from the protection of the city walls, crops were planted where for decades only weeds had grown, and the farmers, who had been reduced to beggars, began to prosper again. The oxen drew the sledges piled high with produce along the roads that were now protected by the legions of Akh-Horus, and the markets were filled with fresh produce.

Some of the profits of the merchants and the land-owners from these ventures were spent in the building of new villas in the countryside, where it was once more deemed safe to take their families to live. Artisans and craftsmen, who had walked the streets of Thebes and Elephantine seeking employment for their skills, were suddenly in demand, and used their wages to buy not only the necessities of life but luxuries for themselves and their families. The markets were thronged.

The volume of traffic up and down the Nile swelled dramatically, so that more craft were needed, and the new keels were laid down in every shipyard. The captains and crews of the river boats and the shipyard workers spent their new wealth in the taverns and pleasure-houses, so that the prostitutes and the courtesans clamoured for fine clothes and baubles, and the tailors and the jewellers thrived and built new homes, while their wives prowled the markets with gold and silver in their purses, looking for everything from new slaves to cooking-pots.

Egypt was coming to life again, after being strangled for all these years by the depredations of Akh-Seth and the Shrikes.

As a result of all this, the state revenues burgeoned, and Pharaoh's tax-collectors circled above it all with as much relish as the vultures above the corpses of the bandits that Akh-Horus and his legions were strewing across the countryside. Of course, Pharaoh was grateful.

So were my mistress and I. At my suggestion, the two of us invested in a share of a trading expedition that was setting out eastwards into Syria. When the expedition returned six months later, we found that we had made a profit of fifty times our original investment. My mistress bought herself a string of pearls and five new female slaves to make my life miserable. Prudent as always, I used my share to acquire five plots of prime land on the east bank of the river, and one of the law scribes drew up the deeds and had them registered in the temple books.

Then came the day that I had been dreading. One morning my mistress studied her reflection in the mirror with even more attention than usual, and declared that she was ready at last. In all fairness, I had grudgingly to agree that she had never looked more lovely. It was as though all she had suffered recently had tempered her to a new

387

resilience. The last traces of girlishness, uncertainty, and puppy fat had evaporated from her features, and she had become a woman, mature and composed.

'I trusted you, Taita. Now prove to me that I was not silly to do so. Bring Tanus to me.'

When Tanus and I had parted at Safaga, we had been unable to agree on any sure method of exchanging messages.

'I will be on the march every day, and who can tell where this campaign will lead me. Do not let the Lady Lostris worry if she does not hear from me. Tell her I will send a message when my task is completed. But tell her that I will be there when the fruits of our love are ripe upon the tree, and are ready for plucking.'

Thus it was that we had heard nothing of him other than the wild rumours of the wharves and bazaars.

Once again it seemed that the gods had intervened to save me, this time from the wrath of my Lady Lostris. There was a fresh rumour in the market-place that day. A caravan coming down the northern road had encountered a recently erected pyramid of human heads at the roadside not two miles beyond the city walls. The heads were so fresh that they were stinking only a little and had not yet been cleaned of flesh by the crows and vultures.

'This means only one thing,' the gossips told each other. 'This means that Akh-Horus is in the nome of Assoun, probably within sight of the walls of Elephantine. He has fallen upon the remnants of the clan of Akheku, who have been skulking in the desert since their baron had his head hacked off at

Gallala. Akh-Horus has slaughtered the last of the bandits, and piled their heads at the roadside. Thanks be to the new god, the south has been cleared of the dreaded Shrikes!'

This was news indeed, the best I had heard in weeks, and I was in a fever to take it to my mistress. I pushed my way through the throng of sailors and merchants and fishermen on the wharf to find a boatman to take me back to the island.

Somebody tugged at my arm, and I shrugged the hand away irritably. Despite the new prosperity sweeping the land, or perhaps because of it, the beggars were more demanding than ever. This one was not so easily put off, and I turned back to him, angrily raising my staff to drive him off.

'Do not strike an old friend! I have a message for you from one of the gods,' the beggar whined, and I stayed the blow and gaped at him.

'Hui!' My heart soared as I recognized the sly grin of the erstwhile robber. 'What are you doing here?' I did not wait for a reply to my fatuous question, but went on swiftly, 'Follow me at a distance.'

I led him to one of the pleasure-houses in a narrow alley beyond the harbour that provided rooms to couples, of the same or of mixed gender. They rented the rooms for a short period measured by a water-clock set at the door, and charged a large copper ring for this service. I paid this exorbitant fee and the moment we were alone, I seized Hui by his ragged cloak.

'What news of your master?' I demanded, and he chuckled with infuriating insolence.

'My throat is so dry I can hardly speak.' Already he had adopted all the swagger and insolent panache of a trooper of the Blues. How quickly a monkey learns new tricks! I shouted for the porter to bring up a pot of beer. Hui drank like a thirsty donkey, then lowered the pot and belched happily.

'The god Akh-Horus sends greetings, to you and to another whose name cannot be mentioned. He bids me tell you that the task is completed and that all the birds are in the cage. He reminds you that it lacks only a few months to the next festival of Osiris and it is time to write a new script for the passion play for the amusement of the king.'

'Where is he? How long will it take for you to return to him?' I demanded eagerly.

'I can be with him before Ammon-Ra, the sun god, plunges beyond the western hills,' Hui declared, and I glanced through the window at the sun which was halfway down the sky. Tanus was lying up very close to the city, and I rejoiced anew. How I longed to feel his rough embrace, and hear that great booming laugh of his!

Grinning to myself in anticipation, I paced up and down the filthy floor of the room while I decided on the message that I would give Hui to take back to him.

 It was almost dark when I stepped ashore on our little jetty and hurried up the steps. One of the slave girls was weeping at the gate, and rubbing her swollen ear.

'She struck me,' the girl whimpered, and I saw that her dignity had suffered more than her ear.

'Do not refer to the Lady Lostris as "she",' I
390

scolded her.

'Anyway, what have you to complain of? Slaves are there to be struck.'

None the less, it was unusual for my mistress to lift a hand to anyone in her household. She must indeed be in a fine mood, I thought, and slowed my pace. Proceeding warily now, I arrived just as another of the girls fled weeping from the chamber. My mistress appeared in the doorway behind her, flushed with anger. 'You have turned my hair into a haystack—'

She saw me then and broke off her tirade. She rounded on me with such gusto that I knew that I was the true object of her ire.

'Where have you been?' she demanded. 'I sent you to the harbour before noon. How dare you leave me waiting so long?' She advanced upon me with such an expression that I backed off nervously.

'He is here,' I told her hastily, and then dropped my voice so that none of the slave girls could hear me. 'Tanus is here,' I whispered, 'the day after tomorrow I will make good my promise to you.'

Her mood swung in a full circle and she leaped up to throw her arms around my neck, then she went off to find her offended girls and to comfort them.

As part of his annual tribute the vassal king of the Amorites had sent Pharaoh a pair of trained hunting cheetahs from his kingdom across the Red Sea. The king was eager to run these magnificent creatures against the herds of gazelle that abounded in the desert dunes of the west bank. The entire court, including my mistress, had been commanded to attend the course.

We sailed across to the west bank in a fleet of small river craft, white sails and bright-coloured pennants fluttering. There was laughter and the music of lute and sistrum to accompany us. The annual flooding of the great river would begin within days, and this expectation, together with the prosperous new climate of the land, enhanced the carnival mood of the court.

My mistress was in a gayer mood than any of them, and she called merry greetings to her friends in the other boats as our felucca cut through the green summer waters at such a rate as to deck our bows with a lacy white garland of foam and leave a shining wake behind us.

It seemed that I was the only one who was not happy and carefree. The wind had a harsh, abrasive edge to it, and was blowing from the wrong quarter. I kept glancing anxiously at the western sky. It was cloudless and bright, but there was a brassy sheen to the heavens that was unnatural. It was almost as though another sun was dawning from the opposite direction to the one we knew so well.

I put aside my misgivings and tried to enter into

the spirit of the outing. I failed in this, for I had more than the weather to worry about. If one part of my plan went awry, my life would be in danger, and perhaps other lives more valuable than mine would be at risk.

I must have shown all this on my face, for my mistress nudged me with her pretty painted toe and told me, 'So glum, Taita? Everyone who looks at you will know that you are up to something. Smile! I command you to smile.'

When we landed on the west bank, there was an army of slaves waiting for us there. Grooms holding splendid white riding donkeys from the royal stables, all caparisoned with silk. Pack-donkeys laden with tents and rugs and baskets of food and wine, and all the other provisions for a royal picnic. There was a regiment of slaves in attendance, some to hold sun-shades above the ladies, others to wait upon the noble guests. There were clowns and acrobats and musicians to entertain them, and a hundred huntsmen to provide the sport.

The cheetah cage was loaded on a sledge drawn by a team of white oxen, and the court gathered around the vehicle to admire these rare beasts. They did not occur naturally in our land, for they were creatures of the open grassy savannah, and there was none of this type of terrain along the river. They were the first that I had ever seen, and my curiosity was so aroused that for a while I forgot my other worries and went up as close to the cage as I could push through the crowd without jostling or treading on the toes of some irascible nobleman.

They were the most beautiful cats that I could

imagine, taller and leaner than our leopards, with long, clean limbs and concave bellies. Their sinuous tails seemed to give expression to their mood. Their golden hides were starred with rosettes of deepest black, while from the inner corner of each of their eyes, a line of black was painted down the cheek like a runnel of tears. This, with their regal bearing, gave them a tragic and romantic air that I found enchanting. I longed to own one of these creatures, and I decided on the moment to put the thought into the mind of my mistress. Pharaoh had never refused one of her whims.

Too soon for my liking, the barque carrying the king across the river arrived on the west bank, and with the rest of the court we hurried to the landing to greet him.

Pharaoh was dressed in light hunting garb and for once seemed relaxed and happy. He stopped beside my mistress and while she made a ritual obeisance, he enquired graciously about her health. I was filled with dread that he might decide to keep her by his side throughout the day, which would have upset all my arrangements. However, the hunting cheetah caught his attention and he passed by without giving my mistress any order to follow.

We lost ourselves in the throng and made our way to where a donkey was being held for my Lady Lostris. While I helped her to mount, I spoke quietly to the groom. When he told me what I wanted to hear, I slipped a ring of silver into his hand, and it disappeared, as though by magic.

With one slave leading her and another holding a sun-shade over her, my mistress and I followed the king and the sledge out into the desert. With frequent stops for refreshment, it took us half the morning to reach the Valley of the Gazelles. On the way we passed at a distance the ancient cemetery of Tras which dated from the time of the very first pharaohs. Some of the wise men said that the tombs had been carved from the cliff of black rock three thousand years ago, although how they reached this conclusion I could not tell. Without making it obvious, I studied the entrances of the tombs keenly as we passed. However, from so far off I could make out no trace of recent human presence around them, and I was unreasonably disappointed. I kept glancing back, as we went on.

The Valley of the Gazelles was one of the royal hunting preserves, protected by the decrees of a long line of pharaohs. A company of royal gamekeepers was permanently stationed in the hills above the valley to enforce the king's proclamation reserving all the creatures in it to himself. The penalty for hunting here without the royal authority was death by strangulation.

The nobles dismounted on the crest of one of these hills overlooking the broad brown valley. With despatch the tents were set up to give them shade, and jars of sherbet and beer were broached to slake the thirst of their journey.

I made certain that my mistress and I secured a good vantage-point from which to watch the hunt, but one from which we could also withdraw discreetly without attracting undue attention to ourselves. In the distance I could make out the herds of gazelle through the wavering watery mirage on the floor of the valley. I pointed them out to my mistress.

395

'What do they find to eat down there?' My Lady Lostris asked. 'There is not a trace of green. They must eat stones, for there are enough of those.'

'Many of those are not stones at all, but living plants,' I told her. When she laughed in disbelief, I searched the rocky ground and plucked a handful of those miraculous plants.

'They are stones,' she insisted, until she held one in her hand and crushed it. The thick juice trickled over her fingers, and she marvelled at the cunning of whatever god had devised this deception. 'This is what they live on? It does not seem possible.'

We could not continue this conversation, because the hunt was beginning. Two of the royal huntsmen opened the cage and the hunting cheetahs leaped down to earth. I expected them to attempt to escape, but they were tame as temple cats and rubbed themselves affectionately against the legs of their handlers. The cats uttered a strange twittering sound, more like a bird than a savage predator.

Along the far side of the brown, scorched valley bottom I could make out the line of beaters, their forms tiny and distorted by distance and mirage. They were moving slowly in our direction, and the herds of antelope were beginning to drift ahead of them.

While the king and his huntsmen, with the cheetahs on leash, moved down the slope towards the valley bottom, we and the rest of the court remained on the crest. The courtiers were already placing wagers with one another, and I was as eager as any of them to watch the outcome of the hunt, but my mistress had her mind on other matters.

'When can we go?' she whispered. 'When can we escape into the desert?'

'Once the hunt begins, all their eyes will be upon it. That will be our opportunity.' Even as I spoke, the wind that had blown us across the river and cooled us on the march suddenly dropped. It was as though a coppersmith had opened the door of his forge. The air became almost too hot to breathe.

Once again I looked to the western horizon. The sky above it had turned a sulphurous yellow. Even as I watched, the stain seemed to spread across the heavens. It made me uneasy. However, I was the only one in the crowd who seemed to notice this strange phenomenon.

Although the hunting party was now at the bottom of the hill, it was still close enough for me to observe the great cats. They had seen the herds of gazelle which were being driven slowly towards them. This had transformed them from affectionate pets into the savage hunters they truly were. Their heads were up, intent and alert, ears pricked forward, leaning against the leash. Their concave bellies were sucked in, and every muscle was taut as a bowstring drawn to full stretch.

My mistress tugged at my skirt, and whispered imperatively, 'Let us be gone, Taita,' and reluctantly I began to edge away towards a clump of rocks that would cover our retreat and screen us from the rest of the company. The bribe of silver to the groom had procured for us a donkey that was now tethered out of sight amongst the rocks. As soon as we reached it, I checked that it carried what I had ordered, the water-skin and the leather bag of provisions. I found that they were all in order.

I could not restrain myself, and I pleaded with my mistress, 'Just one moment more.' Before she could forbid it, I scrambled to the top of the rocky outcrop and peeped down into the valley below.

The nearest antelope were crossing a few hundred paces in front of where Pharaoh held the pair of cheetahs on the leash. I was just in time to watch him slip them and send them away. They started out at an easy lope, heads up, as if they were studying the herds of daintily trotting antelope to select their prey. Suddenly the herds became aware of their rapid approach, and they burst into full flight. Like a flock of swallows they skimmed away across the dusty plain.

The cats stretched out their long bodies, reaching far ahead with their forepaws and then whipping their hindquarters through, doubling their lean torsos before stretching out again. Swiftly they built up to the top of their speed, and I had never seen an animal so swift. Compared to them, the herds of gazelle seemed suddenly to have run into swampy ground and to have had their flight impeded. With effortless elegance, the two cats overhauled the herd, and ran past one or two stragglers before they caught up with the victims of their choice.

The panic-stricken antelopes tried to dodge the deadly rush. They leaped high and changed direction in mid-air, twisting and doubling back the moment their dainty hooves touched the scorched earth. The cats followed each of the convolutions with graceful ease, and the end was inevitable. Each of them bore one of the gazelle to earth in a sliding, tumbling cloud of dust, and then crouched over it, jaws clamped across the windpipe to strangle it while the gazelle's back legs kicked out convulsively, and then at last stiffened into the rigor of death.

I found myself shaken and breathless with the excitement of it all. Then my mistress's voice roused me. 'Taita! Come down immediately. They will see you perched up there.' And I slid down to rejoin her.

Although I was still wrought up, I boosted her into the saddle and led the donkey down into the dead ground where we were out of sight of the company on the hilltop behind us. My mistress could not sustain her irritation with me for very long, and when I slyly mentioned Tanus' name again she forgot it entirely, and urged her mount on towards the rendez-vous.

Only after I had placed another ridge behind us and was certain that we were well clear of the Valley of the Gazelles, did I head back directly towards the cemetery of Tras. In the still, hot air, the sound of our donkey's hooves clinked and crackled on the stones as though it were passing over a bed of broken glass. Soon I felt the sweat break out upon my skin, for the air was close and heavy with a feeling of thunder. Long before we reached the tombs, I told my mistress, 'The air is dry as old bones. You should drink a little water—'

'Keep on! There will be plenty of time to drink your fill later.'

'I was thinking only of you, mistress,' I protested.

'We must not be late. Every moment you waste will give me that much less with Tanus.' She was right, of course, for we would have little enough time before we were missed by the others. My mistress was so popular that many would be looking to enjoy her company once the hunt was over and they were returning to the river.

As we drew closer to the cliffs, so her eagerness increased until she could no longer abide the pace of her mount. She leaped off its back and ran ahead to the next rise. 'There it is! That is where he will be waiting for me,' she cried, and pointed ahead.

As she danced on the skyline, the wind came at us like a ravening wolf, howling amongst the hills and canyons. It caught my mistress's hair and spread it like a flag, snapping and tangling it around her head. It lifted her skirts high above her slim brown thighs, and she laughed and pirouetted, flirting with the wind as though it were her lover. I did not share her delight.

I turned and looked back and saw the storm coming out of the Sahara. It towered into the sullen yellow heavens, dun and awful, billowing upon itself like surf breaking on a coral reef. The wind-blown sand scoured my legs and I broke into a run, dragging the donkey behind me on its lead. The wind thrusting into my back almost knocked me off my feet, but I caught my mistress.

'We must be quick,' I shouted above the wind. 'We must reach the shelter of the tombs before it hits us.'

High clouds of sand blew across the sun, dimming it until I could look directly at it with my naked eye. All the world was washed with that sombre shade of ochre, and the sun was a dull ball of orange. Flying sand raked the exposed skin of our limbs and the backs of our necks, until I wound my shawl around my mistress's head to protect her, and led her forward by the hand.

Sheets of driven sand engulfed us, blotting out our surroundings, so that I feared I had lost direction, until abruptly a hole opened in the curtains of sand, and I saw the dark mouth of one of the tombs appear ahead of us. Dragging my mistress with one hand and our donkey with the other, I staggered into the shelter of the cave. The entrance-shaft was carved from the solid rock. It led us deep into the hillside, and then made a sharp turn before entering the burial chamber where once the ancient mummy had been laid to rest. Centuries before, the grave-robbers had disposed of the embalmed body and all its treasures. Now all that remained were the faded frescoes upon the stone walls, images of gods and monsters that were ghostly in the gloom.

My mistress sank down against the rock wall, but her first thoughts were for her love. 'Tanus will never find us now,' she cried in despair, and I who had led her to safety was hurt by her ingratitude. I unsaddled our donkey and heaped the load in a corner of the tomb. Then I drew a cup of water from the skin and made her drink.

'What will happen to the others, the king and all our friends?' she asked, between gulps from the cup. It was her nature to think of the welfare of others, even in her own predicament.

'They have the huntsmen to care for them,' I told her. 'They are good men and know the desert.' But not well enough to have anticipated the storm, I thought grimly. Although I sought to reassure her, I knew it would go hard with the women and children out there.

'And Tanus?' she asked. 'What will become of him?'

'Tanus especially will know what to do. He is like one of the Bedouin. You can be sure he will have seen the storm coming.'

'Will we ever get back to the river? Will they ever find us here?' At last she thought of her own safety.

'We will be safe here. We have water enough for many days. When the storm blows itself out, we will find our way back to the river.' Thinking of the precious water, I carried the bulging skin further into the tomb, where the donkey would not trample it. By now it was almost completely dark, and I fumbled with the lamp that the slave had provided from the pack, and blew upon the smouldering wick. It flared and lit the tomb with a cheery yellow light.

While I was still busy with the lamp and my back was turned to the entrance, my mistress screamed. It was a sound so high and filled with such mortal terror that I was struck with equal dread, and the courses of my blood ran thick and slow as honey, although my heart raced like the hooves of the flying gazelle. I spun about and reached for my dagger, but when I saw the monster whose bulk filled the doorway, I froze without touching the weapon on my belt. I knew instinctively that my puny blade would avail us not at all against whatever this creature might be.

In the feeble light of the lamp the form was indistinct and distorted. I saw that it had a human shape, but it was too large to be a man, and the grotesque head convinced me that this was indeed that dreadful crocodile-headed monster from the

402

underworld that devours the hearts of those who are found wanting on the scales of Thoth, the monster depicted on the walls of the tomb. The head gleamed with reptilian scales, and the beak was that of an eagle or a gigantic turtle. The eyes were deep and fathomless pits that stared at us implacably. Great wings sprouted from its shoulders. Half-furled, they flapped about the towering body like those of a falcon at bate. I expected the creature to launch itself on those wings and to rend my mistress with brazen talons. She must have dreaded this as much as I, for she screamed again as she crouched at the monster's feet.

Then suddenly I realized that the creature was not winged, but that the folds of a long woollen cape, such as the Bedouin wear, were flogging on the wind. While we were still frozen by this horrible presence, it raised both hands and lifted off the gilded war helmet with the visor fashioned like the head of an eagle. Then it shook its head and a mass of red-gold curls tumbled down on to the broad shoulders.

'From the top of the cliff I saw you coming through the storm,' it said in those dear familiar tones.

My mistress screamed again, this time with wildly ringing joy. 'Tanus!' She flew to him, and he gathered her up as though she were a child and lifted her so high that her head brushed the rock roof. Then he brought her down and folded her to his chest. From the cradle of his arms, she reached up with her mouth for his, and it seemed that they might devour each other with the strength of their need.

I stood forgotten in the shadows of the tomb. Although I had conspired and risked so much to bring them together, I cannot bring myself to write down here the feelings that assailed me as I was made reluctant witness to their rapture. I believe that jealousy is the most ignoble of all our emotions, and yet I loved the Lady Lostris as well as Tanus did, and not with the love of a father or of a brother, either. I was a eunuch, but what I felt for her was the love of a natural man, hopeless of course, but all the more bitter because of that. I could not stay and watch them and I began to slink from the tomb like a whipped puppy, but Tanus saw me leaving and broke that kiss which was threatening to destroy my soul.

'Taita, don't leave me alone with the wife of the king. Stay with us to protect me from this terrible temptation. Our honour is in jeopardy. I cannot trust myself, you must stay and see that I bring no shame to the wife of Pharaoh.'

'Go,' cried my Lady Lostris from his arms. 'Leave us alone. I'll listen to no talk of shame or honour now. Our love has been too long denied. I cannot wait for the prophecy of the Mazes to run its course. Leave us alone now, gentle Taita.'

I fled from the chamber as though my life was in danger. I might have run out into the storm and perished there. That way I would have found surcease, but I was too much of a coward, and I let the wind drive me back. I stumbled to a corner of the shaft where the wind could no longer harry me, and I sank to the stone floor. I pulled my shawl over my head to stop my eyes and my ears, but although the storm roared along the cliff, it could not drown the sounds from the burial chamber.

For two days the storm blew with unabated ferocity. I slept for part of that time, forcing myself to seek oblivion, but whenever I awoke, I could hear them, and the sounds of their love tortured me. Strange that I had never known such distress when my mistress was with the king—but then on the other hand not so strange, for the old man had meant nothing to her.

This was another world of torment for me. The cries, the groans, the whispers tore at my heart. The rhythmic sobs of a young woman that were not those of pain threatened to destroy me. Her wild scream of final rapture was more agonizing to me than the cut of the gelding-knife.

At last the wind abated and died away, moaning at the foot of the cliffs. The light strengthened and I realized that it was the third day of my incarceration in the tomb. I roused myself and called to them, not daring to enter the inner chamber for fear of what I might discover. For a while there was no reply, and then my mistress spoke in a husky, bemused voice that echoed eerily down the shaft. 'Taita, is that you? I thought that I had died in the storm and been carried to the western fields of paradise.'

Once the storm had dropped, we had little time remaining. The royal huntsmen would already be searching for us. The storm had given us the best possible excuse for our absence. I was sure that the survivors of the hunting party would be scattered across these terrible hills. But the search-party must not

discover us in the company of Tanus.

On the other hand, Tanus and I had barely spoken during these last days, and there was much to discuss. Hastily we made our plans, standing in the entrance to the shaft.

My mistress was quiet and composed as I had seldom seen her before. No longer the irrepressible chatterbox, she stood beside Tanus, watching his face with a new serenity. She reminded me of a priestess serving before the image of her god. Her eyes never left his face, and occasionally she reached out to touch him, as if to reassure herself that it was truly he.

When she did this, Tanus broke off whatever he was saying and gave all his attention to those dark green eyes. I had to call him back to the business we still had not completed. In the presence of such manifest adoration, my own feelings were base and mean. I forced myself to rejoice for them.

It took longer to finish our business than I deemed wise, but at last I embraced Tanus in farewell and urged the donkey out into the sunlight that was filtered by the fine yellow dust that still filled the air. My mistress lingered, and I waited for her in the valley below.

Looking back, I saw them emerge from the cave at last. They stood gazing at each other for a long moment without touching, and then Tanus turned and strode away. My mistress watched until he was gone from her sight, then she came down to where I waited. She walked like a woman in a dream.

I helped her to mount, and while I adjusted the saddle girth, she reached down and took my hand. 'Thank you,' she said simply.

'I do not deserve your gratitude,' I demurred.

'I am the happiest creature in all the world. Everything that you told me of love is true. Please rejoice for me, even though—' she did not finish, and suddenly I realized that she had read my innermost feelings. Even in her own great joy, she grieved that she had caused me pain. I think I loved her more in that moment than I had ever done before.

I turned away and took up the reins, and led her back towards the Nile.

 One of the royal huntsmen spied us from a far hilltop, and hailed us heartily.

'We have been searching for you at the king's command,' he told us, as he hurried down to join us.

'Was the king saved?' I asked.

'He is safe in the palace on Elephantine Island, and he has commanded that the Lady Lostris be brought to him directly she is found.'

As we set foot on the palace jetty, Aton was there, puffing out his painted cheeks with relief and fussing over my mistress. 'They have found the bodies of twenty-three unfortunates who perished in the storm,' he told us with ghoulish relish. 'All were certain that you would be found dead also. However, I prayed at the temple of Hapi for your safe return.' He looked pleased with himself, and I was annoyed that he tried to claim the credit for her survival for himself. He allowed us only time enough to wash hastily and anoint our dry skin with perfumed oil, before he whisked us away to the audience with the king.

Pharaoh was truly moved to have my mistress returned to him. I am sure he had come to love her as much as any of the others, and not merely for the promise of immortality that he saw in her. A tear tangled in his eyelash and smeared the paint on his cheek as she knelt before him.

'I thought you were lost,' he told her, and would have embraced her, had etiquette permitted it. 'Instead I find you prettier and livelier than ever.' Which was true, for love had gilded her with its special magic.

'Taita saved me,' she told Pharaoh. 'He guided me to a shelter and protected me through all those terrible days. Without him I would have perished, like those other poor souls.'

'Is this true, Taita?' Pharaoh demanded of me directly, and I assumed my modest expression, and murmured, 'I am but a humble instrument of the gods.'

He smiled at me, for I knew he had become fond of me also. 'You have rendered us many services, oh humble instrument. But this is the most valuable of them all. Approach!' he commanded, and I knelt before him.

Aton stood beside him, holding a small cedar-wood box. He lifted the lid and proffered it to the king. From the case Pharaoh lifted out a gold chain. It was of the purest unalloyed gold, and bore the marks of the royal jewellers to attest its weight of twenty deben.

The king held the chain over my head and intoned, 'I bestow upon you the Gold of Praise.' He lowered it on to my shoulders, and the oppressive weight was a delight to me. This decoration was the highest mark of royal favour, usually reserved for generals and ambassadors, or for high officials such as Lord Intef. I doubted that ever in the history of this very Egypt had the gold chain been placed around the neck of a lowly slave.

That was not the end of the gifts and awards that were to be bestowed upon me, for my mistress was not to be outdone. That evening while I was attending her bath, she suddenly dismissed her slaves and, standing naked before me, she told me, 'You may help me to dress, Taita.' She allowed me this privilege when she was especially well pleased with me. She knew just how much I enjoyed having her to myself in these intimate circumstances.

Her loveliness was covered only by the glossy tresses of her sable hair. It seemed that those days she had spent with Tanus had filled her with a new quality of beauty. It emanated from deep within her. A lamp placed inside an alabaster jar will shine through the translucent sides; in the same way, the Lady Lostris seemed to glow.

'I never dreamed that such a poor vessel as this body of mine could contain such joy.' She stroked her own flanks as she said it and looked down at herself, inviting me to do the same. 'All that you promised me came to pass while I was with Tanus. Pharaoh has bestowed the Gold of Praise upon you, it is fitting that I also show my appreciation to you. I want you to share my happiness in some way.'

'Serving you is all the reward I could wish for.'

'Help me to dress,' she ordered, and lifted her hands above her head. Her breasts changed shape as she moved. Over the years I had watched them grow from tiny immature figs into these round, creamy pomegranates, more beautiful than jewels or marble sculptures. I held the diaphanous nightdress over her, and then let it float down over her body. It covered her, but did not obscure her loveliness, in the same way that the morning mist decks the waters of the Nile in the dawn.

'I have commanded a banquet, and sent invitations to the royal ladies.'

'Very well, my lady. I shall see to it.'

'No, no, Taita. The banquet is in your honour. You will sit beside me as my guest.'

This was as shocking as any of the wild schemes she had thought up recently. 'It is not fitting, mistress. You will offend against custom.'

'I am the wife of Pharaoh. I set the customs. During the banquet I will have a gift for you, and I will present it to you in the sight of all.'

'Will you tell me what this gift is?' I asked, with some trepidation. I was never sure of what mischief she would dream up next.

'Certainly I will tell you what it is.' She smiled mysteriously. 'It is a secret, that's what it is.'

 Even though I was the guest of honour, I could not leave the arrangements for the banquet to cooks and giggling slave girls. After all, the reputation of my mistress as a hostess was at stake. I was at the market before dawn to procure the finest, freshest produce from the fields and the river.

I promised Aton that he would be invited, and he opened the king's wine cellar and let me make my selection. I hired and rehearsed the best musicians and acrobats in the city. I sent out the slaves to gather hyacinth and lily and lotus from the banks of the river to augment the masses of blooms that already decorated our garden. I had the weavers plait tiny arks of reeds on which I floated coloured glass lamps and set them adrift on the ponds of our water-garden. I set out leather cushions and garlands of flowers for each guest, and jars of perfumed oil to cool them in the sultry night and drive away the mosquitoes.

At nightfall the royal ladies began to arrive in all their frippery and high fashion. Some of them had even shaved their heads and replaced their natural hair with elaborate wigs woven from the hair which the wives of the poor were forced to sell, in order to feed their brats. This was a fashion I abhorred and I vowed to do all in my power to prevent my mistress from succumbing to such folly. Her lustrous tresses were amongst my chief delights, but when it comes to fashion, even the most sensible woman is not to be trusted.

When, at the insistence of my mistress, I seated myself on the cushion beside her, rather than taking my usual position behind her, I could see that many of our guests were scandalized by such indecorous behaviour, and they whispered to each other behind their fans. I was just as uncomfortable as they were, and to cover my embarrassment, I signalled the slaves to keep the wine cups filled, the musicians to play, and the dancers to dance.

The wine was robust, the music rousing, and the dancers were all male. They gave ample proof of their gender, for I had ordered them to perform in a state of nature. The ladies were so enchanted by this display that they soon forgot their decent outrage, and did justice to the wine. I had no doubt that many of the male dancers would not leave the harem before dawn. Some of the royal ladies had voracious appetites, and many had not been visited by the king in years.

In this convivial atmosphere my mistress rose to her feet and called for the attention of her guests. Then she commended me to them in terms so extravagant that even I blushed. She went on to relate amusing and touching episodes from the lifetime we had spent together. The wine seemed to have softened the attitude of the women towards me, and they laughed and applauded. A few of them even wept a little with wine and sentiment.

At last my mistress commanded me to kneel before her, and as I did so, there was a murmur of comment. I had chosen to wear a simple kilt of the finest linen, and the slave girls had dressed my hair in the fashion that best suited me. Apart from the Gold of Praise around my throat, I wore no other ornament. In the midst of such ostentation, my simple style was striking. With regular swimming and exercise I had kept the athletic body which had first attracted Lord Intef to me. In those years I was in my prime.

I heard one of the senior wives murmur to her neighbour, 'What a pity he has lost his jewels. He would make such a diverting toy.' This evening I could ignore the words that in other circumstances would have caused me intense pain.

My mistress was looking very pleased with herself. She had succeeded in keeping me ignorant of the nature of her gift. Usually she was not so adroit as to be able to outwit me. She looked down on my bowed head and spoke slowly and clearly, wringing the utmost enjoyment from the moment.

'Taita the slave. For all the years of my life you have been a shield over me. You have been my mentor and my tutor. You have taught me to read and to write. You have made clear to me the mysteries of the stars and the arcane arts. You have taught me to sing and to dance. You have shown me how to find happiness and contentment in many things. I am grateful.'

The royal ladies were once more beginning to become restive. They had never before heard a slave praised in such effusive terms.

'On the day of the *khamsin* you did me a service that I must reward. Pharaoh has bestowed the Gold of Praise upon you. I have my own gift for you.'

From under her robe she took a roll of papyrus secured with a coloured thread. 'You knelt before me as a slave. Now rise to your feet as a free man.' She held up the papyrus. 'This is your deed of manumission, prepared by the scribes of the court. From this day forward, you are a free man.'

I lifted my head for the first time and stared at her in disbelief. She pressed the roll of papyrus into my numbed fingers, and smiled down at me fondly.

'You did not expect this, did you? You are so surprised that you have no words for me. Say something to me, Taita. Tell me how grateful you are for this boon.'

Every word she spoke wounded me like a poisoned dart. My tongue was a rock in my mouth as I contemplated a life without her. As a freed

413

man, I would be excluded from her presence for ever. I would never again prepare her food, nor attend her bath. I would never spread the covers over her as she prepared for sleep, nor would I rouse her in the dawn and be at her side when first she opened those lovely dark green eyes to each new day. I would never again sing with her, or hold her cup, or help her to dress and have the pleasure of gazing upon all her loveliness.

I was stricken, and I stared at her hopelessly, as one whose life had reached its end.

'Be happy, Taita,' she ordered me. 'Be happy in this new freedom I give you.'

'I will never be happy again,' I blurted. 'You have cast me off. How can I ever be happy again?'

Her smile faded away, and she stared at me in perturbation. 'I offer you the most precious gift that it is in my power to give you. I offer you your freedom.'

I shook my head. 'You inflict the most dire punishment upon me. You are driving me away from you. I will never know happiness again.'

'It is not a punishment, Taita. It was meant as a reward. Please, don't you understand?'

'The only reward I desire is to remain at your side for the rest of my life.' I felt the tears welling up from deep inside me, and I tried to hold them back. 'Please, mistress, I beg of you, don't send me away from you. If you have any feeling towards me, allow me to stay with you.'

'Do not weep,' she commanded. 'For if you do, then I will weep with you, in front of all my guests.' I truly believe that she had not, until that moment, contemplated the consequences of this misplaced piece of generosity that she had dreamed up. The

414

tears broke over my lids and streamed down my cheeks.

'Stop it! This is not what I wanted.' Her own tears kept mine good company. 'I only thought to honour you, as the king has honoured you.'

I held up the roll of papyrus. 'Please let me tear this piece of foolery to shreds. Take me back into your service. Give me leave to stand behind you, where I belong.'

'Stop it, Taita! You are breaking my heart.' Loudly she snuffled up her tears, but I was merciless.

'The only gift I want from you is the right to serve you for all the days of my life. Please, mistress, rescind this deed. Give me your permission to tear it.'

She nodded vigorously, blubbering as she used to do when she was a little girl who had fallen and grazed her knees. I ripped the sheet of papyrus once and then again. Not satisfied with this destruction, I held the fragments to the lamp flame and let them burn to crispy black curls.

'Promise me that you will never try to drive me away again. Swear that you will never again try to thrust my freedom upon me.'

She nodded through her tears, but I would not accept that. 'Say it,' I insisted. 'Say it aloud for all to hear.'

'I promise to keep you as my slave, never to sell you, nor to set you free,' she whispered huskily through the tears, and then a beam of mischief shone out of those tragic dark green eyes. 'Unless, of course, you annoy me inordinately, then I will summon the law scribes immediately.' She put out a hand to lift me to my feet. 'Get up, you silly man, and attend to your duties. I swear my cup is empty.'

I resumed my proper position behind her, and refilled the cup. The tipsy company thought it all a bit of fun that we had arranged for their amusement, and they clapped and whistled and threw flower petals at us to show their appreciation. I could see that most of them were relieved that we had not truly flouted decorum, and that a slave was still a slave.

My mistress lifted the wine cup to her lips, but before she drank, she smiled at me over the rim. Though her eyes were still wet with tears, that smile lifted my spirits and restored my happiness. I felt as close to her then as ever I had in all the years.

 The morning after the banquet and my hour of freedom, we woke to find that during the night the river had swollen with the commencement of the annual flood. We had no warning of it until the joyous cries of the watchmen down at the port aroused us. Still heavy with wine, I left my bed and ran down to the riverside. Both banks were already lined with the populace of the city. They greeted the waters with prayers and songs and waving palm-fronds.

The low waters had been the bright green of the verdigris that grows on bars of copper. The waters of the inundation had flushed it all away, and now the river had swollen to an ominous grey. During the night it had crept halfway up the stone pylons of the harbour, and soon it would press against the earthworks of the embankment. Then it would force its way into the mouths of the irrigation canals that had been cracked and dry for so many months. From there it would swirl out and flood the fields, drowning the huts of the peasants, and washing away the boundary markers between the fields.

The surveying and replacement of the boundaries after each flood was the responsibility of the Guardian of the Waters. Lord Intef had multiplied his fortune by favouring the claims of the rich and the generous when the time came round each year to reset the marker stones.

From upstream echoed the distant rumble of the cataract. The rising flood overwhelmed the natural barrages of granite that were placed in its path, and, as it roared through the gorges, the spray rose into the hard blue sky, a silver column that could be seen from every quarter of the nome of Assoun. When the fine mist drifted across the island, it was cool and refreshing on our upturned faces. We delighted in this blessing, for it was the only rain we ever knew in our valley.

Even as we watched, the beaches around our island were eaten up by the flood. Soon our jetty would be submerged, and the river would lap at the gates of our garden. Where it would stop was a question that could only be calculated by a study of the levels of the Nilometer. On those levels hung prosperity or famine for the whole land and every person in it.

I hurried back to find my mistress and to prepare for the ceremony of the waters, in which I would play a prominent role. We dressed in our

417

finest and I placed my new gold chain around my neck. Then, with the rest of our household and the ladies of the harem, we joined the spontaneous procession to the temple of Hapi.

Pharaoh and all the great lords of Egypt led us. The priests, plump with rich living, were waiting for us on the temple steps. Their heads were shaven, their pates shining with oil, and their eyes glittering with avarice, for the king would sacrifice lavishly today.

Before the king the statue of the god was carried from the sanctuary, and decked with flowers and fine crimson linen. Then the statue was drenched in oils and perfume while we sang psalms of praise and thanks to the god for sending down the flood.

Far to the south, in a land that no civilized man had ever visited, the god Hapi sat on top of his mountain and from two pitchers of infinite capacity he poured the holy waters into his Nile. The water from each pitcher was of a different colour and taste; one was bright green and sweet, the other grey and heavy with the silt which flooded our fields each season and charged them with new life and fertility.

While we sang, the king made sacrifice of corn and meats and wine and silver and gold. Then he called out his wise men, his engineers and his mathematicians, and bade them enter the Nilometer to begin their observations and their calculations.

In the time that I had belonged to Lord Intef, I had been nominated as one of the keepers of the water. I was the only slave in that illustrious company, but I consoled myself by the fact that very few others wore the Gold of Praise, and that

418

they treated me with respect. They had worked with me before, and they knew my worth. I had helped to design the Nilometers that measured the flow of the river, and I had supervised the building of them. It was I who had worked out the complex formula to determine the projected height and the volume of each flood from the observations.

Our way lit by flickering torches of pitch-dipped rushes, I followed the high priest into the mouth of the Nilometer, a dark opening in the rear wall of the sanctuary. We descended the incline shaft, the stone steps slippery with slime and the effusions of the river. From under our feet, one of the deadly black water cobras slithered away, and with a furious hiss plunged into the dark water that had already risen halfway up the shaft.

We gathered on the last exposed step and by the light of the torches studied the marks that my masons had chiselled in the walls of the shaft. Each of the symbols had values, both magical and empirical, allotted to it.

We made the first and most crucial reading together with extreme care. Over the following five days we would take it in turns to watch and record the rising waters, and time the readings with the flow of a water-clock. From samples of the water, we would estimate the amount of silt it bore, and all these factors would influence our final conclusions.

When the five days of observation were completed, we embarked on a further three days of calculations. These covered many scrolls of papyrus. Finally, we were ready to present our findings to the king. On that day Pharaoh returned to the temple in royal state, accompanied by his nobles and half the population of Elephantine to receive the estimates.

As the high priest read them aloud, the king began to smile. We had forecast an inundation of almost perfect proportions. It would not be too low, to leave the fields exposed and baking in the sun, depriving them of the rich black layer of silt so vital to their fertility. Nor would it be so high as to wash away the canals and earthworks, and to drown the villages and cities along the banks. This season would bring forth bountiful harvests and fat herds.

Pharaoh smiled, not so much for the good fortune of his subjects, but for the bounty that his tax-collectors would gather in. The annual taxes were computed on the value of the flood, and this year there would be vast new treasures added to the store-rooms of his funerary temple. To close the ceremony of the blessing of the water in the temple of Hapi, Pharaoh announced the date of the biennial pilgrimage to Thebes to participate in the festival of Osiris. It did not seem possible that two years had passed since my mistress had played the part of the goddess in the last passion of Osiris.

I had as little sleep that night as when I had kept vigil in the shaft of the Nilometer, for my mistress was too excited to seek her own couch. She made me sit up with her until dawn, singing and laughing and repeating those stories of Tanus to which she never tired of listening.

In eight days the royal flotilla would sail northwards on the rising flood of the Nile. When we arrived, Tanus, Lord Harrab would be waiting for us in Thebes. My mistress was delirious with happiness.

The flotilla that assembled in the harbour roads of Elephantine was so numerous that it seemed to cover the water from bank to bank. My mistress remarked jokingly that a man might cross the Nile without wetting his feet by strolling over the bridge of hulls. With pennants and flags flying from every masthead, the fleet made a gallant show.

We and the rest of the court had already embarked on the vessels that had been allotted to us, and from the deck we cheered the king as he descended the marble steps from the palace and went aboard the great state barge. The moment he was safely embarked, a hundred horns sounded the signal to set sail. As one, the fleet squared away and pointed their bows into the north. With the rush of the river and the banks of oars driving us, we bore away.

There had been a different spirit abroad in the land since Akh-Horus had destroyed the Shrikes. The inhabitants of every village we passed came down to the water's edge to greet their king. Pharaoh sat high on the poop, wearing the cumbersome double crown, so that all might have a clear view of him. They waved palm-fronds and shouted, 'May all the gods smile on Pharaoh!' The river brought down to them not only their king, but also the promise of its own benevolence, and they were happy.

Twice during the days that followed, Pharaoh and all his train went ashore to inspect the monuments that Akh-Horus had raised to his passing at the crossroads of the caravan routes.

421

The local peasants had preserved these gruesome piles of skulls as sacred relics of the new god. They had polished each skull until it shone like ivory, and bound the pyramids with building clay so that they would stand through the years. Then they had built shrines over them and appointed priests to serve these holy places.

At both these shrines my mistress left a gold ring as an offering, joyously accepted by the self-appointed guardians. It was to no avail that I protested this extravagance. My mistress often lacked the proper respect for the wealth that I was so painstakingly amassing on her behalf. Without my restraining hand, she would probably have given it all away to the grasping priesthood and the insatiable poor, smiling as she did so.

On the tenth night after leaving Elephantine, the royal entourage camped on a pleasant promontory above a bend in the river. The entertainment that evening was to include one of the most famous story-tellers in the land, and usually my mistress loved a good story above most other pleasures. Both she and I had been looking forward to this occasion and discussing it avidly since leaving the palace. It was therefore to my surprise and bitter disappointment that the Lady Lostris declared herself too fatigued and out of sorts to attend the story-teller. Although she urged me to go, and take the rest of our household with me, I could not leave her alone when she was unwell. I gave her a hot draught and I slept on the floor at the end of her bed, so that I could be near if she needed me during the night.

I was truly worried in the morning when I tried to wake her. Usually she would spring from her bed with a smile of anticipation, ready to seize and devour the new day, a glutton for the joy of living. However, this morning she pulled the covers back over her head and mumbled, 'Leave me to sleep a little longer. I feel as heavy and dull as an old woman.'

'The king has decreed an early start. We must be aboard before the sun rises. I will bring you a hot infusion that will cheer you.' I poured boiling water over a bowl of herbs that I had picked with my own hands during the most propitious phase of the last moon.

'Do stop fussing,' she grumped at me, but I would not let her sleep again. I prodded her awake and made her drink the tonic. She pulled a face. 'I swear you are trying to poison me,' she complained, and then, without warning and before I could do anything to prevent it, she vomited copiously.

Afterwards she seemed as shocked as I was. We both stared at the steaming puddle beside her bed in consternation.

'What is wrong with me, Taita?' she whispered. 'Nothing like this has ever happened to me before.'

Only then did the meaning of it all dawn on me. 'The *khamsin*!' I cried. 'The cemetery of Tras! Tanus!'

She stared at me blankly for a moment, and then her smile lit the gloom of the tent like a lamp. 'I am making a baby!' she cried.

'Not so loud, mistress,' I pleaded.

'Tanus' baby! I am carrying Tanus' son.' It could not be the king's infant, for I had successfully kept him from her bed since her starvation sickness and her miscarriage.

'Oh, Taita,' she purred, as she lifted her nightdress and inspected her flat, firm belly with awe. 'Just think of it! A little imp just like Tanus growing inside of me.' She palpated her stomach hopefully. 'I knew that such delights as I discovered in the tomb of Tras could not pass unremarked by the gods. They have given me a memory that will last all my lifetime.'

'You race ahead,' I warned her. 'It may be only a colic. I must make the tests before we can be sure.'

'I need no test. I know it in my heart and in the secret depths of my body.'

'We will still do the tests,' I told her wryly, and went to fetch the pot. She perched upon it to provide me with the first water of her day, and I divided this into two equal parts.

The first portion of her urine I mixed with an equal part of Nile water. Then I filled two jars with black earth and in each of them planted five seeds of dhurra corn. I watered one jar with pure Nile water, and the other with the mixture that my mistress had provided. This was the first test.

Then I hunted amongst the reeds in the lagoon near the camp and captured ten frogs. These were not the lively green and yellow variety with leaping back legs, but slimy, black creatures. Their heads are not separated from their sluggish, fat bodies by a neck, and their eyes sit on top of the flat skull, so that the children call them sky-gazers.

I placed five of each of the sky-gazers in two separate jars of river water. To the one I added my mistress's intimate emission and I left the other unadulterated. The following morning, in the privacy of my mistress's cabin on board the galley, we removed the cloth with which I had covered the

424

jars and inspected the contents.

The corn watered by the Lady Lostris had thrown tiny green shoots, while the other seeds were still inert. The five sky-gazers who had not received my mistress's blessing were barren, but the other more fortunate five had each laid long silvery strings which were speckled with black eggs.

'I told you so!' my mistress chirruped smugly, before I could give my official diagnosis. 'Oh, thanks to all the gods! No more beautiful thing has happened to me in all my life.'

'I will speak to Aton immediately. You will share the king's couch this very night,' I told her grimly, and she stared at me in bewilderment.

'Even Pharaoh who believes most things I tell him, will not believe that you were impregnated by the seeds blown in on the *khamsin* wind. We must have a foster-father for this little bastard of ours.' Already I considered the infant ours, and not hers alone. Though I tried to conceal it behind my levity, I was every bit as delighted with her fecundity as she was.

'Don't you ever call him a bastard again,' she flared at me. 'He will be a prince.'

'He will be a prince only if I can find a royal sire for him. Prepare yourself. I am going to see the king.'

'Last night I had a dream, Great Egypt,' I told Pharaoh. 'It was so amazing that to confirm it I worked the Mazes of Ammon-Ra.'

Pharaoh leaned forward eagerly, for he had come to believe in my dreams and the Mazes as much as any of my other patients.

'This time it is unequivocal, Majesty. In my dream the goddess Isis appeared and promised to counter the baleful influence of her brother Seth, who so cruelly deprived you of your first son when he struck down the Lady Lostris with the wasting disease. Take my mistress to your bed on the first day of the festival of Osiris, and you will be blessed with another son. That is the promise of the goddess.'

'Tonight is the eve of the festival.' The king looked delighted. 'In truth, Taita, I have been ready to perform this pleasant duty all these past months, had you only allowed me to do so. But you have not told me what you saw in the Mazes of Ammon-Ra.' Again he leaned forward eagerly, and I was ready for him.

'It was the vision as before, only this time it was stronger and more vivid. The same endless forest of trees growing along the banks of the river, each tree crowned and imperial. Your dynasty reaching into the ages, strong and unbroken.'

Pharaoh sighed with satisfaction. 'Send the child to me.'

When I returned to the tent, my mistress was waiting for me. She had prepared herself with good grace and humour.

426

'I shall close my eyes and imagine that I am back in the tomb of Tras with Tanus,' she confided, and then giggled saucily. 'Although to imagine the king as Tanus is to imagine that the tail of the mouse has become the trunk of the elephant.'

Aton came to fetch her to the king's tent soon after the king had eaten his dinner. She went with a calm expression and a firm step, dreaming perhaps of her little prince, and of his true father who waited for us in Thebes.

 Beloved Thebes, beautiful Thebes of the hundred gates—how we rejoiced as we saw it appear ahead of us, decorating the broad sweep of the river-bank with its temples and gleaming walls.

My mistress sang out with excitement as each of the familiar landmarks revealed itself to us. Then, as the royal barge put in to the wharf below the palace of the grand vizier, the joy of home-coming went out of both of us, and we fell silent. The Lady Lostris groped for my hand like a little girl frightened by tales of hob-goblins, for we had seen her father.

Lord Intef with his sons, Menset and Sobek, those two thumbless heroes, stood at the head of the great concourse of the nobles and the city fathers of Thebes that waited upon the quay to greet the king. Lord Intef was as handsome and suave as I had imagined him in my nightmares, and I felt my spirits quail.

'You must be vigilant now,' the Lady Lostris whispered to me. 'They will seek to have you out of their way. Remember the cobra.'

Not far behind the grand vizier stood Rasfer. During our absence he had obviously received high promotion. He now wore the head-dress of a Commander of Ten Thousand and carried the golden whip of rank. There had been no improvement in his facial muscles. One side of his face still sagged hideously and saliva dribbled from the corner of his mouth. At that moment he recognized me, and grinned at me with half his face across the narrow strip of water. He lifted his golden whip in ironic greeting.

'I promise you, my lady, that my hand will be upon my dagger and I will eat nothing but fruit that I have peeled with my own hands while Rasfer and I are in Thebes together,' I murmured, as I smiled at him and returned his salute with a cheery wave.

'You are to accept no strange gifts,' my mistress insisted, 'and you will sleep at the foot of my bed, where I can protect you at night. During the day you will stay at my side, and not go wandering off on your own.'

'I will not find that irksome,' I assured her, and over the following days I kept my promise to her and remained under her immediate protection, for I was certain that Lord Intef would not jeopardize his connection to the throne by putting his daughter in danger.

Naturally, we were often in the company of the grand vizier, for it was his duty to escort the king through all the ceremonies of the festival. During this time, Lord Intef played the role of loving and considerate father to the Lady Lostris, and he treated her with all the deference and consideration due to a royal wife. Each morning he sent her gifts, gold and jewels and exquisite little carvings of scarabs and godlets in ivory and precious woods. Despite my mistress's orders, I did not return these. I did not wish to warn the enemy, and besides, the gifts were valuable. I sold them discreetly and invested the proceeds in stores of corn held for us in the granaries of trustworthy merchants in the city, men who were my friends.

In view of the expected harvest, the price of corn was the lowest it had been for ten years. There was only one direction it could go, and that was up, although we might have to wait a while for our profits. The merchants gave me receipts in the name of my mistress which I deposited in the archives of the law courts. I kept only a fifth part to myself, which I felt was a very moderate commission.

This gave me some secret pleasure whenever I caught Lord Intef watching me with those pale leopard's eyes. That look left me in no doubt that his feelings towards me had not moderated. I remembered his patience and his persistence when dealing with an enemy. He waited at the centre of his web like a beautiful spider, and his eyes glittered as he watched me. I remembered the bowl of poisoned milk and the cobra, and despite all my precautions, I was uneasy.

Meanwhile the festival rolled on with all the ceremony and tradition, as it had for centuries past. However, this season it was not Tanus' Blues but another squadron that hunted the river-cows in the lagoon of Hapi, while another company of actors played out the passion in the temple of Osiris. Because Pharaoh's decree was observed and the version of the play was mine, the words were as powerful and moving. However, this new Isis was not as lovely as my mistress had portrayed her, nor was Horus as noble or striking as Lord Tanus. On the other hand, Seth was winsome and lovable in comparison to the way that Rasfer had played him.

The day after the passion, Pharaoh crossed the river to inspect his temple, and on this occasion he kept me close at hand throughout the day. On numerous occasions he openly consulted me on aspects of the works. Of course I wore my golden chain whenever it was proper to do so. None of this was missed by Lord Intef, and I could see him musing on the favour the king showed to me. I hoped that this might further serve to protect me from the grand vizier's vengeance.

Since I had left Thebes, another architect had been placed in charge of the temple project. It was perhaps unfair that Pharaoh should expect this unfortunate to be able to maintain the high standards that I had set, or to push the work forward at the same pace.

'By the blessed mother of Horus, I wish you were still in charge here, Taita,' Pharaoh muttered. 'If she would part with you, I would buy you from your mistress, and keep you here in the City of the Dead permanently to supervise the work. The cost seems to have doubled since this other idiot took over from you.'

'He is a naïve young man,' I agreed. 'The masons and the contractors will steal his testicles from him and he will not notice that they are missing.'

'It is my balls that they are stealing,' the king

scowled. 'I want you to go over the bill of quantities with him and show him where we are being robbed.'

I was of course flattered by his regard, and there was nothing spiteful in my pointing out to Pharaoh the lapses of taste that the new architect had perpetrated when he redesigned the pediment to my temple façade, or the shoddy craftsmanship that those rogues in the guild of masons had been able to slip past him. The pediment was permeated with the decadent Syrian style that was all the rage in the Lower Kingdom, where the common tastes of the low-born red pretender were corrupting the classical traditions of Egyptian art.

As for the workmanship, I demonstrated to the king how it was possible to slip a fragment of papyrus between the joints of the stone blocks that made up the side-wall of the mortuary temple. Pharaoh ordered both the pediment and the temple wall to be torn down, and he fined the guild of masons five hundred deben of gold to be paid into the royal store-rooms.

Pharaoh spent the rest of that day and the whole of the next reviewing the treasures in the store-rooms of the funerary temple. Here at least he could find very little to complain of. In the history of the world never had such wealth been assembled in one place at one time. Even I, who love fine things, was soon jaded by the abundance of it, and my eyes were pained by the dazzle of gold.

The king insisted that the Lady Lostris remain at his side all this time. I think that his infatuation with her was slowly turning into real love, or as close a facsimile of it as he was capable of. The

431

consequence of his affection for her was that when we returned across the river to Thebes, my mistress was exhausted, and I feared for the child she was carrying. It was too soon to tell the king of her condition and to suggest that he showed her more consideration. It was less than a week since she had returned to his couch, and such an early diagnosis of pregnancy even from me must arouse his suspicion. To him she was still a healthy and robust young woman, and he treated her that way.

 The festival ended, as it had for centuries past, with the assembly of the people in the temple of Osiris to hear the proclamation from the throne.

On the raised stone dais in front of the sanctuary of Osiris, Pharaoh was seated on his tall throne so that all the congregation could have a clear view of him. He wore the double crown and carried the crook and the flail.

This time there was an alteration to the usual layout of the temple, for I had made a suggestion to the king which he had been gracious enough to adopt. Against three walls of the inner temple he had ordered the erection of timber scaffolding. These rose in tiers halfway up the massive stone walls, and provided seating for thousands of the notables of Thebes from which they had a privileged and uninterrupted view of the proceedings. I had suggested that these stands be decorated with coloured bunting and palm-fronds, to disguise their ugliness. It was the first time that these structures were built in our land. Thereafter, they were to become commonplace, and they were built at most public functions, along the routes of royal processions and around the fields of athletic games. To this day they are known as Taita stands.

There had been much bitter competition for seats upon these stands, but as their designer, I had been able to procure the very best for my mistress and myself. We were directly opposite the throne and a little above the height of the king's head, so we had a fine view of the whole of the inner courtyard. I had provided a leather cushion stuffed with lamb's-wool for the Lady Lostris and a basket of fruits and cakes, together with jars of sherbet and beer, to sustain us during the interminable ceremony.

All around us were assembled the noblest in the land, lords and ladies decked out in high fashion. The generals and admirals carrying their golden whips and proudly flaunting the honours and standards of their regiments, the guild masters and the rich merchants, the priests and the ambassadors from the vassal states of the empire, they were all here.

In front of the king extended the courts of the temple, one opening into another like the boxes in a children's puzzle-game, but such was the layout of the massive stone walls that the gates were all perfectly aligned. A worshipper standing in the Avenue of Sacred Rams outside the pylons of the main gate could look through the inner gates and clearly see the king on his high throne almost four hundred paces away.

All the courts of the temple were packed with the multitudes of the common people, and the overflow spilled out into the sacred avenue and the gardens beyond the temple walls. Though I had lived almost my entire life in Thebes, I had never seen such a gathering. It was not possible to count their numbers, but I estimated that there must have been two hundred thousand assembled that day. From them rose such a hubbub of sound that I felt myself but a single bee in the vast humming hive.

Around the throne was gathered a small group of the highest dignitaries, their heads at the level of Pharaoh's feet. Of course one of these was the high priest of Osiris. During the past year the old abbot had left this transitory world of ours and set off on his journey through the underworld to the western fields of the eternal paradise. This new abbot was a younger, firmer man. I knew that he would not be so easily manipulated by Lord Intef. In fact, he had collaborated with me in certain unusual arrangements for today's ceremony that I had put in hand while supervising the erection of the Taita stands.

However, the most impressive figure in the group, rivalling Pharaoh himself, was the grand vizier. Lord Intef drew all eyes. He was tall and stately in bearing, handsome as a legend. With the heavy chains of the Gold of Praise lying weightily upon his chest and shoulders, he was like a figure from the myth of the pantheon. Close behind him loomed the hideous shape of Rasfer.

Lord Intef opened the ceremony in the traditional manner by stepping into the clear space before the throne and beginning the address of welcome to the king from the twin cities of Thebes. As he spoke, I glanced sideways at my mistress, and even though I shared her loathing, I was shocked by the expression of anger and hatred that she made no attempt to conceal, and that she directed openly at her own father. I wanted to warn her to make it less obvious to all about her, but I knew that in doing so, I might merely draw further attention to her burning antagonism.

The grand vizier spoke at length, listing his own accomplishments and the loyal service he had rendered Pharaoh in the year past. The crowd murmured and rustled with boredom and discomfort. The heat was rising from so many bodies, and the rays of the sun beating down into the crowded courts were trapped within the temple walls. I saw more than one woman in the press swoon and collapse.

When at last Lord Intef finished speaking, the high priest stepped into his place. While the sun made its noon overhead, he reported to the king on the ecclesiastical affairs of Thebes. As he spoke, the heat and the stench increased; perfume and fragrant oils could no longer disguise the odour of hot, unwashed bodies and running sweat. There was no escape from the crowd to attend urgent bodily functions. Men and women simply squatted where they stood. The temple began to stink like a sty or a public latrine. I handed my mistress a silk kerchief drenched in perfume which she dabbed to her nose.

There was a sigh of relief when at last the high priest ended his address with a blessing on the king in the name of the god Osiris, and, with a deep bow, retreated to his place behind the grand vizier. For the first time since it had begun to assemble before dawn that morning, the crowd fell completely silent. The boredom and discomfort

435

was forgotten, and they craned forward eagerly to hear Pharaoh speak.

The king rose to his feet. I wondered at the old man's fortitude, for he had sat all this time like a statue. He spread his arms in benediction, and at that moment the hallowed chalice of custom and tradition was shattered by an event that plunged the entire congregation—priests, nobles and commoners—into consternation. I was one of the few in the crowd who was not surprised by what followed, for I had done more than my share to arrange it all.

The great burnished copper doors to the sanctuary swung open. There seemed to be no human agency to the movement, it was as though the doors opened of their own accord.

A gasp, a sigh of expelled breath passed like a wind through temple courts, and rustled the densely packed ranks as though they were the leaves of a tamarind tree. Then suddenly a woman screamed, and immediately a groan of superstitious horror shook them all. Some fell to their knees, some lifted their hands above their heads in terror, others covered their faces with their shawls so that they should not be struck blind by looking on sights that were not for mortal eyes.

A god strode out through the sanctuary doors, a tall and terrifying god, whose cloak swirled about his shoulders as he moved. His helmet was crowned with a plume of egret's feathers, and his features were grotesque and metallic, half-eagle and half-man, with a hooked beak and dark slits for eyes.

'Akh-Horus!' screamed a woman, and she collapsed in a dead faint upon the stone flags.

436

'Akh-Horus!' the cry was taken up. 'It is the god!' Row after row, they fell upon their knees in the attitude of reverence. Those on the high tiers of stands knelt and many of them made the sign to avert misfortune. Even the group of nobles around the throne went down. In all the temple only two persons remained on their feet. Pharaoh posed on the steps of his throne like a painted statue; and the grand vizier of Thebes stood tall and arrogant.

Akh-Horus stopped in front of the king and looked up at him through those slitted eyes in the bronze mask, and even then Pharaoh never flinched. The king's cheeks were painted dead white, so I could not tell whether he blanched, but there was a glitter in his eyes that may have been either religious ecstasy, or terror.

'Who are you?' Pharaoh challenged. 'Are you ghost or man? Why do you disturb our solemn proceedings?' His voice was strong and clear. I could detect no tremor in it, and my admiration for him was enhanced. Weak and aging and gullible perhaps, but still the old man had his full share of courage. He could face up to man or god and stand his ground like a warrior.

Akh-Horus answered him in a voice that had commanded regiments in the desperate din of battle, a voice that echoed amongst the stone pillars. 'Great Pharaoh, I am a man, not a ghost. I am your man. I come before you in response to your command. I come before you to account to you for the duty that you laid upon me in this place on this very day of Osiris two years ago.'

He lifted the helmet from his head, and the fiery curls tumbled down. The congregation recognized him instantly. A shout went up that seemed to rock

437

the foundations of the temple.

'Lord Tanus! Tanus! Tanus!'

It seemed to me that my mistress screamed the loudest of them all, fairly deafening me, who sat so close beside her.

'Tanus! Akh-Horus! Akh-Horus!' The two names mingled and crashed against the temple walls like storm-driven surf.

'He has risen from his tomb! He has become a god amongst us!'

It did not abate until suddenly Tanus drew the sword from his scabbard and held it aloft in an unmistakable command for silence. This was obeyed, and in the silence he spoke again.

'Great Egypt, do I have your permission to speak?'

I think by now the king could no longer rely on his powers of speech, for he made a gesture with crook and flail, and then his legs seemed to give way beneath him and he dropped back on his throne.

Tanus addressed him in ringing tones that carried to the outer court. 'Two years ago you charged me with the destruction of those viperous nests of murderers and robbers who were threatening the life of the state. You placed in my trust the royal hawk seal.'

From under his cloak, Tanus drew out the blue statuette and placed it on the steps of the throne. Then he stepped back and spoke again.

'In order better to carry out the king's orders, I pretended my own death and caused the mummy of a stranger to be sealed in my tomb.'

'*Bak-Her*!' shouted a single voice, and they took up the cry until Tanus once more commanded

438

silence.

'I led a thousand brave men of the Blues into the deserts and the wild places and sought out the Shrikes in their secret fortresses. There we slew them in their hundreds and piled their severed heads at the roadside.'

'*Bak-Her!*' they screamed. 'It is true. Akh-Horus has done all these things.' Once again Tanus silenced them.

'I broke the power of the barons. I slaughtered their followers without mercy. In all this very Egypt of ours there remains only one who still calls himself a Shrike.'

Now at last they were silent, gobbling up every word he said, fascinated and intent. Even Pharaoh could not hold his impatience in check. 'Speak, Lord Tanus, whom men now know as Akh-Horus. Name this man. Give me his name so that he may come to know the wrath of Pharaoh.'

'He hides behind the name of Akh-Seth,' Tanus roared, 'His deeds of infamy rank with those of his brother, the dark god.'

'Give me his true name,' Pharaoh commanded, rising once more to his feet in his agitation. 'Name this last of all the Shrikes!'

Tanus drew out the moment. He looked around the temple slowly and deliberately. When our eyes met, I nodded so slightly that only he saw the movement, but his gaze passed on without a pause and he looked towards the open doors of the sanctuary.

The attention of all the congregation was so fixed upon Lord Tanus that they did not at first see the file of armed men that issued swiftly and silently from the sanctuary. Although they wore full armour and carried their war shields, I recognized most of them under the helmets. There were Remrem and Astes and fifty other warriors of the Blues. Swiftly, they formed up around the throne like a royal bodyguard, but, without making it obvious, Remrem and Astes moved up behind Lord Intef. As soon as they were in position, Tanus spoke again.

'I will name this Akh-Seth for you, Divine Pharaoh. He stands unashamedly in the shadow of your throne.' Tanus pointed with his sword. 'There he is, wearing the Gold of Praise about his traitor's throat. There he stands, Pharaoh's sole companion who has turned your kingdom into a playground for murderers and bandits. That is Akh-Seth, governor of the nome of Thebes, grand vizier of the Upper Kingdom.'

An awful hush fell upon the temple. There must have been ten thousand or more in the congregation who had suffered grievously at Lord Intef's hands and who had every reason to hate him, but not a voice spoke out in jubilation or in triumph against him. All knew just how terrible was his wrath, and just how certain his retribution. I could smell the stink of their fear in the air, thick as the incense smoke. Every one of them understood that even Tanus' reputation and his mighty deeds were not sufficient for his unproven accusation to prevail against such a person as Lord Intef. To show joy or open agreement at this stage would be mortal folly.

In that hush Lord Intef laughed. It was a sound full of disdain, and with a dismissive gesture he turned his back upon Tanus and spoke directly to the king. 'The desert sun has burned his brain.

The poor lad has gone mad. There is not a single word of truth in all his ravings. I should be angry, but instead I am saddened that a warrior of reputation has fallen so low.' He held out both hands to Pharaoh, a dignified and loyal gesture. 'All my life I have served Pharaoh and my people. My honour is so invulnerable that I see no need to defend myself against these wild rantings. Without fear I place my trust in the wisdom and justice of the divine king. I let my deeds and my love of Pharaoh speak, in place of my tongue.'

I saw the confusion and indecision on the king's painted face. His lips trembled and his brow was furrowed, for he was not blessed with a swift and incisive mind. After a moment he opened his mouth to speak, but before he could utter any fateful or irredeemable judgement, Tanus lifted his sword again and pointed beyond the throne to the open doors of the sanctuary.

Through the doors came another procession of men so unusual that Pharaoh gaped at them with his mouth still open. Kratas led, with his visor raised and a sword in his right hand. Those who followed him wore only loin-cloths, and their heads and feet were bare. Their arms were bound behind their backs, and they shuffled like slaves on their way to the auction block.

I was watching Lord Intef's face, and I saw the shock assail him and force him to flinch, as though he had received a blow in the face. He had recognized the captives, but he had obviously believed that they were long dead, and their skulls grinning at the roadside. He darted a sideways glance at the small sacristy door in the wall that was almost hidden by the hanging linen bunting. It was his only escape from the crowded inner court, but Remrem moved one pace to his right and blocked his path to the doorway. Lord Intef looked back at the throne and lifted his chin in a confident and defiant gesture.

The six bound captives lined up before the throne and then, at a quiet order from Kratas, dropped to their knees and bowed their heads.

'Who are these creatures?' Pharaoh demanded, and Tanus stood over the first of them, seized his bound wrists and hauled him to his feet. The captive's skin was studded with the old healed scars of the smallpox and his blind eye reflected the light like a silver coin.

'The divine Pharaoh asks who you are,' Tanus said softly. 'Reply to the question.'

'Great Egypt, I am Shufti,' he said. 'I was once a baron of the Shrikes before Akh-Horus scattered and slew my clan at the city of Gallala.'

'Tell the king who was your overlord,' Tanus insisted.

'Akh-Seth was my overlord,' Shufti replied. 'I swore a blood-oath of allegiance to Akh-Seth, and I paid a bounty of one-quarter of all my plunder to him. In return Akh-Seth gave me immunity from the forces of law, and provided me with information on my intended victims.'

'Point out to the king the man you know as Akh-Seth,' Tanus ordered, and Shufti shuffled forward until he faced Lord Intef. He filled his mouth with spittle and spat it on to the grand vizier's gorgeous uniform. 'This is Akh-Seth,' he cried. 'And may the worms feast on his guts!'

Kratas dragged Shufti to one side and Tanus lifted the next captive to his feet. 'Tell the king who you are,' he ordered.

'I am Akheku, and I was a baron of the Shrikes, but all my men are killed.'

'Who was your overlord? To whom did you pay your bounty?' Tanus demanded.

'Lord Intef was my overlord. I paid my bounty into the coffers of the grand vizier.'

Lord Intef stood proud and aloof, showing no emotion as these accusations were hurled at him. He offered no defence as, one after the other, the barons were dragged before him and each made the same declaration.

'Lord Intef was my overlord. Lord Intef is Akh-Seth.'

The silence of the multitudes in the temple was as oppressive as the heat. They watched in horror, or in silent hatred, or in confusion and disbelief. However, not one of them dared yet to speak out against Lord Intef, or to show emotion until Pharaoh had first spoken.

The last of the barons was brought forward to confront the grand vizier. He was a tall, lean man with stringy muscles and sun-blasted skin. There was Bedouin blood in his veins, for his eyes were black and his nose beaked. His beard was thick and curling, and his expression arrogant.

'My name is Basti.' He spoke more clearly than any of the others. 'Men call me Basti the Cruel, though I know not the reason why.' He grinned with a raffish hangman's humour. 'I was a baron of the Shrikes until Akh-Horus destroyed my clan. Lord Intef was my overlord.'

This time he was not dragged away as the others had been. Tanus spoke to him again. 'Tell the king. Did you know Pianki, Lord Harrab, who in former times was a nobleman of Thebes?'

'I knew him well. I had dealings with him.'

'What were these dealings?' Tanus asked, with death in his voice.

'I plundered his caravans. I burned his crops in the fields. I raided his mines at Sestra, and I slew the miners in such amusing fashion that no others ever came to work the copper there. I burned his villas. I sent my men into the cities to speak evil of him, so that his honesty and his loyalty to the state were tarnished. I helped others to destroy him so that in the end he drank the poisonous Datura seed from his own cup.'

I saw the hand of Pharaoh that held the royal flail shake as he listened, and one of his eyelids twitched in a manner that I had noticed before when he was sore distressed.

'Who was it that ordered these things?'

'Lord Intef commanded these things and rewarded me with a takh of pure gold.'

'What did Lord Intef hope to gain from this persecution of Lord Harrab?'

Basti grinned and shrugged. 'Lord Intef is grand vizier, while Pianki, Lord Harrab is dead. It seems to me Lord Intef achieved his purpose.'

'You acknowledge that I have offered you no clemency in return for this confession? Do you understand that death awaits you?'

'Death?' Basti laughed. 'I have never been afraid of that. It is the flour of the loaf I bake. I have fed it to countless others, so now why should I be afraid to feast on it myself?' Was he fool or brave man, I wondered, as I listened to the boast. Either way, I could find neither pity nor admiration for him in my heart. I remembered that Pianki, Lord Harrab

444

had been a man like his son, and that is where my pity and my admiration lay.

I saw the merciless expression in the eyes of Tanus. I knew that he shared my feelings, and his grip upon the hilt of his sword tightened until his fingers turned as white as those of a drowned man.

'Take him away!' he grated. 'Let him await the king's pleasure.' I saw him compose himself with an effort, then he turned back to face the king. He went down on one knee before him.

'I have done all that you asked of me, Divine Mamose, god and ruler of *Kemit*. I wait for you to command me further.' His dignity and his grace closed up my throat so that I could not swallow. It took an effort to compose myself.

The silence in the temple persisted. I could hear my mistress's laboured breathing beside me and then I felt her take my hand and squeeze it with a strength that threatened to crack my finger-bones.

At last Pharaoh spoke, but with dismay I heard the doubt in his voice, and I sensed intuitively that he did not want any of this to be true. He had trusted Lord Intef so deeply for so long that it shook the foundations of his faith.

'Lord Intef, you have heard the accusations against you. How say you to them?'

'Divine Pharaoh, are these indeed accusations? I thought them merely the fantasies of a young man driven insane with envy and jealousy. He is the son of a convicted criminal and a traitor. Lord Tanus' motives are plain to see. He has convinced himself that the traitor Pianki might have become grand vizier in my place. In some perverse fashion, he holds me responsible for his father's downfall.'

With a wave of his hand he dismissed Tanus. It

445

was so skilfully done that I saw the king waver. His doubts were growing stronger. For a lifetime he had implicitly trusted Lord Intef, and it was difficult for him to adjust his thinking. He wanted to believe in his innocence.

'What of the accusations of the barons?' Pharaoh asked at last. 'What reply do you make to them?'

'Barons?' Lord Intef asked. 'Must we flatter them with such a title? By their own testimony they are criminals of the basest kind—murderers, thieves, violators of women and children. Should we look for truth in them any more than we should look for honour and conscience in the beasts of the field?' Lord Intef pointed to them, and they were indeed half-naked and bound like animals. 'Let us gaze upon them, Divine Majesty. Are these not the kind of men that can be bribed or beaten into saying anything for the sake of their own skins? Would you take the word of one of these against a man who has served you faithfully all his life?'

I saw the small, involuntary nod of the king's head as he accepted the reasoning of the man he had looked upon as a friend, the man upon whom he had heaped trust and rewards.

'All you say is true. You have always served me without vice. These rogues are strangers to truth and honour. It is possible that they may have been coerced.' He vacillated, and Lord Intef sensed his advantage.

'So far I have had only words thrown at me. Surely there must be some other evidence to support such mortal charges against me? Is there one person in this very Egypt who will bring evidence against me, real evidence and not mere words? If there is, let him come forward. Then I

446

will answer this charge. If there is no one who has this evidence, then I have nothing to answer to.'

His words troubled Pharaoh deeply, I could see that. He gazed about the hall as if seeking the evidence that Lord Intef demanded, and then he obviously reached a decision.

'Lord Tanus, what proof do you have of these things, apart from the words of murderers and criminals?'

'The beast has covered his tracks well,' Tanus admitted, 'and he has taken cover in the densest thicket where it is difficult to come at him. I have no further evidence against Lord Intef, but there may be some other who does, somebody who will be inspired by what he has heard here today. I beg you, Royal Egypt, ask your people if there is not one of them who can bring forth anything to help us here.'

'Pharaoh, this is provocation. My enemies will be emboldened to come out of the shadows where they lurk to attack me,' cried Lord Intef in vehement protest, but Pharaoh silenced him with a brusque gesture. 'They will bear false witness against you at their peril,' he promised, and then addressed the congregation.

'My people! Citizens of Thebes! You have heard the accusations made against my trusted and well-beloved grand vizier. Is there one of you who can provide the proof that Lord Tanus lacks? Can any of you bring forward evidence against the Lord Intef? If so, I charge you to speak.'

I was standing before I realized what I had done, and my voice was so loud in my own ears that it startled me.

'I am Taita, who was once the slave of Lord

447

Intef,' I shouted, and Pharaoh looked across at me and frowned. 'I have aught that I wish to show Your Majesty.'

'You are known to us, Taita the physician. You may approach.'

As I left my seat on the stand and went down to stand before the king, I looked across at Lord Intef and I missed my step. It was as though I had walked into a stone wall, so tangible was his hatred.

'Divine Egypt, this thing is a slave.' Lord Intef's voice was cold and tight. 'The word of a slave against a lord of the Theban circle, and a high officer of the state—what mockery is this?'

I was still so conditioned to respond to his voice and to succumb to his word, that my resolve wavered. Then I felt Tanus' hand on my arm. It was only a brief touch, but it manned and sustained me. However, Lord Intef had noticed the gesture, and he pointed it out to the king.

'See how this slave is in the thrall of my accuser. Here is another one of Lord Tanus' trained monkeys.' Lord Intef's voice was once more smooth as warm honey. 'His insolence is unbounded. There are penalties laid down in the law codes—'

Pharaoh silenced him with a gesture of his flail. 'You presume on our good opinion of you, Lord Intef. The codes of law are mine to interpret or amend. In them there are penalties laid down for the high-born as well as the common man. You would be well advised to remember that.' Lord Intef bowed in submission and remained silent, but suddenly his face was haggard and drawn as he realized his predicament.

448

Now the king looked down at me. 'These are unusual circumstances, such as allow of unprecedented remedy. However, Taita the slave, let me warn you that if your words should prove frivolous, should they lack proof or substance, the strangling-rope awaits you.'

That threat and the poisonous bane of Lord Intef's gaze upon me made me stutter. 'While I was the slave of the grand vizier, I was his messenger and his emissary to the barons. I know all these men.' I pointed to the captives that Kratas held near to the throne. 'It was I who carried Lord Intef's commands to them.'

'Lies! More words, lacking proof,' Lord Intef called out, but now the edge of desperation was in his voice. 'Where is the proof?'

'Silence!' the king thundered with sudden ferocity. 'We will hear the testimony of Taita the slave.' He was looking directly at me, and I drew breath to continue.

'It was I who carried the command of Lord Intef to Basti the Cruel. The command was to destroy the estate and the fortune of Pianki, Lord Harrab. At that time I was the confidant of Intef, I knew that he desired the position of grand vizier to himself. All these things that Lord Intef commanded were accomplished. Lord Harrab was destroyed, and he was deprived of Pharaoh's favour and love, so that he drank the Datura cup. I, Taita, attest all these things.'

'It is so.' Basti the Cruel lifted his bound arms to the throne. 'All that Taita says is the truth.'

'*Bak-Her!*' shouted the barons. 'It is the truth. Taita speaks the truth.'

'Still these are only words,' the king mused.

449

'Lord Intef has demanded proof. I, your Pharaoh, demand proof.'

'For half my lifetime I was the scribe and the treasurer of the grand vizier. I kept the record of his fortune. I noted his profits and his expenses on my scrolls. I gathered in the bounty that the barons of the Shrikes paid to Lord Intef, and I disposed of all this wealth.'

'Can you show me these scrolls, Taita?' Pharaoh's expression shone like the full moon at the mention of treasure. Now I had his avid attention.

'No, Majesty, I cannot do so. The scrolls remained always in the possession of Lord Intef.'

Pharaoh made no effort to conceal his chagrin, his face hardened towards me, but I went on doggedly, 'I cannot show you the scrolls, but perhaps I can lead you to the treasure that the grand vizier has stolen from you, and from the people of your realm. It was I who built his secret treasuries for him, and hid within them the bounty that I gathered from the barons. It was in these store-rooms that I placed the wealth that Pharaoh's tax-collectors never saw.'

The king's excitement rekindled, hot as the coals on the coppersmith's forge. He leaned forward intently. Although every eye in the temple was fastened upon me, and the nobles were crowding forward the better to hear each word, I was watching Lord Intef without seeming to look in his direction. The burnished copper doors of the sanctuary were tall mirrors in which his reflection was magnified. Every nuance of his expression and every movement he made, however slight, was clear to me.

I had taken a fatal risk in assuming that his treasure still remained in the secret places where I had stored it for him. He might have moved it at any time during the past two years. Yet moving such quantities of treasure would have been a major work and the risk of doing so as great as letting it rest where it lay. He would have been forced to take others into his trust, and that was not easy for Lord Intef to do. He was by nature a suspicious man. Added to which was the fact that, until recently, he had believed me dead, and my secret with me.

I calculated that my chances were evenly balanced, and I risked my life on it. Now I held my breath as I watched Lord Intef's reflection in the copper doors. Then my heart raced and my spirits soared on the wings of eagles. I saw from the pain and panic in his expression that the arrow I had fired at him had struck the mark. I had won. The treasure was where I had left it. I knew that I could lead Pharaoh to the plunder and the loot that Lord Intef had gathered up over his lifetime.

But he was not yet defeated. I was rash to believe it would be so easily accomplished. I saw him make a gesture with his right hand that puzzled me, and while I dallied, it was almost too late.

In my triumph, I had forgotten Rasfer. The signal that Lord Intef gave him was a flick of the right hand, but Rasfer responded like a trained boar-hound to the huntsman's command to attack. He launched himself at me with such sudden ferocity that he took all of us by complete surprise. He had only ten paces to cover to reach me, and his sword rasped from its scabbard as he came.

There were two of Kratas' men standing between us, but their backs were turned to him, and Rasfer barged into them and knocked them off their feet, so that one of them sprawled across the stone flags in front of Tanus and blocked his path when he tried to spring to my aid. I was on my own, defenceless, and Rasfer threw up his sword with both hands to cleave through my skull to my breast-bone. I lifted my hands to ward off the blow, but my legs were frozen with shock and terror, and I could not move or duck away from the hissing blade.

I never saw Tanus throw his sword. I had eyes for nothing but the face of Rasfer, but suddenly the sword was in the air. Terror had so enhanced my senses that time seemed to pass as slowly as spilled oil dribbling from the jar. I watched Tanus' sword turning end over end, spinning slowly on its axis, flashing at each revolution like a sheet of summer lightning, but it had not completed a full turn when it struck, and it was the hilt and not the point that crashed into Rasfer's head. It did not kill him, but it snapped his head over, whipping his neck like the branch of a willow in the wind, so that his eyes rolled back blindly in their sockets.

Rasfer never completed the blow he aimed at me. His legs collapsed under him and he fell in a pile at my feet. His sword flew from his nerveless fingers, spinning high in the air, and then fell back. It pegged into the side of Pharaoh's throne, and quivered there. The king stared at it in shocked disbelief. The razor edge had touched his arm, and split the skin. As we all watched, a line of ruby droplets oozed from the shallow wound, and dripped on to Pharaoh's cloud-white linen kilt.

Tanus broke the horrified silence. 'Great Egypt, you saw who gave the signal for this beast to attack. You know who was to blame for endangering your royal person.' He leaped over the downed guardsman and seized Lord Intef by the arm, twisting it until he fell to his knees and cried out with pain.

'I did not want to believe this of you.' Pharaoh's expression was sorrowful as he looked down on his grand vizier. 'I have trusted you all my life, and you have spat upon me.'

'Great Egypt, hear me!' Lord Intef begged on his knees, but Pharaoh turned his face away from him.

'I have listened to you long enough.' Then he nodded to Tanus. 'Have your men guard him well, but show him courtesy, for his guilt is not yet fully proven.'

Finally Pharaoh addressed the congregation. 'These are strange and unprecedented events. I adjourn these proceedings to consider fully the evidence that Taita the slave will present to me. The population of Thebes will assemble once again to hear my judgement in this same place at noon tomorrow. I have spoken.'

 We entered through the main doorway to the audience hall of the grand vizier's palace. Pharaoh paused at the threshold. Although the wound from Rasfer's sword was slight, I had bandaged it with linen and placed his arm in a sling.

Pharaoh surveyed the hall slowly. At the far end

of the long room stood the grand vizier's throne. Carved from a solid block of alabaster, it was hardly less imposing than Pharaoh's own in the throne room at Elephantine. The high walls were plastered with smooth clay and on this background were painted some of the most impressive frescoes that I had ever designed. They transformed the huge room into a blazing garden of delights. I had painted them while I was Lord Intef's slave, and even though they were my own creations, they still gave me a deep thrill of pleasure when I looked upon them.

I have no doubt that these works alone, without consideration of any other of my achievements, would support my claim to the title of the most significant artist in the history of our land. It was sad that I who had created them was now to demolish them. It detracted from the triumph of this tumultuous day.

I led Pharaoh down the hall. For once we had dispensed with all protocol, and Pharaoh was as eager as a child. He followed me so closely that he almost trod upon my heels, and his royal train fell in as eagerly behind him.

I led them to the throne wall and we stopped below the huge mural depicting the sun god, Ammon-Ra, on his daily journey across the heavens. Even in his excitement, I could see the reverent expression in the king's eyes as he looked up at the painting.

Behind us, the great hall was half-filled with the king's train, the courtiers and the warriors and the noble lords, to say nothing of the royal wives and concubines who would rather have given up all their rouges and paint-boxes of cosmetics than

454

miss such an exciting moment as I had promised them. Naturally, my mistress was in the forefront. Tanus marched only a pace behind the king. He and his Blues had taken over the duties of the royal bodyguard.

The king turned back to Tanus now. 'Have your men bring forward the Lord Intef!'

Treating him with elaborate and icy courtesy, Kratas led Intef to face the wall, but he interposed himself between the prisoner and the king and stood with his naked blade at the ready.

'Taita, you may proceed,' the king told me, and I measured the wall, stepping out exactly thirty paces from the furthest corner and marking the distance with the lump of chalk that I had brought with me for the purpose.

'Behind this wall lie the private quarters of the grand vizier,' I explained to the king. 'Certain alterations were made when last the palace was renovated. Lord Intef likes to have his wealth close at hand.'

'Sometimes you are garrulous, Taita.' Pharaoh was less than captivated by my lecture on the palace architecture. 'Get on with it, fellow. I am aflame to see what is hidden here.'

'Let the masons approach!' I called out, and a small band of these sturdy rogues in their leather aprons came down the aisle and dropped their leather tool-bags at the foot of the throne wall. I had summoned them across the river from their work on Pharaoh's tomb. The white stone-dust in their hair gave them an air of age and wisdom that few of them deserved.

I borrowed a wooden set-square from their foreman, and with it marked out an oblong shape on the clay-plastered wall. Then I stepped back and addressed the master mason. 'Gently now! Damage the frescoes as little as you can. They are great works of art.'

With their wooden mallets and their chisels of flint, they fell upon the wall, and they paid little heed to my strictures. Paint and plaster flew in clouds as slabs of the outer wall were stripped away and thumped to the marble floor. The dust offended the ladies and they covered their mouths and noses with their shawls.

Gradually from under the layer of plaster emerged the outline of the stone blocks. Then Pharaoh exclaimed aloud and, ignoring the flying dust, he drew closer, and peered at the design that appeared from beneath the plaster skin. The regular courses of stone blocks were marred by an oblong of alien-coloured stone that followed almost exactly the outline I had chalked upon the outer layer of plaster.

'There is a hidden door in there,' he cried. 'Open it immediately!' Under the king's urging, the masons attacked the sealed doorway with a will, and once they had removed the keystone, the other blocks came out readily. A dark opening was revealed, and Pharaoh, who had by now taken charge of the work, called excitedly for torches to be lit.

'The entire space behind this wall is a secret compartment,' I told Pharaoh, while we waited for the torches to be brought to us. 'I had it constructed on Lord Intef's orders.'

When the torches were brought, Tanus took one of them and lit the king's way into the gaping secret door. The king stepped through, and I was the next to enter after him and Tanus.

It was so long since I had last been in there that I looked around me with as much interest as the others. Nothing had changed in all that time. The chests and casks of cedar and acacia wood were stacked exactly as I had left them. I pointed out to the king those cases to which he should first devote his attention, and he ordered, 'Have them carried out into the audience hall.'

'You will need strong men to carry them,' I remarked drily. 'They are rather heavy.'

It took three of the biggest men of the Blues to lift each case and they staggered out through the jagged opening in the wall with them.

'I have never seen these boxes before,' Lord Intef protested, as the first of them was carried out and laid on the dais of the grand vizier's throne. 'I had no knowledge of a secret chamber behind the wall. It must have been built by my predecessor, and the cases placed there at his command.'

'Your Majesty, observe the seal on this lid.' I pointed it out to him and the king peered at the clay tablet.

'Whose seal is this?' he demanded.

'Observe the ring on the left forefinger of the grand vizier, Majesty,' I murmured. 'May I respectfully suggest that Pharaoh match it to the seal on this chest?'

'Lord Intef, hand me your ring if you please,' the king asked with exaggerated courtesy, and the grand vizier hid his left hand behind his back.

'Great Egypt, the ring has been on my finger for twenty years. My flesh has grown around it and it cannot now be removed.'

'Lord Tanus.' The king turned to him. 'Take

457

your sword. Remove Lord Intef's finger and bring it to me with the ring upon it.' Tanus smiled cruelly as he stepped forward to obey, half-drawing his blade.

'Perhaps I am mistaken,' Lord Intef admitted with alacrity. 'Let me see if I cannot free it.' The ring slipped readily enough from his finger, and Tanus went down on one knee to hand it to the king.

Pharaoh bent studiously over the chest and made the comparison of ring to seal. When he straightened up again his face was dark with anger.

'It is a perfect match. This seal was struck from your ring, Lord Intef.' But the grand vizier made no reply to the accusation. He stood with his arms folded and his expression stony.

'Break the seal. Open the chest!' Pharaoh ordered, and Tanus cut away the clay tablet and prised up the lid with his sword.

The king cried out involuntarily as the lid fell away and the contents were revealed, 'By all the gods!' And his courtiers crowded forward without ceremony to gaze into the chest, exclaiming and jostling each other for a better view.

'Gold!' The king scooped both hands full with the glittering yellow rings, and then let them cascade back between his fingers. He kept a single ring in his hand and held it close to his face to study the mint marks upon it. 'Two deben weight of fine gold. How much will this case contain, and how many cases are there in the secret store-room?' His question was rhetorical, and he was not expecting an answer, but I gave him a reply nevertheless.

'This case contains—' I read the manifest that I

had inscribed on the lid so many years before. 'It contains one takh and three hundred deben of pure gold. As to how many cases of gold, if my memory serves me well, there should be fifty-three of gold and twenty-three of silver in this store. However, I have forgotten exactly how many chests of jewellery we hid here.'

'Is there no one I can trust? You, Lord Intef, I treated as my brother. There was no kindness that you did not receive from my hands, and this is how you have repaid me.'

 At midnight the chancellor and the chief inspector of the royal taxes came to the king's chamber where I was changing the dressing on his injured arm. They presented their final tally of the amount of the treasure and Pharaoh read it with awe. Once again, his emotions warred with each other, outrage vying with euphoria at this staggering windfall.

'The rogue was richer than his own king. There is no punishment harsh enough for such evil. He has cheated and robbed me and my tax-collectors.'

'As well as murdering and plundering Lord Harrab and tens of thousands of your subjects,' I reminded him, as I secured the bandage on his arm. It was perhaps impudent of me. However, he was by now so deep in my debt that I could risk it.

'That too,' he agreed readily enough, my sarcasm wasted upon him. 'His guilt is deep as the sea and high as the heaven. I will have to devise a suitable punishment. The strangler's rope is too kind for Lord Intef.'

'Majesty, as your physician, I must insist that you rest now. It has been a day that has taxed even your great strength and endurance.'

'Where is Intef? I cannot rest until I am assured that he is well taken care of.'

'He is under guard in his own quarters, Majesty. A senior captain and a detachment of the Blues have that duty.' I hesitated delicately. 'Rasfer is also under guard.'

'Rasfer, that ugly drooling animal of his? The one who tried to kill you in the temple of Osiris? Did he survive the crack that Lord Tanus gave him?'

'He is well if not happy, Pharaoh,' I assured him. 'Did Your Majesty know that Rasfer is the one who, so long ago, used the gelding-knife upon me?' I saw the beam of pity in the king's eye, as I blurted it out.

'I will deal with him as I deal with his master,' Pharaoh promised. 'He will suffer the same punishment as Lord Intef. Will that satisfy you, Taita?'

'Your Majesty is just and omniscient.' I backed out of his presence and went to find my mistress.

She was waiting for me and, although it was after midnight and I was exhausted, she would not let me sleep. She was far too overwrought, and she insisted that for the rest of the night I sit beside her bed and listen to her chatter about Tanus and other topics of lesser importance.

Despite the dearth of sleep, I was bright and clear-headed when I took my place in the temple of Osiris the following morning.

If anything, the congregation was even larger than it had been the day before. There was not a soul in Thebes who had not heard of the downfall of the grand vizier, and who was not eager to witness his ultimate humiliation. Even those of his underlings, who had most prospered under his corrupt administration, now turned upon him, like a pack of hyena who devour their leader when he is sick and wounded.

The barons of the Shrikes were led before the throne in their rags and bonds, but when Lord Intef entered the temple, he wore fine linen and silver sandals. His hair was freshly curled, his face painted, and the chains of the Gold of Praise hung around his neck.

The barons knelt before the king, but even when one of the guards pricked him with the sword, Lord Intef refused to bend the knee, and the king made a gesture for the guard to desist.

'Let him stand!' the king ordered. 'He will lie in his tomb long enough.' Then Pharaoh rose and stood before us in all his grandeur and his rage. This once he seemed a true king, as the first of his dynasty had been, a man of might and force. I, who had come to know him and his weaknesses so well, found that I was overcome with a sense of awe.

'Lord Intef, you are accused of treason and murder, of brigandage and piracy, and of a hundred other crimes no less deserving of

461

punishment. I have heard the supported testimony of fifty of my subjects from all walks and stations of life, from lords and freemen and slaves. I have seen the contents of your secret treasury wherein you hid your stolen wealth from the royal tax-collectors. I have seen your personal seal upon the treasure chests. By all these matters your guilt is proven a thousand times over. I, Mamose the eighth of that name, Pharaoh and ruler of this very Egypt, hereby find you guilty of all the crimes of which you are accused, and deserving of neither royal clemency nor mercy.'

'Long live Pharaoh!' shouted Tanus, and the salute was taken up and repeated ten times by the people of Thebes. 'May he live for ever!'

When silence fell, Pharaoh spoke again. 'Lord Intef, you wear the Gold of Praise. The sight of that decoration on the breast of a traitor offends me.' He looked across at Tanus. 'Centurion, remove the gold from the prisoner.'

Tanus lifted the chains from Lord Intef's neck and carried them to the king. Pharaoh took the gold in his two hands, but when Tanus started to withdraw, he stayed him with a word.

'The name Lord Harrab was tarnished with the slur of treason. Your father was hounded to a traitor's death. You have proven your father's innocence. I rescind all sentences passed against Pianki, Lord Harrab, and posthumously restore to him all his honours and titles that were stripped from him. Those honours and titles descend to you, his son.'

'*Bak-Her!*' shouted the congregation. 'May Pharaoh live for ever! Hail, Tanus, Lord Harrab!'

'In addition to those titles which now come

462

down to you as your inheritance, I bestow upon you new distinction. You have carried out my charge to you. You have destroyed the Shrikes and delivered their overlord to justice. In recognition of this service to the crown, I bestow upon you the Gold of Valour. Kneel, Lord Harrab, and receive the king's favour.'

'*Bak-Her*!' they cried, as Pharaoh placed the jangling gold chains, that had so recently belonged to Lord Intef, but to which he had now added the star pendant of the warrior's decoration, about Tanus' neck. 'Hail, Lord Harrab!'

As Tanus withdrew, Pharaoh turned his attention back to the prisoners. 'Lord Intef, you are deprived of your title as a lord of the Theban circle. Your name and rank will be erased from all the public monuments, and from your tomb that you have prepared in the Valley of the Nobles. Your estates and all your possessions, including your illicit treasure, are forfeited to the crown, except only those estates that once belonged to Pianki, Lord Harrab, and which by fell means have come into your possession. These are now returned in their entirety to his heir, my goodly Tanus, Lord Harrab.'

'*Bak-Her!* Pharaoh is wise! May he live for ever!' the people cheered wildly, and beside me my mistress was weeping unashamedly, but then so were half the royal women. Very few of them could resist that heroic figure whose golden hair seemed to dim the chains upon his breast.

Now the king took me by surprise. He looked directly at where I sat beside my mistress. 'There is one other who has done the crown loyal service, the one who revealed the whereabouts of the stolen treasure. Let the slave, Taita, stand forth.'

I went down to stand before the throne, and the king's voice was gentle. 'You have suffered unspeakable harm at the hands of the traitor Intef and his henchman Rasfer. You have been forced by them to commit nefarious deeds and capital crimes against the state, by conniving with bandits and robbers and by concealing your master's treasure from the royal tax-collectors. However, these were not crimes of your own inspiration. As a slave, you were forced to the will of your master. Therefore I absolve you from all guilt and liability. I find you innocent of any crime, and I reward you for your service to us with a bounty of two takhs of fine gold to be paid out of the treasure confiscated from the traitor, Intef.'

A murmur of astonishment greeted this announcement, and I gasped aloud. It was a staggering amount. A fortune to match those of all but the wealthiest lords in the land, enough to buy great tracts of the most fertile land along the river, and to furnish magnificent villas upon that land, to buy three hundred strong slaves to work the land, enough to fit out a fleet of trading vessels and send them to the ends of the earth to bring back more treasure. It was a sum large enough to boggle even my imagination, but the king had not finished.

'As a slave, this bounty will be paid not to you, but to your mistress, the Lady Lostris, who is a junior wife of Pharaoh.' I should have guessed that Pharaoh would keep it in the family.

I, who for a fleeting moment had been one of the richest men in Egypt, bowed to the king and returned to my place beside my mistress. She squeezed my hand to console me, but in truth I

464

was not unhappy. Our destinies were so entwined that I was a part of her, and I knew that we would never again want for any material thing. I was already planning how I would invest my mistress's fortune for her.

At last the king was ready to pass sentence on the line of prisoners, though he looked only at Intef as he spoke.

'Your crimes are unparalleled. No punishment before meted out is harsh enough to fit your case. This then is the sentence I pass upon you. At dawn on the day after the end of the festival of Osiris, you will be marched through the streets of Thebes, bound and naked. While you still live you will be nailed by your feet to the main gate of the city, with your heads hanging downwards. You will be left there until your bones are picked clean by the crows. Then your bones will be taken down and ground to powder and cast into Mother Nile.'

Even Intef paled and swayed on his feet as he listened to the sentence. By dispersing their earthly bodies so that they could never be embalmed and preserved, Pharaoh was condemning the prisoners to oblivion. For an Egyptian there could be no harsher punishment. They were being denied for all eternity the fields of paradise.

 When my mistress expressed her determination to attend the executions and to watch her father being nailed upside-down to the main gate, I do not think that she truly realized the horror of what she would witness. I was equally

determined that she should not be there to see it. There had never been a sadistic streak in her. I believe that her decision was influenced by the fact that most of the other royal women were going to enjoy the diverting spectacle, and that Tanus would be in command of the execution. She would never pass up an opportunity to gaze at him, even from a distance.

In the end I persuaded her only by employing the most poignant argument in my arsenal. 'My lady, such cruel sights as these will certainly affect your unborn son. Surely you do not wish to blight his young unformed mind.'

'That is not possible,' she faltered for the first time in our argument. 'My son could know nothing of it.'

'He will see through your eyes, and the screams of his dying grandfather will pass through the walls of your stomach and enter his tiny ears.' It was an evocative choice of words, and they had the effect I was striving for.

She thought about it at length, and then sighed. 'Very well then, but I shall expect you to bring me back a full description of it all. You are not to miss a single detail. Especially I will want to know what the other royal wives were wearing.' Then she grinned at me wickedly to prove that she had not been totally gulled by my arguments. 'You can whisper it all to me, so the child sleeping in my belly cannot overhear us.'

At dawn on the day of the execution the gardens of the palace were still shrouded in darkness when I left the harem. I hurried through the water-gardens, and the stars were reflected in the black surfaces of the ponds. As I approached the

466

wing of the palace where Lord Intef was being held in his own quarters, I saw the blaze of torches and lamps lighting the windows, and heard the frantic yelling of orders and invective from within.

I knew instantly that something was seriously amiss, and I broke into a run. I was almost speared by the guard at the door to Lord Intef's private quarters, but he recognized me at the last moment before he skewered me, and lifted his weapon and let me pass.

Tanus was in the centre of the ante-chamber. He was roaring like a black-maned lion in a trap, and aiming blows with his clenched fists at whoever came within range. Even though he had always had a stormy temper, I had never before seen him so incapacitated by rage. He seemed to have lost the power of reason or of articulate speech. His men, those mighty heroes of the Blues, cowered away from him, and the rest of the palace wing was in an uproar.

I went straight up to him, ducked under another wild punch, and shouted in his face, 'Tanus! It is I! Control yourself! In the name of all the gods, are you mad?'

He almost struck me, and I saw him wrestle with his emotions and at last take control of them.

'See what you can do for them.' He pointed at the bodies that were scattered about the ante-chamber as though a battle had raged through it.

With horror I recognized that one of them was Khetkhet, a senior captain of the regiment and a man I respected. He was curled in the corner clutching his stomach, with such agony etched on his rigid features that I hoped never to see again. I

467

touched his cheek and the skin was cold and dead.

I shook my head, 'He is past all help that I can give him.' I lifted his eyelid with my thumb and gazed into his dead eye, then I leaned forward and smelled his mouth. The faint musty odour of mushrooms on it was dreadfully familiar.

'Poison.' I stood up. 'The others will be the same.' There were five of them curled on the tiles.

'How?' asked Tanus, in a tone of forced calm, and I picked up one of the bowls piled on the low table from which they had obviously eaten their dinner, and I sniffed it. The smell of mushrooms was stronger.

'Ask the cooks,' I suggested. Then, in a sudden access of anger, I hurled the bowl against the wall. The crumpled bodies reminded me of my pets who had died the same death, and Khetkhet had been my friend.

I took a deep breath to calm myself before I asked, 'No doubt your prisoner has escaped?' Tanus did not reply, but led me through into the grand vizier's bedchamber. Immediately I saw the painted panel that had been removed from the far wall of the empty room, and the opening behind it.

'Did you know that there was a secret passage?' Tanus demanded coldly, and I shook my head.

'I thought I knew all his secrets, but I was wrong.' My voice was resigned. I think that in my heart I had known all along that we would never bring Intef to justice. He was a favourite of the dark gods and enjoyed their protection.

'Has Rasfer escaped with him?' I asked, and Tanus shook his head.

'I have him locked in the arsenal with the barons. But Intef's two sons, Menset and Sobek, have disappeared. Almost certainly they were the ones who arranged this murder of my men, and their father's escape.' Tanus had full control of that wild temper of his once more, but his anger was still there beneath it. 'You know Intef so well, Taita. What will he do? Where will he go? How can I catch him?'

'One thing I know, he will have made plans against such a day as this. I know he has treasure stored for him in the Lower Kingdom, with merchants and lawyers there. He has even had commerce with the false pharaoh. I think that he sold military information to him and his generals. He would receive a friendly welcome in the north.'

'I have already sent five fast galleys to the north, with orders to search all vessels that they overtake,' Tanus told me.

'He has friends across the Red Sea,' I said. 'And he has sent treasure to merchants in Gaza on the shores of the northern sea, to be held for him. He has had dealings with the Bedouin. Many of them are in his pay. They would help him to cross the desert.'

'By Horus, he is like a rat with a dozen escape-routes to his hole,' swore Tanus. 'How can I cover all of them?'

'You cannot,' I said. 'And now Pharaoh is waiting to witness the executions. You will have to report this to him.'

'The king will be angry, and with good reason. By allowing Intef to escape, I have failed in my duty.'

But Tanus was wrong. Pharaoh accepted the news of Intef's escape with remarkable equanimity. I cannot fathom the reason for this,

469

except perhaps that the vast quantity of treasure he had acquired so unexpectedly had mellowed him. Deep in his heart he may still have cherished some sneaking affection for his grand vizier. On the other hand, Pharaoh was a kindly man, and may not have truly relished the prospect of watching Lord Intef being nailed to the city gates.

It is true he showed some passing annoyance, and spoke of justice being cheated, but all the time we were in his presence, he was surreptitiously studying the manifest of the treasure. Even when Tanus admitted his responsibility for the prisoner's escape, Pharaoh brushed it aside.

'The fault lies with the captain of the guard, and he has already been sufficiently punished from the poison bowl that Intef provided for him. You have sent galleys and troops in pursuit of the fugitive. You have done all that can be expected of you, Lord Harrab. It remains only for you to carry out my sentence on these other criminals.'

'Is Pharaoh ready to witness the execution?' Tanus asked, and Pharaoh looked about him for an excuse to remain with his manifests and tax-collectors' reports.

'I have much to do here, Lord Tanus. Proceed without me. Report to me when the sentences have been carried out.'

So great was the public interest in the executions that the city fathers had erected a Taita stand in front of the main gates. They charged a silver ring for a seat upon it. There was no lack of customers, and the stand was packed to capacity. The crowds who could not find a seat upon it overflowed out into the fields beyond the walls. Many of them had brought beer and wine to make a celebration of it, and to toast the barons on their way. Very few of them had not suffered from the ravages of the Shrikes, and many of them had lost husbands or brothers or sons to them.

Stark naked and bound together, as Pharaoh had ordered, the condemned men were led through the streets of Karnak. The crowd lined their way and hurled dung and filth at them as they passed, screaming insults and shaking their fists. The children danced ahead of the procession singing bits of doggerel made up on the spur of the moment;

Nails in my tooties, bare bum to the sky,
I am a baron, and that's how I die.

Obedient to my mistress's wishes, I had taken up a place on the stand to watch the sentence carried out. In truth I had no eyes for the clothing and jewellery of the women of fashion around me when the prisoners were at last led through the open gates. I looked instead at Rasfer and I tried to revive and inflate my hatred for him. I forced myself to recite every cruel and wicked act that he

471

had ever committed against me, to relive the agony of the lash and the knife that he had inflicted upon me. Yet there he stood with his white belly sagging almost to his knees, with excrement in his hair and filth streaking his face and running down his grotesque body. It was difficult to hate him as much as he deserved.

He saw me on the stand and he grinned up at me. The paralysed muscles on one side of his face made it only half a grin, a sardonic grimace, and he called, 'Thank you for coming to wish me godspeed, eunuch. Perhaps we will meet again in the fields of paradise, where I hope to have the pleasure of cutting off your balls once again.'

That taunt should have made it easier for me to hate him, but somehow it failed, although I called back to him, 'You are going no further than the mud in the river bottom, old friend. The next catfish that I roast on the spit I will call Rasfer.'

He was the first prisoner to be lifted on to the wooden gate. It took three men on the parapet of the wall, straining on the rope, while at the same time, four more shoved from below. They held him there as one of the regimental armourers climbed the ladder beside him with a stone, headed mallet in his fist.

There were no more jokes from Rasfer when the first of the thick copper nails was driven through the flesh and bones of his huge, calloused feet. He roared and swore and twisted in the grip of the men who held him, and the crowd cheered and laughed and urged on the sweating armourer.

It was only when the nails had been driven home and the hammerman had climbed down to admire his handiwork that the flaws in this novel form of

472

punishment became evident. Rasfer howled and roared, swinging upside-down, with the blood trickling slowly down his legs. The hang of his pendulous paunch was reversed, and the huge hairy bunch of his genitalia flapped against his belly-button. As he twisted and struggled, the nails slowly ripped through the web of flesh between his toes, until finally they tore entirely free. Rasfer fell back to earth and flopped around like a beached fish. The spectators loved the show, and howled with mirth at his antics.

Encouraged by the spectators, his executioners lifted him back on to the gate, and the armourer with his hammer climbed back up the ladder to drive in more nails. In order to pin Rasfer more securely and to prevent him struggling, Tanus ordered his hands as well as his feet to be nailed to the gate.

This time it was more successful. Rasfer hung head down, his limbs spread like some monstrous star-fish. He was no longer bellowing, for the mass of intestines in his belly were sagging down and pressing on his lungs. He struggled for every breath he drew, and had none over for shouting.

One at a time, the other condemned men were lifted on to the gate and nailed there, and the crowd hooted and applauded. Only Basti the Cruel made no sound and gave them poor sport.

As the day wore on, the sun beat down upon the crucified victims, and the heat grew steadily stronger. By noon the prisoners were so weak with pain and thirst and loss of blood that they hung as quietly as the carcasses on butchers' hooks. The spectators began to lose interest and drifted away. Some of the barons lasted longer than the others.

Basti went on breathing all that day. Only as the sun was setting did he take one deep shuddering breath and finally hang inert.

Rasfer was the toughest of them all. Long after Basti was gone, he hung on. His face was filled with dark blood so it swelled to twice its normal size. His tongue protruded from between his lips, like a thick slice of purple liver. Once in a while he would utter a deep groan and his eyes would flutter open. Every time this happened, I shared his agony. The last of my hatred for him had long ago shrivelled and died, and I was racked with pity, as I would have been for any other tortured animal.

The crowd had long ago dispersed, and I sat alone on the empty stand. Not attempting to hide his disgust at such a brutal duty thrust upon him by the royal command, Tanus had stood to his post until sunset. Then finally he had handed over the death watch to one of his captains, and strode back into the city, leaving us to our vigil.

There were only the ten guards below the gate, myself on the stand and a few beggars lying like bundles of rags at the foot of the wall. The torches on either side of the gate guttered and flickered in the night breeze off the river, casting an eerie light over the macabre scene.

Rasfer groaned again, and I could stand it no longer. I took a jar of beer from my basket and climbed down to speak to the captain. We knew each other from the desert, and he laughed and shook his head at my request. 'You are a soft-hearted fool, Taita. The bastard is so far-gone, he is not worth worrying about,' he told me. 'But I will look the other way for a while. Be quick about it.'

I went to the gate, and Rasfer's head was on a level with my own. I called his name softly, and his eyes fluttered open. I had no way of telling how much he understood, but I whispered, 'I have a little beer to wet your tongue.'

He made a soft gulping sound in his throat. His eyes were looking at me. If he still had feeling, I knew his thirst must be a torment of hell. I dribbled a few drops from the jar over his tongue, careful not to let any of it run back into his nose. He made a weak and futile effort to swallow. It would have been impossible, even if he had been stronger; the liquid ran out of the corners of his mouth and down his cheeks into the dung-caked hair.

He closed his eyes, and that was the moment I was waiting for. I slipped my dagger out of the folds of my shawl. Carefully I placed the point behind his ear, and then with a sharp movement drove it in to the hilt. His back arched in the final spasm, and then he relaxed into death. I drew out the blade. There was very little blood, and I hid the dagger in my shawl and turned away.

'May dreams of paradise waft you through the night, Taita,' the captain of the guard called after me, but I had lost my voice and could not reply. I never thought that I would weep for Rasfer, and maybe I never did so. Perhaps I wept only for myself.

At Pharaoh's command the return of the court to Elephantine was initially delayed for a month. The king had his new treasure to dispose of and was in buoyant mood. In all the time I had known him, I had never seen him so happy and contented. I was pleased for him. By this time I held the old man in real and warm affection. Some nights I sat up late with him and his scribes, going over the accounts of the royal treasury, which now emitted a decidedly rosy glow.

At other times, I was summoned by Pharaoh to consultations on the alterations to the mortuary temple and the royal tomb that he was now better able to afford. I calculated that at least half of the recently revealed treasure would go into the tomb with Pharaoh. He selected all the finest jewellery from Intef's hoard and sent almost fifteen takhs of bullion to the goldsmiths in his temple, to be turned into funerary objects.

Nevertheless, he found time to send for Tanus to advise him on military matters. He had now recognized Tanus as one of the foremost generals in his army.

I was present at some of these meetings. The threat from the false pharaoh in the Lower Kingdom was ever-present and preyed on all our minds. Such was Tanus' favour with the king that he was able to make the most of these fears and to persuade Pharaoh to divert a small part of Intef's treasure to the building of five new squadrons of war galleys, and to re-equipping all the guards regiments with new weapons and sandals—

although he was unable to persuade the king to make up the arrears in pay for the army. Many of the regiments had not been paid for the last half-year. Morale in the army was much boosted by these reinforcements, and every soldier knew whom to thank for them. They roared like lions and raised their clenched right fists in salute, when Tanus inspected their massed formations.

Most times when Tanus was summoned to the royal audience, my mistress found some excuse to be present. Although she had the good sense to keep in the background on these occasions, she and Tanus directed such looks at each other that I feared they might scorch the false beard of the Pharaoh. Fortunately nobody but myself seemed to notice these flashing messages of passion.

Whenever my mistress knew that I was to see Tanus in private, she burdened me with long and ardent messages for him. On my return I carried his replies which matched hers in length and fire. Fortunately these outpourings were highly repetitive, and memorizing them was not a great hardship.

My Lady Lostris never tired of urging me to find some subterfuge by which she and Tanus might be alone together once more. I admit that I feared enough for my own skin and for the safety of my mistress and our unborn child, not to devote all my energies and ingenuity to satisfying this request of hers. Once when I did tentatively approach Tanus with my mistress's invitation to a meeting, he sighed and refused it with many protestations of love for her.

'That interlude in the tombs of Tras was sheer madness, Taita. I never intended to compromise

477

the Lady Lostris' honour, but for the *khamsin*, it would never have happened. We cannot take that risk again. Tell her that I love her more than life itself. Tell her our time will come, for the Mazes of Ammon-Ra have promised it to us. Tell her I will wait for her through all the days of my life.'

On receiving this loving message, my mistress stamped her foot, called her true love a stubborn fool who cared nothing for her, broke a cup and two bowls of coloured glass, hurled a jewelled mirror which had been a gift from the king into the river, and finally threw herself on the bed where she wept until suppertime.

Apart from his military duties, which included supervising the building of the new fleet of galleys, Tanus, these days, was much occupied with the reorganization of his father's estates that he had at last inherited.

On these matters he consulted me almost daily. Not surprisingly, the estates had never been preyed upon by the Shrikes while they belonged to Lord Intef, and accordingly they were all prosperous and in good repair. Thus Tanus had become overnight one of the most wealthy men in the Upper Kingdom. Although I tried my best to dissuade him, he spent much of this private fortune in making up the arrears in pay to his men and in re-equipping his beloved Blues. Of course his men loved him all the more for this generosity.

Not content with these profligate expenditures, Tanus sent out his captains, Kratas and Remrem and Astes, to gather up all the crippled and blinded veterans of the river wars who now existed by begging in the streets of Thebes. Tanus installed this riff-raff in one of the large country villas that formed part of his inheritance, and although slops and kitchen refuse would have been too good for them, he fed them on meat and corn-cakes and beer. The common soldiers cheered Tanus in the streets and drank his health in the taverns.

When I told my mistress of Tanus' mad extravagances, she was so encouraged by them that she immediately spent hundreds of deben of the gold that I had earned for her, in buying and equipping a dozen buildings which she turned into hospitals and hostels for the poor people of Thebes. I had already earmarked this gold for investment in the corn market, and though I wrung my hands and pleaded with her, she could not be moved.

Needless to say, it was the long-suffering slave Taita who was responsible for the day-to-day management of this latest folly of his mistress, although she visited her charity homes every day. Thus it was possible for any loafer and drunkard in the twin cities to scrounge a free meal and a comfortable bed from us. If that was not enough, they could have their bowl of soup served to them by my mistress's own fair hand, and their running sores and purging bowels treated by one of the most eminent physicians in this very Egypt.

I was able to find a few young unemployed scribes and disenchanted priests who loved people more than gods or money. My mistress took them into her employ. I led this little band on nocturnal hunts through the back alleys and slum quarters of

479

the city. Nightly we gathered up the street orphans. They were a filthy, verminous bunch of little savages, and very few of them came with us willingly. We had to pursue and catch them like wild cats. I received many lusty bites and scratches in the process of bathing their filth-encrusted little bodies and shaving their hair that was so thick with lice and nits that it was impossible to drag a comb through it.

We housed them in one of my mistress's new hostels. Here the priests began the tedious process of taming them, while the scribes started on the long road of their education. Most of our captives escaped within the first few days, and returned to the gutters where they belonged. However, some of them stayed on in the hostel. Their slow transformation from animals to human beings delighted my mistress and gave me more pleasure than I had suspected could ever come from such an unlikely source.

All my protests against the manner in which my mistress was wasting our substance were in vain, and I vowed that if I were to be embalmed and laid in my tomb before my allotted time, the blame would surely rest entirely with these two young idiots whom I had taken under my wing, and who rewarded me by consistently ignoring my best advice.

Needless to say, it was my mistress and not me whom the widows and the cripples blessed and presented with their pitiful little gifts of wilting wild flowers, cheap beads and tattered scraps of papyrus containing poorly written texts from the *Book of the Dead*. As she walked abroad, the common people held up their brats for her blessing and tried to touch the hem of her skirt as though it were some religious talisman. She kissed the grubby babies, a practice which I warned her would endanger her health, and she scattered copper pieces to the loafers with as much care as a tree drops its autumn leaves.

'This is my city,' she told me. 'I love it and I love every person in it. Oh, Taita, I dread the return to Elephantine. I hate to leave my beautiful Thebes.'

'Is it the city you hate to leave?' I asked. 'Or is it a certain uncouth soldier who lives here?' She slapped me, but lightly.

'Is there nothing you hold sacred, not even love that is pure and true? For all your scrolls and grand language, you are at heart a barbarian.'

Thus the days passed swiftly for all of us, until one morning I consulted my calendar and discovered that over two months had passed since my Lady Lostris had resumed her marital duties on Pharaoh's couch. Although she still showed no evidence of her condition, it was time to apprise the king of his great good fortune, his approaching paternity.

When I told my mistress what I intended, only one matter engaged her consideration. She made me promise that before I discussed it with the king, I must first tell Tanus that he was the true father of the child she was carrying. I set out to fulfil my promise that very afternoon. I found Tanus at the shipyards on the west bank of the river, where he was swearing at the shipwrights and threatening to throw them into the river to feed the crocodiles.

He forgot his anger when he saw me, and took me on board the galley that they had launched that morning. Proudly, he showed me the new pump to remove water from the bilges, if the ship should ever be damaged in battle. He seemed to have forgotten that I had designed the equipment for him, and I had to remind him tactfully.

'Next you will want me to pay you for your ideas, you old rogue. I swear you are as stingy as any Syrian trader.' He clapped me on the back, and led me to the far end of the deck where none of the sailors could overhear us. He dropped his voice.

'How goes it with your mistress? I dreamed about her again last night. Tell me, is she well? How are those little orphans of hers? What a loving heart she has, what beauty! All of Thebes adores her. I hear her name spoken wherever I go, and the sound of it is as sharp as a spear thrust in my chest.'

'There will soon be two of her for you to love,' I told him, and he stared at me with his mouth agape like a man suddenly bereft of his senses. 'It was much more than just the *khamsin* that struck that night in the tombs of Tras.'

He seized me in a hug so powerful that I could not breathe. 'What is this riddle? Speak plainly, or I shall throw you into the river. What are you saying, you old scallywag? Don't juggle words with me!'

'The Lady Lostris is carrying your child. She sent me to tell you so that you should be the first to know it, even before the king,' I gasped. 'Now set me free before I am permanently damaged.' He released me so suddenly, that I almost fell overboard.

'My child! My son!' he cried. It was amazing how both of them had made that immediate assumption of the poor little mite's gender. 'This is a miracle. This is a direct gift from Horus.' It was clear to Tanus in that moment that no other man in the history of the world had ever fathered an infant.

'My son!' he shook his head in wonder. He was grinning like an idiot. 'My woman and my son! I must go to them this very moment.' He set off down the deck, and I had to run to catch him. It took all my powers of persuasion to prevent him from storming the palace and bursting into the royal harem. In the end, I led him to the nearest riverside tavern to wet the baby's head. Fortunately a gang of off-duty Blues was already drinking there. I ordered and paid for a butt of the tavern's best wine and left them to it. There were men from some of the other regiments in the tavern, so there would probably be a riot later, for Tanus was in a rumbustious mood and the Blues never needed much encouragement to fight.

I went directly from the tavern to the palace, and Pharaoh was delighted to see me. 'I was about to send for you, Taita. I have decided that we have been too niggardly with the entrance-gates to my temple. I want something grander—'

'Pharaoh!' I cried. 'Great and Divine Egypt! I have wonderful tidings. The goddess Isis has kept her promise to you. Your dynasty will be eternal. The prophecy of the Mazes of Ammon-Ra will be fulfilled. The moon of my mistress has been trodden under the hooves of the mighty bull of Egypt! The Lady Lostris is bearing your son!'

483

For once all thought of funerals and temple-building was driven from Pharaoh's mind, and, like Tanus, his very first instinct was to go to her. Led by the king, we rushed through the palace corridors, a solid stream of nobles and courtiers turbulent as the Nile in spate, and my mistress was waiting for us in the garden of the harem. With the natural wiles of the female, she had composed the setting perfectly to show off her loveliness to full effect. She was seated on a low bench with flower-beds around her and the broad river behind her. For a moment I thought the king might throw himself to his knees in front of her, but even the prospect of immortality could not cause him to forget his dignity to that extent.

Instead, he showered her with congratulations and compliments and earnest enquiries after her health. All the while his fascinated gaze was fastened on her belly from which the miracle would in the fullness of time emerge. Finally he asked her, 'My dear child, is there anything that you lack for your happiness? Is there anything I can do to make you more comfortable during this trying time in your life?'

I was filled once more with admiration for my mistress. She would have made a great general or corn trader, for her sense of timing was impeccable. 'Your Majesty, Thebes is the city of my birth. I cannot be truly happy anywhere else in Egypt. I beg you in your generosity and understanding to allow your son to be born here in Thebes. Please do not make me return to Elephantine.'

I held my breath, the siting of the court was an affair of state. To remove from one city to another

484

was a decision which affected the lives of thousands of citizens. It was not one to be made on the light whim of a child not yet sixteen years of age.

Pharaoh looked amazed at the request, and scratched his false beard. 'You want to live in Thebes? Very well, then, the court will move to Thebes!' He turned to me. 'Taita, design me a new palace.' He looked back at my mistress. 'Shall we site it there, on the west bank, my dear?' He pointed across the river.

'It is cool and pretty on the west bank,' my mistress agreed. 'I shall be very happy there.'

'On the west bank, Taita. Do not stint yourself in the design. It must be a fitting home for the son of Pharaoh. His name will be Memnon, the ruler of the dawn. We will call it the Palace of Memnon.'

With such simple ease my mistress saddled me with a mountain of labour, and accustomed the king to the first of many such demands in the name of the child in her womb. From this moment on, Pharaoh was not disposed to deny her aught that she asked for, whether it was titles of honour for those she loved or liked, alms for those she had taken under her protection, or rare and exotic dishes that were fetched for her from the ends of the empire. Like a naughty child, I think that she enjoyed testing the limits of this new power she wielded over the king.

She had never seen snow, though she had heard me speak of it from my fragmentary childhood memories of the mountainous land where I had been born. My mistress asked for some to be brought to her to cool her brow in the heat of the

Nile valley. Pharaoh immediately commanded a special athletics games to be held, during which the hundred fastest runners in the Upper Kingdom were selected. They were despatched to Syria to bring back snow to my mistress in a special box of my design, which was intended to prevent it melting. This was probably the only one of all her whims that remained unsatisfied. All we received back from those far-off mountain peaks was a damp patch in the bottom of the box.

In all other things she was fully accommodated. On one occasion she was present when Tanus presented a report to the king on the order of battle of the Egyptian fleet. My mistress sat quietly in the background until Tanus had finished and taken his leave, then she remarked quietly, 'I have heard it said that Lord Tanus is the finest general we have. Don't you think it may be wise, divine husband, to promote him to Great Lion of Egypt and place him in command of the northern corps?' Once again I gasped at her effrontery, but Pharaoh nodded thoughtfully.

'That same thought had already occurred to me, my dear, even though he is still so young for high command.'

The following day, Tanus was summoned to a royal audience, from which he emerged as Great Lion of Egypt and the commander of the northern wing of the army. The ancient general who had preceded him was palmed off with a substantial pension and relegated to a sinecure in the royal household. Tanus now had three hundred galleys and almost thirty thousand men under his command. The promotion meant that he stood fourth in the army lists, with only Nembet and a couple of old dodderers above him.

'Lord Tanus is a proud man,' the Lady Lostris informed me, as if I were completely ignorant of this fact. 'If you should ever tell him that I had any hand in his promotion, I shall sell you to the first Syrian trader I come upon,' she threatened me ominously.

All this time her belly, once so smooth and shapely, was distending gradually. With all my other work I was obliged to relay daily bulletins on this progression, not only to the palace, but also to army headquarters, northern command.

I began work on the construction of the Palace of Memnon five weeks after Pharaoh had given me the original instructions, for it had taken me that long to draw up the final plans. Both my mistress and the king agreed that my designs exceeded their expectations, and that it would be by far the most beautiful building in the land.

On the same day that the work began, a blockade runner who had succeeded in bribing his way past the fleets of the red pretender in the north docked in Thebes with a cargo of cedar wood from Byblos. The captain was an old friend of mine and he had interesting news for me.

Firstly, he told me that Lord Intef had been seen in the city of Gaza. It was said that he was travelling in state with a large bodyguard towards the East. He must therefore have succeeded in crossing the Sinai desert, or he had found a vessel to carry him through the mouth of the Nile and thence east along the coast of the great sea.

The captain had other news that at the time seemed insignificant, but which was to change the destiny of this very Egypt and of all of us who lived along the river. It seemed that a new and warlike tribe had come out of an unknown land to the east of Syria, carrying all before them. Nobody knew much about these warrior people, except that they seemed to have developed a form of warfare that had never been seen before. They could cross vast distances very swiftly, and no army could stand against them.

There were always wild rumours of new enemies about to assail this very Egypt. I had heard fifty like this one before, and thought as little of this one as I had of all the others. However, the captain was usually a reliable source, and so I mentioned his story to Tanus when next we met.

'No one can stand against this mysterious foe?' Tanus smiled. 'I would like to see them come against my lads, I'll show them what the word invincible truly means. What did you say they are called, these mighty warriors who come like the wind?'

'It seems that they call themselves the Shepherd Kings,' I replied, 'the Hyksos.' The name would not have slid over my tongue so smoothly if I understood then what it would mean to our world.

'The shepherds, hey? Well, they will not find my rascals an easy flock to herd.' He dismissed them lightly, and was much more interested in my news of Lord Intef. 'If only we could be certain of his true whereabouts, I could send a detachment of men to arrest him, and bring him back to face up to justice. Wherever I walk on the estates that once belonged to my family, I feel the spirit of my father beside me. I know he will never rest until I avenge him.'

'Would that it were so easy.' I shook my head. 'Intef is as cunning as a desert fox. I don't think we will ever see him in Egypt again.' As I said this, the dark gods must have chuckled to themselves.

 As my mistress's pregnancy advanced, I was able to insist that she limited her many activities. I forbade her to visit the hospitals or the orphanage, for fear of infecting herself and her unborn infant with the vermin and the diseases of the poor. During the heat of the day I made her rest under the barrazza that I had built in the water-garden for the grand vizier. When she protested at the boredom of this enforced inactivity, Pharaoh sent his musicians to the garden to entertain her, and I was persuaded to leave my work on the Palace of Memnon to keep her company, to tell her stories and to discuss Tanus' latest exploits with her.

I was very strict with her diet, and allowed her no wine or beer. I had the palace gardeners provide fresh fruits and vegetables each day, and I carved all the fat off her meat, for I knew that it would make the child in her belly sluggish. I prepared each of her meals myself and every night when I saw her to her bedchamber, I mixed a special potion with herbs and juices that would strengthen her infant.

Of course, when she suddenly declared that she must have a stew made from the liver and kidneys of a gazelle, or a salad of larks' tongues or the roasted breast of the wild bustard, the king immediately sent a hundred of his huntsmen into the desert to procure these delicacies for her. I refrained from telling Lord Tanus of these strange cravings of my mistress, for I dreaded to learn that rather than prosecuting the war against the false pharaoh, the northern army had been sent into the desert to hunt gazelle or larks or bustard.

As the day of her confinement approached, I lay awake at night worrying. I had promised the king a prince, but he was not expecting his heir to arrive so expeditiously. Even a god can count the days from the first of the festival of Osiris. There was nothing that I could do if the child turned out to be a princess, but at least I could prepare Pharaoh for her early arrival.

Pharaoh had now conceived an interest in the subject of pregnancy and parturition, which temporarily rivalled his obsession with temples and tombs. I had to reassure him almost daily that the Lady Lostris' rather narrow hips were no obstacle to a normal birth, and that her tender age, far from being prejudicial, was highly favourable to a successful conclusion to our enterprise.

I took the opportunity to inform him of the interesting but little-known fact that many of the great athletes, warriors and sages of history had been prematurely exposed to the light of day.

'I believe, Your Majesty, that it's rather like the case of the sluggard who lies too long abed, and thus wastes his energy, while the great men are invariably early risers. I have noticed that you, Divine Pharaoh, are always about before sunrise. It would not surprise me to learn that you were also a premature birth.' I knew that he was not, but naturally he could not now contradict me. 'It would be a most propitious circumstance if this prince of yours should imitate his sire, and start early from his mother's womb.' I hoped that I had not belaboured my point, but the king seemed convinced by my eloquence.

In the end, the child cooperated most handsomely by overstaying its allotted term by almost two weeks, and I did nothing to hurry it along. The time span was so close to the normal that no tongues could wag, but Pharaoh was blessed with the premature birth that he had come to believe was so desirable.

It was no surprise to me that my mistress began her labour at a most inconvenient hour. Her waters broke in the third watch of the night. She was not in the habit of making matters too easy for me. At least this gave me the excuse of dispensing with the services of a midwife, for I had little faith in those hags with the black, dried blood crusted under their long, ragged fingernails.

Once she had begun, my Lady Lostris carried it off with her usual despatch and aplomb. I had barely time to shake myself fully awake, scrub my hands in hot wine and bless my instruments in the flame of the lamp, before she grunted and said quite cheerfully, 'You had better take another look, Taita. I think something is happening.' Although I knew it was much too soon, I humoured her. One glance was enough, and I shouted for her slave girls.

'Hurry, you lazy strumpets! Fetch the royal wives!'

'Which ones?' The first girl to answer my call

tottered into the room half-naked and half-asleep.

'All of them, any of them.' No prince could inherit the double crown unless his birth had been witnessed, and it was formally attested that no exchange had taken place.

The royal women began to arrive just as the child revealed itself for the first time. My lady was seized by an overpowering convulsion, and then the crown of the head appeared. I had dreaded that it might be surmounted by a shock of red-gold curls, but what I saw was a thick dark pelt like that of one of the river otters. It was much later that the colour would change and the red would begin to sparkle in the black locks, like points of polished garnets, and then only when the sun shone upon it.

'Push!' I called to my mistress. 'Push hard!' And she responded lustily. The young bones of her pelvis, not yet tempered to rigidity by the years, spread to give the infant fair passage, and the way was well oiled. The child took me unawares. It came out like a stone from a sling-shot, and the tiny, slippery body almost flew from my hands.

Before I had a good hold on it, my mistress struggled up on her elbows. Her hair was plastered to her scalp with sweat and her expression was desperate with anxiety. 'Is it a boy? Tell me! Tell me!'

The roomful of royal ladies crowding around the bed were witness to the very first act the child performed, as it entered this world of ours. From a penis as long as my little finger, the Prince Memnon, the first of that name, shot a fountain almost as high as the ceiling. I was full in the path of this warm stream, and it drenched me to the skin.

'Is it a boy?' my mistress cried again, and a dozen voices answered her together.

'A boy! Hail, Memnon, the royal prince of Egypt!'

I could not speak yet, for my eyes burned not only with royal urine, but with tears of joy and relief as his birth cry rang out, angry and hot with temper.

He waved his arms at me and kicked out so strongly that I almost lost my grip again. As my vision cleared I was able to make out the strong, lean body and the small, proud head with the thick pelt of dark hair.

 I lost count long ago of how many infants I have birthed, but there had been nothing in my experience to prepare me for this. I felt all the love and devotion of which I was capable crystallized into that moment. I knew that something which would last a lifetime, and which would grow stronger with each passing day, had begun. I knew that my life had taken another random turn, and that nothing would ever be the same again. As I cut the cord and bathed the child, I was filled with a sense of religious awe such as I had never known in the sanctuary of any one of Egypt's manifold gods. I feasted my eyes and my soul upon that perfect little body and upon the red and wrinkled face in which the signs of strength and stubborn courage were stamped as clearly as upon the features of his true father.

I laid him in his mother's arms, and as he found

493

and latched on to her swollen nipple like a leopard on to the throat of a gazelle, my mistress looked up at me. I could not speak, but then there were no words that could frame what passed silently between us. We both knew. It had begun, something so wonderful that as yet neither of us could fully comprehend it.

I left her to the joy of her son and went to report to the king. I was in no hurry. I knew that the news would have been carried to him long since. The royal ladies are not renowned for their reticence. He was probably on his way to the harem at this very moment.

I dawdled in the water-garden, possessed by a dreaming sense of unreality. The dawn was breaking, and the sun god, Ammon-Ra, showed the tip of his fiery disc above the eastern hills. I whispered a prayer of thanks to him. As I stood with my eyes uplifted, a flock of the palace pigeons circled above the gardens. As they turned, the rays of the sun caught their wings and they flashed like bright jewels in the sky.

Then I saw the dark speck high above the circling flock, and even at that distance I recognized it immediately. It was a wild falcon, come out of the desert. It folded back its sharp wings and began its stoop. It had chosen the leading bird in the flock, and the dive was deadly accurate and inexorable. It struck the pigeon in a burst of feathers, like a puff of pale smoke, and the bird was dead in the air. Always a falcon will bind to its prey and drop to earth with it gripped in its talons.

This time that did not happen. The falcon killed the pigeon and then opened his talons and released

494

it. The shattered carcass of the bird fell free, and, with a harsh scream, the falcon circled over my head. Three times it circled and three times it uttered that thrilling, warlike call. Three is one of the most potent magical numbers. From all these things I realized that this was no natural occurrence. The falcon was a messenger, or even the god Horus in his other form.

The carcass of the pigeon fell at my feet, droplets of its warm blood splattered my sandals. I knew that it was a token from the god. A sign of his protection, and patronage for the infant prince. I understood also that it was a charge to me. The god was commending him to my care.

I took the dead pigeon in my hands, and lifted it to the sky. 'Joyfully I accept this trust that you have placed upon me, oh Horus. Through all the days of my life I will be true to it.'

The falcon called again, one last wild shriek, and then it banked away and on quick, stabbing wing-beats, flew out across the wide Nile waters and disappeared into the wilderness, back towards the western fields of paradise where the gods live.

I plucked a single wing-feather from the pigeon. Later I placed it under the mattress of the prince's cot, for good luck.